The Music of
Remember

Philip & Rosita,

   I hope you enjoy some of
the stories — & don't recognise too
many of the characters.

      Many thanks.

         Liam.

GUILDHALL PRESS

First published in May 2006

Guildhall Press
Unit 15
Ráth Mór Business Park
Bligh's Lane
Derry BT48 0LZ
T: (028) 7136 4413 F: (028) 7137 2949
info@ghpress.com www.ghpress.com

The author asserts his moral rights in this work in accordance with the Copyright, Designs and Patents Act 1998

Copyright © Liam Black / Guildhall Press
ISBN 0 946451 93 1

We gratefully acknowledge the financial support of the Arts Council of Northern Ireland under its Multi-Annual Lottery Programme.

ACKNOWLEDGEMENTS

Many thanks to Paul, Declan, Michael, Aaron and Joe at Guildhall Press. Special thanks to Tom McLaughlin.

———•———

A teacher for many years, a businessman for longer, Liam Black has taken to writing by accident of chance.

Also by the author: *Syllables* (1994); *Training* (2001); *How To Be A Summer Dad* (2003); *Testimony* (2004).

———•———

Please embrace the sprinkle of unusual patois so the lifeblood of language may be enriched.

For Tom, the brother.

Contents

THE HANGING TREE

On a good day, the old house at Carrickmaquigley was the most beautiful place on earth; however, on a bad day, something malevolent held the air, caught the back of your neck and rippled down your spine. By the time our generation found its use, musty smells had the house in their grip. Fifty years of summer holidays, plus the occasional weekend occupation, left it feeling very lonely.

Knowing generations past had lived and built all that lay around instilled a sense of pride in me, a belief that here there was real, tangible proof my forefathers (and mothers) had worked and lived. Hereabouts for centuries past, my ancestors toiled the earth, making it into fields and farmland. A farm that provided well for them. Witness here Bangor Blue slates on the barn as well as the long house; witness also the fact that one hundred and fifty years ago they could all read and write.

At the road side of the barn was a large pile of stones that lay in sad testimony to a plan unfulfilled. What had gone wrong? Why had three sons fled the farm? What could have made them give up their inheritance, leave family, friends and a secure future? This question haunted me as I played with watchful eyes around the grounds. I always felt someone, something ethereal perhaps, was watching me rather than watching over me; something indistinct was continually breathing down my neck.

When I was very young, it was easy to convince myself this was just the effect a great number of trees of a great size had on a single boy of a small size. In my heart, as in my stomach, as well as in my head, I knew this was not the case. I thought it was the countless generations of ancestors peeping, watching, looking, studying, to see how the living measured up to what had gone before. I had the feeling they weren't pleased with just day-trippers into our past and our lack of any real living on the farm.

This wasn't a house to be tickled by the occasional visit; it was a farm that needed living, working, toil, sweat, love and perhaps every so often a generous helping of tears. Although a fire was always blazing and crackling out its good intentions summer and winter, the house was unhappy, for it always retained its dank, musty air. Houses that are not treated as homes tend to get that way; it's inevitable when they spend too much time on their own. The same with people, I suppose.

So, senses were kept on constant red alert when not out patrolling the perimeter and foraging for signs of the past around the orchard, along the stream, aside and under the bridge. Goose-pimples had my body on a state of high alert when I entered among the fallen remains of the stable or the preying darkness of the interior of the chicken coop. Alarm bells rang inside my head when I went into the cavernous interior of the old barn, and when I climbed the lofty ladder, I didn't dare take even one hand off it in case I disappeared forever. Instead, I let my eyes blaze around and through the darkness of the interior while my two hands squeezed all blood from my fingers. It was worth putting my nerves through a good workout, because it was only in here I could catch the sweat and toily smell of lost ancestors amid their work.

Outside again, I could ease my nerves back into their proper place. I could breathe properly; I could think clearly, I could see the world as bright and lovely as it really was. But only so long as I didn't go near the old chicken coop. Into that place, tiny as it was, I would not let body and soul enter; my eyes were the only part of me that ever ventured in there.

The rusted hinges of the rotting door squealed at me as I pushed sunlight into its dreary depths with the aid of a long and strong sycamore branch. As I peeped into its deep dark intensity, all sorts of images flashed before my eyes.

Sometimes I would throw small, heavy sticks in, sometimes stones; and then I would wait, listening for movement, for the sound of something I knew not what, for the fear of this place was in me. More often than not, I was off and away, yelping to myself, convinced I had heard something move. I ran like the clappers, catching nettle stings on arms and legs as I raced towards the consoling whitewash of the house. I knew, as all children know, whenever something strange, something old, unknown and sinister lurks inside a place, because it sets your mind aknocking and your legs ashaking.

The sad, dilapidated beauty of the whole place still caught my sense of history and mixed it with pride and every other available emotion in a young boy. The tumbling outbuildings. The chicken coop without its window. The stable with its fallen roof. The orchard with branches covered in moss. The massive perimeter trees unruly in size, bullying all around. The logs that pretended to be a gate at the main entrance. The broken back gate. The immoveable remains of a gate down into the fields that sustained generations. Somehow I could tell we would be the last to witness its love.

The long house with bedrooms snugly set upstairs under one of the best roofs in the vicinity. The low, drooping windows that shed years of light onto the beautiful smoothness of a stone floor polished by generations of family footwork. The enormous hearth, so big you could stand up straight while you hung the looped half-moon handles of pots onto the blackened metal bars. The pine dresser with its willow-patterned crockery and far too many eggcups.

The whole place, inside and out, was teeming with history, my history, created and sustained and vacated by my relations. It was another world for me, a past cocooned in time by the enormous trees all around which held jealous guard over part of my heritage, their black lookouts squawking at my every move.

I enjoyed dipping an old pail into the well on the far side of the road, dip, dip, dipping, until satisfied with the fewness of water flies that had nothing better to do than spend their Sunday afternoons skating across the surface of our drinking water. Inside the barn was another pail, but this one was kept for special occasions inside a homemade wooden seating arrangement you had to empty and clean out after use. Unless it was raining, it was a lot less bother to go behind a wall, or down behind a tree near a patch of dockens if it was a big job. This antiquated contraption was probably sheer luxury for its day, but, like so much else about the house and grounds, its day had long since been and gone.

So, what had happened? Why had three brothers left the land? This question I never directly asked granny of her brothers, but it was often asked of mum, partly because I never fully believed what she told me and partly because I liked what I heard.

The line I was fed was that the three brothers got involved in the IRA, and this answer satisfied me enormously at first. The story goes that at the time of Partition, the three brothers, Peter, John and James, all in their early twenties, became involved firstly in anti-British and then anti-Partition activity. The net result of all this was they had to flee across the water, taking the steamer to America, over to relations already established there.

Something about this didn't add up; it never flowed properly, so it was never told properly, so it never seemed to fit. Only one of the brothers ever came back to visit, not very often, and when he did so, he never once paid a visit to the home house. The other two brothers had long since died in America and left no kin of their own.

As I got older, cracks began to appear in this story. My improving knowledge and study of local history showed no record of IRA activity in this remote part of Ireland. It was a very sedate little outcrop of our island where there was no great wealth and no real poverty – the land saw to that. Decent farmland and some fishing, no big houses, colonial or otherwise, no big centres of population, and most importantly, no uniforms. It was, as it had been and still is, a quiet neck of the woods where law and order was, and still is, the mainstay of sheepdogs.

One of the great things about granda was that he liked to talk, to tell stories, *his* stories. Granny, on the other hand, liked company, someone around her and especially if they headed out somewhere together. As I grew older, it was more and more frequent that granda had the lend of my ear as he told his stories of the countryside, the hard work, land, farm and folk thereabouts. Always, just as he was getting to the nitty-gritty, granny would interrupt: 'That's enough of your old stories; let's talk about something nice.'

It didn't matter that *this* was nice, interesting and relevant, that it was something I wanted to hear. It was something granny didn't want to hear (or, as I got older, I felt it was something she didn't want *me* to hear). Although the not knowing didn't bother me, I knew the time for telling would one day arrive, and so, on a dark November evening when granny was off visiting a relative of hers – who also had made the great leap into town – the truth finally came out. I was nearly man-big now and sat in with granda when opportunity needed or arose.

He told me it was a night that started off like the one we were in, where the rain swept hard and steady and the wind made whips out of every branch in the trees. Of the three brothers, only James, the youngest, was in the house all evening, having taken care of the animals before settling in at the hearth with the rest of the family. Peter, the eldest, was in a house but a few fields away, courting the most beautiful girl of the locality, Mary Rose, his betrothed, for they were to be married the following spring.

Early in the evening, Peter returned. He had a sensible head on him and knew his being out on such a night would worry the family. As time ticked on by, young and old left the dying embers for the snugness of their beds and Peter told them he'd sit up to see John in.

Later, the latch was heard dropping on the door as Peter made his way out into the tempestuous night to look for John. No-one knows why he went to look for him where he did, but he did, and when Peter found him, John was not alone; Mary Rose was in his arms.

At the sight of the two of them together, Peter said not a single word but turned and left. Back into the torrent of wind and rain he went, with God knows what rage going on inside his head. Thoughts uglier than the weather, no doubt. The madness of the night tore open his heart, letting it bleed into his mind. It didn't get a chance to blow over with the storm, but had an effect on generations to come.

From what Mary Rose said after, John waited a bit with her before going out into the violent, destructive elements of the night after his brother. Nobody knows for certain what happened next; those around at the time had differing views and it took years for talk to die down. Whatever the truth of it was, when the house rose early the next day to the calm of a winter morning, the two brothers were hanging by the neck beside one another, from the same tree by the main gate.

One explanation is that Peter went back to the barn, got a length of rope and hanged himself because he had lost the two people closest to him in life. John, when he made it back to the house and saw what his actions had caused, could see no way out but to follow the course of his older brother. Both brothers ended up hanging from the same length of rope tied up on the same tree.

As granda finished his story, there was a loud creak from a floorboard outside the open door, and, to our astonishment, granny's voice led her back into us.

'That's one side of the story and, as everyone knows, there's another side, but truth lies somewhere in between. Partition is what really killed them. The split that came after breaking up the country set friend against friend, neighbour against neighbour. Everyone knew where my brothers stood. Many in the area didn't like it and some decided to take out the leaders so the rest would fall into line with their view.

'James has never gone back down there because he knows it was those around that murdered his brothers and made him flee. Some even said your granda's family had a hand in it too. All I can say for sure is there was a lot of blood spilled and a lot of tears shed. It does no good to keep harking back to the past. Love is what needs to flourish, for it is all that matters. Isn't that right, Johnny?'

There followed a hug and kiss of a warmth so deep it made my heart fill with the pride of their courage, the last of their together. I didn't want to leave, but I knew my place was not with them, not now, not at this, their moment. I said my goodbyes and left them to the silent study of their own thoughts, the bond and witness of their togetherness.

The truth I have found is that with regard to places as well as people, the past matters only if you want to keep going back into it. All that is here, now, is all that matters.

A DOG'S LIFE

'Do any of you want to come out and help me with the dogs?'

It wasn't very often Uncle Mick – or Great Uncle Mick, as he really was – took us under his notice, not to mention involve us in anything he was doing. This was partly my family's fault, because it seemed we visited less and less often than we had done years before.

Days away are to be spent enjoying yourself, not moping around an old farmhouse where nobody ever smiles. No-one could argue with this assertion of mum's.

This wasn't fully true, for I had sometimes seen Auntie Mary smile, not very often, though, just sometimes. Auntie Mary was married to Uncle Peter, Uncle Mick's brother, and they all lived together in the family farmhouse in the country. The three of them, two collie sheepdogs, one old and one young, loads of farm animals and too many hens cluck, cluck, clucking about every square inch of dry ground outside.

In the summer months, when the front door lay open to the brightness of the world outside, hens would investigate inside, nodding their way up the hall. Hearing their clucks, Auntie Mary would call, 'If you come into the kitchen, I'll wring your neck and you'll be on the table tonight!' It was as if they understood her, because they didn't cluck any further in.

From a very early age, one thing I understood that was very different about living in the country was the smell. Thick farmyard smells caught inside your nose as you drove in and stuffed it full of pungent odours. When these kinds of smells happened at home, windows were opened and fancy smelling sprays were pulled, like guns, out of drawers to attack the smells so keenly sensed by some. In the countryside, there wasn't the same element of control.

There wasn't the aural distraction of a far and distant radio station blasting away or the comfort of a television pulling at our visuals. No-one had control over our taste buds, not even mum, because if she had, she would not have allowed us even one of Auntie Mary's sugar sandwiches. If it was up to us, we would have eaten another and another, and if it had been up to Auntie Mary, she would have kept them coming all day. They did things differently in the country; we certainly knew that much.

Smell was free, unlimited, and abounded in every corner of every relative's house we visited. It said a lot about those in the house and pretty much determined whether you liked them or not. I definitely liked the wafting coming from Auntie Mary's kitchen at certain times of the year. Sometimes, around autumn, it was the sweaty smell of jam plumping dangerously in the big pot on the kitchen stove that permeated the house and drew us near so we could hear its hissing, bubbling, gurgling and complaining sound. Sometimes it was the heavy bubbly odour of washing powder and thick chunky bars of soap scrubbing and rubbing in the scullery that caught the smelly part of my brain and made me follow it around. I knew this smell didn't travel well and could never make its way up beyond the first few stairs. Maybe it was just plain lazy.

If we were lucky, as soon as the car door was opened I knew we had timed our visit correctly, because all around the house hung an aura of deliciousness; it was as if the house was held in the wrap of my favourite cake. The smell, which escaped with every peep into Auntie Mary's oven, had a magnetic force that discreetly made itself known in all corners of the house and beyond, in all corners of the body and beyond.

Throughout my formative years, visits to the country introduced me, through my senses, to areas of learning I would otherwise never have experienced. In the country, all my senses were utilised to full advantage and became part and parcel of the familiars of learning. Smell, though, was in a little league of its own, because this was one area where adults could not control, an area where perhaps children had more control than grown-ups.

Now, after all the years of play and being unnoticed, of staying in the house with Auntie Mary and mum, finally I was being noticed by one of the men in the house. There was no doubting the question asked by Uncle Mick was directed at me and I wasn't going to miss my opportunity. I was up like a shot and out the door in front of him.

The day was dry again; it had rained heavily in the morning on our drive out, but now there wasn't a drop falling from the sky.

'Don't get yourself mucked to the eyeballs!' Mum's shout fought its way out through the deliciousness of baking hanging in the air from the kitchen.

'Don't worry, I won't.' My head only half-turned as I threw my call casually behind me. *This is an improvement*, I thought. *At least now mum recognises it is inevitable that some muck and dirt is going to stick to you when you're out and about on a farm.*

'Come on, boy. Don't be slackening.' Uncle Mick's deep voice shook me from my daydream. I had to quicken my step to keep apace with him as we rounded the back yard, along the line of old outhouses until we reached the second-last one.

'Fetch me one of those sacks, there.' A finger ordered from an outstretched arm, and it belonged to this gruff voice. Again, I noticed he didn't wear a watch; I had always wondered at this. Uncle Mick must have had a way of telling the time, just as he must have had a wealth of words stashed away inside his head, because he certainly didn't waste them on small-talk. He was like a creature from the past in the way he dressed and chewed tobacco and rarely took anyone under his notice; a creature that might soon be extinct.

I lifted the folded potato sack and caught a mouthful of dust and dirt, and something connected to dead and rotten came alive again. After handing the sack to him, we went into the last of the outhouses, and here I couldn't believe my eyes. Blackie, the younger of the sheepdogs, was lying on a bed of straw and around her nestled six of the most beautiful little puppies you ever did see.

Uncle Mick reached into the middle of them. 'Let me see, now. Right, you'll do.' He sat his chosen pup beside its mother's nose and she began licking her young one. 'Hand the rest of them up to me.'

I did as I was told. I pulled them away from their suckling business at their mother and, one by one, into his big, broad hands, which dropped them carelessly into the sack. I looked at him disapprovingly, but I knew better than to say a word against him or his manner.

With a few twists of the neck of the sack, it was thrown over his shoulder and we were off, back round the front of the house again and down the lane until we got to where it met up with the main road. All the time we were walking, not a word was spoken between us. Inside

15

my head, I had fooled myself into thinking we were taking them down to the shop, where they would be sold and go to happy homes and have fun and be well-fed for the rest of their doggy days.

Down by the roadside, he stopped; so I stopped; I didn't want to, I wanted to keep going until we reached the shop. He dropped the sack down on the dry side of the ditch, the side coming up off the road.

'Reach me one out at a time.' There was no emotion in his voice, good or bad.

When I opened the bag, the sight and sounds of the yelping little pups made me smile; they were so small and playful and loving and helpless and licking and sucking at my fingers when I dipped in to ladle the first one out. This made me laugh. I wasn't laughing on the inside, though.

As I handed the first puppy over to Uncle Mick, I knew in my heart what was coming next. I watched him plug a fresh slither of chewing tobacco into his stained mouth and a broad run of dark spittle jumped from his lips before he spoke.

'Watch this.'

His words were few, but I saw excitement flicker through his eyes as he took the puppy in his strong hands and soused its tiny head in through the lying water of the roadside ditch and into the soft, brown gooey stuff underneath.

I stood watching with eyes that couldn't believe what was happening. My heart had stopped beating. My mind had stopped letting me think this was real and happening. And yet, like a machine, I handed the puppies out to him and, one by one, they had the makings of a wonderful, happy life soused out of them in the murky shallowness of ditch water. Little legs pedalled like mad at clean, fresh air, with nothing and no-one around to help them, and so their batteries very quickly ran out. Without taking the bother to inspect if there was even a hint of life left in any one of them, their glossy remains were unceremoniously pitched onto the other side of the ditch.

Five glossy puppies lay looking as though the paint was still wet on them. They were beautiful and shiny and healthy looking and they were, of course, dead. Even in death, these poor little creatures had to suffer the ignominy of Uncle Mick's awkward nature. He had them on display as signposts for all to see.

We didn't stand on ceremony. I folded the sack, tucked it under an arm and we headed back up the lane towards the house. All this time, I had the feeling he was waiting for me to say something, to disagree with what he was doing, to say it was wrong. Or maybe it was that little bit of truth inside me wanting out, wanting its airing. I wasn't going to give in to either. I bit my tongue and said nothing.

When we neared the house, he said what had been mulched into spit with his chew. 'Read your Heaney if you think it wrong!'

There was just a hint, a small but detectable note, that what he had done wasn't to his taste either. It was enough to keep me on his side.

I had nothing to say in response to his meaning. I had to join him in his smile, though, as we entered the house. I handed him the empty sack, which he flung under the stairs.

'What have you two been up to?' Auntie Mary had a plateful of the sweetest home baking in her hand as she spoke.

'Oh, we had to get rid of a few pests, there. Isn't that right?' Uncle Mick's last three words were directed at me.

I stalled in my thoughts for a moment before responding. 'We had farm business to take care of.'

Uncle Mick and myself sat with the rest, after we had washed the smell of dogs and spuds and other debris from our hands, and tucked into the most delicious display of fancy home-cooking. It's strange the different things that give you an appetite.

I often thought about those five puppies many times after. And each time, I've moved further and further away from my initial reaction to this as a cruel and heartless act carried out on poor defenceless little puppies. Those on a farm live a very different life to those of us living city lives not too great a distance away. When a farmer saw a litter of pups, not puppies, he saw a number of pests that had no place in the natural order of things, plus the one that had the right to stay. He isn't judge, jury and executioner. He is a survivalist who has rules and regulations that must be rigidly adhered to if they are all to survive.

It wasn't too long after when I saw Uncle Mick for the last time; it was also the first time I saw him that he was not in his working clothes or chewing tobacco. Dressed in his best suit, clean-shaven and no dark tobacco stains around his mouth, he looked the picture of good health. But he wasn't. He was laid out in his coffin.

Somehow, and it remains a mystery, Uncle Mick was rolling home from his local at the dead of night with Blackie, his loyal collie, when he fell and landed in the ditch at the bottom of the lane. Loyal to the end, Blackie sat on top of the ditch, watching over her fallen master; she didn't run off and leave him. And there, face down in the stillness of the lying water in the ditch by the side of the road, Uncle Mick was found the following morning.

Seal of Death

Shroove. It's a little spot at the top of Ireland's head that has a lonely beauty about it, because once you're there, you're not going anywhere else except back. Even the houses have a great loneliness of aspect as well as distance about them, and the road that feeds their long laneways hugs the coast at sea-level, loops round, and goes back the direction it came only one hundred and fifty feet higher up the land.

To some minds, Shroove is a dead-end where nothing happens, but at a young age you learn to make the most of wherever you are and eventually you manage to enjoy yourself. In reality, where there are even a few people, there are always going to be plenty of things happening, and even more to do.

At least once a week, we'd head off, out into the north Atlantic in a small boat, owned, captained and ruled with a harpoon tongue by Tom Gallagher, the man who occasionally gave brother Tom, friend Niall and myself a lift the twenty-or-so miles down from home. No matter what way you mathematise it, four into an E-Type Jaguar doesn't go, but it had to, and so it did. All sorts of bodily contortions were required of the one, normally me, who drew the short straw and spent the journey curled up on the parcel shelf in the back. Thank God the car was quick. At journey's end, on stepping out, I was about three foot tall and I had to spend my time tweaking, twisting and turning muscles and other body parts back into their rightful six-foot position.

Fishing was thrilling stuff, especially since none of the three of us had a liking either for fish or the sea. Great long lengths of line were thrown over the sides of the small fishing boat, each line with at least thirty or forty barbed hooks enticing the poor fish to us. The trick, as we learned from the shouts and roars of our captain, was all in the timing. Timing it right to pull the lines in was easy, because he shouted it at us from his standing steering-wheel position. Timing your technique to pull in the line without letting one fish unhook itself was something that was obviously a long time in the making.

'Take the wheel!' was the roar that pulled me aside as his big hands grappled over mine and took over from my undoing. I was happy!

Standing steering the boat meant I could look out along the beauty of the coast, from the blackened rocks jutting and pointing out to sea, to the magnificent stretch of cliffs rising, rising as we chugged along and then falling, falling away dramatically into a narrow smugglers' bay or cove.

'Keep her steady!' roared from behind didn't matter, because I could see out across the vastness of the ocean, and on a really lucky day, the funny big eyes of a seal would periscope the water. The course of our craft was set along the steady line of my eye, towards this fine creature; but it never lasted.

'Keep her steady! Away from the rocks!' was generally enough to pull me from the trap of my wandering mind. I never understood why our bold captain always threatened to bring his shotgun and shoot the beautiful seal on every subsequent outing.

When finally he did stand true to his word and take a few pot-shots at the poor creature, we decided we had had enough; we wouldn't be casting off with such a madman ever again.

Instead, we made the days and nights our own and we were determined not to waste them on unnecessaries of existence such as fishing and all that went with it. It was a time when even we could notice a change in ourselves, could see ourselves growing up in every way, shape and form.

At last, we were able to make the long pilgrimage out to Culdaff for a Horslips concert. In terms of being a musical extravaganza in a plush setting, it probably didn't amount to very much in either sense. But in terms of sheer raw musical energy and action, it was brilliant. I'm not sure whether their music was a mixture of Irish with a stream of rock running through it or more a river of rock that was sourced in the mountains of traditional Irish music residing hereabouts. Either way, audience participation was a big part of the entertainment and the sweat on our clothes stood testament to that. But the road home gave clothes plenty of time to dry.

The awful part of this, our first big night out, was thumbing the fifteen-or-so miles back to our beds at three o'clock in the morning. It wasn't the walking that bothered us; we didn't mind that at all for it occasioned us plenty of time for chat and craic. It was taking a lift that frightened us.

Three cars provided a lift for us in the general direction of home that moonlit night. The first two cars were driven by culchies, who weren't anything less than half-drunk. Dead drunk is the only possible way to describe the inebriated state of being of each of these men, whose vehicles somehow managed to retain a semblance of control over them. Most of the distance, travelled on four wobbly wheels, was spent swerving, dodging from ditch to ditch as we said our prayers for the whole year in between. An infinite sense of relief was felt when the car braked suddenly in the straightest piece of driving of the evening, and our second driver slurred that this was as far as he was going.

Third time lucky was definitely in our minds after this night of razzle-dazzle entertainment concerting in Culdaff. Myself, the brother and our buddy had only a couple of miles left to trek along the silent road back to Shroove. With seldom occasion to extend a thumb for a lift, there was a great sense of anticipation, accompanied by a step back from the road, that greeted the announcing lights of a car approaching from behind. Our surprise was even more real when the lights of the car slowed and then stopped just ahead of us. We sprinted up to it and the three of us nearly exploded with excitement when we opened the doors and saw three young ladies – not too much older than ourselves – inside. Well, it was the early hours of the morning in the middle of nowhere – what do you expect to happen?

'Where are you going?' This wasn't the most intelligent of opening lines because the road ran nowhere except back along itself.

'Down to the beach for a swim. Coming?'

There was no point in seeing opportunity and not seizing it. Before they said a word we knew they were up for it; their giggles told a lot.

On the drive down to the beach, the girls didn't stop nattering: about where they were from, what they were doing in life, and everything else about themselves except for one thing – their names. For reasons best known only to themselves, they wouldn't divulge their names.

What did we care? We wouldn't be seeing them again after that night and the small matter of a name wasn't going to interfere with the luxury of time spent alone with a lovely female.

As soon as we stopped at the beach, three male hands grabbed three female hands and instinctively we headed for different snugs of a sandy shore we knew well.

'I thought we were going for a swim…' A little tug in the direction opposite to the one I was heading stopped me in my tracks.

Just my luck, I thought. *Trust me to get the lippy one.*

Her words had been uttered loud enough to stall the other two couples as well. Eyes danced off the delight of each other's wanton smile.

'That's for afters; this is for now.' With that I had her scooped up in my arms and off, to the delight of her own cries and the favour of her friends. We nestled together over behind a large clump of rock and did all the things you're supposed to do, and before we knew it, there was the sound of splashing and rollicking about in water catching our ears.

It didn't take us too long to catch up with the others; their sounds made them easy to find in the darkness of the early hours. Brightness had not yet begun to break upon the day and only the whiteness of the moon's light shone upon our world that night. Thank goodness too, because our whiteness would have been on display as we skinny-dipped together in the bracing sea. The reddish glow of embarrassment from our cheeks must have made us shine like little beacons in the dark. Our hearts were certainly aglow on the inside. We were having the time of our lives in this, one of the nights of our lives. It was turning out to be a night to remember. It certainly wasn't a night we were ever going to forget.

Boys being boys, or nearly men being nearly men, we soon reverted to type by carrying on with one another, showing off how manly we were by indulging in juvenile behaviour. We were ducking each other and doing all manner of unmanly things while the three girls looked on, bemused; but not for long. Soon, they were off, away from our frolicking about and heading straight out from the shore, calling to us as they went.

'Come on, boys. We'll meet you out at the rocks!' They must have been three mermaids if they thought they could reach the far-off rocks. We knew where these were and we knew where we stood in relation to the distance of cold, choppy water between – firmly on the shoreline! One thing was for sure, we weren't mermen and we knew there was no point in swimming halfway there to show ourselves up and then have to swim all the way back to shore.

'Come on, boys. We'll be waiting. Where are you, boys? Come and get us!' The girls' calls taunted and teased us over the growing distance of water between. There wasn't much for us to do on shore except run about trying to dry ourselves as best we could before donning the covers of respectability and warmth again.

Then we had a brainwave. We gathered up all the girls' clothes and hid them in a bit of scrub near the parked car. A few souvenirs were stuffed into pockets for the value of having them teased out of us later. We then made our high-spirited way back down to the sandy oasis of fun, expecting our three mermaids to be there on our return.

The beach was all alone but for the strong crash of wave after wave washing the foreshore. We stood silently in the comfort of the moon's light, listening, hoping to catch a giveaway giggle. Then, it caught us.

Cries. Long deep cries for help carried over the surface of the water and caught the stillness of our hearts in their wake. We each turned pale, then – as we caught the look of each other – one by one, smiles melted away our frowns of concern.

'Ha-ha! We heard that one before. Come on out.' Laughing and pulling and hauling at each other again, we smiled profusely as we called back: 'You nearly had us there!'

Waves continued their relentless wash onto the shore; not another sound disturbed the air. Then distant calls swept over us.

'Help! Help! Please help!'

It was the real, fullness of fear contained in that one word "please" that emptied us of our want of fun.

Together we ran down into the water and swam out towards the alarming calls that kept on coming. Onward and onward we pushed and pushed ourselves out towards these most distressful sounds. Soon, I was falling behind as the other two were strong swimmers, but, despite their splashes, I could still hear the distant cries.

The rocks the girls swam out to must have disappeared under the incoming tide for there was no outline above the water ahead. My arms felt as if they were about to fall off and it was all I could do to stay afloat and keep breathing. I knew I didn't have the strength to continue out and swim back to shore, definitely not with someone desperately clinging onto me. I wanted to go back. I knew I should go back now. But I had to go forward. So, summoning all the strength I could, I pushed on ahead.

It was hard, it was sore, it felt as if I was not moving, but something inside made me push on and on. Suddenly, I could see heads bobbing out of the water over on my right, and they were heading back. It was the others. I knew it was the others, they had reached two of the girls and were taking them back.

Great, I thought, *I'm nearly there.*

Somehow, a great surge of encouragement made me push harder with my legs, forced my arms out wider and faster in a sweeping, waving, swimming motion. I was determined I wasn't going to be beaten. Then, straight ahead, I saw a head bobbing up and down with the motion of the sea.

From my eyes to my mind, to every sinew in my body, a new sense of vigour was instilled in me and I pummelled the water with my utmost strength. Closer and closer towards the head I forced myself with every reserve of muscular force I had. It wasn't shouting or crying out, it wasn't even calling or waving toward me, but it was there, and I was nearly there.

I stalled for a moment, glad of the chance to catch my breath, but knowing I shouldn't stop for too long, because this could finish off the last bit of strength I had. Pushing myself up well above the surface of the water, I stretched an arm as far as I could into the air and waved.

At this the head slipped away and disappeared under the surface of the sea. I was stunned. I nearly disappeared under myself. To have come so far, been so close and to have lost at the last moment, I couldn't believe what was happening.

Something inside my head told me to stop, to turn back, give up and save myself while I still had strength enough in my veins to do so. I wanted to turn back, but I knew I had to go on. Just another few strokes, then another few, then another…

Not more than a couple of arms' lengths away, the head again rose out of the sea. I was stopped in my stroke by this reappearance and then I cursed and swore and struck out at it with my fist, for I couldn't believe what I was seeing. It was the head of a seal, probably the same seal from our fishing expeditions.

Rage filled my heart as I looked round me one last time, but all I could see was the blackness of the sea. I pounded and fought through myself, my tiredness, through all the emptiness now inside me, and I mustered enough strength to see me back to shore.

Lying sprawled on the sand, waves lapping around me, I heard noise, voices, crying.

'You didn't find her?' The power of sadness held the question. The gentle sobs that held the background erupted into wails of woe.

'A seal. I swam out to that cursed seal!' The venom in my voice only momentarily held back the flood of sorrow that swept through me, that swept through all five of us as we cried and mourned the loss of what wasn't there.

What was left of the summer was supposedly spent fishing. Out on the boat with old Tom; not noticing his ways, his words and unchanged manner. Glad now for the presence of the shotgun. A different interest lay all around now in the steal of the sea.

INHERITANCE

'Why couldn't you make it back before he died?' Brigid's shallow look stared through the picture of her brother after wiping away the notion that his dress sense hadn't improved with age. 'It would have meant a lot to him; he would have seen you towards the end.'

'Aye, sure, he would have seen me then. Of course he would have when he wasn't fit to speak; when he wasn't able to say he was sorry for the great wrong he did.' Brian's anger rose with his words as feelings he thought were long since exhausted rose up inside him and found their way out. And yet, he was surprised at himself. Surprised he hadn't felt anything from where he was standing. This place had once been home, had become the target of so much annoyance, and now had the feeling of just another call-out. The same front door leading into different expectation. People expected from him and he had to give. But not here; not even now.

It was the day after their father's funeral and Brian, the eldest, stood in the dimly lit hallway with his sister Brigid and brother Brendan. As well as the look, there was a definite air of mourning about the house; nothing had changed in that respect.

'I don't know how the two of you ever stayed in this dark, depressing dungeon of a place, and having to look after that cantankerous old brute. Did he mention me at all?' Brian's look changed, but his tone stayed the same.

Brendan rolled his eyes to heaven. 'He nev… ver mentioned yo… you at all.'

Brian stared into Brendan; he could hardly believe fifty years had made no difference to his brother; he was still just a boy. A little nod inside him agreed he was right to ignore Brendan's big half-century last year. Or was it the year before? Whatever the way of it, Brian stumbled back upon the knowledge that Brendan still had a child's deviousness and devilment about him at times. The stutter helped enormously, too, allowing him to lie without recourse to little tell-tale smiles that warned you of what he was at.

Brendan turned and headed in towards the kitchen so Brian couldn't see the form of his face. Brigid moved alongside her big brother.

'Of course he did. He mentioned you often, but perhaps not in the way you might have wanted him to.' Brigid caught hold of his arm. 'You know what he was like, Brian. He was never going to change and he never did. You were the wise one got away from here. He only got worse as time went on.'

It was some years since Brian had felt the warmth of his sister's touch, of any woman's touch, for that matter, and it stirred an interest deep within him. Then his feeling moved off as his eyes caught the look of the kitchen, unchanged in the two decades or so since he had last set foot in it, and only then through the hallucinations of sentiment, when his mother had died. It had been a mistake, and one he never dared repeat on himself.

'Brian, you weren't listening. Do you like the new curtains?' Brigid's tug on his sleeve pulled him out of his reverie.

'Those aren't new; they're the same ones I remember.' Brian caught his sister's eye as he spoke and knew at once he had got this one wrong. Wrong in terms of what needed to be said. 'I'm only joking, sis; they're lovely. They change the whole room.' He desperately sped his eyes around, hoping to spot something else that had changed before it had to be pointed out to him. But he noticed nothing new.

'Thanks for trying. You always were a poor one for hiding the truth.' Brigid pulled out a chair at the head of the table as she passed it on her way to the kettle.

'I still can't forgive the old buzzard for not going to Mary's funeral. I thought he liked her.' Brian looked over, first at Brigid and then at Brendan. Brigid's eyes were downcast; Brendan's seemed to be following the invisible flight path of a noiseless fly around the room.

'Well, at least for the boys' sake he should have come. How do you think Donal and Patrick felt when their grandfather didn't appear at their mother's funeral? They were only boys, for God's sake.' The last part of his statement lost its hold on hope in Brian's voice.

Brigid smiled as she looked over at her older brother and she continued setting plates and cups on the table as electricity drove its charge through the water in the kettle. 'How are the twins? Did they like their jumpers last Christmas?' For the first time that day, a feeling of affection showed through in Brigid's voice. The turbulence in the kettle held the moment. 'I think I'll knit them red this year. I suppose they're fed up always wearing brown, but it's a good practical colour.' Brigid's smile lost its breadth on seeing Brendan's face out of the corner of her eye. 'Sit down, Brendan, and stop your gawking. You're making the place look untidy.' Brigid's smile settled again in her, but her look was beyond Brian as she still sought an answer to her question.

'I wouldn't bother with red or any other colour.' Brian tried to stretch himself back from the table in his chair, but it refused to budge for him. The confusion of his mind took control of his features.

'Rubber pads on the feet of the chairs; he didn't like the sound of them dragging on the floor.' Brigid shrugged her shoulders as if to say that was the way of it and sure what can you do?

Brian smiled. 'I put cork tiles on my kitchen floor; there's no noise nuisance with them and they're warmer on the feet.' Brian caught the look of his boys in Brigid; he had never before noticed the similarity of expression around the mouth.

'Would you for God's sake make a pot of tea, Brendan, and stop that blessed kettle boiling?' Without reply, Brendan set to with kettle and teapot, and Brigid was able to turn her thoughts and her eyes back to Brian. 'I thought university students all loved big warm jumpers to wrap up against the cold of dingy flats. What should I get them instead?' Brigid's thoughts ran away inside her as she considered the freedom of Christmas ahead and the hope that the only two of her own name she had to bother about should be able to join them.

A long, hollow silence followed.

'Give me the first cup, Brendan. I prefer mine weak these days.' When Brian turned his head and his attention back to the table, the question was still there waiting for him. He had to answer. 'Last year's presents are still in the house, along with the year before. They never bothered to collect them.' Brian's tone dropped with the weight of his thoughts as well as the price of his words.

'What?' Brigid's sharpness made Brendan stop pouring. 'Did they go off skiing again?' Consideration made her brighten a bit.

'They've never been away skiing; that was a lie of mine.' Brian sat slumped in his chair. He didn't raise his head as he continued to speak. 'They both had the grades to do med. They went against my wishes and the better judgment of careers advisers and all at their boarding school and went off together to study art. Can you believe it? Ability like that and they throw it away on a course for… well, you don't need much of a brain to get into Art College.'

With the look of right on his side, Brian stared into his sister's eyes. He noticed them well up, and then, one by one, large tears traced their way down her cheeks. *Oh, God, here we go*, he thought. *The emotional trauma of a spinster sister of a certain age!*

'I can't believe it. I can't believe you would be so stupid!' Anger forced itself out through the tears Brigid was now flinging off with the back of her hands.

'Get her some hankies, Brendan!' Brian was very offhand with his words.

Brendan turned one way, then another, as his brain twisted and skipped within him and he tried to think where to go to get a box of paper hankies. Strips of kitchen roll were presented to the table instead.

'And get us a biscuit or something to eat, Brendan. Is there any cake?' Brian's voice tried to brighten the scene; it was but a flutter in the wind.

'What are you telling me, Brian?' Brigid tried to reason with her brother with her expression.

'I'm not spending my hard-earned on some bum arty-farty degree when they should be studying medicine and helping to make a difference in the world.' Brian found the words came out very easily, but he wasn't sure if they were his.

'You've fallen out with your sons over stupid education? Is that what you're telling me?' As a rage grew inside her, so Brigid's tears stopped.

'Come on, Brigid. What are you going to do with an art degree? Get a teaching job? Is that what you want for them when they could be earning the respect of the community in a profession that means something to people?' Brian could have continued, but he sensed he probably had said enough.

'I never thought I'd see the day.' Brigid rose from the table, shaking her head, took a plate off Brendan and proceeded to fill it with a variety of sweet home-baking from a tin in the larder.

Brian knew what she meant, but he was busy trying to gather his thoughts into a defensible argument around his own position. 'Didn't the old man make a difference? I know I certainly did. Saving lives: there's no greater way of making a difference in society.' Brian felt cornered; he couldn't remember when he last had to defend his role and function in life.

'Sa... s... aving people's li... lives so they can di... die another day. That's all doctors do.' Brendan packed a few laughs onto the end of his words.

Brian knew to ignore this; it wouldn't be fair picking on poor Brendan. He turned his look back onto his sister. 'I told them I'd pay their way through medicine and nothing else, for it wouldn't be right to waste the talents God gave them.' The last bit was thrown in as an appeal to the holy streak in his sister.

'Oh, so it was good enough for their mother to be an art teacher, but boys must follow in their father's and grandfather's footsteps. Is that what you're saying?' Brigid stood over her brother, offering from the plateful of delicious home-baking as she spoke.

'Come on, Brigid. You know Mary was never serious about her art; it was just something for her to do.' Brian tried a teasing smile as he lifted three buns off the plate.

'You never could see people, could you, Brian? You never could go beyond the surface. You're a veneer man, always superficial. God bless Mary, but if she hadn't been so beautiful on the outside, you never would have seen her.' A note of sorrow slipped into Brigid's soundings.

'I really miss her, Brigid.' Brian's eyes began to fill up and he dragged a deep breath in from the air around to try to keep himself steady.

'I bet it's not half as much as the boys miss her.' Brigid wasn't used putting her older brother down: she liked the feeling of it; she enjoyed the taste of it; she was going to savour it a little longer. 'Let me get this straight then: you're not supporting your twin sons at university because they aren't doing the course you'd like them to do?' There was almost a sneer in Brigid's voice.

'It's not as simple as that, Brigid, and well you know it.' Brian didn't feel able to explain himself fully.

'And when it comes to them wanting a wife, will you be doing that choosing for them, too, like your own father?' Disdain threaded Brigid's words together.

'He had nothing to do with Mary and me; you're wide of the mark there, Brigid.' A ray of hope raised in Brian's voice.

'Her one redeeming feature was that her mother and father were both doctors. He often said it, just maybe not within earshot of you.' Brigid didn't want to be hurtful to the memory of her sister-in-law, because Mary had been a loving girl.

'Mary's gone. We'll not tarnish her memory by bringing her into this.' Brian added a measure of firmness and control to his speech and his face.

'Well, you should be more like her and a lot less like your own father when it comes to your two sons.' Brigid's words were sharpened, as well as being packed with firmness as she fired them out.

'It wouldn't be ri... right for the twins to tur... tur... turn out like their mammy inste... instead of their daddy.' Both Brian and Brigid's heads swung round together to catch the end of Brendan's words. Brendan smiled a watery smile at them before departing the room.

Brian immediately caught what he meant and called after him. 'It wasn't easy bringing up two teenage boys on my own; you should try it sometime.' The kitchen door threw the last of his words back at him and put a lid on the remainder of what Brendan said on his way out.

'The big bits are easy, Brian. There's right and there's wrong, and this nonsense of yours falls deep into the wrong end of things.' Brigid's voice held firm.

She always did seem to have right on her side, probably because she never did any wrong, because she never did anything much with her life except go to work and Mass. Brian wanted to publish his thoughts there and then for his sister to have to eat a bit of the humble pie she was always so fond of dishing out to others. He stopped himself, because he knew it would be too hurtful, especially now.

'I honestly thought they'd learn sense once they were away and found how difficult it is to fend for themselves, but it doesn't look like they're going to learn now, does it?' Sadness held Brian's countenance.

31

'Do you mean to tell me you haven't seen your boys in over two years? Jesus, Brian! What sort of a father are you?' Brigid moved away in disgust from her brother.

'What am I meant to do, Brigid? How am I going to get them to see sense?' After catching the look in her face, he was appealing to his sister not to back away from him but to help him.

'*Them* see sense? It's *you* who needs to waken up to the world. You haven't got them for long. Go and apologise for what you've done and accept your two boys for whatever it is they want to be!' Brigid slammed her words into her brother's face; there was no doubting the strength of her feeling.

Brian held his peace – but only for a few moments before exploding back at his sister. 'How dare you take their side against me, your own brother! I don't remember anyone saying anything different when it was decided *I* would follow the old man and become a doctor. *I* had dreams too, you know!' It was an emotional outburst that exploded out of him and back at his sister.

'So now the sins of the father should be repeated on the children. Is that what you believe?' Brigid stopped there. She knew her brother and decided it best to give him space enough to come round. She waited.

There was a noise in the hallway as Brendan's discretion led him away again from the kitchen and out of the line of fire. It was the shouting that had made him stop, but it was the sound of his brother crying, his big brother, the smart one in the family, that drove him up the stairs and made him retreat into his bedroom.

Tears were now dappling the tabletop under Brian's nose, but these were not tears of grief or sorrow, nor were they tears of joy. They were the emotional expression of not knowing what to do, and perhaps not for the first time. This had been the case with his treatment of his sons. And in the lack of certitude, nothing had been done. He knew there was a twist to his character that didn't mind conflict, that relished the prospect of discord, and that functioned perfectly well in the dissonance of family strife. It was all beginning to gel in his head.

'Do you know what you've done?' Brigid wasn't about to give up the cause.

Brian's eyes entreated his sister to go easy on him, that today of all days he didn't need it and he most certainly didn't want it.

'You've continued the unworthy, the wicked, resolve of that old burden we buried. You had a chance to make things different, you got away from here, from him, and yet, inside you, you took him with you.' Brigid began to sob heartily. 'God, if you only knew how he was after you left! Hating you because he loved you so much, but you were gone and so he turned his black soul on us. Why do you think Brendan's the dithering fool he is? He needed me, but he neither needed nor wanted poor Brendan.' Brigid's tears got the better of her and her arms fell flat on the table and her sobbing head on top of that.

Brian's murmurings of sorrow stopped. He wanted to put his arm around his sister and hold her and tell her it was all over now, that everything was changed from now on, but he couldn't. He just sat there, thoughts stuck inside themselves, inside his head, motionless, emotionless on the outside.

It was another few minutes before Brigid took control of herself.

'God, you're just like him. Cold and unmoving! You think you're sitting at your desk in the surgery dealing with a patient. How can you be so heartless? How can you be so cruel with the twins, your own two boys?' Brigid's whole body, her whole person, was pleading with Brian to move, to change, and to make a break with the past.

There was no response. Not a word, not a sound, not a movement; just a stare.

'It's now or never, Brian. You'll never have a better chance than this to rid yourself of the past.'

Silence ensued.

Brian felt trapped. He was ensnared by a darkness within.

Brigid waited. The whole house was in silence, waiting for Brian to make his move, to come to a decision. For Brigid, the silence was unbearable, but she held her pleas within, which was easy enough for her; she had had plenty of practice at this in her world of home.

Brian's head began to move. In a long, slow, deliberate movement, it shifted slightly from one side to the other, picking up speed as it did so, until an over-obvious shaking of the head was on show. The more his head shook, the quicker the look of sorrow faded from Brigid's demeanour and the stronger was the determination that rose inside her. She said nothing.

A mournful firmness stared out from Brian when he looked up. 'I'm sorry, I can't. It's they who have to change.' There wasn't much sense of sorrow in his voice.

'Sorry you're not, but sorry you'll be. Thank God the old blackguard did something right, even if it was for the wrong reason. He cut you out. Did you know that? In his will, everything's divided into three equal parts, between the three of us, except you don't get your share; it goes directly to the twins. You don't receive a penny!'

An enormous smile broke across Brigid's face and the goodness it brought spread through her whole body; she felt entirely uplifted. 'Isn't there a wonderful irony in that? Isn't that brilliant? The boys will never have to look to you again, and all thanks to the warped mentality you so ably display along with our dead father. That's your inheritance!' Brigid began to laugh heartily.

Brian couldn't stay in this past any longer. He had to leave, to get away from their lives forever. He rose slowly from the table, gave Brigid one last glance, and silently left the house.

Brigid immediately pushed in his chair. Silence stood still in the house. This was only disturbed when creaking stairs announced the burden of a weighty person's arrival. Soon Brendan stood by the kitchen door.

'Wh... wh... what happened?' His eyes darted around as the rest of him stood perfectly still.

Brigid moved slowly towards her younger brother. She could feel the presence of youth before her, although what she saw was a man growing old on the outside.

Brigid lifted Brendan's hands into hers. She squeezed tightly while lifting them up to waist height. Drawing in a deep breath lifted her up close to the level of her younger brother.

'We've buried two people today, two halves of the same whole.' There was pleasure, real conscious enjoyment in Brigid's voice as she spoke. 'Now we have two young bodies to unearth.'

A delightful smile energised Brigid's look and spread its message into Brendan's thoughts. He smiled his belief back upon her.

THE BOGMARTIN

My acquaintance with a smattering of Irish, gained at the tenderest of ages in a local community centre, was enough to lodge me away for the full of a summer month with other such likelies in an area of Ireland officially designated a Gaeltacht. Here, fires burned turf, the toilet was an outside loo, travel was by tractor, and everyone spoke Irish; everyone that is, except us. There was one rule: if you were caught speaking English, automatic expulsion would follow. The possibilities of procedure for the offence of talking French, German, or whatever, were left deliberately vague so that we would not partake of such a crime. Life was definitely harsh enough around these parts without losing any of the advantages our collective existence gave us in terms of numbers.

So, with six of the likeliest lads of my generation, I was cut off from the rest of civilisation by bogs and mountains, plus an invisible language barrier that shackled us to an almost forgotten way of life.

We were installed in a house about a two-mile walk to the old schoolroom we attended daily lessons in, and it was God knows how much further to the nearest neighbour. A farther five-mile walk would take us to the main centre, where ceilis were held and the main body of the Irish college existed, especially the female bits. Despite its undoubted attractions, we walked into the main centre on just a couple of occasions, and spent the remainder of our free time bog walking or playing cards.

Seven city lads, lodged away in the middle of nowhere with a family who couldn't communicate with us because they only spoke Irish, it's enough to make you bog crazy!

During our month-long existence of walking everywhere, not once were we successful in hitching a lift along the main road. Therefore, every time we had to be somewhere, we made sure we had more than an hour to spare to get there, and so we took up the challenge of the long, narrow road with determined gusto. This meant placing the puniest of our number on the roadside, while the rest of us submarined down the nearest ditch. Then, when a car did stop, the other half-dozen of us clambered up, feet slopping and slipping, eyes ablaze with smiling hope, excitement emblazoned across our faces. To look at us, you'd think not one of us had seen the inside of a car before; and that's certainly how it felt. However, the driver spotted us on each occasion and took off, gravel firing back from under the rear tyres, leaving us cursing our luck and hurling insults, verbal and gestured, whilst spitting dust. Incidents like this made us all the more aware of ourselves, our situation, and what life in this godforsaken barren wilderness really held in store for us.

It was not all empty road and frivolous gestures, though.

One afternoon changed us, along with our perception of the world, forever. After lessons that afternoon, as we straggled our talkative way back from class to delight our taste buds with whatever delicacy the *bean an tí* had hard boiled for us, we stopped and gazed. Together, we caught the view of something grand, glowing and glistening and glinting its magnificent way along the narrow, bendy, flat road ahead. It was a beautiful, white and very large coach of the sort we only ever managed a close-up view of on television, and it was headed our way.

We moved off the edge of the road, knowing this massive machine would be the full of it, thereby allowing the driver enough room to pass with ease. As it approached and passed, we waved our balanced blessings from the top of a soaky ditch. None too often would we have seen a vehicle of this size and beauty – even at home – so it was a real rarity hereabouts. Imagine our surprise, then, when this giant of a beast lurched to a halt just past us. We stared in wonder and awe, not knowing what was going to happen next.

Our amazement was almost complete when, one by one, a whole troupe of people, mainly elderly and overweight, clad in sunglasses, caps, outrageous tartan trousers, gaudy tops and Arran cardigans, appeared as if by magic from round the far side of the bus. If the clothes weren't enough of an indicator, the accents sure were a dead giveaway, for these were Americans. But they were well-balanced Americans, because they all had cameras hanging round their necks, and these bounced off their bellies and other protuberances as they strode toward us.

The driver was then sent over to ask if we would group together for a photograph. He was probably chosen for this task because he spoke our lingo: English. Back he went and translated our answer for them: Yeah. Sure. No problem.

What then followed was a five-minute photo shoot that would have put the highest A-list celebrity to shame. We stood together, our enormous sparkling grins disguising the fact there was not much in a twenty-mile radius, apart from bogland, worth photographing. Around these parts, they would have stood a better chance seeing a bald eagle than a sheep, so treacherous was the bogland.

Where we were was a great place if you wanted to get away from it all. But a coachload of Yankee tourists were only over in this quaint little Ireland place because they wanted to see it all. There are a lot of sights to see, but not out in the middle of boggish wasteland where they now found themselves. And once you've seen one bog, you've seen them all.

They thought we were locals, which indeed we were, for the time being at least. They probably thought we were members of the same family, and there was no point in us confusing the issue for them by stating otherwise. Then, as the clicking and snapping began to die down, one of the Yanks took off her fancy hat and passed it around the beg of her compatriots.

Imagine our astonishment when they all reached into their pockets and put coin after coin into the hat. In the main, these were big coins of the wonderful silverish variety, and then, low and behold, a couple of notes fluttered down from heaven and landed on top of the coins.

Our smiles grew even larger. We could hardly contain the joy that was bursting from our hearts, for never before had we seen so much money gathered together in the one place. The basket passed around the church on Sunday paled to insignificance in comparison to what was passing our way.

The lovely lady, who had used her flamboyant hat for our purpose, emptied the contents into the cupped hands of the eldest of our number: Martin. We couldn't believe it – this was turning out to be one of the best days of our lives. Now we would be able to afford to buy presents to take home for grandparents as well as siblings. Now we would be able to afford to buy bars of chocolate and bags of crisps after Mass on Sunday to keep us going all week. Now we would be able to afford the occasional bus ticket into ceilis at night, where all the action was, where all the girls were. Now would see an end to our Spartan existence in this desolate blight of a nothingness of landscape.

As the four big tyres of the bus took up the strain again, we waved the happiest goodbyes of our lives until the bus re-emerged from the first bend, and we danced with glee as we continued waving until the great white coach was well out of sight. Now there was only one thing on our minds: money, lots and lots of lovely money.

It was almost beyond our comprehension that strangers, total strangers, people we had never seen before in our lives and would never see again, had handed us loads of money. We all had relations, close relations, who had never given us a penny in our whole existence, and yet complete strangers from a different country, from a different continent, had made us all rich beyond our wildest dreams.

It was all true. All those years of listening to stories about relatives heading off to the U S of A to seek their fortune made sense now. What a wonderful world this must be!

We continued our trek again, only more slowly now, and much more closely grouped together than before.

'Show us the money, Martin,' one of us chirped.

We all stopped and stared deeply, lovingly, longingly, into the pot of gold cupped between his hands. We could hardly believe our luck, but we could believe our eyes as they tried to visualise the strain of the weight that awaited our pockets.

'Come on, we'll divide it out now,' I enthused.

Our minds were bubbling over, our mouths dripping wet at the prospect of so much money, so much hope, so much comfort, ready for our take. And the closer our eyes took us into the magnificence of it, the more eager we were to have our share.

'What?' Martin squawked.

'We'll share it out now,' a number of voices rejoined.

'It's *my* money. She gave it to *me*!' Martin squealed back at the rest of us.

'*They* gave it to *her* and *she* gave it to *you* to share with *us*,' we chorused, eyebrows knitting.

'It's *my* money! You're not getting a penny of it!' Martin cried back at us.

We could see he wasn't joking; we knew what had to be done.

'No, it's bloody not!' Our gang of voices bellowed back at him.

Martin began to take long, deliberate strides in the direction of the house, but, as we followed, our bodies instinctively spread out in a quick encircling movement, cutting off this option.

Immediately, we made our move for him, but being the eldest gave him that split second of sharpness on us and he was off and away across the bog. This was the one route we didn't expect him to take, and he had the beating of us now, but not for long. In a flash, we were off and after him, the line of us following along directly behind him, and gaining on him with every stride.

It might not have been a minute later and we were nearly on him, feet soaking, trousers wet up to the knees when – whooaaa! – he vanished. As quickly as he had taken off from us, Martin disappeared down one of the bog holes we had often been warned about.

It was amazing. One moment he was there, in front of us, and a moment later, he was gone. Then, as strangely as he had disappeared, his head bobbed up behind a big gluck of air, onto the surface of the brown boggy bubbly liquid. The sound of water breaking and slopping soon disappeared with the racket of Martin's gasping cries for air. By now, our gathering encircled the bog hole; it wasn't much more than five feet wide.

'Help!'

There was hardly enough time for the whole word to escape from Martin's terrified, filthy face. But his hands didn't reach out for help, they didn't grab at his own rescue, they weren't open to our grasp; that much was more than plain and obvious to us.

Something in me wanted to help him, but I wasn't going to break our bond, none of us were, and none did. We watched as Martin swore and splashed and spluttered and yelped and gulped. We watched as his eyes pleaded with us to help him, just one of us, any one of us, to reach out a hand to save him. But still his hands stayed hidden; they didn't reach out for us, they held on to what they had.

We watched in earnest as the fight washed out of him, as the splashing stopped, as Martin disappeared, as the bubbles faded and the bog went back under the hush of its hold. We stood there a while longer wondering, absorbing, taking in the disappointment of Martin's behaviour, of his disappearance. We stood shoulder to shoulder around the bog hole until we knew it was time for us to leave.

Not a word was spoken then or after by any one of us concerning our disappointment with Martin. All we knew was the truth, which was that he hadn't bothered returning with us to the house after lessons. He had disappeared, vanished without a trace.

It's a lonely world out there in the bog. No-one saw us go in, no-one saw us come out, and only ourselves knew what went on in between.

It was easy enough explaining away Martin's disappearance. We didn't know anything. The first day's investigations were conducted in Irish, which suited us fine, because we really didn't have a coherent explanation – in Irish at least. On the second day, the investigation took a more serious twist when the Garda sergeant questioned us in English. We explained that Martin, being the eldest, did what he wanted and only sometimes told us about this afterwards. He was a law onto himself. In fact, most of the time he insisted that we do whatever it was he wanted to do, but that was only when he wanted to include us in his doing.

We told the sergeant that we knew Martin did have a special place out in the bog, a place he called his "wishing well", for he had twice taken us along with him to throw coins in and make a wish; the second time was quite recent. The big Garda got very excited at this news and hurried us all off into the bog to show him exactly where this was. Eyes watched worried eyes as we quick-stepped along and off towards the well, especially when we passed close by the spot of Martin's disappearance.

The first time he examined the wishing well carved into a clump of granite during the Ice Age, out in the midst of the desolate, lonely bog, there was no obvious evidence to back up what we had told him, the money we definitely chucked in having suspiciously disappeared; almost. Further investigation with the poke of his stick under some craggy bits unearthed a couple of English coins of recent minting. This proved us right and, more particularly, it told the sergeant the type of person Martin must surely have been. For now the garda knew the money-taking enterprise that Martin was up to with his wishing well.

On the way back, just to pursue the point, I thought I'd add a bit of measure to our moment. A great splash accompanied an almighty roar from me as I disappeared down one of the bog holes. It was a chance worth taking.

My deliberate stroke of genius, not pre-arranged or even mentioned to anyone, worked a treat. Very quickly, the Garda and as many hands as could grab onto any piece of me, had me dragged out of the bottomless hole of water. With great care, he ushered us away and out of the bog, swearing to God in heaven and all the holy saints he could think of, that townies should never put a foot near a bog, for he knew now exactly what had become of poor Martin in the bog.

BLACK AND WHITE

Smell was what he missed most, was what he couldn't remember, was what he didn't want to forget. And yet he had forgotten, he most definitely had forgotten. For a long time after his arrival in the new country, his new life, all he had to do was get his sense of smell into his head and so transport himself back thousands of miles, to home, back to where he belonged. The comfort of his old existence comforted him with the hold of belong, where he would belong again one day. Had the smell died away inside him? Was it want of the smell that was dying? Or... had he finally moved on from where he swore he never would?

Once it had all been black and white to Mickie McGrew: who he was, who he would be again one day, the day he returned to Ireland; and in between times, he worked and saved. What was it now, fifteen? No, twenty-plus years since he had left. He could hardly believe it. It was like getting older. Time and the mirror were in it together against you and backed each other up with the lie. It was how you felt inside, that was where real truth lay, that was where all the real answers lay, secretly stored and ready for the big telling when need arose.

This reminded him of the guys he worked with, some of them, who couldn't remember how long they had been married, or the ages of their children. Mickie had always reckoned this was an act of bravado, but now he wasn't so sure.

Black and white, everything in big-city America was black and white. It had to be. This was the only way to survive there, and this is why Mickie got on so well with America. Work hard, get paid, keep yourself to yourself, spend as much as you must, save the rest. He had seen others, better men than him, as soon as they eased off on themselves, that was it. The slippery slope took them down into a hole they had to get out of themselves, because no-one else was going to help them. He used to be able to laugh about this with others, the fact that there wasn't anyone to pull you out of a hole, but there were plenty willing to fill it in.

This wasn't the old way; it was a new, hard way; the way of a new country like America. Ireland was blessed with the old way, the good way, where everyone still looked out for everyone else. Ireland was still burdened with the old way, the bad way, where everyone knew the business of everyone else; where, if you did a wrong, you would have to do a lot of right to rebalance the equation. Mickie hoped that was how it worked, hoped he had put enough right into his life to go forward into the past. Old Ireland still survived for him in full colour, where the whole spectrum of existence functioned differently, yet functioned together. Somehow, whatever the way of it was, it all came together to work as one, simply because the people wanted it to, they needed it to, in themselves, for others. Or was it that those who didn't fit into its narrow pattern simply left to find and fulfil themselves elsewhere?

America was bolstered every year by hundreds of thousands of these brave new idealists who needed colour in their black-and-white existence. In the beginning, this suited Mickie and his purpose well enough, and it lasted for a long time, but recent years had been different. Anyway, that's the way life works in America, because that's the way life works. If you want different, you have to keep going elsewhere.

Like Mickie, most of the workers he knew had memories that over the years changed black-and-white images to full colour. It's strange what goes on in the mind sometimes. Unlike most of his workmates, Mickie had never been back to visit, not in the twenty-odd years; not for funeral, not for wedding. He had kept his word to himself thus far and nothing was going to see him break it now. Day one, he had told himself, and many another, that when he went back, it would be for good. In his own mind, this meant he would be able to buy the only business back home that was in his heart that meant anything to him. Mickie was convinced he would return and buy a pub, not just any old pub, but Dan McCafferty's lounge bar and saloon, complete with seven-day liquor licence for the sale of intoxicating spirits on and off the premises. Nothing else would do for Mickie McGrew, and until this and another bit of business were done, he knew he would never be content with the life that was in him or the life he had to live.

Unlike many another of his kin, Mickie hadn't become a regular regular in McCafferty's in his hometown of Ballysaggart prior to his departure for the States. Maybe this was because he was too young then to have fallen fully under the influence and into the flow of life lipped out of a glass; maybe not. He certainly hadn't lived his life that way in America, although he could hold his own with the best of them.

Work was the real curse of life in recent years. For when your mind knows it's time to stop what you're doing and move on, then there's no hiding this fact from your body. And once your inners of conscience get hold of this message, there's no room for retreat; there's only one thing to do and that is to give in. Giving in was falling off the edge of Mickie's mind this long time, falling off his mind and into every thought that came, unconsidered, into his head. When this gets a hold of you, there's no recourse but do something about it, and for good.

So, letters were written, phone calls made, bank managers consulted, lawyers paid. And the single proviso Mickie put on the whole proceeding was that no-one should know. No-one meant just that: absolutely no-one. Neither friend nor family, not supplier or staff, none on this earth except the few whose business it was to know, were to know. Mickie knew the way things had to be for himself. It was he who was paying; it was he who had paid, paid dearly too. So long was this in the making, in the coming together, that he could see only one way for it to be.

On the set date, a Monday morning, Mickie would open the doors to his newly acquired licensed premises, and as the customers came in, they would all know it to be his; they would all know Mickie McGrew had returned. This was important; this was mighty important to him. What was of vital importance was that he could see their faces, catch the truth of twenty-odd years rise in their look and vanish into the thin air of recognition. Face after face as they came in would recognise him, would see it all to be his, and he would know it all to have been worthwhile. Word would spread and before long, the whole town would be aware of his return, especially the straggles of kinsfolk he still had thereabouts. He couldn't wait.

Over the weeks and months that dragged on until the big move, every face he had ever known back home popped into his head in a curious visit of the mind. It was smiles all round at this, the sight of one of their own having done so well being back in amongst the fold.

'We always knew you had it in you,' would smile O'Malley the schoolteacher.

'Well done, but be careful,' Fr Kelly, the parish priest, must be ancient by now.

McKinnon the grocer, McLaughlin the hardware, Jones the barber, all would be there waiting, wanting to extend hellos and best wishes to him personally.

Would his father, whom he hadn't seen all these years, be there for him, to wish him well, welcome him back? The bit of dust that rose before his leaving had had a long time to settle; it must be long gone and well dispersed by now. His father was only one picture in the montage of home. There were other, bigger, brighter faces his mind's eye needed to contend with. Mickie knew in his heart of hearts he was right in doing what needed to be done, but a slight hesitation inside indicated the measure of his unsureness about the outcome.

Stalling didn't take you anywhere in life except backwards, and this was the opposite direction to the one in which he was headed. He had more than done his bit in terms of working hard and earning his fare home, to a bright life, to pick up where he left off, but in his new standing in his old society.

So it was with a great swelling of his heart that he left America, that he said goodbye to its magnificent shores, built upon by men like himself until it was the truly splendid spectacle Mickie was turning his back on. It was this great swelling of the heart that rose through the rest of his being, lifting his spirits to feelings unknown before, lifting him up to the height of an angel when Mickie's eyes caught their first sight of the shores of home. When he landed on home ground, he wanted to immerse his whole body, his whole person, in the goodness of every speck of soil underfoot.

The grass was so green, the turf so luscious, he felt he could eat it, be part of it, make him part of it again. It was so thoroughly true: Mickie was home at last, in mind and spirit, in body and thought, beautifully, wonderfully, and almost totally.

The road home rose up through Mickie like a stroll into a dream as all the normals of place re-entered his mind through eyes that could see, could see it all, could see it all for the first time since... it had been a long time left unseen. It lifted him in a way he didn't think was possible. It swelled his heart so he felt it was about to burst inside him, until he felt as if his ribcage was about to burst open with the emotion of too many years of away coming back in on him, all at once, all in one, inside him. This was a feeling a long time gone. A feeling that had deserted him since... he knew exactly when.

A great distance of years was in that journey home. A great distance of emotion was in every twist and turn of every road taking him back through time and space until he was there, back where it all began, back where he had left it all behind. Like a bolt from beyond, the strength of feeling caught up with Mickie, caught him unawares, and a sleeve was needed to quickly wipe away all evidence in the flow of tears.

Grown men don't cry. Where did that surface from? When did he last hear that?

He knew rightly where it came from, from the sore at the very heart of his heart, the very core of his being, a long time there, waiting and wanting to be cured. Mickie knew the strength of his self that had seen him through all the miseries of alone, taken him all those thousands of miles from home and left him with nothing but the ache of work as a comfort to his mind. Mickie knew the basis on which that self existed, the young fellow in him who was forced to go, coerced into going away from all that was his, all that he wanted, all that he knew. And all because of love.

All through the years, hardly a day had gone by without that want in him grabbing hold of every ounce of his possession, his mind, body, spirit, and every bit of him beyond the seeing, and bled him with the regret of what he had done, what he hadn't done. Every day, he expected change to be just around the next corner, then the next, then the next, waiting for him, to lift him out of the purgatory of his existence, put his life in the happy, smiling order it should be in. Day by day, little bit by little bit, it wore away inside him until it had all but left him, all but gone away as time and the trials of life took their toll with new burdens and made him into a new blend of an old self.

****

Mary: that was the name behind it all.

Mary Madigan, the loveliest girl in town, was Mickie's girl. From no age, they were together, even though their families were very far apart. Whereas his father laboured, her father was undertaker and land agent to the best part of the diocese. Somehow a few streets can equate with many miles distance in terms of their upbringings, leaving them worlds apart inside the heads of others. From the start of them being together, something niggled at Mickie's mind that he wasn't good enough. It was nothing inside himself, nothing inside Mary, but it was a disease of the air of small towns like Ballysaggart.

The fact that no-one ever said anything was a big part of the problem, but this was part and parcel of living in a close-knit town. For all Mickie knew then, this was the way of the world, for it seemed to be inherent in every bit of what passed for life hereabouts. There were those who have, and those who mustn't.

No-one said anything, because no-one minded, because it wasn't going anywhere as far as all the leading minds of the day were concerned. Two young ones, so much together in their own eyes, so far apart in the eyes of those who could only see through their constrictions of mind, in a small speck on the map, in a small spot in time.

Go and have your bit of fun while you're young. He wondered now what thoughts really lay behind these words he had heard so often. Encouragement like this was not needed, but it made life all the tastier for what was hidden in his mother's telling. A warm feeling of hurt on the inside reminded Mickie of so much then. How one bit of fun led onto another and another until he and Mary were firmly part of the one heart, and to such an extent that even those with an opposing view couldn't help but notice.

So the beauty of all their togethernesses grew and flew with the short time they had with each other until one Friday evening while out walking, heads down and snuggled into the warmth of each other's share, through the soft drive of wind and rain, Mary spoke two words to end the dream, to begin the nightmare, 'I'm late.'

The glance that came with her words caught Mickie's head, his brain, his reality, and chucked it around inside him. He wasn't ready for, hadn't expected, couldn't handle, didn't want to know any of this. Why did she have to go and ruin it all, their lovely dream, by saying this? Why couldn't everything go on as before? Why couldn't everything continue on along the same lines as it had done, as it was meant to do?

'Are you sure?' What else was he meant to say? What else could he say? He didn't want it to be true.

'Positive.' There was no real feeling in Mary's voice; she was speaking plainly and simply.

'What do we do now?' Mickie couldn't think for the mishmash of thoughts smashing about inside his head.

'I don't know.' That was the truth of it: Mary didn't know. Mickie didn't know either, and so together they went and sat by themselves in a darkened corner of the picture-house, glad for all the silence they had, happy to be cut off from the rest of the world. But when the lights came on again, they had to return to the world of outside, of opposites, without a clue where they were going.

It was a tremble of a kiss Mickie laid on Mary's lips that evening at her door. He didn't like to go in with her, even at the best of times, but now he wanted away, he wanted out of there, he wanted off with himself along streets that didn't notice, didn't know any of what was going on inside his head.

And when the last bit of life was pulled out of the last cigarette and the empty packet crushed and kicked away, only then was there room for thoughts of home, bed, comfort, sleep and lights out to cut his mind off from the tumult of it all.

Over the following days, the telephone line was busy with words of wonder not getting the response they wanted.

'Is it there yet? Is there any sign? Are you sure you haven't got your dates mixed up?' Looking for any little glimmer of hope to light the way for them out of this mess. Mickie then remembered something, a little something he had heard, in an aside, a pick-up, probably only a bit of bravado nonsense young men of that certain age go in for. But worth a go nonetheless. The first chance he had, he bought a bottle of vinegar, a big bottle of brown vinegar, because he reckoned this looked stronger, and slipped it into Mary's possession. Her hands were cold – he always remembered that – freezing cold, so cold she should have had gloves on.

'If you put this into a hot bath, a very hot bath... it can do the trick.'

48

Mickie couldn't bear to look near Mary's face as he spoke.

Nothing was said in response.

They stood so close together yet so far apart in terms of the thoughts going on inside their heads. Each held by the burden of knowing yet not knowing, and wanting to know what was going on inside the thinking of the other. Perhaps it was the cold, perhaps not. Whatever the way of it, the plastic bag containing the bottle of brown vinegar fell, smashing onto the pavement. Neither made a move to stop it, to catch it before it broke. Each watched, catching only the strong stench of vinegar that sparked their clothes as the breakage fed off along the lines of the pavement beneath. Before they moved off, Mickie kicked the broken remains, bag and all, off the pavement and into the gulley at the side of the road. He then walked Mary the short distance back home. They held hands, not knowing this would be the last time. This was when Mickie noticed the cold that was in Mary's hold, the heat that was in his own.

They said their goodbyes on her front doorstep, short and to the point, for there wasn't much point; there wasn't much of a kiss to come out of either of them. And so Mickie left.

Over the following days, he tried as best he could to put it all to the back of his mind and to reintroduce a bit of normality into his existence. So he caught up with a few friends he hadn't bothered about in a long time. It was just what he needed. It did him good to get out and about, to have a bit of a laugh again and enjoy the feeling of being young and alive and able to enjoy life. Then, one evening, there they all were in the kitchen at home, waiting for him. Mary, her mother and father, sitting glum-faced and serious around the table with his mother and father. Mickie wanted to beat a hasty retreat, to head back outside. But he couldn't, he knew he couldn't, he had to act as if he cared, which he did, about Mary, but not about the rest of them, every last one of them who only wanted to mess up his life, wreck the happiness he and Mary had together.

'So what's all this, then?' He thought it best to hit them with a question rather than have them start on him. As he finished his words, he threw a casual smile out in Mary's direction, the type that had always worked effortlessly before.

Mary's eyes caught it but didn't hold onto it, then her eyes rebounded off the look of her father.

There was one thought in Mickie's head and it was that he had never seen Mary look as beautiful as she did at the table, stuck between the tight-lipped, sour faces of supposedly worthy others around her. He could see it in their eyes, that self-righteous look of determination, showing off the fact that they had never made even one small mistake between the lot of them in their entire lives.

'That's no way to talk, young man.'

His father's chair seemed to move of its own volition. But the gentlest touch of his mother's hand on top of his father's, which only Mickie could see happen under the table, brought a quick end to his notion – for now, at least.

'Mr Madigan here has just been filling us in on a few details, on one particular detail, you neglected to share with us.'

Mickie was caught by the look of his mother's eyes upon him. He could see she was staring at him, but her look was elsewhere, off beyond the notice of everyone else in the room, except perhaps her husband.

'Well, these things happen, don't they?'

The cheekiness in Mickie's words was a disappointment to himself, but he couldn't help his feeling of being let down by Mary, by her not forewarning him. Still, he wished he hadn't said what he just had; he wished he could take it back, take it all back. At that particular moment in time, he wished he could take a lot of things back, but he knew wishes like his were never going to be granted.

'So that's the way of it, is it? That's all you've got to say about the state you've left my daughter in. You've ruined her, ruined her life, but not for the world to see.'

That was the long and the short of what was said before Mary was marched out between her parents; her father with the devil at work in his eyes, her mother with the sorrow of a broken heart bleeding out through her look. Mary, the last look Mickie had of her, showed him they were all over and done with, that this was an end to them, completely.

All the years he had to think back on it, all the years on his own, all the years with other girls, women, gave Mickie plenty of occasion to reflect on Mary's look as she stepped out of his life forever. It tore the heart from inside him for years after, for he knew he could have, should have, done better by her.

Nothing more was said on the subject.

Mickie didn't want to know what had been said in his absence, before his arrival home; he certainly didn't want to know then. There may have been a few times later, later on when he wouldn't have minded knowing, when the greed of wanting to explain away his situation caught up with an empty darkness inside. However, it was never enough, never strong enough to carry him through to actually asking, to finding out. It had never registered with him during the early years of his time away that it might have been he who wasn't strong enough. And when it might have mattered, it was too late, there was no-one there, not in America; he was well away from it all.

There had always been an inkling in him to head off, away, free himself from the claustrophobic wrap of Ballysaggart and this provided him with the perfect opportunity to do so. He knew he mightn't get another chance like this in his life. Mickie also knew it was what was expected of him and if he didn't go it could be insisted on. Words were never spoken regarding the matter, but it was always there, all the more said for remaining unsaid.

A brave little romantic twist inside suggested more than once that he and Mary might head off together and live happily ever after, but he knew this was never on. He had been brought up in the real world of hard knocks where life had a certain habit of spoiling the good times. He had learned young they were never meant to last, certainly not for his sort.

Before Mickie had to up and go, Mary was gone, off to England to live with an aunt and study in college over there. So he was told.

So, he was free. Nothing was going to hold him back anyway, but now he had his freedom, he headed immediately to America. He had done with Ireland, done with Ballysaggart and all it held against him. He was off to the promise of a brave new life in a brave new world and he wasn't going to look back.

****

51

That was the way of it then.

Now it was all change again; now was different; now was the time for renewal.

Catching a glimpse of himself in the rear-view mirror pulled Mickie out of his reverie. He looked older. The years hadn't been kind to him, so much so that he wondered if many would recognise him when he arrived back.

Thoughts like these didn't sit long in him. His eye was soon off himself and down the fading road behind, watching it fall away into the distance.

Stopping at the summit of Slieve Finn, travelling the back road into Ballysaggart, Mickie could see the spread of lights below, some moving, most firmly fixed. It had grown, it looked twice the size he remembered it, but, he thought, perhaps this was just a trick of the light; perhaps the light had spread into the areas where there had been none before. Forward he travelled, keys and deeds and thoughts all his own and there with him to comfort him, taking him back as someone he had always wanted to be, a man of note, of worth, of value amongst his own. A big man in a small town.

It was late. A few youths hurried along the wet pavement, feet moving in double-quick time under the constancy of the fall of rain. He saw fragments of an old self in this movement, when all the goodness had been wrung out of a night, trying to quick-step it back home under the blight of rain. They looked as young as he had been when last he strode the streets around here. A shiver caught him from within. He shook the old notion out of himself with a final thought: he hoped they would fare better in the romance stakes than he had done; at least they were better equipped for it than had been the practice back then.

Mickie took a wrong turn. It was deliberate. He found himself driving down the road Mary had lived on all those years before. The car stopped in front of a house; it was Mary's house. It looked brighter, done up somehow, definitely a world away from the drabness of before. The old sign for undertaking was gone; this brought a little pang of pleasure.

He must have been sitting there a while when a light struck on upstairs. Mickie's heart, on overdrive before, now nearly jumped out of his mouth. With a rush of fuel to the accelerator, the car jerked to a standstill. He cursed it for all he was worth. A rush of blood flooded his thoughts. He cursed himself for having driven there in the first place. Then, at the corner of his eye, he thought he saw a shaft of light sneak out. A glance round wasn't chanced. Off like a shot the car screeched, spitting small stones back in its wake. Away from there Mickie rushed, away from all thought of there and back onto the main road he knew he shouldn't have deviated from.

Not another second was wasted in getting to the bar and getting into it. That moment, that proudest moment so long dreamt of, so long dwelt upon in the subconscious of his mind, didn't arrive with him. It wasn't in the turn of the key in the door, wasn't in the bend of the heavy handle, but it was ever so slightly rekindled with his reacquaintance with the smell inside. It hadn't changed much; he was glad of that. In fact, it was better than he had imagined it. Mickie could feel echoes of the past rise through him, echoes enhanced by his touch as he felt his way around each corner of the past.

At last he was home, back where he belonged and in charge, not just of his own situation but of his destiny for the first time in his life. It was the best of feelings. And ahead lay the joy of all the many faces coming in through the front doors. Tomorrow was the day when truth would be on display, real, immediate, unmasked feelings and faces as they walked in for their usual and caught a glimpse of their past. Mickie couldn't wait.

There was a knock at the door. His thoughts ran cold and straight out of him. He stalled, looking at his watch; it was well after one in the morning.

'We're closed.' It felt good being in control.

There was a second knock at the door.

'We're closed.' Mickie's shout would have been heard a lot further away than the front street.

There was a third knock at the door.

Mickie eased himself off the stool he was perched on. Unbolting the door, he opened it slightly, wedging a foot firmly behind. He had forgotten himself for that moment; he thought himself back in the States. Removing his foot, he opened the door wide. A woman stood alone out in the mizzle of the night.

It took a few seconds, a few seconds that pulled Mickie back through the barren years between, back to when he last enjoyed this new feeling of comfort and joy in his heart. Back through all the years he now knew, in that lonely instant, had been wasted in America, had been thrown away in pursuit of an empty dream, a dream that was real and here, now.

'Jesus, Mary. I'm looking at you and I don't know what to say. Come in, come in.'

Mickie wanted to rush straight into his past, his long lost past. He wanted to wrap his arms around Mary and squeeze away all that had happened in between. He wanted to say all the thousands of words he had thought of saying when eventually he got to this moment in time. Now it was here, he had nothing to say.

Mary stepped inside. She looked thinner, somehow smaller; she certainly had lost the freshness of appearance bursting from her when last they were together.

'How have you been?'

Mickie was pushing the door, locking it as he spoke. He knew this wasn't much to say after so long apart. Thought crashed on thought in his mind.

There was a pause.

'I've been myself, Mickie. How have you been?'

The sound of her voice tore shreds off Mickie's heart, so lovely did it sound. He wanted to cry.

Looking out from under his gaze into the past, Mickie saw the warmth in Mary's face; the honesty of those eyes was not lost on him either. He knew it was all there, that Mary had not changed; goodness still lived in her heart, love still flourished in her soul.

'I've been working, working away. I found something I was good at and stuck with it for as long as I could. And now I'm back.' The last few words settled heavily into the air around.

Mary was about to say something, but Mickie's anxiousness interrupted the moment.

'I'm sorry. I've forgotten my manners. Sit down, Mary, and I'll get you a drink. What would you like?' Mickie was all shuffley and awkward within himself and it shone through in his actions.

'A mineral will do fine, Mickie. I'm here to talk. We need to talk.' The firmness with which Mary messaged her words fixed Mickie's mind on the greater need there now was for a drink.

Two large glasses were poured and carried shaken-handedly to the small table where Mary had sat down. There wasn't room for Mickie to sit beside. It was either pull up a chair alongside or sit opposite. He sat opposite.

Cometh the moment, disappeareth the man.

All sorts of thoughts rose and fell within his mind. He followed up on this by reaching across the table. It stayed there, all alone and unforgiven. There was no reaction to it, certainly no movement towards it.

'You look more beautiful than I remember, Mary.' Mickie's smile held the sadness of all he felt.

'I see you haven't changed.' Mary's smile rippled out into a cover of creases around her face.

Mickie chastised his inner self for homing in on an irrelevancy such as this.

Mary's touch seemed further away than ever. A small table carried a greater distance than a large ocean.

'Was that your car drove up outside the house?' Very little lightness had managed to enter Mary's voice.

Mickie burned with embarrassment inside. Outside, his hand withdrew from across the table and his large frame froze solid.

'Are you still living in the same house, then?' The hope in his voice blended nicely with the telling tones of wanting her to go easy on him.

'I've been back in the house this number of years. After father died.'

Sadness hung onto every word Mary uttered.

Mickie didn't want to go there; he didn't want to go back. He didn't want to start raking through the ashes of all that was all but dead and gone. He wanted to go forward, to look ahead, to make something of what might still be. He wanted to focus all his energies, all their combined energies, on the hope that lay in each new day, in as much togetherness as possible. But could he say this? Could he say any of it? It was too early to tell.

'I've come back for you, Mary.'

That was the way with him. He knew he should have waited, gauged what was what, but no, he had gone ahead and spurted out what was on his mind. Still, he was well enough pleased with himself, not just for choosing such pointed words, but for saying them with such direction, such strength.

'You've come back for yourself, Mickie. If you were thinking of me, you would have come back for me twenty-three years ago.'

Mickie was wrong; it was Mary's words that held strength, Mary's voice that held power. He was lost inside his thoughts. He knew she was right. She shouldn't have said it, though; she shouldn't have cut him like that; it hurt him. Then again, perhaps she had a right to hurt him, perhaps she had a right to cut him down to size, perhaps he did have a right cheek on him coming back after so long away, and coming back hoping, expecting things to go his way. He saw now he had assumed rather a lot.

'I always wanted to... I always meant to... It's just that one day you're there, and then the next thing you know, you've been there five years, then ten, then twenty. Every day you were in my thoughts. Honest, Mary.'

Mickie was beginning to struggle. He could feel the desperation rising within. He could hear his voice start to crack under the strain. In a brave effort to clear himself, he announced, 'I thought you were in England.'

'I was. And I hoped and prayed each and every day that you would show up and save me from the hell of loneliness I was lost in, with the business I had to do.'

Their eyes caught across this small table – but way back in time. Twenty-odd years were held in the stare of each other.

Mickie was afraid to ask. He most definitely wanted to ask. He needed to know. All those years, all the years of wondering: was it a boy, was it a girl, who did it look like, was it at school now, was it happy, did it do well at exams, did it play sport, did it grow up good and honest and nice? All these thoughts and hundreds of thousands more had plagued and pleased Mickie's mind. There had been a sorrowful comfort in them, a kind of sour sweetener to take him through the dark moments of life.

'Was it a boy?'

His mind had always come down on the side of it being a boy. He always had it in the front of his mind that it was a boy, his son. The back of his mind was reserved for the softer moments in life when he thought in terms of his little baby, his child, his little girl.

'What?'

Disbelief jumped back at him. There was almost a squeal screwed onto the end of her sound.

Mickie sensed he had got it wrong, got it totally wrong. All these years, and there he was thinking to himself and not telling another soul he had a child. All this time thinking he had a son somewhere, growing stronger with each day, a piece of himself who, no doubt, would come looking for him one day. A son who would want to know who his father was, his real father. A son who probably looked like him and had some of his ways, his good ways, he hoped. And all this time it wasn't a son that he had, it was a daughter, a beautiful, darling girl who was now grown to be a young woman. Mickie smiled as he wondered if she had her mother's beauty or her father's fine features. He was just about to ask.

'I had an abortion, Mickie.'

This was real. What Mary was saying was real. He could see it in her eyes, he could see it in her face, he could see it in how she leaned across the table and then threw herself into the back of the chair.

'Jesus, Mickie! You knew that was what I was sent to England for.'

The silence of all the years past hung between their two faces. Mickie was lost in thoughts without words as Mary's words stuck in the forefront of his mind. In the moments that followed, tears began a steady trickle down Mickie's face. So lost was he in the torment of the truth, he made no attempt to wipe them away.

'Mary, I'm so sorry. I had no idea that... It never entered my head that you... Dear God, what you must have been through.' Mickie's tears were matched by those now on full flow across the table.

'My father wouldn't let me keep it. It was all arranged. I was to come back after as if nothing had happened. I couldn't come back, not with the torment that was in my mind. So I stayed in England, lived there, didn't come back until he was dead.'

That was it, the sum total of twenty-odd years broken down into a line of words and tears. A line that contained a lot more tears than words.

'I know we all have to atone for our sins, but I didn't think I would have to pay so dearly.'

'Mary, I'm sorry. I'm so very, very sorry.'

Mickie's words were for Mary but his thoughts were completely within himself. His pain, his grief, his sorrow, the misery that now existed within him, all the emotion of leaving, as well as return. All the feelings welled up with being back where he once belonged, back in the land of his birth, the place he had once known and had once known him. All this did was bring back his loneliness, his emptiness, and for this void inside then to be filled by... such unbelievable sadness.

'You need to go back to America, Mickie. You should never have come back here. There's nothing but pain and sorrow for you here.'

Mickie tried to understand Mary's words, tried to understand them fully. He hoped they were sent out to test his resolve. He wouldn't fail her this time. Yet he could hardly believe the strength in her sound, the fullness of thought contained in their message. He was caught by the firmness of her look, the drive of her control. He realised that time had undoubtedly changed them, had definitely blended them to a new form, but he still expected something a bit more inviting than this.

As the tears dried in both of them, Mickie could see the sallow, pale look of Mary's face. They were both far removed from the full flush of youth when they had last seen each other. This wasn't the face or the form or the sound that he had remembered all those years.

'I'm here to stay.'

He said the words, he had the look, but within himself, he didn't know whether he really meant them or not.

'What are you back for, Mickie? Don't try and tell me it's this place.'

He truly did love the sound of her voice. It seemed like he had waited an eternity to hear it. The way Mary said his name held him, took him straight back into the memory of youth she had known so well, and one he had not found part of himself in many years.

'I'm back for you, Mary.'

As much feeling as he could muster, as much as he could master, was put into saying her name. He had forgotten how much he enjoyed saying Mary, for there were too many Marias around where he lived in America. It didn't seem to work.

'Don't talk nonsense. You know nothing about me. I'm far removed from the young girl you knew a lifetime ago. And I bet you're as different on the inside as you are on the outside.'

Mary was standing, poised to leave.

Mickie didn't want to rise, he didn't want to see her out, he wanted her to stay to hear him out. He had so much to say, he didn't know where to start. This wasn't the reception he had expected. Perhaps he had been foolish to expect any other sort of reception.

'You need to give me a chance, Mary.'

Mary turned.

'This isn't about you, Mickie. There are others besides yourself who have lives that they want to be getting on with. The town of Ballysaggart doesn't revolve around your needs or the needs of men like you. You and your big secret that everyone knew. You can't keep a secret around these parts. I know that only too well, and to my cost, and now your coming back will do nothing but rake up all the dirt again.'

There was no sign of Mary heading for the door; she obviously had plenty more in her to say, perhaps a lot more than Mickie's ears needed to hear.

'Mary, if you tell me to go, I'll go for good.'

Mickie was on his feet.

'Men and their amateur dramatics! Is that all you're good for?' Arms high in the air, Mary was now definitely moving to leave.

'It's not like that. I'm not like that. You can't know how much you mean to me.'

Mickie was hurting, it was all turning out so wrong, so far removed from what he had anticipated. He wanted to touch her, to hold her, to show her how much she meant to him. Instead, he stood motionless, wanting something to happen.

Mary stopped a little away from him; she stood still, her eyes heavy with sadness. Perhaps she knew that waiting for Mickie to make the right move would be a waste of time. Perhaps she was waiting for him to say the right words, words that would sweep away all the knowledge and doubt she had in her mind.

Mary realised nothing had changed. She wondered how on earth Mickie had ever managed to take the decision and make all the necessary moves to bring him back. There was only one answer. With this in mind, she spoke.

'I have a life here that I am happy with, a life I have worked hard to make for myself. I have enough to deal with in my life without trying to cope with you and all the baggage you bring with you. Go back to America, Mickie. I'm going back home and I don't expect to see you again. Goodbye.'

All he could do was watch her leave. All he could hear was the door slam firmly shut and the fall of her feet disappear into the distance of darkness outside.

After standing a long time drowning in the pain of his sorrow, dreams shattered, more and more lost in misery, he eventually made his way to the door and bolted it, closing himself off from the world outside. Then Mickie retreated to the bar, poured himself a drink, and stayed there.

****

The drink Mickie poured himself that sad and sorry night lasted a long time. There were many knocks on the door of the pub the following day, accompanied by shouts and calls growing in voice and number. Names, names that took Mickie back, way back beyond football and drinking, back in amongst the warm security of solid rows of desks irremovably linked to childhood and all that was good in life. These were the many he had most wanted to catch up with, for it seemed to him that the further time took you away from the past, the fonder the memories grew in warmth and number.

Days later and he was still pouring his heart into a glass without making contact with even one person. His head was in the drink, for it took his mind off what mattered. Now nothing mattered, and it never would again.

The days that were in him grew into weeks, and these weeks left him in a roaring, sorry state that disappeared without a thought from him. He knew what he needed, what he wanted, what he had come back for, but all he could now see was that it never would be his.

A whisper ran through the town about a drunken, bitter man who had come back from America to drink McCafferty's dry. The young boys of the town sent their shouts in through the letter-box, and their jumps outside the lounge window were lost on the poor, drunk, besotted foreigner inside.

Poor Mickie. For even drunk, he couldn't shift the wonder of Mary from the front of his mind. And all this time there was but one face burning its way through Mary's heart, one person, returned, in every breath she took. But Mary had no wish to be kind to be cruel, certainly not to her one, first and truest love, most definitely not to herself. There were moments when she might have slipped, when the strength of her resolve might have failed her, but she dug deep, and love won through every time. Love would not let her mend his heart for it to be broken all over again.

In the end, as he knew it would, the drink eventually ran out, and Mickie was left with the sober light of day to bring him to his senses. As he had known, perhaps even before he arrived, as he had been left in no doubt after his arrival, as all the weeks of internal abandonment couldn't hide him from the truth, whilst his heart lay somewhere in Ballysaggart, his fate lay elsewhere.

In the small hours of a miserable morning, Mickie left the pub, left the town, left the dying hint of hope it held for him, never to return.

PESIAIL

A big, fit-looking lump of a man, not burly, but honest in figure and look, and having the eye for being able and willing to handle whatever situation landed on his ecclesiastical shoulders, Fr Ignatius was all he was ever known as. And as well as being a man of the cloth, he was an Englishman, born and half-bred.

It wasn't very often that one came the other way, this way, from over there across the water; this was one such time. The truth of it was that Fr Benedict, the parish priest in the parish of Kiltemper, had to take off suddenly, because of his nerves, it was rumoured, and his return was not expected for a couple of months at least. In stepped Fr Ignatius; he was just the man for the job and he didn't mind a trip into a past he had only heard tell of, the countryside his mother hailed from.

Kiltemper it was, then, for a short stay, and the idea of it suited him fine, especially the idea of fresh air and clean living to take the place of inner city pollution. Kiltemper wasn't much of a village and it certainly wasn't a town; in fact, it was more of a crossroads that had spread itself out in a couple of directions until it assumed the identity of a horseshoe around the lake of the same name. Or perhaps it was shaped like a big, old-fashioned magnet that drew in folk from all the outlying areas of mountain, hill and vale.

The best way of conducting a census was by counting the throng attending eleven o'clock Mass on Sundays. Why this Mass? Because there was only one Mass held on the Sabbath in Kiltemper and it was at eleven o'clock. So everyone had to learn to suit it or go without, and in these parts, it didn't do to go without.

It was here, then, Fr Ignatius arrived, armed with the religious message that was his calling, into the background that had been in his mother's telling as he grew up. Well he knew the locals would have every last detail on him before he ever got the length of the place. So when he stood up on the altar in front of their packed gathering, a surly sense of what life was once all about was clustered before him.

In seconds, all but a few faces had turned sour with the first words uttered by their temporary priest. It wasn't what he said, it was the way he said it, for his accent had a knack all its own in these parts. This English twang was associated with uniforms and taxes and other unwanteds that went back a long way and most certainly didn't go down too well in the present parish of Kiltemper – or any other unurban setting in Ireland.

Fr Ignatius looked around from the upper level of the altar. He knew now he had made the right decision. Immediately, he was caught by the lack of brightness, of lightness of colour, by the heaviness of the drab and darkly dressed gathering of locals he looked down on. Perhaps he was still taken with his last mission, with the casualness of city-centre colour and cut, its spaciousness of pew.

Memory jolted worry into his head and his eyes darted down the centre aisle. To his eternal relief, there was no coffin on its way in. He had been caught out once before, when he hadn't remembered being told. An oversight on his part, never to be repeated again. Then, half-awake, he had started Mass only for a coffin to walk in on him.

Looking around, it had been all too obvious then. Looking around now, that same funereal dismay was all-present before him. And he hated funerals.

On second thoughts, it wasn't just the people. What a drab, dreary, dismal, dark, dreadful looking interior this was, with the very paint leaving the walls. The dirt and grime of the sacristy had left him in no doubt that the present full-time incumbent smoked his lights out, and probably mostly in that one little room behind the altar. Eyes to heaven showed him the lights were actually on, only somehow this made the church seem darker. A glance around the windows told him it was a very long time since sunlight had found its way through their stained glass, the stains being *on* the glass rather than *in*.

Strangest of all was the peculiar catch of mustiness that had definitely grown as the church had filled up. Perhaps they brought it with them. Perhaps they stirred it up as they shuffled and manipulated themselves into the narrow rows. Perhaps this was what the mix of church and congregation brought – staleness.

Ah well, here goes, he thought.

'In the name of the Father, and of the Son, and of the Holy Ghost. Amen.'

As his head went down, slightly, an eye went up to see what sort of a bunch Kiltemperans really were. This told him a lot. Their heads dropped. They were an earnest, God-fearing lot.

This will do nicely, he thought to himself. Soft, low, gravelly sounds came out with their responses. *There shouldn't be too much bother with them.*

All the way through the workings of the Mass, Fr Ignatius's mind was on a "will he, won't he?" strategy, on how best to deal with his new charges. He decided it best to get their surrounds sorted first before turning their attention on themselves.

'You're a disgrace! Each and every one of you gathered here today. You should be ashamed of yourselves!'

There was a pause, a momentary break as heads looked round at heads, astonished by what they had just heard.

'Do you call this a church? Do you call this a House of God? It's a disgrace to religion! A disgrace to Ireland! A disgrace to call yourselves Catholics!'

Numbed silence killed off the last of the light chatter as the congregation's attention absorbed the full force of every word thundered upon them in that English prattle.

'In your defence, all I can say is that this is the outward representation of your souls. God help me when I try to make a job of saving those.'

Few sat comfortably with what he was saying, because they weren't used to hearing the likes of this; not here, not now. A lot of fidgeting was taking place inside heads. A lot of scratching was going on inside thoughts. Heads swung round in short, sharp angles, looking to see how those in their immediate vicinity were taking it all. There was a lot of looking going on; there was a lot of thinking going on; but there was still only one person saying anything. Everyone else was quietly taking it and dying for Mass to be over so they could escape back out into the world and vent their true feelings.

They were all of one mind and it was: *The cheek of this one, this outsider! Who was he to come among them and criticise them for how things were? Who the hell did he think he was, this Englishman, coming into their parish and telling them in no uncertain terms that none of this was good enough for him?* The Irish had had a bellyful of English history dictating to them how the world and all in it should be. Centuries it had taken them to rid most of the island of the sorts who dictated what was what without reference to what was already there.

However, when they looked up at their sermoniser, they focused in on the white collar and this told them he was one of their own. It was the accent lambasting all from on high that caught them hardest, because it wasn't their own. So, heads went down and stayed down.

It was only when the slow start turned into the torrent for communion that most of them availed of the opportunity to look around and see exactly what he was complaining about. The inside of the church looked as it always had done, grand, almost, good enough for all the years it had been so. Slowly but surely, eyes began to see what the priest could see, the detail of his earlier ranting. There were parts, corners and the like, plus long bits extending out from the corners, that would have looked better for the wipe of a damp cloth. In fact, the whole interior could probably have done with a good spring clean, and a drop of paint wouldn't have gone amiss in some parts either.

By the time Mass was over, most minds had moved off from the confusion of earlier thoughts to the embarrassment of an outsider, and a Sassenach at that, having to come into their midst to put them right about their own place. It was a bitter pill to swallow, something they were far from used to, but it was exactly what they knew they were going to have to do.

As the final blessing was pronounced, and Fr Ignatius's polished shoes were off the altar, there was a stampede to get out before the new priest got a chance to make it round to the front steps. Apart from the few stragglers who were either too deaf or too taken with their own importance to have absorbed the priest's words into their worth, the church and grounds were empty within a matter of minutes.

Fr Ignatius knew he had managed perfectly well to captivate his audience, because they couldn't miss the faults he pointed out to them. In future, they would be listening attentively and picking up on points when he made them aware of what might not be so obvious at first.

It didn't take the parish long to get gathered. Next day, ladders of a great length, buckets of enormous depth, cloths of a mixed variety, pots of paint of the one bright white colour, arrived accompanied by able-bodied men, women and children, who straight away put their backs into what needed to be done. Soon dustsheets were spread out over wide areas as the pots of paint found a new home, spread out over great surfaces of wall. There was hardly room to move in the church with the effort and endeavour of so many. And so, by the following Sunday, the transformation was there for all to see. It may not have been totally complete, but it was well on the way to being finished.

For themselves, the delight was there and theirs and a very conscious blessing came upon them as they found their way into the light, bright cleanness of a building that seemed fresh and reborn. A bit of a brighter effort had been made by a good chunk of locals gathered for Mass and it was a favourable impression not lost on Fr Ignatius. However, he had no intention of letting them know this of themselves, not at this early stage.

So, the Mass of his second Sunday jittered along as uneventfully as it should have, and smiles were on the faces of all as they basked in the brightness of their own creation, their new surrounds. Then Fr Ignatius settled himself for his sermon.

'Cursed and damned is the soul of every one of you who doesn't see the inside of a confessional from one year's end to the next. If I don't hear you in the confessional during the coming fortnight, then I don't expect to see you anywhere near this altar for the sacrament of Holy Communion. There are no special spiritual benefits on offer for anyone whose soul is not spotlessly clean. No doubt some of you regard it as your heathen human duty to damn body and soul to eternal fire and damnation, but let me tell you, it is my solemn duty on this earth to make sure you don't succeed!

'In consideration of this, Confession will be heard during the hour before evening Mass every night this week. I expect to hear each and every one of you there.'

As his words finished in a great flourish of tone, his eyes led off around the congregation, and one by one they could tell that what was said was aimed specifically at them. A horrible feeling of embarrassment gripped the minds of all present. Now it had been brought to their attention, they understood just how remiss they had been in terms of personal duty, and many minds immediately resolved to do better by themselves, by their family, by their priest, by their Church.

In the days following on from his second sermon, pews were lined out with bodies of persons awaiting use of the confessional, to the extent that Fr Ignatius almost regretted his own doing. He offered up their sins for the repose of holy souls close to his heart.

The delight and lightness and brightness of feeling coming out from the holy sacrament of Confession was such that many were hard pressed to contain their joy and stay on for evening Mass. Some even stayed on after Mass, but this was mostly in prayerful pose to work their way through the wonderful number they had to recite as penance for forgiveness of their sins; and all this before the church was locked up for the night.

The following days saw the number of bright colours prosper in the pews, even though spring was still a long way off. However, there were those who reckoned against this being a proper way to proceed and, to this end, they spent their time in deliberate rejection of all things bright and beautiful in their lives, internally as well as externally. These numbers were only significant in the fact they were a growing minority. The vast majority of Kiltemper's faithful fell in with the new priest's ways, even though, or perhaps because, they knew he was only there on a temporary basis. Mind you, they still would have preferred him a bit more guarded in his method of delivery.

The following Sunday, there was a good feeling amongst most entering the church. Smiles of satisfaction blended with smiles of self-contained smugness along rows of bright eyes. Voices were louder and diction a lot clearer in the general responses of all gathered together in the Lord's name.

When it came to the sermon, backs sat up straight, chins rose up to the angle of the priest's, and an expectant hush quelled the mood of the congregation in preparation for a positive twist to the priest's tongue. He began.

'Well, aren't we the smug lot! All nice and bright and clean on the outside, all white and good and holy with the slate wiped clean on the inside. But what do you do with all this goodness? I look down on each and every one of you and I ask myself: what is the point in your living, your working, your striving, when you don't make time for God in your life? How many of you, gathered here today, ever bother with even a couple of decades of the rosary at night? How many? How many of you copy the good sense of the few decent households that haven't fallen in with today's easy ways?

'Take a step back to understand. Take a moment to notice the price that has been paid by others in lives without a love of God. Is it a price worth paying?

'My dear people, remember your rosary, and if this means rhyming off a string of prayers, so well and so good. But a real rosary is when you kneel down in the presence of God every evening and you offer up for his consideration a list of all the good works and deeds you have done that day.'

Silence hung on the features of every face before him.

Fr Ignatius's words stopped; his mind seemed caught up somewhere inside his head, inside his throat. He gave a few little twists of his neck that sent his head round in awkward angles off the altar, but his eyes were firmly fixed and continued to hold the gaze of all before him.

'By next Sunday, I expect to have heard of a lot of action: I expect to see you bothering about those you haven't bothered about in a long time; helping those you've managed to get out of the way of helping; visiting those you no longer bother to visit; talking to all who need a word spoken, who need more than just a passing nod. Make the effort, and make it count.'

So much for so many of the congregation feeling good about themselves in the days, hours and moments before Fr Ignatius's sermon put their minds through the mill of self-worth. Deep within, inside whatever little parcel of brain or mind, or whatever it was that held their essence intact, they knew the big, bold priest was right. He might not have won any prizes for the way his message was delivered to its target audience, but they could not rightly deny its validity.

Heads went down as minds wondered and wandered off into the recall that had stained their conscience. All the many times they could have, but decided against, bothering with that neighbour, that friend, that relation. In their minds, the same answer always came through: there was something else they needed to be doing, something more important than that which was of genuine importance. At least they recognised this much, so there was still some hope for them. They understood perfectly well what Fr Ignatius was saying. All hearts before him resolved to do better, to do right by themselves as well as by others.

As the congregation left the church after Mass, their thoughts paced them out more slowly than the expectation that had taken them in. Small groups gathered and smiled their goodbyes to the many others passing, and stood on chatting to those they had found no reason to chat to in a long, long time. A marvellous sense of good feeling came with the few words that flowed between the different bodies of folk, and immediately, they began to feel the better of themselves for the good feeling brought about by these few words.

Days ambled along in their inevitable way through the week and there was a noticeable movement throughout many parts of the parish as folk went out of their way to meet and greet and talk and chat to one another. Acts of kindness followed on from the new means of sharing many found at their disposal, and a great section of people felt a lot better within themselves for the change.

A genuine feeling of warmth came upon the people of Kiltemper as they took to chatting and gossiping and finding out about and doing for others in a way that almost came naturally. Then, as a follow-on to this, they found they didn't want the company of much television of an evening; they found they didn't need its empty feed.

Instead, they found they began thinking about the lives of those around. These lives became real and physical and part of them again, and this had the double effect of making their own lives feel worthwhile in making someone else's important to them. By the time the following Sunday came around, a great many of the parish felt they had made a positive and definite change to their lives and for good, and this they could barely contain in their interaction with others.

The demeanour of the priest seemed little changed from previous weeks and his hollow countenance furrowed the same frightful face down on his parishioners. The sounds of the Mass followed along the normal format except for the hurriedness of words recited back by the packed gathering. There was only one thing on the minds of all kneeling before him and this was to quicken proceedings along to the important part, the sermon, to find out what blessing he had to bestow on them that day.

Eventually they got there.

'I have noticed an air of change come amongst you in recent days. I can see it chasing the air around, because it has not settled, because it cannot settle itself. There is still too much cut-off and drift among many in the parish. Some tried to listen to my words last Sunday, but many were not able to understand their true meaning. For those who cannot understand what I said, I will spell it out to you.

'The road outside is worn thin with the travel of cars. Big, fat, ugly, expensive-to-run, waste-of-your-time cars, that do nothing but choke the roads, the lungs, and the bodies, and stifle the minds of all connected to them. Stand up anyone who has a broken leg!'

The priest's words paused for a few seconds, but his eyes continued their sweep of all before him.

'No-one? So why can I not see the road for the cars? What need is there for all those lumps of metal lying out there? Are you trying to tell me something? Are you trying to tell each other something? Or are you simply trying to tell yourself something?

'Well, let me tell each and every one of you something. We know already. We all know what's what and who's who around here. It's no use trying to bluff those who know you, with your expensive suits of engined armour. But I know that inside the hollow shell you hide in, there is a might of goodness wanting to grow. Inside each stem, there is a bud waiting to open, a flower waiting to burst into bloom and shine its goodness on the world. For this to happen, the sun needs to shine on you; the rain needs to fall on you.

'If you need to travel a short distance in life, do it with your own two feet under you; you'll find you're much the better person for it. You never know what good thoughts and prayers will pop into a mind that has room for more. Try it and see.

'And finally, today, my dear people, remember this. You only need a small fire to keep you warm. A big fire will burn the backside off you.'

Fr Ignatius seemed more subdued than his previous Sunday deliberations had shown him. Perhaps the people of Kiltemper were having a good effect on him. Perhaps the changes he had called for were working their way slowly but surely into the lives and dealings of those thereabouts, and this was paying off in terms of his attitude towards them.

In terms of the general attitude towards their priest, the people knew they had most definitely changed. Even his accent was no longer a matter of note to them. All other issues aside, there were very few who would have even attempted to deny him the truth of what he was saying, and so, within their own good and the strength of themselves as a parish community, they attempted to resolve the issues their priest brought into their focus to the best of their ability.

Sore feet and achy limbs were the order of the day – every day that followed the Sunday sermon. Some tried a lot harder than others and were glad they had. Some weren't fit enough to try too hard, but try they nonetheless did and were encouraged enough within themselves to determine to try even harder next time. The roads thereabouts, and a lot further afield, were a lot less travelled by tyre and a lot more trampled by shoes.

Somehow, by spending less time dashing about trying to do too many things, the days seemed longer. A lot of people were much happier in their own worth, and value was afforded to time as they took to thinking about where they were going and what they would be doing when they got there. Life no longer had to be travelled at a rate of rotations determined by a machine.

So, a lot longer was needed in terms of time for some to arrive on time for eleven o'clock Mass the following Sunday. Slowly, cheerfully, expectantly, they chatted their way along in small droves, working their way up in the gather of together.

Getting to Mass was becoming part of a meaningful, worthwhile experience for many.

As the flow of his vestments hovered onto the altar, Fr Ignatius's arrival was greeted with an almost continuous smile on the faces of those before him, something that was by no means a true reflection of the priest's facial expression.

Mass duly began and flowed along until hearts began to beat at a greater pace than before. It was nearing time for his sermon. When eventually he did get there, he stung the many happy minds before him into numbness with one word.

'Drink!'

There was an enormous draw-in of disappointed breath from

the congregation. Mostly it was the men whose lips pursed in dried anticipation of what was to follow, but many women's eyes glazed over in vexed readiness for the thrashing their ears were about to receive.

'It used to be a common sight along roads around here for men and women to be seen carrying two pails, or two pitchers, or two young'uns in their arms. Now, the disgusting sight of heavy-grade blue plastic bags from the off-licence is all pervasive; in fact, it is so common a sight, I wonder how there is money left over for anything else.'

The priest's words cut deeply into the embarrassed silence of his gathering of parishioners. Not one would break the air to release a choking cough.

'I can see the good of drink in measured form. But I'll be damned from heaven if I will stand back and do nothing while the weak among you spread the curse of this disease through the rest of the parish. What you do in public after closing hours is bad enough. What you do in the privacy of your homes I can only assume to be ten times worse. Therefore, this is not a private matter.

'You have children who suffer in least form from bad impression, in worst form from the neglect and cruelty that goes with it. This must stop!

'What I have heard in Confession these recent weeks tells me that drink is the greatest scourge hereabouts to decent family life, and that this curse is well on its way to ruining the futures of many of the young. This has to stop, and now!'

The whole interior of the church hung with silence. The roars of the priest's words were still ringing more personal messages of intemperance in the ears of his listeners quite a bit later when the Prayers of the Faithful continued. Although eyes were empty on many of the altar-facing faces, heads were angled upward, so Fr Ignatius knew he was in with a good chance.

As the feet of the folk of the parish of Kiltemper slow-stepped out in one general throng after Mass, heads were held higher than they needed to be, and the biggest smiles they could muster were unfurled in the sure and certain hope this would mask all. In the minds of these definite hopefuls, it appeared that they most probably had changed the drinking course of the rest of their lives, or for as long as the notion held firm.

During the week that followed, Fr Ignatius didn't hear even one word about what he had said from the owner of the pub and off-licence. This came almost as a disappointment to him. The close eye he did keep on these premises revealed his words were having the desired effect, for, even at the unsettling hour of most evenings, there was a fall-off in foot-fall thereabouts. If anything, there was an increase in foot-fall for Confession during the week as the sober truths of what amounted to many lifetimes of overindulgence emerged.

Despite so many changes following on in rapid succession from one another, the people of the parish seemed well-enough pleased with themselves, because the underlying belief was that the priest was right in his manipulations. Maybe it was the right time of year for change, the deadness of winter giving way to the hopes coming in a new spring. Whatever the way of it, the priest's words were having no end of an effect on Kiltemper, and the locals reckoned he must be well-pleased with his efforts by now. They reckoned wrong.

Sunday came, and with it, smiles of meeting and greeting and glad to see. But still a significant little something was held back in the eyes of some of the smiles. It was obvious what they all wanted to hear. It was far from obvious what they were going to hear.

Eventually Fr Ignatius readied himself to deliver his sermon.

He smiled. His smile was broadcast back to him many hundredfold from the bright pack of the pews beneath his gaze. His smile broadened, catching the look of so much hope. Then, reaching in under his cassock, he pulled out something and held it out for all in the church to see. Eyes at the back strained forward, eyes at the front strained back. A hushed murmur spread along the pews and off in all directions from the altar.

'A condom! I found this... somewhere... which led me to believe they are being sold somewhere hereabouts; which led me to believe they are being used hereabouts; which leaves me with just the one conclusion left in my head: that some of the good Catholics of this parish are breaking the holy laws of their Church, and oftentimes not even in the confines of the matrimonial bed.'

Here, the condom Fr Ignatius was holding aloft fell onto the floor of the altar. It was obvious he didn't know whether he should pick it up. A couple of the altar boys nudged at each other, but it was soon obvious that none of them was going to do the necessary to alleviate their priest's dilemma.

Anxious sniggers erupted from different parts of the congregation. Embarrassment pervaded the air. Then, deftly, Fr Ignatius lifted his right foot in a long swinging motion, caught the said object with the polished toe of his shoe and landed it way beyond, in the general direction of the sacristy door.

'That's what should be done to these curses of modern convenience. Throw them all out! Have nothing to do with their empty ways. Anyone who sells this sort of filth, anyone who needs to use this sort of filth, anyone whose life is so untruthful he or she feels they have to base their existence, their future, on the failings of a piece of stretched rubber, God help them!'

The only members of the parish whose faces were not aglow with too much blood inflating into rosiness in their cheeks were those too young or too old to understand what it was their priest had held up in front of their noses. This remaindered the greater chunk of the congregation who knew exactly what Fr Ignatius was on about. Pews became distinctly more uncomfortable for some. For others, they were in a blind sweat over the contents of a wallet or handbag, for they hadn't a clue what a priest of the calibre of Fr Ignatius was liable to do next.

'I don't want to see, I don't want to hear of, I never again want to know that the likes of this... unnatural creation, ever came into the parish of Kiltemper again. Let us pray.'

A great sigh groaned from the congregation as they stuttered and muttered their way through the rest of the prayers of the Mass. They didn't know how much more they could take, but more to the point, they didn't know how much more they would *have* to take.

There were a few who felt like saying something, and a few more who felt like rising and walking out, but they knew this was the priest's turf and he could say what he liked. Anyway, it wouldn't do to let the cat out of the bag with regards matters of a sensitive and private nature. People hereabouts had long memories, and a private knowledge – publicly stated – could stick with a whole family connection for generations to come. They had all been witness to this with even the most trivial of matters over the years.

As they said locally: 'One sheep…' Everyone knew only too well this was all it took for even the best of them to fall from grace in the eyes of others, and so no-one was going to pop a head up above the parapet on this or any other matter.

The week that was in it went well and went quickly, because they all had their heads down on this one. A bit of shopping might have to be ventured a lot further afield than normal, but this was not a bad thing either. It wasn't the sort of subject families could touch on with one another. It wasn't the sort of subject friends would touch on with one another. Sex and its derivatives were still too personal to be the general order of conversation around countryside such as Kiltemper.

The following Sunday saw great heart in so many smiles of the locals who obviously hadn't been affected in the slightest by Fr Ignatius's sermon the preceding Sabbath. For many there was a bit too much "hail fellow, well met" as tongues that normally only existed in generalities rattled off along the smalls of detail. So, as Mass began, it was a case of chins out, noses in the air, and necks stretched to the full of their hold to show the priest, and everyone else, that they weren't in the least bit put out by what had gone before.

Smug smiles were well settled into many of the faces of the congregation as Fr Ignatius readied himself for his sermon. Unlike his parishioners, he had a whole week to prepare himself for it.

'When I look around the parish, in every part of it, in every street, in every farm, in every house of whatever size, my eyes bulge. They find it difficult to comprehend what they see. They find it difficult to contemplate that a body, even a large family of large bodies, could need so much.

'Well, my disappointment is as nothing in comparison to the disappointment you are going to feel when you eventually get inside St Peter's pearly gates. Heaven will seem as nothing when compared to the great hoards of wealth you have amassed here on earth. Don't get me wrong. Of course it's good to strive: it's good to do well; it's good to improve your situation and do better for your family and others. Remember, though, that it's good to share, to share with those less fortunate, those who are unable, for whatever reason, to better themselves in the tangibles of modern existence.

'Remember, too, true wealth is being happy, being content. Ask yourself: am I really happy with all that I have, with all the excess I have accumulated? Do I really need more and more and more? Am I doing my children any favours, creating in them the belief that it is necessary to have so much?

'It is all madness! This consumerist hell of gluttony is perverse. It goes against the true nature of God's message. Cupidity has captured your heads, it has melted your minds, it has banished your souls into the nether regions of yourselves, and if it hasn't already done so, it will most surely break your heart. Excess kills. It defeats all essence of good there is in you.

'Moderation is what is needed, so, at very least, moderate your excesses. Cut back. Give away. Give to those less fortunate, give to those in need, give a lot to those you love, give a little to those you do not respect. Give to the Missions, the needy, the poor; give to those you passed on the way up, for on another day this might be you. Be generous of yourself, your time, your money, anything and everything connected to you that you can be generous with. There is no point in having it just to lock it away. Don't be a hoarder. Above all, be magnanimous in your dealing with all, especially yourself. Let us pray.'

There was hardly a heart or a mind in the congregation that wasn't inwardly stunned into silence, that reality check which linked up heart and mind and soul and all aspects of function and came up with... the truth. The truth was felt deep within, there was no hiding from it, an enormous weight of guilt hung over their minds and only faint and broken whispers managed to join in with the Prayers of the Faithful.

Fr Ignatius's message had certainly hit home on this one.

It was a quiet and subdued lot that slow-paced their way out of church after Mass. Consideration was in their heads of how well they had done. This may have been answered in a way during the sermon, but feelings were that it would take time to satisfy their minds to the right and wrong of all they had acquired through thrift, hard work, and a lot else besides.

Minds were definitely hooked onto the priest's angle and decisions were made in the first instance not to add to the overall show of wealth. Time would make a better show of it all for them and this was a definite path they set out in themselves to follow. It would take a distance of time, but at least they were set back upon the true path of conscience.

A lot of good thoughts were brewing in the minds of the decent folk in the parish of Kiltemper as the days wore on towards the end of the week. And when Sunday eventually arrived, the church was well-packed with backs straight and heads held on an even keel. Thoughts were concentrated on one particular aspect of the Mass and so prayers were ushered into their minds and out of their mouths as quickly as possible.

Fr Ignatius readied himself at the pulpit. A smile of sorts came upon him as creases of skin erupted in lines around the shape of his face. His smile was reflected in the hundreds of insecure smiles set before him.

'The last lesson I had to teach you, you have taught yourself.'

As the priest stood in silence again, his congregation fell into a mumble of not understanding but wanting to know what their spiritual director was talking about. It was obvious, too, from the rumble of their mumble, they weren't advancing very far with their own thoughts on this matter.

'Ire. Anger. Wrath. This is the last of the seven deadly sins that I wanted to bring back into the focus of your daily lives. There is no need to do this now. Over recent weeks you have taught yourself how to deal with real anger. In learning how to deal with the preachings of your priest and the ways in which I have made you observe yourself, you have shown true fortitude of manner and depth of purpose.'

Fr Ignatius stopped and stared up into the packed gallery, then down into the packed pews before him, and finally along the lines of hopeful faces of those standing in the aisles.

'I can do no better than you have done for me, than you have done for yourself. My mission here, to the beautiful parish of Kiltemper, is accomplished. I can go away in the sure and certain knowledge that your souls are rightly mended, that you have all the means of coping within you that are necessary to deal with the years ahead.'

Again the priest stopped as he saw the parade of smiling eyes and faces before him. For the parishioners of Kiltemper, the strange thing was that Fr Ignatius seemed to have lost his accent, he no longer sounded like the Englishman recently come amongst them. The thought of their outsider leaving sent a sadness through them, for they no longer relished the prospect of his departure.

'I must tell you, I didn't think my leaving could be so well-accomplished in the short space of time we had together. I have you and you alone to thank for this. Thank you for taking my words into your hearts and into your heads and making them your own.

Now, let us pray.'

Well, hardly a word was uttered by the good folk of Kiltemper, so choked were they with the emotion of the moment. Gradually, though, they caught hold of their voice and soon every square inch of air inside the church was filled with the dedication of one exultant voice.

There is a worthy tradition in good parish churches throughout the length and breadth of Ireland, where only in exceptional circumstances would you hear the sound of two hands clapping. This, then, was one of those rare, exceptional cases; one where it was only but right and proper that a total and sustained outburst of applause erupted after the final blessing. Just before the embarrassed features of Fr Ignatius walked off their altar for the last time and out of their lives for good.

BEYOND

I knew I shouldn't have stayed up late; I knew I should have gone on to bed and let them chat themselves off into the small hours of the morning.

Thirteen years of this five o'clock-in-the-morning early rising behind me and it doesn't get any easier. If truth be told, it's more difficult, with the demands of a young wife and young family, plus the greater demands of a growing business that I'm still working on my own. It's a different life when you're your own boss: you work ten times harder for yourself than you do for others. All decisions are yours, all debts are yours, and everything falls on your shoulders. But that's grand, because when there's light at the end of the tunnel, you can see where you're going. It doesn't half leave you tired in between times, though.

Tiredness is bad, because it makes you make mistakes, and that's bad for business. I'm not too bad today, though. I think I've gotten away with only four hours' sleep.

One night doesn't empty you. It's the accumulation of all the one nights that leaves you feeling totally drained – as if you're running on empty. Young children don't help in the night-sleeping stakes either, but that, too, will change soon enough. In fact, it's already getting better. How time flies these days!

Anyway, a good strong cup of tea in mum's when I leave these cakes up for dad to sell will put me back on course for the day, for our long overdue day away. I can't wait to go up and get this over and done with, because I can tell what's going to happen. I know what's expected of me up there where they live, just as I know what's expected of me down here where I live, and I'm lost somewhere in between. Personally, I'd be more than happy to spend the whole day at work rather than head off a distance in this November weather. What's it going to be like on the way back? What am *I* going to be like on the way back? That's enough of the negative thoughts. I haven't done much on the family scene lately, and a young wife has needs as well.

Mothers are the most selfish creatures known to man. They want for everyone but themselves, but it's in the getting for everyone else that mothers feed themselves. I know what's ahead of me: it's going to be a full-frontal assault on me as a son, as a brother, to take my little sister with me, with us. Oh, the asking will all come from a mother who doesn't want anything for herself, only what's best for her children.

That's the way I said it would go and that's the way it went. There is a lot in this life we men should stop kidding ourselves about, thinking we have control over. We can only do what we're let do, which is exactly the same thing as what they want us to do. And we're suckers for it. By God we are!

She knows I'll make it up to her; she knows I will. I'll make sure she gets everything, absolutely everything, for our new house. This is the whole point of our day away today, getting a few of those extra specials for the new home that aren't available in the local shops.

I know. I know I should have said we'd take her the next time, any time except this time. Always put off until another day what you don't want to face today, and I really don't want to face this today, or any other day, for that matter. I know I should have said no.

My little sister certainly expected me to say no, and, judging by the size of the smile on mum's face, she certainly didn't expect me to say yes. She could see it was a very reluctant yes. She knew by the look of me I didn't want to be asked that question. Why did she insist on putting me on the spot? Why do mothers have to be so pushy? Why didn't little sister back off and stay? Why didn't she try to help the situation and stay and help look after the children, or lend a hand to the younger brother who's running the shop? Why didn't we head off without telling anyone? It would have been worth it afterwards to pay someone to look after them instead of having to go through all this nonsense.

I know the face that's going to greet me when I get back home and she sees little sister plumped up like a queen in the front seat. She needn't think for one moment she's going to get sitting there. It's all right for now, but when we get back down, she had better make it into the back, and sharpish.

Why does it have to be like this? Why do women expect so much from men? And when they get that, they want more! Why do I feel as if I've done something wrong? I've done nothing wrong. I'm hard working; I do for all, everyone, whenever I can. And this is the thanks I get in return.

Up early. Work, work, work. No football to play or watch – don't get to matches anymore. In fact, time off is all spent at her mother's, or mum's. Of course, we spend more time at her mother's than we do anywhere else, than we do *everywhere* else. Does any of this count? Of course not!

Sometimes I think there'd be more thought of me if I rolled in drunk every weekend. But no, I wouldn't do that. Money would have been better appreciated if I had stayed in my dead-end job instead of striking out on my own with all the worries and strains that brings. I think I've had more sleepless nights in the past two years than most people have in a lifetime. And for what? Exactly! So I can just feel put upon by those who are meant to be closest to me, those who are meant to be my greatest support.

I expect this from the customers, some of them, anyway. You accept them diddling you and pretending they'll pay you when you know they know they have no intention of doing so. You expect it from suppliers. That they'll deliver a couple of this short and a few of that will be missing. You don't expect this from your own. You don't expect those closest to you to try to diddle an extra bit of you this way and that. It's not bloody fair!

I don't make demands on any of them. I don't hold love up to ransom. I don't say you'll do this for me because if you don't, you really don't love me. Okay, they don't say it in so many words, but that's what they mean. That's the message they're putting into my head by pressing this out of me and demanding that from me.

All it does is make me feel tired, more tired, even though I didn't think this was possible. And the more tired you are, the less use you are to anyone, especially yourself. But what I've found out from all of this is that anything's possible when you know you have to do it, when you've no option but to do, or else.

I can see it all now. A blazing row that'll last for days and nobody happy at the end of it; and everyone offended during it; and then everybody else taking sides; and giving advice on what should have been done; what *I* should have done to avoid all this family mayhem and falling out; over one stupid day away.

Why did I agree to any of this in the first place? Why didn't I stick to what I do best and say: *No. I work. I'm the worker; that's what I do best. And today, that's all I want to do.* I can feel it all rising up inside me now as we're nearly home. This is where the fun starts.

****

Look, look! I saw her head move behind the curtains. I can see her. I know that face. I know the mood she's in. I know she stayed there long enough to make sure I saw her. I'll hold my temper. I won't roar or shout. I won't react. I'll say nothing. I'll stand and take it, because the sooner it's over, the sooner we're away. And the sooner we're away, the sooner we're back tonight, because I'm up early for work tomorrow morning. As usual!

I stand and take it, and take it. How many times does a person have to say the same words over and over again? It doesn't matter, because I will keep answering the same question with the same answer, over and over and over again.

I didn't think it mattered. Honestly, I didn't. Yes, I know what you wanted. Yes, I know it's our first day away since whenever. Mind you, I could have sworn it wasn't as long as that. I know. Yes, I know. But what was I meant to do? I didn't think it mattered, that's all. On and on, round and round it goes, and all that is happening is time being wasted, time we can ill afford. If the going's good, we might make up for some of the lost time on the way there.

Over and over and over again, until it runs out of steam or trips on another angle of logic it just caught up on. Why should you be done out of your day away because of a spoilt little whatever? Of course, no-one has to talk. There's no need for anyone to talk.

All was not lost. We had movement towards the car, and little sister had the good sense to jump into the back. At least we're on our way. Things will undoubtedly pick up as we progress and time works its way through us.

****

Boys-oh-dear! I have never found lack of conversation so absorbing, and so difficult, as it is today. Two people so close and yet so far away from each other. I've lost count of the number of single "yes" and "no" answers I've teased from them. This two-hour journey could last for an eternity if the present state of company is anything to go by. I don't know why I bother.

I certainly don't know why I'm playing along with the imbecilic behaviour of the two of them. If they don't want to talk to each other, that's fine; if they want to ignore each other, that's fine too; but why do *I* have to be piggied about in the middle of it?

They could take it in turn. Even a couple of words every couple of minutes would show a little bit of movement towards common ground. No chance. Not with either of these two. Necks rigid, eyes frozen, mouths clamped firmly shut, and me, like an eejit, trying to play Mr Niceguy. As usual!

Why do I bother? What the heck possesses me to bring all this nonsense down on myself? What sort of a docile cretin am I? Stuff them! Stuff the lot of them! Stuff them and their game of silence! I can play that game too.

It's no problem for me to keep quiet, but only as long as I'm in a room full of noisy people. Or if I'm given a little corner of peace and quiet. I can hold my tongue for ages as long as I'm sleeping. This, on the other hand, is eating me from the inside out because of the lack of outside coming in. I can't stand it! It's driving me berserk! This is the last time I'll be taking anyone out with me.

It serves me right. I knew I should have bought a van. That's what the business needed, that's what I wanted to buy. But oh, no. A van was not allowed; an estate car would do the same job and serve the growing needs of the family as well. She didn't reckon on the family growing to include her sister-in-law for the big day away, though!

Still not a word, not a syllable, not a sound, and certainly not even a bag of mints being passed around. Three people in the car and no-one exists for two of the occupants, apart from their silly selves, of course.

Oh, right. So that's the game, is it? The ante has just been upped with polishing or filing or whatever it is females do to their nails. Done for my benefit, no doubt! Well, stuff them! I'll show them what's bloody what! And stuff this bloody rain and these damn wipers that don't know what their sole purpose in life is meant to be. A bit more acceleration should bring them to life. I'll show the two of them!

'Aaaaarrrhh!'

That turned out to be much more of a corner than I expected. And as we slid through it, a lorry blocked our path in the opposite direction. A big lorry it was. A very big lorry, loaded with coal so it didn't give much on impact. Fortunately, the front driver's side took the brunt of the crash.

I don't know whether it was the old car, the lack of sleep or the rush of blood to my head. Perhaps a bit of all three, plus an overgenerous helping of bad luck. But there was no possible way of avoiding what came next.

Luckily, there was only one fatality.

Right now, I am watching from a growing distance as my life fades and leaves with the thunderous sound of the crash. Below, I look down upon the lifeless form sitting in the driver's seat.

After the noise of the crash came a deafening silence. Strange, that.

BEANS

What makes mum think I want to go to my bedroom and play with toys?

That's all they are: toys with electricity running through them, and I don't want their electricity running through me; I've enough of my own recently to last until I'm fifteen, thank you very much.

What do they think boys are made of?

I'll show them what I'm made of! I'm made of hurt and kindness and all the good and bad things that happen every day, plus whatever I get for dinner. Some days I'm just a tin of beans, but that isn't bad, because I know the next day I'll probably be made of fish and chips or pizza. Yippee!

It's best not to think about what you're going to be made of, because there's always the bread bin later on to take care of the grumbles inside the tummy. It's the grumbles inside the head that have been getting to me recently – big time.

Mums are all right when you're young and for all sorts after, but they don't understand, they can't understand, because they've never been inside a boy's head. They think they know by looking in from outside, but that's impossible; they're just guessing and they haven't a clue what they're talking about.

From dad, all it took was a nod; you just had to watch the eyes to know what was what. But with mum, her eyes are all over the place and her shouts throw you into a distraction. It's only got worse since dad left.

I'm the only one in the house now with mum, and yet, we're never alone. You can never be alone with a woman who has friends plus a significant other at her beck and call all day – and night-time too.

Every day since dad left has been the longest day of my life. It's not so bad during school time when I'm busy and I know dad is busy at work too, but when I get home, it's different. At the kitchen table for dinner, all I do is stare into the space of the place where dad should be sitting. The emptiness of that one place is like a ginormous cliff which has opened up at the side of the table; and I spend all my time staring in, wondering and worrying.

Dad's leaving was never spoken of to me; it might have been shouted about in my company often enough, but this was never anything serious, it was never real – until it happened – and one day mum told me dad was gone for good. For good? For whose good? It certainly wasn't for *my* good. I didn't want dad to go. But oh, no. Nobody thought to involve me in any of the decisions of the family, because I'm too young. Imagine, that's what they said: 'You're too young to understand.'

If they were going to burn the house down, would I be too young to understand that? Not a bit of it. But that doesn't matter; because all parents today care about is themselves. That's right: they don't give a damn about anyone but themselves.

I've never seen *them* eating a tin of beans for *their* dinner. *I'll go without* or *don't you worry about me* is all I get when I know there's something cooking in the kitchen, but it's nowhere near the cooker. I know rightly they'll be stuffing themselves later on after wherever they've been out to.

None of this would matter if dad was here. But he's not. And he hasn't been this long time. And the worst bit, or part of it anyway, is that nobody cares what *I* think. I have to remain the little boy who does what he's told and says nothing, and has to fit in with all the subtle changes making way for the big one. Stuff them! Things have been changing so much round here recently I'm going to have to say something, because that's all I can do.

Do you know, all I was told was *mummy and daddy are fighting too much, so daddy is moving out*. Do they think I don't know? Do they think I don't care? Do they think I don't see things, hear things, put two and two together and come up with two separate twos? Because that's what this is all about.

Imagine, two big stupid faces of parents staring in at me when I was in my bedroom and that's all they had to say. Plus, I didn't get beans that night. Oh, no! It was more like somebody's birthday, with pizza and chips.

Look, he's crying now. I knew this would happen. Get out of here before you do any more damage! Mum immediately went into one of her ranting and raving moods and grabbed me into herself so I didn't see dad leaving. I couldn't run after him and stop him going. I couldn't even say anything to him before he left home – his home, our home.

Of course I was crying! What did they expect me to do? What else was I meant to do? What else could I do?

I wasn't allowed any say in what was going on. I wasn't given a chance to say what I thought. I wasn't even stuck in the middle with the two of them fighting over me. No, I was cast aside and shown I didn't matter.

Mummy and daddy are fighting. Of course they are! What else are they meant to do? What's wrong with fighting, anyway? Boys and girls fight all the time: in school, on the way home, outside playing. That's the way things are, but we don't go off in a huff, never to play with each other again; of course not; we're out and at each other and others the next day again. That's just the way things are.

They might have fought more than even I wanted, but so what? Sometimes, when I got up during the night to go to the toilet, I would hear them at it, fighting. One time, when a nightmare threw me out of bed, I ran into their bedroom and there was dad on top of mum and they were fighting then too, in bed, in the middle of the night when they should have been asleep.

But so what?

If they liked fighting so much they should have stayed together and enjoyed it as much as they could. But no, they hadn't enough fight in them for that.

The worst part, the *really* worst part, has come since dad left, because after him not being here was the finding out of where he was; that was hard to take. As it turned out, everyone knew except me; I was the last person in the world to find out. Plenty of ones at school knew the names of the two girls, Simone and Natalie, who go to a posh secondary school and are older than me, whom he is playing daddy to now. I didn't believe it until I saw the four of them together in dad's car, and I can't understand, because the woman in the front seat looked older than mum. What does dad want with a strange woman like that and her two daughters? And why hasn't he bothered to visit when I'm not at school? It isn't right, and it certainly isn't fair!

I didn't mention to mum that I'd seen them all together in dad's car, just in case, but I still can't believe how they all looked so happy. It wasn't right not seeing mum's long black hair in the front seat of the car. How could dad like a woman with short blond hair who has two daughters? Mum should have kept the car and learned to drive instead of letting them parade around the town in our car while we have to walk everywhere.

Buses are for rainy days and *every penny is precious* and *keep every pound a prisoner* are mum's new watchwords, because there's something important she is saving up for. Well, mum thinks it's important, but I know what I think about it and it wouldn't be right for me to say.

When I mentioned it quietly to some friends in a corner of the playground at school, two of them laughed a bit too loudly and the third looked as if he had a bad taste in his mouth. I knew right away I shouldn't have bothered saying anything, but it was too late. The next day at school, funny looks were coming from every direction and one little girl even came up and said, 'My uncle's marrying your mum!'

I stared at her as she chorused out to the rest of my friends, 'You're going to be my cousin.'

My head was about to burst and I couldn't think what to say, so I just blurted, 'Clear off or I'll thump you!' What else was I meant to say? I don't need any second-hand cousins, and certainly not ones like that.

I don't know what's gotten into mum this past while since this David guy came along. It's as if she isn't grown-up anymore, because all she wants to do is talk, talk, talk about wonderful David and how great life is going to be when he moves in for good before they get married. I wonder what she ever saw in dad, because this David looks nothing like him; but I think mum has it the wrong way round.

Isn't David really nice? Hasn't he lovely hair? Isn't he so good looking? Did you see the way his eyes lit up when I came into the room? Is what I'm wearing all right? Is my hair nicer up or down? Do these trousers make my bum look fat? All the things a mum isn't meant to say to a son are being said now and I don't know what to say or think and I don't know who to turn to. I feel like telling her she *has* a fat bum, because she *is* fat; but I know there's no point.

I can't stand and shrug my shoulders like dad always did when these were *his* questions. I have to pretend to look, and sometimes I have to watch what I say.

It used to be different. I used to be able to say he was really nice, because every time he appeared, he had a great big tube of Smarties for me, not one of the ordinary small ones, but a great big one. Now he doesn't bother. All that changed when I told mum one day that David was great. Well, what was I meant to say? She kept on and on at me until I gave her the answer she wanted.

They used to take me out with them wherever they were going, but all that stopped when mum got Charlie Maggot's older sister, Elaine, in. An ugly big cow she is, because she sends me to bed early and then sits on the phone all night talking to her friends.

As if things weren't going badly enough, recently all mum and her friends have to talk about is wedding dress this and honeymoon that, and the giggles and silly laughs of them is enough to put an army of men off. They're so stupid when they go on like that.

I know primary-school girls who act more grown-up than mum and her lot. At least I can go out and do whatever I want whenever mum's pals are around, thank God, because I don't think I can stand much more of them.

Oh, you're going to look so good in your new clothes for the wedding. What colour would you like to wear? It mustn't clash with the beautiful bride. And so it goes; on and on and on.

Mind you, mum did say that after the wedding I can have my own TV in my bedroom, which David will buy, and maybe a video player too, if he gets the promotion he's after at his work. She did add on at the end that I would have to call him dad.

I don't know. It ties me up in little knots inside every time I say it; it just doesn't feel or sound right, even though I've only ever said it to myself.

It's not his name, he's not my dad. And what's more, I don't see why I should have to have the same name as him. It's so stupid! How am I going to call myself Seamus Brown when my name has always been Seamus Green? It would mean having to change the register at school as well as all my books. I tried writing it on old bits of paper and it didn't look right; it looked stupid. I tore them into shreds right away.

Mum says this is the first thing that brought them together: she was Green and he was Brown. *Isn't that fate?* she said. *Two colours drawn together like that from a big crowd in a pub.* She looked at me, all smiling and lovely and waiting for me to give her the answer she wanted.

How was I meant to tell? I wasn't there. I didn't see what went on and I haven't a clue what fate is, but I couldn't tell mum that. All I could do was smile and agree with her, because that's what she wanted, that's what good boys are meant to do and so that's what I did.

Granda says if I'm to take anyone's name, I'm to take his – Doherty. I think it suits me better and there's a lot more of them around here. They've even got a coat of arms and there's been all sorts of famous people called Doherty. They used to be chieftains and had their own forts and a castle, and plenty of them still have shops around the town. It's a lot better than being called Brown; there were never any famous people called Brown, certainly not around here.

You get used to the sound of your name and the look of it on your books, but I really wouldn't mind changing mine from Green to Doherty. I don't know what mum would say about it, but I have a fair idea what dad would say. The few times I've seen him recently, he's been in bad form, but maybe that's just around mum and me; he looked happy enough with those others. I know now he doesn't want to bother about me, because he doesn't bother about me. He doesn't even phone me anymore to say something stupid has come up and he can't see me. He must think I'm stupid. He must think I'm thick. I know he doesn't want to spend his money on me. I know he's got two new daughters with their fancy ways and fancy school and he thinks all that is brilliant, because he's all newfangled with it. Once, only once since Christmas, has he taken me out, and then he bought me a McDonald's.

Do you want a Happy Meal, son? That's what he'd said. Imagine! I told him I'm not a baby and I'd have a Whopper with extra everything, but he went and bought me an ordinary burger. I bet he buys them a Big Mac each; he wouldn't let them down by buying ordinary burgers. Oh, no. That wouldn't be good enough for the two fancy-haired Miss High-and-Mighties!

Granda's right: I'm going to end up as bad as them. He keeps telling me to smile at them all and say nothing, but that's easier said than done; it's certainly not easy smiling when other people want you to. In fact, recently it's not been easy to raise a smile at all.

I know I'm to blame, but it's not my fault. The thing is this: I always kissed mum goodnight before I went to bed every night, until recently, and now mum says it's because I'm too grown-up that I don't. I'm not! I haven't changed. I'm not the one getting married again and I'm certainly not the one kissing other people. I've seen them. Yuk! Him and mum, you know, kissy-kissing, and then she expects me to kiss her goodnight. No chance! It would be like kissing Kelly's dog next door, and it's a dirty wee mutt, always sniffing about where it shouldn't. How could I kiss mum when she's been kissing him? I can't do it, but I can't tell her why not; she mightn't understand. She would call me silly, like she did when I told her I knew she didn't want me around; she just told me I would have to get used to change.

Every weekend for a couple of months, I had to stay in granny and granda's because mum had "something else planned". I knew what it was. I knew she didn't want me around. Every sort of excuse was tried on me. *You'll have to stay with granny and granda because I'm invited away for the weekend*, or *because I have to go and visit a friend who's sick*, or *because I have to help so and so with such and such*. I forget all the stupid excuses.

Still, granny and granda are great. They take me everywhere with them and even buy me a Whopper after school; imagine, not even for dinner. Isn't that great? Granny helps me with homework and I help granda in the garden and they let me sit up late if there is anything good on TV. It's super; but it would be better if mum was there too. Just mum.

I know when I grow up I'm not going to get married. No chance. All that arguing and fighting, plus all the... yuk! If I do get married, I'm not going to have children, because, well, because it's not fair having children and then not wanting them. I used to feel sorry for all the ones round where we live whose parents split up and divorced, because I didn't know what they were going through; it shouldn't be allowed. I used to feel really sorry for Joey Dillon and the like who never had a father, but now I know they're the lucky ones; at least they don't have to go through all this nonsense. It's not fair! They shouldn't be allowed to do it to children, their children, anyone's children.

How would they feel if we spent our time shouting and roaring at them, slamming doors, smashing plates and saying terrible things? How would they like it if we walked out, and then came back, and walked out, and then didn't come back? They wouldn't put up with it, so why should we have to?

I wish I could go back and change it so I didn't have a dad; then we all wouldn't be in the mess we are now. Then I wouldn't be missing dad and wanting him to come and do things with me, take me places so we could enjoy being together. Then I wouldn't be jealous of those two horrid-looking girls being chauffeured around the place by *my* dad in *our* car. Then mum wouldn't be getting married again and so there would be no David. He would have to stay with *his* family and look after *his* children like a proper dad should. I think his three children must feel sad about missing their dad, even though they're still young. I hope they don't cry when he comes to live here; that would mean we all cry because he is coming to live in my house. I hope they don't think I want him as my daddy.

I only cry at night-time in my bed. Not every night, just the odd night when I think about what has happened, plus what's going to happen. I don't want it to happen, but I can't say anything, because mum thinks she's so happy. And anyway, I know. I know why she's going to get married. It's because she has to. I heard her saying to one of her best friends, Sheila, the big fat one, that she is going to have a baby. She called her a poor fool and then hugged her, and then I cleared, because I couldn't stand the thought of a brand new crying baby in the house. I know from what they were saying that David had something to do with it; I bet you it was all *his* fault. I bet you it was all that kissing. Yuk! I'm never going to kiss anyone ever again, apart from granny.

I told granny and granda what I had heard, but they must already have known, because granny said, 'Not again!' I guess mum must have told her in the first place. That was all they had to say about it.

I know I'm meant to smile and pretend everything is okay and everything a mum does is a good idea. It's not! It wasn't a good idea to get rid of dad, to throw him out, even though granny did say she never liked him and that he was never good enough. She only said this after dad was gone and I know she didn't really mean it; I know it was her temper talking. Anyway, he's my dad.

Granny and granda are good to me – great to me – but it's not the same thing: they're meant to be there as well as, not instead of. Of course, I'm glad they're there, it's just that, well, you need more than that. I know I certainly want more than that. There's plenty in my class that have two grannies and grandas doing for them, and aunts and uncles, and big brothers and sisters, as well as their mum and dad. One boy in my class, Jim Maloney, has a big brother who takes him out on his motorbike with him. I saw them; he's dead lucky.

Mum thinks I'm dead lucky because I have my own bedroom over in granny and granda's house and it used to be her bedroom. That's typical of my luck: I get a girl's room!

Granda hasn't said it to anyone else, but he's definite he's not going to the wedding; I think granny knows too. I heard him saying to her, 'If she thinks I'm going to give her away again...' and then I came into the room.

'Your granda doesn't like greed. He thinks one wedding is enough for everyone.'

I remember granny smiling at me as she spoke, but that put an end to it. Nothing more was said about it. I wonder if granda thinks having a baby is greedy, as this will be mum's second. I'm with him on this one if he does.

I've just remembered something. There are only two bedrooms in our house. How could I have been so stupid? How could I not have seen this one coming? I'm going to have to share my room. That's not fair, it's *my* room!

Bunk beds, it'll have to be bunk beds, because there isn't enough room for another bed. According to granda, there isn't enough room to swing a cat in my bedroom; I would like to have seen that. I know he says it because he would like me to move in with them, and the way things are going, anything is possible.

Whoops, that's mum calling me for my dinner. It's only the first call, so I'll be all right for a few more minutes. In fact, I'd say I'll not be missed for a good while, because we have an unexpected visitor for dinner; well, *I* didn't expect him and *I* don't want him here.

If there are beans on the plate, I'll know he probably wasn't expected, but I know rightly it'll be something fancy to please him, something hot and spicy and with a sauce that's more like soup. Yuk! I bet it's that horrible Chinese stuff with skinny worms in it. Since that David guy started coming round here more and more for dinner, we can't give our scraps in next door for the dog; even the crows don't bother our bin anymore. I know how they feel.

'Pizza and chips will do me rightly, mum.' She probably didn't hear me, but I won't shout it any louder in case she would. I'll wait another while until... there, that's shout number two. I'll go after number three.

'Your mother's been calling you for your dinner!'

How dare he come into my room and shout at me! Imagine the cheek of that! He came into my bedroom and shouted at me! And that's not the worst of it. You should have seen his eyes. They weren't the eyes he has for mum; there was no lovey-doveyness in them; they were full of hate.

That was no mask he had on; he showed his real self for the first time and I know, now, I was right all along. I don't want him in this house; he doesn't belong here – certainly not while I'm here.

We haven't had any shouting in the house for a long time, not since dad left. It's been so long, my ears didn't know what was hitting them. Mum shouting doesn't count, that's part and parcel of being a mum; everyone's mum shouts, and sometimes dads, but not strangers from outside; other children's dads are not meant to shout at you.

I'll show him. I'm going to the kitchen to see what mum has to say about this. She'll soon sort out this David whatever-colour his name is!

'Mum, he shouted at me and...'

I shouldn't have burst into the kitchen like that. I probably shouldn't have pointed my finger at him in a cheeky way, especially when he and mum were wrapped in each other's arms, kissing, kissing in the kitchen; dad would never have done that. I definitely shouldn't have shouted at mum, because she sprang at me, hit me a hard thump, pushed me out of the kitchen and told me not to come back until I was ready to apologise – to both of them!

What am I meant to do now? I don't know what to do, because before I was landed out on my ear, I saw my dinner waiting for me on the table and it's my favourite; pizza and chips... and beans.

STERLING SERVICE

When you're young and know best, your primary-school headmaster has to have been the smartest person in the whole world. This was certainly the case where I came from: small country school delights on the edge of big city ways.

We delighted in the terror of the sight and sound of him patrolling the corridors with his cane, curled to form a perfect handle at one end. When he approached from behind, we didn't dare look round, but stood up straighter than we should and didn't utter a sound.

If there was too much noise, he appeared as if from a conjurer's trick, with the crack of his cane against his baggy trouser leg announcing him first. Then our teacher reappeared, smoking at the nostrils, his face cast in anger and revenge, and although we wanted to laugh, we very quickly couldn't because of the sickness we felt in our stomachs at the thought of extra maths that afternoon.

Headmaster only ever came into our classroom for one of two things. Occasionally he would enter and, while someone from the front of the class kangarooed in a vertically challenged and therefore vain attempt at cleaning the blackboard, mumble words with our teacher as together they eyed us with suspicion while their heads nodded in unison.

Then our teacher would disappear off out of the classroom, pulling the door quietly shut as he went. So would begin thirty to forty minutes of proper handwriting. Headmaster's handwriting was so perfect and accomplished, was of such quality, that it belonged in the Book of Kells rather than on our blackboard, and so it made me want to hide my own raspings. Fortunately, he had the good sense not to go around the class inspecting our jotters.

More often than not, though, only half a headmaster's person appeared round the classroom door and, in a much softer tone of voice, he asked our teacher if it would be all right if he borrowed me for a short while. Of course he could. As I curtailed the impulse to run up the classroom, I stepped along proudly, having to tighten the muscles around my lips and bite down hard on my teeth to control the big grin that was trying its best to burst out onto the rest of the class.

Instead, a puzzled, almost worried, look would pretend its way onto my face as I passed through the rows of admiring seats. This admiration was tinged with just the slightest hint of jealousy, but this would not last for more than a couple of seconds, because it was generally recognised, on the subconscious level that children function best on, that I was different.

I was the only boy in the class who didn't have a father. Not on this earth, anyway. It didn't bother me in the way that it seemed to bother a lot of others. I didn't know any better, so I didn't mind.

Once outside the confines of the classroom, my tongue pointedly poked my goodbyes back in at my classmates.

My calling from class was always for the same thing. I was sent off on a mission to purchase sixty Sterling cigarettes from the local, although not the closest, shop. On this errand for headmaster, rain, hail, snow and sometimes even sunshine, I would run virtually the whole way to and from the local shop, Norrbys; people we knew but who didn't know us. This wasn't so that I would receive my 3d, then 6d, and later 5p, all the quicker, but because I knew that he called on me because I was the quickest. I had to be; the look of want and desperation in his eyes told me so, and I often saw this as well. As his door closed, the sight of him picking through the remains of his ashtray, trying to unearth the longest butt, remains with me still.

Appropriately enough, the footpath I raced along margined a main highway called the Racecourse Road, but I don't think this had very much to do with my fleetness of foot. Getting to the shop was dead easy; it was all down hill. Getting back up the hill in the same time scale wasn't so easy, but I would push myself to my absolute limit before desperately trying to catch my breath as I loped back into the school, along the long, long corridors, past photographs of Confirmation smiles that caught my eye with every stride.

At the end of my journey, at the end of the great distances of footpath and lengths of corridor, I stopped, knocked, waited and listened for the throaty call telling me to enter. In those days, we hadn't learned to mind the smell of smoke, which was just as well, because thick clouds of it were blown into every corner of the room. Whilst a packet was immediately and unceremoniously cracked open, and the beauty of its contents brought a deep, sonorous sensation from headmaster, I had to stand for at least five minutes, answering questions. These questions followed the same line of communication every time. They began with schoolwork and soon shifted tack to concentrate on the main area of inquiry, the family – and with particular reference to one. After thanking him profusely, I always left with the same goodbye: 'And I won't forget to tell mum you were asking for her…' I knew there was something there. But what he didn't know was that it was all one-sided, and it doesn't take a genius to work out whose was the one side.

****

After leaving primary school, it was some years before I met up with headmaster again, and I could hardly believe my eyes when they saw a wizened, frail old man. He looked ancient beyond his years. Before we got into our chat of times old and not so long gone, I took out my packet of cigarettes and proudly offered him one.

His hand instinctively reached out for one. 'Oh, no. You've only a couple left, yourself.'

'Don't be silly.' I pulled a full packet out from an inside pocket.

'I'm meant to be off them. In fact…' He didn't have a chance to finish what he was going to say.

'Off them? Nonsense, it'll kill you going off them at your age!' I had eased a cigarette up so it was protruding from the packet.

In a sure and simple way, he had the cigarette out, and with just a slight flutter in his fingers, he had it between his lips. As I leant forward with my lighter, I could see the essence of desire in his whole body draw up to the lit end. We smoked a couple of cigarettes together as we mused on the ways of the changing world around us. Before we parted, I insisted he take my fresh packet of cigarettes.

'That'll get me started again,' were his departing words that day.

****

A year or two later, as I left church one Sunday, departing down an aisle, I noticed a pair of eyes, not much else except a pair of eyes, from a far and distant past. Headmaster it was, although now a mere shadow of his former self, sitting forward in his seat, two arms leaning over the back of the row in front. He was like a machine, an old-fashioned mechanical steam-driven machine that exists for one singular purpose.

The sadness that held his eyes was nothing compared to the sadness I had fluttering through my mind and going down into the depths of my heart. His whole body, his whole spirit, was given over to the solitary purpose of pulling in just enough air from between earth and the heavens to keep his lungs going.

Immediately, my mind could see only lungs, black and putrid, as the decay of decades of tar and nicotine filtered through them until there wasn't room for any more. I could see his lungs were so full of noxious putrefaction they could no longer function normally; in fact, they could hardly function at all. Now I was thankful for the little bit of sanity still inside me that made me give up smoking not too many months before. Although the desire was far from gone, there and then I was wholly glad I had always shown the strength to see these moments off.

I smiled my old, schoolboyish smile and spoke of how long it had been, and what I had done and become in between times. He didn't speak. Only with his eyes did he answer with a soft and sad smile. Then he pointed. My eyes, my mind was so appalled by the sight of his finger, long and purple and devoid of the essence of life, that at first I didn't notice what he was pointing at. It was his throat. There was something on it, something stuck to the skin, something man-made and horrible was cut through the skin on his neck and attached into his throat.

It was a voice box or something to help him breathe, or some contraption that comprised a bit of both. The horror of seeing this must have been staring out of my eyes, because he immediately attempted to rise to leave. I couldn't help myself, because the sight of this truly terrified me and sickened my mind deep into my stomach. Too feeble to see through his grand move to leave, headmaster had to hold onto my arm while I led him out of the well-emptied church.

As we left the grounds, I offered to drive him home. He patted my arm in a thanking way and reached into the pocket of his coat. Amongst some mint papers, which fell away as his hand drew out, was a card with his name and address on it. The address was of a nearby nursing home; it also stated that all taxi fares would be paid. It all seemed a terribly long way from the cracking sound of approaching headmaster that froze us to the spot where we stood all those years before.

When he was settled in the car and I was about to start the engine, I nearly shot out through the roof with fright at the sound that hit my ears. It took me back to my childhood, but to the sound that Daleks scared me with. This time it wasn't a Dalek, but headmaster with something pushed into the contraption in his throat.

'Have you got a cigarette?'

I don't know whether it was the shock of the question, or my confusion as the sound of the question caught me, but I could only squawk, 'What?'

I wanted to tell him to wise up, to catch himself on, that he could hardly breathe, and did he not know it was these accursed little killers that were doing it to him. I said nothing.

I drove the car as fast as I could down the length of the Racecourse Road, all the while listening to the shrill, mechanical raspings of air being caught and dragged in to feed his clapped-out, clogged-up lungs. I stopped outside Norrby's shop, and as I got out of the car, I couldn't help but notice the line of a tear follow a steady course down the sallow complexion of his skin.

Inside the shop, I asked for twenty Sterling cigarettes, but the assistant didn't know what I was talking about; obviously they hadn't been on the market for quite some time. I stood undecided, not knowing what suitable substitute to ask for instead.

'Give me a packet of those gold ones, please. Ten will do.'

I hurried back out to the car, opened the door, and as I moved to sit down, the thought came to me that I didn't want to call him "sir". I didn't want to call him "headmaster". In fact, I didn't want to talk to him at all; I didn't want him anywhere near me.

Perhaps because there wasn't enough care or thought in my head as I got in, my shoulder nudged against him. He was so frail his body tipped to one side and his head knocked against the side window; yet there was not a murmur from him as it happened, or after. In fact, there wasn't the ear-wrenching sound of him trying to breathe now.

If there wasn't much life in him before I got out of the car, there definitely wasn't much left in him now. *Just my luck,* I thought, *what am I going to do with this now?*

I turned and turned the knob on the side of his seat until it was levelled and he was lying there, on his back, in the recovery position. I knew what needed done next, just as I knew what I wasn't going to do. I knew I should give him the kiss of life, but I hadn't a clue whether this should be administered through his lips or the contraption stuck to his throat. Instead, I chose to do what any sensible person would do. I floored the accelerator pedal, and headed straight for the nearest Accident and Emergency department.

The doctors and nurses there were brilliant. They took him off my hands straight away. While I went and provided as many of the necessary details as I possibly could, they disappeared off with his lifeless form to perform all the necessaries of trying to reintroduce the elements of existence into a goner.

Afterwards, a very junior doctor tried to explain to me that he had been dead on arrival. And he went on to say the end had been very quick and he hadn't suffered, however he came by that information. Then, before he left me in the relative's room, he handed me a piece of paper, and on it was a telephone number and details for bereavement counselling.

In the short space of time it took me to get from the hospital back home, I had three cigarettes smoked and I was dying for more. For some reason I couldn't help but feel a small twinge of guilt over the cigarettes, but this didn't last long. The comfort of their feel in my pocket was more than enough to get me over anything.

Viva España!

The phone call came out of the blue, which is probably how it seems to an uninitiated mind like mine, and so I reasoned it better to lift the receiver than let it keep ringing.

'Quickly, hurry. He's collapsed!'

There was angst in mum's voice. It wasn't panicky, it wasn't shouted, it wasn't squealed, it wasn't crying or sobbing, and yet a sense of all of these swept through me from their meaning, if not their sound. I thought for a moment, a split second, maybe even less.

Phone down, jacket on, calling to Pam what was what, out the front door, running, my mind racing ahead of me, not knowing what to think, not knowing what lay ahead of me. I played the words over and over again inside my head, with the same voice, with mum's voice, with the voice I had heard all my life, the voice I had always jumped in response to. Now was different, this was different, what she said was different, wasn't the normal *oh, jump when your mother calls and run like a good boy* Pam liked to rattle my cage with.

There was no doubting whom she was talking about; it was her husband, her second, and my first stepfather. One of these would do quite nicely, thank you very much.

When you're hurrying beyond your normal pace, when you're running as fast as you can, which is not as fast as you could but a lot faster than you should, something inside tells you to slow down, not be too hasty. You are neither trained for this means of getting there nor what awaits you when you do get there; a collapsed heap of flesh and bone that you'll have to touch, to help, to work with.

Like a bad smell, these thoughts held my focus as I ran on, ran hard, ran fast past the eyes in cars staring through their passing at me. At the sight of someone running hard along the street. The sight of someone old and heavy and bald enough to have known better than to run for all he was worth, along footpath, between parked cars, across traffic indulging its favourite pastime of moving slowly along. And eyes, all the eyes within their engined boxes, staring, and my wonder was in them, in the focus of minds stalled, stopping and starting, because they couldn't possibly know, they couldn't possibly understand, because they couldn't possibly see my purpose.

As my breathing got heavier, more laboured, drawn from deeper within, I knew I was getting close, I knew I would soon be there. It was many years – how many I couldn't say for sure, they pass so quickly, but ten or twelve or more – since I last ran this distance. I used to run it regularly, trying to keep up with bicycles. The distance hadn't changed but it was easier then because I was different, I was... I don't want to think about it because I need to keep going; I'm nearly there.

Traffic wasn't as bad then, mustn't have been as bad then when I last ran round, when I last had to run round. Then, it had been a bed that had caused the emergency and very funny it was, too, for many; everyone catches enjoyment from the thought of a bed catching fire. Not me, not then and certainly not now.

Okay, a bed catching fire by spontaneous combustion is a bit of a laugh, a bit of craic and worth a yarn. However, your mum's bed catching fire is in no way funny, especially not when this is the bed she shares with your stepfather; it's frightening. It frightened the life out of me when I got the phone call then and ran, ran, ran, just as now. Then, it ended up harmless enough; a little bit of property is easily replaced. It was only a bed that needed renewing, only a bit of paint in a room and a lot of washing and airing. Mind you, I don't think the airing worked too well, because it's almost impossible to remove the smoky stench of burning from curtains and fabric and clothes. And I think the CFC-unfriendly air fresheners only made matters worse. No matter, there was no-one too much the worse for it all and eventually a new electric blanket was trusted back into the bed. It was never left on for long after that scare, and it certainly wasn't left on too long.

My children got most mileage out of the story. They took teams of friends round to stare and marvel at the big black hole in granny's bed, in their granny and granda's bed. It must be twelve or more years ago now, maybe more, because the three of them are up and have flown the nest. The last went last year, off to uni, to another part of the country that might as well be another part of the world if the aways of the other two are anything to go by.

'We're only a phone call away. Come and visit, but phone first.'

That's how they treat us now, that's all I hear, that's all there is. They're too young yet to realise there aren't any memories in phone calls, there's only sadness and missing the voices you associate with childhood and play and loving and growing up, when they always were there. Perhaps it is nice to know they're still alive, to hear the voice, hear the news of life away, hear all the happenings you are no longer a part of. At least it provides fodder for neighbours when they ask about them, and they always do when they have something to tell you themselves.

Our streets seem to be full of people like us, all of a certain age and ilk where the chicks have flown the nest and we've moved on to talk about ourselves, except now it's *our* pains and ills, and how long *we'll* have to wait for the first grandchild to materialise. I think it'll have to come free with something, because the next generation are not at all like how we were. Children and christenings and birthday parties and showing them off around relations and friends and constantly visiting grandparents – both sets lived round different corners in different directions – that was how we lived. Of course, that was until we realised how much hard work it all was, on top of all the hard work we had to do at work, and eventually we found a way to stop, after three, and while we still had a chance to catch a bit of life.

Some chance!

We weren't brought up to that, to be like that, live that way, think that way, act that way. It was probably too late anyway, too late for us inside ourselves, and so all we could do was stick our heads into work. The object of this exercise was promotion, which equated with more money for less work, and this easier time all round would mean more energy for home, for each other, and thus wonderful happiness all round.

Some chance!

The little bit of promotion you were fed at work, meant you worked harder, leaving less time and thought and energy for home. It meant happiness stayed further away than it had done. It meant all that had changed was that you had made things worse. So, life progressed down that path, until the children found their bit of happiness elsewhere and were determined to hold on to it, and good luck to them for not falling into our old trap.

It's only then, when you've found plenty of happiness, that you can afford to share some with others. Thank God, they aren't making all the mistakes we made. Me, always running over to a home I never felt at home in because it was never a home, it was more of a... I'm not going there; I'm not going down that line, that track, that dead-end. Why? Because I'm too busy keeping myself going, keeping myself running, running there.

That's it, I'm nearly there. I'm totally puffed but I'm nearly there – almost. There's no point in hammering myself and leaving myself too knackered to be of any use, any help, not that I will be much help.

I'm not looking forward to this. I don't want this. I haven't room inside me for this. If I walk these last few houses, if I take it slowly, I'll not be out of breath, I'll be fit enough to do something to help. Maybe the ambulance will have arrived by then and I'll only have to comfort mum; holding mum instead of having to touch, to hold, to do whatever it is I'll have to do with him.

I'm nearly there and still there's no sign of an ambulance, no sound of siren near or far.

Damn it! I've no key with me. It's in the car. I keep it in the ashtray of the car because it's handier, it's always there, I'm always in the car when I go round. Every time mum phones to see if we're finished with the newspaper, because someone forgot to buy it, the key is always there in the front ashtray of the car.

Bloody door bell! I hate door bells you can't hear, you don't know where you are with them. Imagine having to ring mum's front door bell, it doesn't seem right, doesn't feel right, doesn't look right, especially not at a time like this. I wonder how many eyes are watching, how many curtains will fall back straight, how many hands will have to wave if I turn round quickly now. There, two! I saw two move.

Enough of my games. Enough of these thoughts. I'd better run round the back and see if the door is open there.

The garden doesn't look so good at this time of year. It looks tatty, a bit of a mess, but spring will soon be along and growth will cover up a multitude of boredom. When I was young, living here, growing up hereabouts, I always wondered why none of my friends would be bothered to come round here and play or hang out; why we all went round to smaller gardens and smaller houses. It isn't much of a mystery. At the time, I thought it was because we weren't allowed to destroy the grass. I thought grass was something sacrosanct, like the altar in chapel.

Now I remember: it wasn't just the grass, it wasn't just the straight edges of all the flower-beds, it wasn't just the tears and scrapes from the array of different-coloured, dung-heaped, perfume-headed rose bushes that lined the drive and pathways in rigid formation and which deflated more footballs than all the neighbourhood gardens put together. It was that sense of senses you have when you're small, when you're young and innocent and knowing enough to absorb truth in full measure and not have it conditioned by what people say. When it's there, staring you in the face so you can't miss it, and before you are drawn in by the platitudes of olders, having to listen to them so much you end up passing their nonsense off as real, as your fake understanding, to try and make sense of it.

Of course there are *plenty of other gardens to play in*, but they belong to other people; I knew what I was being told and so did all my friends, but that's what friends are for, looking after you when you need it.

It took me years of coming to terms with all the little wrongs I was always told I'd done before I wised up and saw it for how it really was. Unfortunately, it was too late for me, much too late. Unfortunately also, it was just too late for my children, for they too had been infected by the poison I had swallowed and thence passed on as my own.

And now the damned back door is locked. I'll have to run around the front again. They must be upstairs, for I couldn't see any sign of life through any of the windows I looked in. I'm just thinking, I hope to God mum is okay. She certainly didn't sound her usual self on the phone, but I suppose that's understandable enough.

What'll I do if I find the two of them collapsed?

I won't. I won't. I'd better not.

'Quick, son! Where were you? I've been calling you for ages!'

I couldn't tell the truth: that I'd been daydreaming my way over, my way around the house; daydreaming back the decades in the garden.

'I was round the back trying to get in. I've no key with me.'

Even though she had obviously been upset, was upset looking, I was relieved to see there was no sign of tears. She still managed to throw me one of those *silly boy* looks before she backed in through the front door.

I tried to hurry myself in after her, behind this smaller, frailer version of the mum I had always followed. I was surprised when mum didn't go upstairs, this didn't tally with my glances through the downstairs windows. I then felt a surge of relief washing through me that mum was okay. Something enormous eased in me only for it to well up and rattle my brain, my head, all my senses, all my feelings, most of my fears.

'I can't get the door open, son, you'll have to do something.'

I couldn't believe what I was almost seeing. There was a body, his body, slumped in a heap, all curled up wrong, on the floor of the downstairs toilet. It wasn't going to be easy getting into him, but, yuk, he was in the middle of something, of doing something when it happened, when he collapsed. His trousers and underbags were down round his ankles, I could see that much. I didn't want to see any more.

'Did you call an ambulance?'

I could hear a quiver of panic in my voice. I could taste the unsavouriness of my dilemma as the words came out.

'Before I phoned you, son.'

A blind nothingness was staring out from the two of us, but it was obviously up to me to do something, because there still wasn't even the trace of the sound of a siren. Mum looked as white as a ghost; thankfully, she wasn't the spectre of grey that lay heaped before me.

'Mum, go you out and make sure the ambulance comes to the right house.'

As obediently as my young self in childhood, mum shuffled slowly off through the hall and out the front.

I turned to my task in hand. He was all wrong, he looked all wrong, all upside down with a hand turned into itself the wrong way round. There was no movement, no sign of anything moving. I called out as I pushed my way in; his body moved as his legs, the bareness of his legs, caught against the sweep of the door.

I called his name. It always felt unnatural, awkward, saying his name, calling him by the name his friends did. That's all I could ever call him. I wouldn't call him dad, not from day one, because I knew I couldn't, not from inside. I couldn't call him step-dad, I knew that wouldn't be fair. It was a thing apart from me, something I couldn't reconcile internally, in a little corner of my heart, or inside my head.

I spent years listening to friends rattling on about *dad this* and *daddy that* and always my smile joined in with their conversation and always my lips fell silent to the notion of the mention of one. Always my mind took off in another direction as I tried to think up a new angle to take the conversation off on.

There was no angle out of this one. I was firmly stuck with it as I stepped back momentarily to twist and tweak my brain to see if there was any escape, any way round the situation that presented itself to me. I had never touched a dead body before, never actually physically pressed skin on skin and felt the cold deadness of life gone missing from a person. There was no avoiding it now. I had to get stuck in straight away in case there was any chance, in case there was any hope, of a flicker of life left in his body. First of all, I was going to have to get his twistedness out of the toilet.

I grabbed his jumper at the shoulders and gave a great tug. It was like dragging and turning a length of unrolled carpet, except that the head slung low, the two arms didn't hang the way they should have and his feet were twisted the wrong way round and did nothing to help themselves. I didn't look at anything else. I kept my eyes firmly fixed on matters clothed and pulled and tugged until I had him clear of the toilet door and lying on his back in the hall.

'Is he all right? Is he alive?'

The sound of a voice coming through the midst of dead silence made my heart jump from its sunken hold.

'Mum, I thought you were...' I couldn't say anymore; I was glad she was there. With that, the phone rang in the kitchen. 'I'll get it. You fix his trousers.'

I was content to be leaving, even just to move a few feet away. I dived out and grabbed the receiver off its hold on the wall. It was the ambulance men, or paramedics, or whatever they're called now. They were caught up in traffic and it would be another few minutes before they could get to us. Had I put him in the recovery position?

What? What's that?

I listened, I listened carefully to what they told me and then slammed the phone down. As I moved to rush back out to the hall, the receiver jumped off its hold on the wall and bungeed down to smack itself on the floor. I had to slam the brakes on my forward momentum, grab the phone and hook it carefully onto its slot on the wall. I hoped it still worked.

'That was the ambulance men, they'll be here any minute; they said to lie him flat on his back in the recovery position. They just rattled off a list of commands, a list of things to do, to check, and they said they'd be here in a couple of minutes.'

Back into the hall I threw myself with the concentration of a bit of knowledge, with the mind of someone who might know a little of what needed done, with the zeal of remembering that I didn't want him to die. Of course I didn't want him to die. What would that do to mum? It might destroy her, or it could very well destroy more than just her, because, as she always said, she could never live on her own. That was the most telling remark she had ever come out with, because it struck fear into the household of those closest, and I knew this because mine was the closest in every way.

Thank God! Mum had finished her doing. His trousers were up and secured in a sort of fashion, so now I didn't have to take in the look of his nakedness.

'He's still warm, son. I saw his lips move when you were on the phone. Do you think he's still alive?'

The terror on mum's face made me want to hug her, to hold her. I wanted to tell her not to worry, that everything would be all right, that she could come and live with me, with us, but I couldn't, because I knew *us* wasn't true, *us* would be a lie. I had to avert my eyes, I had to snap out of my emotions and get on with what needed doing.

When I got him over and onto his side, some sort of liquid, a yellow bile-like fluid, discharged itself down his nostrils as well as out his mouth. I didn't know whether this was a good or a bad thing. As I turned his body, pulling at the corners of his jumper again, putting my strength into manipulating his shoulders round, as his body swung over, I had to touch his head to ease its turning. I was surprised, because he was still warm. I hadn't expected him to be cold, certainly not ice-cold, but I did expect him to be cool to the touch. When I lifted his hand to try to find a pulse in his wrist, it, too, was warm but lifeless.

'See if you can get a pulse; they told me to pinch him under the arm.'

I pinched up under his arm. It wasn't easy to do; I wasn't sure if I was doing it properly or if I was nipping at a lump of jumper and shirt.

There was no response. So the second time I did it, I was none too nice about it. He was sure to have a bruise from that one. Still, there was no response.

'I can't find a pulse, I don't know where I'm meant to get it.'

Mum looked better, she obviously felt better of herself. We are both like that. We are better at something, doing something with our time, our selves. We weren't great ones for sitting around waiting for something to happen.

'They said to make sure his airwaves are clear.'

I distinctly meant this as something for mum to do. She knew what I meant and it was clear she didn't relish the prospect much; but it was more obvious I fancied the idea even less. Poking her forefinger into his mouth she pulled out his top row of teeth, the bottom row was his own.

I hadn't looked at his face, hadn't concentrated my eyes on his look until now. There was a cut on his head, his forehead, maybe more of a gash than a cut, and a little trickle of blood followed a crooked line of descent but it wasn't bleeding. Perhaps it wasn't deep enough to bleed for long.

He hadn't swallowed his tongue, this was another thing they'd mentioned, but I had forgotten until I noticed that it was protruding slightly through his lips. It wasn't sticking out very far, though. His eyes, on the other hand, his eyes were very definitely dead in his head.

'Should we give him the kiss of life or something?'

Mum most certainly was in control of herself as she spoke, but truth was contained in the look in her eyes. These words, her words, these thoughts, the thought of what she was proposing, what she was thinking, what she had just said, made me want to snarl grotesquely, made me want to laugh and ridicule and make nonsense of what she had said.

'I think I hear a siren... in the distance.'

The last three words were added, as an immediate afterthought, when I saw her face needed escape, probably the same way as my own. My words provided relief for both of us, and release for me. My breathing returned as I left the room, as I walked out into brightness and light and wonderful freedom inside, which must be how a convict feels having paid his dues when he walks out into the vast openness of life. I wanted to run and jump and gulp down all the loveliness of air hovering in empty abundance everywhere.

Instead, I wandered into the garden, touching leaves and bushes as I went, slapping the bareness of spindly branches until I reached the bulk of my old favourite, the horse chestnut in a corner at the front. I loved that tree, loved all the fun of its fruit, so copiously supplied without fail every autumn over my long lifetime. I loved all its climbing, as a child, as a youth, as an adult, with children reminding me of things I had done. I loved that tree enormously, but never before enough to hug its trunk; never before enough to find my face hard pressed against the roughened surface of its bark.

I stepped back, quickly scanning around to see if I had been seen, if anyone had been witness to antics outside my normal self. I didn't know where this had come from, but I wasn't for hanging about in case any of the neighbourhood nosies were on the scan. Strange, that; I had never fancied myself as one of those tree-hugger types. It was only when the door slammed shut after me that I realised it needed to stay open.

'It must have been a fire engine in the distance.'

I didn't have to say anything. There she was, mum, my mum, down on the floor, mouth to mouth with him. It's strange how you are, how you expect yourself to be with something, and then, when it happens, when you're right there in the middle of it, you're not how you expected yourself to be.

'Are you sure you know what you're doing?'

Mum was listening for breathing, she hadn't time or space to listen to what I was saying; my words were pointless anyway. Then, she looked up with those eyes I had known every important moment of my life. I immediately knelt down and set to with both hands pumping hard into his chest. Together we worked it, mum providing the mouth to mouth and myself the heart massage, and before we knew it, we were surprised by two paramedics.

A great sense of relief went out with every word as we filled them in with the detail of all that had happened, with as much background information as we could recall and no, he wasn't on any medication. Within seconds they had oxygen hooked up to a mask over his mouth and two wired patches were stuck onto his chest and hooked up to a machine. Then, they reckoned it best if I took mum inside to sit down. I was glad to escape, and so we moved off slowly into the living room, keeping the door open slightly in case they needed us.

Mum sat down, I paced around the room, but we were a world away now from what was happening in the hall and we were both mighty relieved to be even a small distance from it. His chances of survival had suddenly taken a turn for the better. Now, I felt there was a real chance of life returning to his limbs, of air returning to his lungs, of blood recirculating through his heart, of a bit of bright returning to his eyes.

The sounds from the hall were encouraging; they brought hope into the room with us, filtering normality back into our view of the world. The sound of work was encouraging, of a simple compressor chugging away to recharge its machine of pads and wires that jolted volts of electricity into his veins. I could see mum's thoughts straining out into the hall with the stretch of her eyes; I could see the little light of hope fade back into her look as she observed the lack of reaction to the work in progress. I pushed the door; we had no need to be caught up in the work of others. It was enough we could hear it all as it happened, enough we were drawn back into this world of... dying; a world I had never known before and most definitely had no wish to remain in. We were there, caught up in the unexpected horror of its happening, second- and third-hand witnesses to a darkness we had managed quite well without, thank you.

Death had always been at a distance, sad for others, but normal for some, the way it should be. Any time it had come before it should, there had been a rational explanation along the lines of age, or bad luck, or some such simplicity. Age and misdeed seemed understandable, explainable, perhaps even excusable, occasions for death to take its fancy somewhere. Anyway, its appearance, sudden or otherwise, was never close enough in proximity terms to touch upon my existence. This was different.

This could have huge and far-reaching consequences if he didn't pull back from the brink. If he died, it was more than unlikely mum would stay on her own; it was a sure and certain thing she would have to move in with someone, a family, and she wouldn't want to move far. I could see it all coming, it all happening, could see what lay ahead and might very soon start slotting into place. I shuddered at the thought and tried to fix my thoughts back on the hopeful happenings out in the hall. How was I meant to walk away and leave mum on her own, today, tonight?

If he is taken to hospital, even short-term, where is he going to recover afterwards? And mum, she can't stay on her own. Is it going to be for a week, a couple of weeks, or months, maybe more? And if he dies, what's going to happen then? I can hear it all now, someone's tongue sweeping into action and miscry coming out of it to make my life unbearable. For a wife who doesn't see eye-to-eye with her mother-in-law is a misery for those caught in between and I've been in the middle of it for a lifetime. I'm not saying it's all one-sided, it's not; I know it's not, and anyway, whom could I say that to?

They were made for each other, but I wasn't made for being stuck in between, not quite in the middle, more like a powerless referee, always on my toes, dancing around the two of them. I should put the two of them in a house together, a flat together, a room together and let them slug it out. Let them wear each other down for a change with their sly and silly little demands and the stupid nonsense they enjoy making so real; that would solve the problem, solve two problems with the one fix.

It'll never happen, I know it will never happen, but it's not a bad idea, and it has given me a better idea. If he has to go into hospital, I'll offer to sleep over here tonight, for a couple of nights maybe, so mum can get used to the place on her own, because I'll make sure I'm not around much; perfect. I could even go back to being my old self before I left home, that would be a challenge, and then mum would be only too glad to see the back of me. Why didn't I think of this before? It's a great idea, for all concerned, unless, of course, unless he dies. That takes me back to square one.

I know, I'll stop over here for the few nights and mum can stay over in my house; that should give them the chance to bond a bit, with each other's throats, probably.

'I remember the first time we met, well, it wasn't actually the very first time, but I thought for a long time it was. It happened at just the right time and, oh, he was lovely. It's not normal to call a man beautiful, but he certainly was. Beautiful black hair and so handsome, wasn't he, you remember, what age were you then?'

The encouragement in her tone lifted me out from my own thoughts but her words made me retreat back somewhere else, away from what I didn't want to hear, couldn't bear to listen to.

'Your father and I were married too young. It happened a lot in those days because there wasn't any choice, not really. Go off and give it up for adoption or stay and get married, that's what choice amounted to then. We were innocents, we didn't know what we were at, we hadn't the first notion what life was about.'

'Okay, mum. Can we talk about something else?'

She couldn't feel how my stomach was when she went down this line of past enquiry. She didn't know how it curdled my thoughts and made my stomach shudder. She never wanted to know either, because, first and foremost, she is, was, and forever will be, a woman, pure and simple. Only a woman could have thought that the way out of one failed relationship was to enter into another, to burden herself and another with the ways and moronic demands of another man coming in to try to change our set-up.

All the excuses in the world amount to nought, mere words trifling around the nonsense of hope, of want, of need; of one person's desire impacting upon others. I can understand it all now, I still don't like it any better, but I can understand it, which is a world away from how I

114

felt then. Then, I had a father, he was the only one I needed, the only one I wanted, the only one there was. Of course he had faults, everyone has, it's just that you have to get on with them, mix them with your own and see what blend of understanding comes out the other end. At least, for a child these faults are part and parcel of what life is about, because, having grown up with them, they are part of you.

When mum started down this old line of thought, questions seemed to come at me from all directions inside my mind. Lots and lots of questions, which all had the same answer: that we should have stayed how we were. Why did you do it, mum? Why did you have to change *my* life just because you weren't happy with yours? Why did you have to marry someone else? Why did you have to bring a complete stranger into our house and wreck the little bit of normality we had left, with his alien notions of what was what? Weren't we happy enough the way we were? Didn't it all work perfectly well in our own little world, in our own little way?

For years after, I was consumed by the guilt you burdened me with, that it was *my* fault. *Growing boys need a father. I only did it for you!* I was too stupid then to comprehend, and by the time I was smart enough to know better, I was still too stupid to do anything about it.

I had to stop myself. I had to stop the line of thought that tore me apart when I was younger, when I was too young to understand, too emotional to know how to control it, too lost inside to take on board the fact that others had needs too, and that mum's needs superseded mine. Now that I was old enough to know better, it didn't matter, because it was too late, childhood had long since said its goodbyes to me and left me with its sweet-bitter taste to remember it by.

I wanted done with these thoughts. I wanted away from these negatives of purpose that had a beginning and no end; at least I hoped there was no end in sight for them.

'Do you know, the first time he asked me out, I didn't go with him? I just thought to myself, what does the likes of him want to be taking me out for?'

I don't want to hear this, mum. I don't want to know, don't want to see all the little bits of the jigsaw that blended together to make the picture you see, the one you lived, the one you believe. As far as I'm concerned, we had a bigger and better jigsaw, but bits of it were lost or discarded through carelessness or stupidity and, instead of finding them and putting them all back together, a new jigsaw was bought. Unfortunately, my bit didn't fit into the new jigsaw until it was twisted and turned and cut so that it slotted on to the edge. But I can't say this. I have never been able to say this and now certainly isn't the time to start thinking such thoughts; it wouldn't be fair on mum. So, I smile. I don't know why I'm smiling, but I smile an enormous loving smile, because no matter what, this is mum, my mum, and I love her dearly, even though she was now off in a little world of her own.

'Of course, you know how we met.'

This was probably meant as a question, but I couldn't be bothered to answer it, I couldn't be bothered to give it the dissatisfying glance it so richly deserved. Instead, my stare went off around the room, hoping for some insignificance to rescue my thoughts, and so I stared into the distance in the photographs framed around me. I could hardly believe how young I looked in some of them, the some I was in. Most of the others were the same two faces trying on the same smile in bright and sunny places, showing off where they had been, through decades long gone, in a world long gone; life distanced through travel. Through getting away from what wasn't here, not having any children of their own, of his own. Through getting away from what was here, and seeking meaning in self-satisfying pleasure elsewhere.

It's funny how this is always sought in away, somewhere else, never here, especially not at home, not until I was up and away and they were left with the reality of having themselves to themselves.

'It was through the drama club.'

Of course it was the drama club, otherwise it would have been the golf club or the bridge club or the dancing club or any one of the list that ended at a time of year when something else took over. There was always a reason, always an excuse, to be heading out at night to wherever with whomsoever. I didn't mind, not at all. I loved the freedom of it, of having the house to myself and myself to myself; even if the whole neighbourhood was my babysitter in those days.

'He was adjudicating at one of the festivals we were competing in.'

I remembered those early days well. Remembered being shunted off to big and bumpy grandparent beds with a burden of blankets weighing down heavy on me. There was never a problem with this, not with me and not with them, but I registered the look of disapproval in old eyes each time. From time to time, I caught a few words, but I immediately put them out of my mind.

My eye caught activity in the hall. His jumper was pulled right up, his chest was rising with the pump of oxygen entering through the mask over his mouth, and then his torso seemed to jump a couple of inches off the floor with a shock of electricity charging through him. It was a strange sight to see, I stood staring – in the silence inside myself. Always, I had thought that a sight such as this would horrify me, but it didn't, it saddened me, I was truly sorry for the sad state in which he lay.

Then, one of the paramedics beckoned me out. I stole a look over toward mum, she was still talking, still reminiscing, but only with herself, certainly not with me. I wasn't part of what she was talking about or what she was thinking of, I wasn't even on the periphery of it; I just happened to belong to a time and a phase that was gone, long gone, long dead and gone. So, I slipped out into the hall.

'The cardiac ambulance is on its way.'

I nodded, tried to smile my thoughts that this was good, that they mightn't be doing so well themselves but at least they hadn't given up hope.

I wanted to dive in, to tell mum, to break the lonely spell of her mind and help focus her back on what was real, but, within myself, I had doubts about this. I knew, too, it was probably better she should dream of things past than focus in on the reality of things present.

I had long known there was a little twist in me, perhaps not even so little at times, when I felt like it, when I wanted something my way, my own way. Mum knew about it, I think she openly encouraged it in her own peculiar fashion. She said I was like this because I didn't have a father, not in the way it mattered, not when it would have mattered when I was young enough to get to know, to listen to, when my character was finding its measure.

Don't knock the spirit out of them were oft repeated words, said in defence of grandchildren, my children.

117

I don't want them turning out like me was my defence of the offence I was deemed to have been on the verge of committing, if not in the middle of the angst associated with just having committed it.

I looked into the room. This was how it was going to be; mum on her own, sitting, waiting for me or mine, someone or something, to relieve the stress of boredom, to break the monotony of being on your own, waiting for time to pass until it was time to do whatever.

Am I really so selfish? Have we all become so selfish within ourselves that we have no time for others, not even for those who dedicated enough of their lives to see us through to some form of completion? Then again, what did they actually do? They had us, fed us and clothed us to the best of their ability, made sure we earned ourselves a good-for-whatever education, and they were never too far away for the laterals. In short, they did as much as they had to do and this was probably a lot more than had ever been done for them. If I'm honest, it's not too far off the mark in relation to what I did for my lot.

So, what do I owe in return? What do I owe mum if this ends up wrong and her settled world goes pear-shaped today? What does the standard duty of care for a son toward his mum entail? Can I get away with less than is expected of me? Will I have an overwhelming desire to do more? I think I would need to answer these plus any associated questions on my lonesome own, and definitely not in close proximity to my dearly beloved who still hasn't arrived, even though she said she would drive over as soon as she could manage. I think she'll be along any day now!

I'm being uncharitable. She and mum have been getting along famously well these past few years, but maybe that is just in comparison to how they got on in earlier years. They seem to have mellowed to each other's interference in recent times; not bad, it only took them twenty-odd years to accept each other's aspect.

'Would you get me a glass of water, son?'

I didn't think I was out of the room that long. She couldn't possibly need her tear-tank topped up, because I hadn't noticed one drop being shed. I'm not surprised, and I don't blame her one little bit.

I had to excuse myself as I stepped over legs on my way to the kitchen, and again on my way back in. The paramedics were working hard, although I did think it strange that every time I looked out on them or stepped into their presence, one of them was just beginning his cardiac massage; purely a coincidence, I'm sure.

'The cardiac ambulance will be here soon.'

The one at his head, the one working with the oxygen mask, pointed to his mobile phone as he spoke. I wanted to tell him he shouldn't have bothered, there's a telephone right there beside them, he should have used that, but I didn't think there'd be any point. It was very decent of him using his own phone like that, and mobile calls aren't cheap either. They both seemed decent sorts. They were working well as a team. At least they were doing something, and something positive at that, which was a damn sight more than I could manage. I knew I should ask them how he was doing, but I held back, I decided that if they didn't have anything to tell me, then there wasn't much point in asking.

Back into the room, back in to mum, back into the sadness of her look, back into the saltiness her reminiscences released in me. I hoped against hope she had done with looking back at a time I didn't want to know about, didn't want to hear about, didn't want to remember.

'He was the perfect gentleman, most of the time.'

It was the little glint in mum's eyes that made me think, made me wonder. I had to dispel all inkling of such thoughts from my mind.

'Mum!'

She was like that, she held no thought for the fact that you were her son, for the fact that you, as every other son on this earth, looks upon his mum as a form of reincarnation of the Virgin Mary. Even though this ideal had been well challenged in my youth.

I wiped things like that clean out of my head, then. I wasn't brought up to question some of the things adults got up to, especially not when they regarded themselves as functioning on some sort of parental basis with you. I knew what they were at, heading off on holiday during term-time so that I couldn't go with them. This was perfectly acceptable, I didn't mind the fact that I had to move in with grandparents for the duration; it was okay, but they didn't know what to do with me. It always worked out all right, though.

What I did mind was the *we got a cheap holiday, a cancellation, so we have to go now* scenario they insisted on feeding me. Fine, good, go, off you go and enjoy your time together, have a brilliant time in Spain, just bring me back something decent and not the normal tourist rubbish you usually find so alluring.

What I really minded was the holiday snaps. From about the age of fifteen, I had to refuse to look at any and all photographs, just in case. I was being bored out of my eyes one year with all the sunny photographs of them on holiday being pressed in front of my nose.

This is our room, isn't it lovely? Look at the view from here, you could see right the whole way over to Africa if you were up high enough. This is our swimming pool where we swam every morning and evening. This is our beach, it's a bit stony but if you put enough towels down, you would hardly notice.

It took a second look, a third one of enquiry, a fourth one of disbelief, and a fifth one of *Ah, mum, that's disgusting!*

What are you meant to do when your mum shows you photographs of herself running around topless on a beach? It's not easy knowing how to react to this and so the safest bet was to avoid eye contact with all summer holiday snaps from that day forward. I'll have to burn the lot of them when mum goes, God knows what the children would say if they saw them.

This policy worked well until, a couple of years later, on their return from a winter skiing holiday when their photographs were eagerly being pushed into the hands of myself and some other unsuspecting relatives. Suddenly, a chorus of horror howls was heard from the gathering.

In the aftermath of this, mum tried to make out it was customary to sauna naked in the part of the globe they had been skiing in. What need was there for a group of them to pose starkers in the sauna? It was bad enough actually going naked in the sauna, it was worse than bad photographing it, it was beyond a son's conception how a mother could pass these round people she knew for general visual consumption. I never understood this aspect of mum and I still don't. Perhaps I should broach the subject with her now; it might be a good time to relieve the tension, the distress. It might put her on track for remembering some of the more awkward moments.

Then, when I looked at mum, I thought to myself we'd all be a lot better off if we didn't have photographs to remind us of how things used to be, how we used to be. Age might do us plenty of favours on the inside but it does no favours on the outside. Mum looked the full of her years, and more. For myself, as I stood there, the lone child with his mum, I felt very lost and lonely, very much on my own.

She was probably right to go and do the things she wanted to do, live life the way she felt it should be lived. After all, what had boring acquiescence to everything normal ever achieved? I had always needed to feel that I was in control so that I could keep life at a moderate temperature every day in every possible way, not letting myself or my situation get too hot or too cold.

I shouldn't knock it, boring mediocrity has its rewards too; it must have, otherwise how could so many be attracted to it for so long? I'm better not thinking about these things, it's okay in relation to others but doesn't feel so good in relation to oneself. In fact, there's a lot to be gained from considering the blights of other people's lives, but there's only more blight to be gained by chewing over your own.

'Is he dead?' Mum's eyes were pleading with me to tell her the truth.

I wouldn't hide anything like this from her, I couldn't, it wouldn't be fair, certainly not on her and definitely not on me. I had to give her an answer; she was waiting for my answer.

'It's a good sign they've been working with him for so long, and the cardiac ambulance will be here soon; they'll get him sorted.'

I knew from mum's face this was not enough and yet it was too much. She needed a simple *yes* or *no* answer. I didn't have one to give. I knew I couldn't get away with whatever one I spilled out. Thankfully, I was saved by the bell.

With a renewed burst of enthusiasm, I dashed out of the room, out of the house, into the street, to greet the arrival of the experts, so long awaited, so long anticipated. As they rushed out of the ambulance, some words earlier spoken by the first paramedic team were brought into focus inside my head. I don't know whether he had spoken them to me or to his partner or whether they were of general issue, not knowing or caring whose ears they fell on. He said, let me get it exactly, *we'll get the cardiac team over, if they're not busy* or words to that effect.

This hadn't meant anything to me at the time, except in the hope it brought, in the specialised nature of their care, and inside my head I had built upon this and kept building until I passed it on to mum as something real, something worthy, something that could well save the day.

As I watched the cardiac team leave their ambulance, I understood what the paramedic must really have meant. *If they were doing nothing else they might as well be here seeing what they could do, seeing what they could learn.* The doctor in the paramedic team looked as if he should still be wearing a school uniform and not a suit that ill-fitted his gangly frame. Confidence drained from my whole person.

When the experts moved in, the first two paramedics stepped back as they filled the new team in on his history, especially his most recent history on the hall floor. There was no brightness in their looks, no words of hope, no mention that everything would be all right.

'Right, we'll take over from here.'

The young doctor didn't need an audience, didn't want anyone inspecting his handiwork, I'm sure he had had enough of that. So, as the paramedics packed up their belongings, I knew it was time for me to vacate the hall too.

'Can I give you a hand with that?'

'No, we're fine.'

Thank you was in the sound of his voice. I took this as a positive. I sidled up alongside. 'What do you think?' My nod indicated down toward the patient.

'They'll do all they can.'

This wasn't much of an answer, it didn't tell me anything much to pass on to mum; it certainly didn't give me any hope. He knew by my reaction that it wasn't enough, that I needed more. But it was all I was getting.

I don't know why I asked, I think there was something telling in his eyes, but I cannot say for sure where my next question came from.

'Is it time to call a priest?' An enormous distance around us seemed to come down as I spoke. A great void in distance, in thought, came down between us.

Slowly his head nodded in reply. He didn't say anything, he merely let his head do the talking, then turned away and got on with what he had been doing.

I was unmoved, my mind lost in a lazy limbo as the full strength of the situation started to present itself to me. I found myself hurrying, rushing in to find the phone. I paused. I would need to consult mum on this one, perhaps she'd be better doing it herself, because if I phoned, it definitely wouldn't register with any of them who I was. Whom should I ask for? I knew mum had her favourites, but I hadn't a clue who was presently top of the list. I knew some of their names, just as I recognised some of their faces, but I couldn't match one to the other. *Hello, Father* in a bright and smiley voice was normally more than enough to pass myself when I happened upon one or other of them here.

'Mum, I think we should phone Father what's-his-name, just in case?'

I wouldn't have thought it possible beforehand but this brought even more vacance to mum's eyes. Any fear that had been on show quickly vanished with all colour from her face. She knew what I was saying, because she knew where I was coming from, because she knew this wasn't where I'd place my trust, where I'd pin my hopes. She knew this was real and immediately rhymed off the parochial house phone number.

There was the catch of a short stare between us. I phoned the number and was told by a very uninterested female voice that she would pass on the message to whichever one of the priests she could. She didn't seem in the least bit put out by what I had said.

And so, we sat in silence, and I wanted mum then to torture me with some of the stories she needed to tell. The need seemed to have gone for the moment; I'd have to see if I could raise it again.

'You didn't wait very long until you got married.'

My words fell on deaf ears, her look lost to me, her mind off in another dimension.

'Mum, are you okay?'

I touched her hand, she seemed cold to the touch, colder even than he had felt. Instinctively, I withdrew my hand. I don't know whether it was my action of pulling away quickly, but she seemed to come round.

Her head looked up and she started speaking. No, hold on a minute, she wasn't talking, mum was praying; she had started the Rosary.

Now it was the turn of my mind to go blank, for my head to jump into a spin, for my body to want to follow my thoughts out of there, quickly. I knew prayer had a place, and probably a purpose, too, although I had never felt its appeal, most likely because I had never needed its measure. Mum needed it now and, more to the point, she needed me with her on this one, not just in terms of the responses but also in terms of my self. I had no option but to join her and together we indulged in a chant-like separation of our two selves from the situation we found ourselves in.

Soon, I had forgotten myself, forgotten my old self, or perhaps found my old self, in the midst of our determined blatherings. It was almost like song, we delivered it in perfect beat and momentum and with the shortening of word sounds peculiar to ourselves. At the start of a set of prayers like the Rosary, time passes slowly, very slowly, as your mind deliberately focuses you in on the length of the recital ahead. When you either lose focus or refocus, you ascend to automatic pilot as the lift of how you are saying what you are saying, takes control. Then, before we knew it, a priest walked in and took charge of the ending.

'Thank you, Father Patrick, for coming over so quickly. I'm afraid it's...'

'There, there, now. I've been with him. I've been with him and prayed over him. I prayed over him. There, there, now.'

I wanted to ask if it was the last rites he had been praying over him. I didn't need to be told, because I already knew it must. I thought I'd leave them to it, praying, something they had in common, something they were both good at, something I was useless at. I wanted to see if he had managed a minor miracle in the hall. As I went to step out, nodding a silent hello as I passed, in stepped the long, thin drink of water of a young doctor, and that's exactly what he was doing too.

He stood between us, between mum, with the priest on the couch side, and myself, standing over near the door side of the room, and the poor doctor with lips parched but man enough to do what needed to be done, even though his nerves were trying to get the better of him.

'I'm very sorry, but I have some very bad news.'

I remember reading once, *Reader's Digest* or some such waiting room piece of easy nonsense, that you are meant to let people down gently, create the climate first of all and, once you have prepared the ground with this, give them a moment before hitting them with the full force of truth. He had just prepared the ground.

'Despite our best efforts and attentions, he died...'

My mind couldn't absorb the rest of what he was saying, it was off on a tangent of its own. What's going to happen now? What's mum going to do now? Where's she going to live? Who's going to look after her? This house is too big, far too big now that she's on her own. I had to catch control inside my head.

I knew also that now, the immediate aftermath of something terrible, is not the time to be emotional, and certainly not in terms of making any life-changing decisions. This is the moment Pam had always warned me of. And where was she anyway? She should have been here by now. When you are at your softest, most vulnerable, when you can make disastrous decisions based solely upon the false premise of a heart-rending moment, beware.

I found myself over with mum. She looked lost, forlorn, I didn't know whether she should be crying or not. I wanted to hold her, to hug her, to tell her everything was going to be all right, that I would look after her, but I knew if I started to say it, Pam was bound to walk into the room. So, I said nothing.

'Well, that's the end of that.'

She was looking at me, but she said it for all to hear. I didn't know what she meant, didn't know what she was thinking, what she was saying. My mind was racing about all over the place, thoughts bouncing off thoughts, not knowing what to say, yet knowing what needed said. I wanted to tell mum she could come and live with me, with us, in my house, in our house, for there was plenty of room now the young ones were all up and away.

'Don't worry, mum, everything will be okay; it'll all work out.'

I knew I wasn't saying anything much, in fact I knew I wasn't saying anything at all. Guilt hung heavy in me and I had to say something, even just to pretend to myself and so I hugged mum even closer than before, trying to hide the shame surely staring from my face. I wanted to say more, I needed to say more, I couldn't say another word.

Before I hugged mum in close, I caught the look of her eyes, the look only a child can relate back to when it falls from a mother's stare. In those few seconds, I hated myself for who I was pretending to be.

I bet the priest has cast his watchful eye over this very situation dozens of times; when all concerned know exactly what needs to be said, needs to be done. Like so many other times in life, I bet he has watched muddle take over as the best most have to offer by way of a solution; fuddle and muddle somehow take us through that which we cannot properly see our way through.

'I think we might need to phone the undertaker.'

As the young doctor tried discreetly to back out of the room, the priest released another awkward situation for us to deal with. At least it brought the benefit of breaking the spell with mum. He needed an answer.

Everything was happening at a furious pace. A short while ago, life was normal, as it always more or less had been. Now, it had taken a twist for the... well, it remained to be seen what it had taken a turn for. There was hope, there was always hope, wasn't there? Even when there was just a little glimmer of hope, it didn't matter, it was still something to hold on to, something positive to help us through the awkwardness of time present. I was looking for that little glimmer.

'Could you do that for us please, Father.'

He would know whom to phone. He would know who was the best at dealing with these situations. He looked happy as he moved off to do the necessary. All I could think of was the hope, my greedy hope, that mum wouldn't ask me any awkward questions, wouldn't put me on the spot with regard to finding out what on earth she was going to do with herself now he was gone.

'Maybe you'd like to go and see him?'

This was cruel of me, heartless, sore. I knew how mum was about seeing the dead because she always refused point-blank to be in the same room as a body. So why did I say it? Was I so desperate to fend off the inevitable question? I knew I couldn't avoid it forever, perhaps not even for very long, but I knew I would shy away from being open and honest about what needed to be said for as long as I could manage.

Gutless, spineless; I could call myself these and a lot more besides but I'll not bother because only I know what I have to live with. It's only me who has the inside line on what would become of me, sandwiched between two enormous female personalities for God knows how long. No, thanks, I'm not offering up the rest of my lonely existence for the sake of the conflicting interests of the two women who have spliced parts of themselves into my personality.

It's not always necessary to do what is right, that blend of morality is dead, but perhaps not yet buried. Do the smart thing, that's what life is about these days and it's certainly the best model for survival in the modern world. Chances are, we're not always capable of being smart, just as we're not always sure of being right. Doing the smart thing normally means looking after number one and letting the other numbers follow on from that. Doing the right thing normally means looking after everyone else before yourself, where number one is lucky to end up in the top ten.

'Would it be okay to take down some details?'

The poor young doctor was back in again, his awkwardness in how he felt coming through in how he presented himself; but it was more than welcome, given the present circumstances.

Details he wanted and details he most certainly got from mum; it seemed to give her a real buzz, dealing with the incidentals of his passing. She always did have a forte for dotting every *i* and stroking every *t*; she was nothing if not fastidious about the minutiae of life.

If a job's worth doing, it's worth doing well was the standard she stood over herself and insisted on all others in the house following. Junior doctors were no different, even now.

'I'll have to contact his GP.'

These were the only words that made me turn round from my daydreaming out the front window. *What does he need that for?* I thought. *It's a bit too late for a house call now.*

Mum's mind registered the same question, except her vocal chords followed through from her thoughts.

'It's routine. In a case like this, your GP has to attend the scene and, depending on what he says, the coroner might have to do an autopsy. The police are on their way.'

I could see from mum's face she didn't know whether to cry, shout, squeal or just throw the whole lot of them out of her house. I had to say something – and quickly – before mum did.

'Is all this really necessary?'

I wanted to ask him what exactly he thought had gone on here. Did he think murder most foul had been committed in a quiet little suburb like this? Then I remembered all the detective series and decided to keep my mouth shut.

'In a case of sudden death, the police have to be informed.' Now he was looking at me, had turned his attention toward me as he continued. 'And there are signs of a blow to the head which are not consistent with where he has fallen.'

Although aimed at me, this was said in a way that was meant to put him, the squeaky-clean junior doctor, in his place, above us all. I wasn't having any of it.

'He was on the toilet when he toppled over and so he hit his head on the sink. We had to get him out of there. We couldn't leave him with his trousers down, could we?'

I led him through the hall, over the body and into the toilet, and I showed him where and what exactly had taken place. The other members of the cardiac team kept their heads down, busy packing away their gear; at least they had the decency to cover his face and most of his body with a blanket. Only his feet and ankles could now be seen, his well-polished shoes pointing heavenward.

I wonder if he really believed all that handsome nonsense religion fed us. I wonder was he up there now enjoying the benefits of, as he would see it, never having done much wrong in his life. Never having done too much right to do too much wrong because he didn't do too much with his life. I wonder was his spirit hanging around the hall like a bad smell, for there was definitely a bad smell lingering.

'Look, there you are; his last will and testament on this earth.'

I took the young doctor by the arm and showed him what was lying down the toilet. In all our frantic effort and disorder we had failed to notice the distinctive smell emanating from the load down the toilet.

'I see now what happened. I can assure you I was only doing my job.'

With that, the doctor leaned across me and flushed away all thoughts he may have had of something untoward having happened, along with all else that needed disposed of.

When we stepped back into the hall, two police officers were waiting. Bad enough the small pinge of guilt you feel when you pass them in the street, it's ten times worse when they're standing waiting for you in the hallway of your old home and the only thing between you and them is a dead body. I could feel my breathing getting heavy. I could feel a burden of guilt taking hold of my features, playing with my eyes.

Thankfully, it was detail they were after, so it was detail they received, as much detail as they could manage, because, by this stage, there was bucket loads of it about. I added my lot to the some the priest had already given them, the doctor added his to the list, and mum filled the lot out with all that only she could know. We all then waited for the GP, which wasn't long, and after he smiled and laughed and deliberated with the rest of the emergency services for quite some time, it was decided enough was enough and no post-mortem examination was necessary. I breathed a deep sigh of relief. Now, all we had to do was wait for the undertaker.

It's only in moments of silence, of getting in touch with something quiet inside ourselves, that we can truly reflect on the realities of life. It's only in seeing death that we can appreciate life properly, but how long it remains in our focus is another matter. I could feel this in myself, for myself, but I could see it also in mum. For mum, the truth of life lost, life no longer there, must have set her apart from the world she had known, the world she had been in this morning but found herself thrown out of. This was only the start of it, of the change of life from death, of knowing the balance each day would bring and then being cast into the unknown. I shuddered as I thought of all the variations of change that might lie ahead.

There was plenty of movement, of coming and going in the house, which didn't leave room for chat, for talk and delving into the structures of all the maybes ahead. Then, two medium-sized, dark-suited men entered: there was no mistaking these were the undertakers, even though they seemed a bit on the slight size for the job in hand.

Extremely polite and respectful they were in all they did and said, and off on a stretcher they lifted him into one of the bedrooms for preparation.

Before this got underway, I stood by as mum choose a suit for him to wear. Naturally, I had lifted out his newest, for your wake is the one time in your life when you want to look your best.

'No, not that one, it's too good; he has only worn that a few times.'

I looked at mum, stared at her, trying to see if she realised what she was saying. She did. It wasn't in her nature to waste, even scraps of food from plates were scraped into an old bread bag and kept for a neighbourly dog. A special obsession was kept for clothes. Throughout my younger years, the scissors and the sewing basket were at hand to squeeze another few weeks, another few months, maybe even another year, out of garments any normal household would have regarded as having lasted well beyond their natural lifespan. So, long trousers had a new lease of life cut into them as short trousers, long-sleeved shirts became short-sleeved shirts, sometimes with an extra piece down the back so that I could breathe.

'Someone else can have the good of it now that he's finished with it. Put that old one out for him, no-one will know the difference and if they do, they will have the decency not to mention it.'

Mum was probably right. Anyway, what did it matter what I thought? She could lay him out in one of her dresses for all I cared. The old shirt and tie I supplied to go along with it brought a smile of recognition to mum's face. Perhaps how she felt wasn't so very far away from how I felt. It's one thing being blind when you have to be, it's another after the event; time would tell.

'We'll put the coffin in the back room. There'll be more room in the lounge for everyone that way.'

I smiled my agreement. 'I'll tell the undertakers.'

I felt that, today especially, I was always leaving mum, avoiding her presence, avoiding my presence with her. I was hoping against hope that others would come, that Pam would arrive and help break the agony of decision avoidance on my part. There was no-one, no-one related had arrived yet.

Wherever I went in the house, I took my guilt with me, it was impossible to avoid because it was real; it was family and therefore it dealt with feelings; you don't get much more real than that. It was a good thing I offered to take the clothes in to the undertakers. A sack of potatoes is the best way I can describe how they manipulated him to undress him of his old clothes, the casuals he had been wearing. I wanted to laugh and joke with them about the nature of the work they had to do, about the job in hand, but I said nothing, only smiled, nodded down and beckoned up at the offering of old suit and stuff in my hands.

'Just leave them there, thanks.'

And so they continued what they were doing, the way they had been doing it, which must be the way things are done. I suppose it's not easy working with a dead person: trying to get part of a body to move in the angle and direction you deem necessary for what you have to do must be very difficult. I left them to it; they could cope much better on their own and I could cope much the better for not seeing what they were at.

If you don't mind that sort of thing, dealing with the dead, it must be a great business to be in, you certainly don't have the problem of customer complaints. I was silly enough to mention this to them before I left the room.

'Customers are wonderful, nothing but the best is demanded for them by their grieving loved ones. Brothers and sisters all trying to outdo one another when mother or father dies. The most expensive coffin with all the best trimmings, and three funeral cars plus anything else they can think of. Wonderful, great for business, until afterwards, when the dust has settled and you go looking for your money, that's when people show what they're made of. Oh, no, it's nothing to do with me, you'll have to talk to the rest of the family or come and see us when the will is sorted. I sometimes wonder why I bother.'

I had obviously touched a raw nerve. I was out of there as quick as a shot, back in to see how mum was. I suppose these guys don't get much of a chance to talk to people about their business. They're probably avoided by the general masses in case they think they're out eyeing up potential business opportunities. *I've a lovely little wooden number that would fit you perfectly. What are you, a six-footer?*

131

I didn't realise either there's a hidden compartment that runs the length of the hearse underneath where the coffin sits in proud display. It's like a double-decker and must be very handy for busy days.

It was deliberate, my staying away from mum for a lot longer than was necessary, but it was because I saw Pam go in to her. I wanted to give the two of them a chance to catch up on times new. In a way, it's really Pam's place to broach the subject of afterwards with mum, one woman to another, because what she is leaving is the same as what she is going to, which is a woman's domain; they run them and they rule them.

Police and doctors and paramedics were thanked enormously and forms were signed before they left and the body was ours, almost, as soon as the undertakers were finished with him. When I re-entered the lounge, I couldn't decide if Pam was in one of her upright or uptight moods; time would very soon tell.

'I'm not taking no for an answer, you're coming to stay with us, for a while.'

Why did she have to spoil it by adding those last three words? If you are going to invite someone, be good and gracious enough to do just that; don't put indecent stiplifiers onto the end of the invite.

Mum looked up at me with eyes dead in her head and I wanted to think it was from the death scenario which she found herself in and not her immediate situation, in the room, listening to a daughter-in-law babbling on about what she wanted.

'What would you like to do, mum?'

I positioned myself close enough to wrap an arm around mum's shoulder.

'Don't be silly, your mother's in no fit state to make her own mind up, she's coming over to stay with us, for a while.'

There it was again, *for a while*. It's not a proper time frame, in fact, it is no time frame at all and there's only one message that can be taken from its inclusion. Mum looked at me and I stared my sorrow back at her.

'I have no reason to move to anywhere, and I have no wish to, either.'

There remained something unfinished about the way mum said

her words. It was probably just the truth of knowing she wouldn't be grand, not after a lifetime of having been with someone, gotten used to doing, seeing, being, hearing, avoiding, plus all the banals and normals of existence marrieds go through to pass themselves off as being together. Mum would manage because she could manage on her own, there was absolutely no doubt about that, but it would be lonely, terribly, terribly lonely, living on her own.

'You speak to your mother, she doesn't seem to be listening to me.'

Pam thought about leaving the room. She had almost forgotten she wasn't at home trying to get her own way with me. My advice, for what it's worth, is never marry an only child, because she is too used getting her own way. She will have absolutely no negotiating skills. She is not used finding out what's best for all concerned, she only wants what she knows, which is what's best for her. All that has ever mattered in her life is what she wants, no-one else enters the equation, because there never has been anyone else to enter the equation, certainly not in the formative years, and these years last a whole lifetime.

Now wasn't the time to try to right the wrongs of a selfish upbringing, it never was, there never could be a right time for that. All that should matter now was a proper consideration of mum's needs.

'What would you like to do, mum?'

I tried to make my voice as loving as possible. It wasn't the way we functioned, but mum knew I meant well and wanted to know her true feelings on the matter.

'The deal is done.'

There was almost a smile running through mum's words, but I hadn't a clue what she meant, and I knew to look at Pam that she had no background to what was said either.

'What deal is done, mum?'

The subtlety of mum's words intrigued me and brought a smile of wonder to my face. Pam didn't go in much for subtlety or intrigue, so her face held its natural scold at the world.

'Your auntie Nora and I are selling up and going to buy a place together, in Spain, where we will live. It was all arranged on the phone last night, and I must say I am quite looking forward to the change.'

I had to stare for a moment, I had to take a few seconds out to try to piece together the truth of what I had just heard.

'I don't understand, mum. What about Uncle John, isn't he going with Auntie Nora?'

None of it was fitting into my head the way thoughts are meant to.

'I'm expecting a phone call from her sometime today. I hope everything has gone as smoothly at her end.'

Mum smiled a gentle smile as she looked up through her words at me, at Pam, at the two of us staring disbelievingly at each other.

'Right then, who's for tea? I think I'll make a good strong pot.'

As if it was the easiest thing in the world, she was off, out to the kitchen, leaving Pam and myself to absorb what she had said through what she hadn't said but had discreetly passed on to us.

'I'll join you.'

As Pam left the room, following mum, I was left wondering if she meant Spain or tea.

I'll have to watch her from now on.

FAKING IT WITH THE GREEN BERET

A FAKING IT ROMANTIC COMEDY

TRACY BRODY

Copyright Page

This novel is entirely a work of fiction. The incidents portrayed in it are the work of the author's imagination. Any resemblance to actual persons, living or dead, events or localities is entirely coincidental, unless you're my friend as I do occasionally, with their permission, name a character after friends as a thank you for their support. So be nice to this author and you can show up in a book.

Faking it with the Green Beret

Copyright © 2022 by Tracy Brody Books

ISBN: 978-1-952187-11-7

First Edition

Also available as an ebook

ISBN: 978-1-952187-10-0

❀ Created with Vellum

Praise for Tracy Brody

"The song references are spot on throughout this page turner. John is a perfect mixture of a tough military man with a big heart and a soft side. ... This is a must read and leaves you feeling so good about people and proud of our military." ~ Carol H., Goodreads

"Brody incorporates ... impeccable comedic timing, over-the-top secondary characters, heart-tugging emotion, razor-sharp wit, sigh-worthy declarations, awkward situations, and did I mention humor? So delicious. So addictive. So much fun." ~ PJ – The Romance Dish (Faking it with the Bachelor)

"In this touching, at times heartbreaking as well as heartwarming story, the reader gets a chance to see these two seemingly opposites, be perfect for each other." ~ Yvonne C, Goodreads

"Faking it with the Green Beret provides feels, enlightens, entertains and is good for the soul." ~ Cheryl, Goodreads

To the survivors of abuse. May you heal and thrive.

To those with a heart for helping others – both human and animals.

To my supportive husband and family.

Music Playlists

I'm sharing the playlist of over 100 songs used as chapter titles and referenced in the book so you can sing along with John and Elizabeth. There are country, classic and song rock 'n roll, pop, dance music, and even some show tunes. You can also find links on my website https://tracybrody.com/

Spotify:

Full Playlist

Chapters

YouTube:

Amazon Music:

Chapters

Song Mentions

Trigger Warning

This is a romantic comedy book; however, it also deals with the sensitive subjects of physical and sexual abuse. Elizabeth is an abuse survivor and works with other women who've left abusive situations. While the abuse is not shown on the page, it is discussed in the book and is part of what Elizabeth has to overcome through counseling, EMDR therapy, and with encouragement from John.

The intent is to show women supporting one another and that there is help and hope for healing. Should the idea of a character sharing abuse in their past be a trigger for you, this may not be the book for you—at least not at this time. I do hope you will get to a place of happiness, joy, and strength.

Blessings,
Tracy

Bonus Scene Note

Dear Reader,

I decided not to have sex on the page in this book. Sex happens and is essential to Elizabeth and John's story, but the specifics aren't. However, I know many readers can take the heat and may feel cheated *not* to see what happens. I wanted readers to have the option of keeping it sweet or reading the tastefully-steamy scene.

You can get the free bonus chapter Shen you see a note to "Open the bedroom door." And this link: https://bookhip.com/LFWLHPF. You'll also receive my monthly newsletter, and get access to other bonus material, alerts about sales and upcoming release.

I have to say that I really do love this scene and hope you enjoy John rocking Elizabeth's world. 😉

Chapter One

BACK IN THE USA – Chuck Berry

CAPTAIN JOHN BRYSON waited for the plane to stop taxiing on the runway at Pope Air Base at Fort Bragg. Home, sweet home, North Carolina. He stood and turned around to face the men on his Green Beret team. As was his ritual when they touched down on US soil, he played Chuck Berry's version of "Back in the USA" and sang the first stanza loudly enough to be heard throughout the plane. The lyrics perfectly matched how good it felt to be home after an overseas deployment.

"I am not going to miss your singing," his first lieutenant groused, shaking his head.

"Too bad. It's a team tradition. Right, Top?" John looked to his first sergeant.

"Definitely. I'd miss it if you didn't sing," First Sergeant Rodriguez said. "Next deployment won't be the same without you."

1

"I was *born in the USA*," John broke into song, worse than usual—on purpose. His six-foot-five stature typically gave him license to massacre the melody and lyrics without fear of reprisal, though his off-key singing could be why someone had put a toy snake in his bunk two months into their deployment. It'd looked real enough to fool him for nearly three seconds.

There was one more tradition John would introduce his new lieutenant to once his combat boots hit the tarmac. This had been a good deployment with zero casualties and only two minor injuries on his team.

Unlike the formal welcome home ceremonies given to traditional Army battalions, his operational detachment, or ODA, unit arrived without fanfare due to the classified nature of their missions. They'd be like roadies carrying their gear off the airfield to go home to their families.

"All right, let's move. Let's move," he ordered. Mechanical problems had delayed their flight a few hours. Long enough to derail his plans to get home, surprise Britney, play with Boss, then don his dress uniform to accompany Britney to the charity gala and auction she'd spent months organizing. While he hadn't communicated the date of their return with her due to operational security—something she hadn't grasped the importance of and he'd have to explain again—he had kept abreast of the event via her social media accounts. Rather than let the delay tank his idea, he adapted his mission plan. He'd go straight there, in camouflage, and see his dog when they got home.

Maybe he'd find a trip he could bid on at the auction. Take Britney away for romance, rest, and relaxation and get things back on track since she had a rough introduction to life with—and without—a military man. He'd tried to prep her, but the separation was hard. He blamed the newness of

their relationship. Next time he deployed, things would go smoother.

First, he needed to get his men off this plane and on their way.

"Don't do anything stupid tonight," he warned his team, "because Top and I have plans with our ladies. We'll let your butt sit in jail overnight."

"Amen to that," Rodriguez concurred.

After spending six months in Chad, Africa, those with families would head straight home, but the prospect of catching a buzz and getting laid appealed to the single guys. John had headed to Jumpy's Bar in the past. This time, he had someone waiting for him and damn, it felt good.

His men waited on the tarmac as he descended the steps last.

John took three steps, then dropped to his knees and kissed the nasty asphalt to the cheers of his team. He sang "American Soldier" as he slipped his rucksack onto his back and hefted the strap of his other bag over his shoulder. Rifle in hand, he continued singing as he strode through the lingering men.

When they reached the parking lot for where their freshly washed vehicles waited, most of his team were already on their phones. Though operational security no longer applied with their safe return, he refrained from calling Britney. She would be busy putting finishing touches on tonight's event. The reunion was going to rock. Hell, his surprise entrance might turn into one of those welcome home videos of soldiers that went viral.

Chapter Two

An hour after the event started, John parked his truck in the country club lot. His Ford F-250 stuck out amid all the luxury sedans and SUVs. As he mounted the smooth, marble steps between impressive white columns, he was a jumble of excitement and nerves, in a different way than going out on a dangerous mission. Instrumental music played. The soft chatter of voices was unlike anything he'd heard in the last six months.

"May I help you?" asked a woman in a chic black dress at the hostess stand. Her gaze roved over his uniform, down to his worn combat boots, wordlessly pointing out this was a classy affair.

"My girlfriend's here for the gala and auction."

"Do you have an invitation?"

"Not with me," he fudged. "I just landed an hour ago. I've been deployed overseas for months, and our flight was

delayed. Would you be willing to use my phone to film me surprising her?"

"Oh," she sighed, smiling and bringing a hand to her heart. "That's so sweet and romantic."

They moved to the entrance of the huge ballroom. For a second, his breath stalled in his lungs. There had to be nearly three hundred people seated at round dinner tables. Others mingled and checked out auction items on the room's perimeter tables. While there were probably a few executives with concealed carry permits and socialites packing pistols in purses, no one brandished AK-47s or rocket-propelled grenade launchers. It was nice to be on friendly soil.

With his height advantage, he scanned the guests until he finally picked out Britney in a group near the back wall.

"Follow me." He set his phone to record a video and handed it to the hostess. "She's the woman with long, dark hair in the red dress." He started his stealthy approach, keeping out of Britney's line of sight. As if on cue, the crowd parted and gave him a clear path.

Three more steps to reach the group and John had a clear view of her profile and the man at her side: her cheating ex-boyfriend, Richard James McCall, the third, or fourth, or maybe the fifth. His hand rested possessively on Britney's hip.

John's racing heart backpedaled, and he froze in place.

Dicky boy gulped, and his eyes widened to show white around his irises. His hand dropped to his side and nudged Britney's thigh. Okay, maybe not so ex anymore.

Britney's jaw dropped open and the champagne glass in her hand slipped.

Liquid and glass crashed to the floor. Based on how her

head swiveled to the faces of those around her, the fear in her eyes was for a different reason than Dicky.

"John! What are you doing here?" Her voice warbled, and her spray tan paled a shade or two.

"We just got back from deployment. I thought I'd surprise you. I see it worked."

"You didn't tell me when you were coming back." She edged away from Richard.

Too late, baby. I already saw. "Operational security. I explained why I couldn't communicate on this mission." And had to go dark on her after she posted on social media that he was deployed to Africa. Man, had he gotten his ass handed to him from command on that.

John looked down at Dicky in his tailored tuxedo. Dicky gave an awkward, nervous smile, revealing his gleaming, chemically whitened teeth, and took a half step back.

"I see the bigger surprise is on me." John held his hand out to the hostess. "You can stop filming."

She darkened the screen and placed the cell phone in his palm like it might explode.

A scene showing he'd survived a deployment unscathed only to have a bomb dropped on him the night he got home wasn't the kind of video either he or Britney wanted going viral. He snagged a glass of champagne from a passing server.

"This auction is to raise money for children's cancer research." Britney kept her voice low as she glanced around. "Can you go without making more of a scene?"

"Go where? Home?"

"No. I—I didn't want to send you a Dear John letter while you were deployed. Your stuff's in boxes in the garage."

The air whooshed from his lungs. Whoa. His stuff was

packed? *Dayam*. He hadn't been kicked this hard in the nads in a long time.

"We can talk later." She gave a little shooing motion with her fingers.

"No need." Things were pretty clear. "I'll go by the house, load my boxes, get my dog, and be out of your life by the time you get home from your swanky party."

"Ohhh, shit." Her gaze shot to Richard, who took another small step back. Red tinged her cheeks. "Um, about Boss," she stammered, shifting her weight from one high-heeled foot to the other.

"You're not keeping Boss." Caring for Boss for a few months didn't give her custody of his dog.

"He, uh . . . he died."

The words sucked the life out of him like an M-4 kill shot through his skull. "What? No!"

"I'm sorry."

"How could you not tell me my dog died?" She had to be lying.

"I couldn't video chat or call due to operational security." Sarcasm dripped from her lips. "And I didn't want to tell you in an email or letter."

That Britney had used him as a rebound or maybe an angle to get back with her ex was an ego buster. Finding out his dog was dead? Might as well cut out his heart. "How?"

"He was hit by a car. Or a truck," she offered lamely.

Numbness took hold. John downed his champagne in one gulp. He sure as hell didn't have anything to celebrate, but alcohol might take the edge off. Champagne wasn't going to cut it. Not one glass, anyway. He snatched Richard's glass from his hand and drank it on his way out of the ballroom, ignoring curious stares as people cleared a path for him.

He drove straight to Britney's house, hoping that for some sadistic reason she was lying about Boss. Maybe she'd gotten so attached to the oversized mutt she didn't want to give him up.

John used his key for what would be the last time to let himself into the two-story house. Boss didn't meet him at the front door

"Boss!" He held his breath and listened.

Silence. No signs of Boss. No bowls. No dog bed. Not even dog hair on the hardwood floor.

John climbed the stairs on legs that grew heavier with each step. The bed in the master bedroom was unmade and empty. Discarded clothes covered the floral print chair where he often sat and laced up his combat boots to keep from waking Britney. He plucked a pair of boxer briefs—not his—from a laundry pile and held them up by the waistband.

"Good things come in small packages, eh Dicky?"

He dropped the briefs back to the floor and headed to the closet. Instead of his civvies, expensive suits, starched dress shirts, and pressed polo shirts hung at half-inch intervals. The size of Dicky's bank account bested the small size of his package.

Checking the dresser and bathroom and finding no trace John had lived there confirmed that Britney was another woman who viewed him as an inconsequential blip in her life.

They were from different worlds. He'd known it. His friends knew it. Britney, especially, knew it. It'd been fun while it lasted, a whole three months prior to his deployment. Her friends made it clear from the start that they considered him Britney's rebound guy, and he'd been an idiot to think he could make a relationship last by moving in

together. He was an officer, but her family wanted her with a professional—an executive, lawyer, or doctor. Someone who offered a bigger paycheck to support her in the style she'd become accustomed to.

In the garage, he found large cardboard boxes with his name scrawled on them. He hauled the boxes to the back of his truck.

His life, in eight boxes. That was all he had left after he rented out his house, sold his furniture to another guy in Third Group, and moved in with Britney. It wouldn't be the first time he had to start over. It didn't hurt much—at least not compared to losing Boss.

He rummaged through the boxes, dug out jeans and a T-shirt, then stripped out of his uniform and changed right there in the driveway. Was it too much to expect her to save Boss's stuff? Checking the remaining boxes, he didn't find a single toy. The realization that he'd dodged a hollow point bullet grew as he slammed the gate of his truck closed.

Glancing in the rearview mirror, he gave the house a middle-fingered salute as he peeled out, leaving tread marks as a reminder Britney could live with for a while.

Chapter Three

DRUNK LAST NIGHT – Eli Young Band

"Not that one again, please," John's nameless new drinking buddy pleaded.

"I thought you were my friend." John dropped another quarter in the jukebox. The crowd at Jumpy's had dwindled to a handful of people.

"Not if you sing that again."

"Fine. I'll pick a new song." He'd played "Friends in Low Places" at least three times. Appropriate, since he'd showed up in combat boots and ruined Britney's black-tie affair.

He scrolled the blurry song titles and landed on one he meant to play earlier. "That's it." He tapped the glass and carefully pressed the number for Luke Bryan's song "Little Boys Grow Up and Dogs Get Old," even though he didn't know the words well enough to sing along.

According to the vet, Boss was around six. About forty

in people years. He hadn't gotten the chance to get old. It wasn't fair.

While the song played, John sipped his whiskey and showed pictures of Boss to his new friend. "He was part Rottweiler—see his squarish face? Part springer spaniel. That accounts for his spots."

"Are his eyes different colors, or am I that drunk?" He passed John's phone back to him.

"One blue and one brown. He might not have been the most handsome dog, but he was loyal. And big. A man's dog. Not some sissy, yappy dog. We were brothers by different species of mothers." John tried not to cry in his whiskey.

"To Boss."

"To Boss! The best dog ever." John raised his glass. "He deserves a proper burial."

"Hell yes, he does."

"I'm gonna tell her that." He swiped the screen on his phone.

♫

JOHN WOKE and stretched the best he could, crammed as he was in the passenger seat of his truck. He pulled the bill of his ball cap low against the morning sun beating through the windshield, further aggravating the pounding of his brain against his skull.

He opened the door, poured himself out of the vehicle, and stood on shaky legs. When he'd warned his men not to do anything stupid, he hadn't planned to be the one sleeping it off in his truck outside Jumpy's. Most of last night was a blur thanks to a few too many bourbons. It'd

seemed like a good idea in the moment. And he'd made a friend, not that he remembered the guy's name.

With his mouth desert-patrol nasty, he opened the door to the back of the cab and found a bottle of water that had been in his truck for months. He chugged that to ease the headache.

At least he hadn't done anything totally stupid. Had he? A memory lingered just out of reach. He patted himself down. Where the hell was his phone? He found his cell on the truck's dash and checked the call log.

His heart beat against his ribs. Shit.

Double shit.

And triple shit.

He had a vague recollection of calling Britney, but three times?

Surely, he hadn't begged her to take him back. No. It had to do with Boss. John rubbed his temple as his brain gonged harder in his head. He sat on the edge of the seat and tried to remember.

He'd asked about Boss's remains. What had she said before she hung up on him?

His deployment might be over, but he had a new mission: find out what happened to his dog.

♫

Whiskey still leached from John's pores as he walked down the hospital's administrative hallway to Britney's office. She'd likely come into work to bask in the accolades from organizing the auction.

She looked up from her computer, all smiles until she saw him standing in her doorway. Her body deflated, and her smile dissipated. "What are you doing here?"

"Boss. What did you do with his remains?"

"Why?"

"I need closure. I want to bury him or visit his grave."

"I—we—didn't bury him." Britney wouldn't look him in the eye.

His arm hairs stood at attention. "Then what did you do? Cremate him?"

"Yes," she answered quickly.

"I want his ashes."

"I didn't get them."

John growled. "What's the name of the crematorium?" Maybe they still had the remains.

"I don't remember. Richard took care of it."

That figured. "Call and ask him."

"I'll, uh ask him tonight and call you."

"Now. Or I'll go by his daddy's company and ask him myself."

"I know I said I'd think about moving to Florida with you getting promoted and transferred, but I can't. My job, my friends, my family are all here. Then you got mad about the post and stopped calling. That's why Richard and I ended up back together."

"What does that have to do with Boss?"

"He and Richard didn't get along." She paused between words and sank into her chair as if trying to disappear. "He didn't die."

John would have made a wisecrack if he wasn't so damned relieved. "He—he's alive? Where? Who's got him?"

"Um, I asked around, but I couldn't find a foster. . ."

"A dozen of my buddies would have taken care of him."

"Except I couldn't exactly ask you," she said lamely.

"Where. Is. He?"

"Richard took Bruce to the county animal shelter."

Leave it to Dicky to call Boss by his formal name. Shelter. A chill swept through John For *Richard's* sake, it had better be a no-kill shelter.

♫

JOHN'S FOOT tapped on the concrete floor while the middle-aged woman manning the shelter's desk helped the family ahead of him.

Damn Richard. Damn Britney. Had he thought Britney taking care of Boss would somehow cement their relationship?

I'm sorry, Boss. I screwed up.

Another volunteer showed up to escort the family off to get their new pet. John's gut twisted as he stepped up to the counter.

"Can I help you?" The middle-aged woman asked.

"I'm looking for my dog. My girlfriend's not-so-ex boyfriend brought him here."

"He what?" She gave a disgusted sigh. "How long ago was it?"

"Around two months. I was deployed." It'd been a little longer since Britney jammed him up with her social media post, making him cut communication to almost nil. Had she done that purposefully, trying to get him to break up with her?

"Oh."

The woman's increasingly sympathetic and concerned tone slammed him in the chest like a sledgehammer.

"This is a no-kill shelter, right?"

"It is. You said this was your girlfriend taking care of your dog?"

"She's my ex now. And forever more."

The kennel worker nodded in understanding. "What was the dog's name?"

"Boss."

She typed and scanned the computer records. "I don't have an animal named Boss in our records for the past year. What type of dog was he?"

"Rottweiler mixed with springer spaniel and part something else. Like a mastiff. Wait!" Hadn't Britney said Richard turned *Bruce* in? "Try under Bruce." Maybe Richard used his full name rather than think of him as The Boss.

She turned the monitor for him to see. "Is this him?"

"Yes! That's my Boss! He's here?"

"No. He was here two weeks before he was adopted."

"Adopted?" It was better than Boss being dead or languishing in an animal shelter for months, but the word delivered a kill shot to his hope. He grasped at the only life-line available. "Can you give me information on who adopted him?"

She frowned and sighed. "They didn't have permission to relinquish him?"

"Hell no!"

"And you were deployed overseas?"

"Yes, ma'am." He pulled out his military ID to prove his story. "I'm in a unit that can't communicate much when we're on assignment, so I didn't know what she and her new dick boyfriend had done."

"I can't give you the adopter's information, but if you give me your name and phone number, I can contact them and explain what happened. Then it's out of our hands."

"Anything. I can give you pictures of me with him. I can even get his records from my vet." He'd give her a kidney if it meant he'd get Boss back. He wrote down his name and

15

phone number on the scrap of paper the woman gave him.

Then he scrolled through his phone's picture gallery and pulled up his favorite picture of him with his arm around Boss, their heads together. He'd been smiling at Britney when she took it. Still, it showed the love between him and Boss. "Can you send them this picture?"

"Aww. Sure, I'll send it from my phone." The worker snapped a photo.

He couldn't see her phone screen when she tapped in the number, but he stood ready to answer questions if Boss's new owner answered the call.

"Voicemail," she mouthed. It sounded like a woman's voice on the message, but he couldn't make out the name. "Hi. This is Seana at Cumberland County Animal Services. I'm here with a soldier who just returned from deployment, and it's possible the dog you adopted was his. He says his girlfriend—"

"Ex-girlfriend," he clarified. Okay, maybe he growled, but they'd given away his dog. Couldn't get much lower than that.

"—didn't have permission to relinquish him. I'll give you his contact information and try to text you a picture he has with the animal. I'm sorry about this. We had no idea." She read off John's rank, name, and telephone number before hanging up and texting the photo.

"Thank you. I appreciate you contacting them," he choked out. It wasn't a victory yet, but at least he had a fighting chance to get his dog back.

Chapter Four

LIFE CHANGES – Thomas Rhett

"AFTER HE CAME BACK, what did you do?" Elizabeth asked her client.

"I finally told him how I feel when he storms off when we're fighting." Shannon drew in a shaky breath. Tears formed in the young woman's eyes. "He said the reason he leaves is to get control of himself and not say—or do—something that will hurt me."

"And did hearing that change anything?"

"Definitely. Once I understood he did that to protect me, not that he doesn't care and wants to leave me, I saw things differently. I got out of the crazy cycle, and we talked —really talked—instead of me freezing him out when he came home. I tend to expect him to read my mind, and then I get mad when he doesn't do things I want him to do. He wants me to ask for help with things around the apartment. That way, we can work together."

Elizabeth noted the relief in Shannon's voice and her straighter posture.

"Patterns of behavior can be hard to break," said Elizabeth. "Knowing what to look for, practicing, and then seeing that it goes well can help change those old habits. It sounds like you've done that and made progress. I'm proud of you for being assertive in telling James what you're feeling and what you need."

"Since we weren't fighting, I felt hopeful about things and wasn't stressed at work. That made things better between us the past week, if you know what I mean." Shannon blushed and tucked her hair behind her ear.

"I do." Though that was definitely good for Shannon, and her situation was vastly different than Elizabeth's, the mention still triggered a tightness in Elizabeth's chest. "Keep working on those communication skills. When would you like to come in again?"

A few minutes later, Elizabeth escorted a smiling Shannon to the lobby. Ending with a client moving toward a healthier and happier life was an excellent way to finish her day.

She made notes on her computer, then checked her messages before heading out. She had a text from Jillian about dinner and a message from a number not in her contacts. There was also a missed call, along with a voice-mail notification. She started with the voicemail, expecting a pre-recorded scam call about forgiving student-loan debt or extending her car's warranty.

Her brain refused to process the caller's words, so she restarted the message.

No, she'd heard correctly.

"Oh, my. Oh, Bruce."

ELIZABETH DIDN'T see Jillian enter the busy café until her friend set her order pager on the table.

"I'm starving." Jillian slid into a chair. "My lunch got interrupted when I had to respond to a call about someone passed out in their car at a gas station."

"He was drunk in the middle of the day?"

"Plastered. We asked him who the president was. He said he didn't know because he's from Missouri, not North Carolina."

Elizabeth shook her head. Her friend's police call stories always helped take Elizabeth's mind off her clients.

"He blew a one point two on the breathalyzer, so I had to book him. At least this one didn't pass out and pee himself in my squad car. So, give me an update on Ariana."

She had a vested interest in Elizabeth's newest resident at The Oasis since Jillian had connected them in hopes that having a place to go would encourage Ariana to leave her abusive boyfriend.

"She's settling in. She opened up a bit at the monthly dinner last Friday. It sounds like she hasn't had anyone there for her in a while."

"Probably why she stayed after her boyfriend hit her the first time. Is she going to stick?"

"I hope so. I think she feels safe now. She blocked J.R.'s number so he can't text or call."

"That's a good start, but she can always unblock him," Jillian pointed out.

"True. She went to the animal shelter and adopted a cat."

"She should have gotten a hoss of a dog like you."

She opened the text message and handed Jillian her phone.

"They sent a picture, and it definitely looks like Bruce."

"Any chance he's not legit?"

of and might have done to Ginger.

her first rescue dog back to the shelter, but she'd had no choice after seeing what her now-ex-husband was capable made you do hard things. Elizabeth hadn't wanted to take shelter than dump him out in the country." Sometimes life demands of a pet Bruce's size. Better to take him to the

"Or maybe the girlfriend couldn't keep up with the taking a guy's dog to a shelter is a cold-hearted move."

more a case of the ex not giving the dog back. Though "Maybe they parted on friendly terms. Usually, it's

explains everything."

him to the shelter. I guess the ex-girlfriend part of the story the guy was deployed and didn't have permission to take

"The message said his ex-girlfriend kept Bruce while

"Hmm." Jillian's mouth shifted. "Could be legit."

with a picture."

"No, it was a local cell number, but she also sent a text

"Did caller ID say it was the shelter?"

his dog, and they think it's Bruce."

worker at the shelter. She said a guy showed up looking for from the shelter. "Speaking of Bruce, I got a call from a

Maybe she should get Jillian's read on the messages but now . . .

her some time getting used to a dog five times Barkley's size, mixed breed dog after losing her beloved poodle. It'd taken Elizabeth hadn't planned on adopting a hundred-pound

"Imagine that." Jillian cracked a grin.

size."

"I can tell she's not comfortable around a dog Bruce's

"He even has the different color eyes. The guy's cute." Innuendo laced Jillian's statement.

"Is he?"

Jillian tsked and turned the picture back around.

"Are you interested?" The café pager vibrated noisily on the table, and Elizabeth snatched it up.

"I meant for you. You know he's not my type."

"Not interested." Even if the guy was handsome with a great smile and soulful brown eyes, he was trying to take away her dog. She'd had Bruce less than two months, but she'd grown attached. Having a big, intimidating dog around had made her feel safer if Ariana's abusive ex managed to track her to The Oasis.

"What are you going to do?" Jillian asked when Elizabeth returned with her food.

"I just listened to the message before coming to meet you. I haven't called him yet." She knew she was making excuses.

"Guys like J.R. are always coming up with new angles to play people. Don't give this guy your name or address."

"I wouldn't. Any suggestion for a public place with plenty of people around?" No way she'd allow someone to snatch her dog if this was bogus.

"Let me know when you're meeting this guy claiming Bruce is his, and I'll check him out first."

"Can you do that?"

"I can dig up something with his name and phone number. But if I get his license or registration? Jackpot. I wouldn't want you to give your dog back to an irresponsible owner. Or worse."

Chapter Five

AIN'T NO MOUNTAIN HIGH ENOUGH   Marvin
Gaye and Tammi Tarrell

AFTER HOURS of sitting in a sandwich shop calling online rental listings and praying he'd need one that allowed big dogs, John grabbed his phone the moment it rang. It read RESTRICTED on the screen, and his mouth suddenly went dry. "John Bryson." He held his breath, waiting for a response.

"I'm calling about a message from the animal shelter about the dog I adopted," a woman spoke hesitantly.

Thank you, God! "Yes. Thank you for calling." He could breathe again, though this didn't mean she would give him Boss. "When I returned from deployment yesterday, my ex-girlfriend told me he died before admitting her new boyfriend took him to the shelter."

"If he is your dog, he's very much alive," she assured him. "I guess we should meet to work this out."

Some of the weight lifted off him, like dropping a forty-pound rucksack. He'd thought of a dozen reasons she might refuse to give Boss back to him. Boss might be her kids' beloved pet. Or she would blame him for leaving Boss with Britney in the first place—like he was blaming himself. "Name the time and the place, and I'll be there. I can come now or in the morning."

"Hang on a second."

He couldn't make out her muffled exchange with another person. *Please don't let her be talking with her kids.* He wanted Boss, but he couldn't break kids' hearts. He'd suck it up if Boss were in the loving home he deserved.

"I can bring Bruce to meet you at Arnette Park near the airport in half an hour."

"I'll be there. I'm driving a black truck. Wearing jeans, a reddish T-shirt, and a black ball cap."

"I'll have Bruce. I'm sure you can't miss him."

"I'll see you there. And—thank you."

John headed straight there. After he parked, he debated. Was waiting inside or outside his truck friendlier? He got out and tried to look chill, leaning against the truck rather than pacing as the minutes slowly ticked past.

Even though he arrived fifteen minutes early and the woman hadn't given her name, nor had she said what kind of car she drove, that didn't keep him from checking for Boss when a vehicle arrived.

Except it was a police officer who cruised slowly past. He nodded to her. His empty stomach clenched when she backed up, stopped a few feet away from him, and put her window down.

"Good evening, officer," said John.

"Can I see your license and registration?"

Shit, not now. "What's the problem?"

"Your registration sticker is expired."

He looked down at his plate. Yep, last month. She had to notice this now? "I just got back from an overseas deployment yesterday," he explained, opening his wallet and handing over his license and military ID." "I haven't gotten my mail yet." He didn't have a clue what Britney had done with his mail.

"Registration." The officer didn't let up.

"It's in my glove compartment."

"Do you have any weapons in the vehicle?"

"No ma'am." There was a locked gun case in one of the boxes still in the back of his truck, but he didn't know which one. He retrieved his registration and handed it to the officer, who had already had his license and history displayed on her iPad screen.

"You can wait by your vehicle." She rolled up her window and was on her phone in seconds. He didn't have a record, so she couldn't run him in, which was good because he was not leaving this park for anything.

Could he not catch a break? Give me a warning or— heck, a ticket. Just move on. The last thing he needed was for the woman who adopted Boss to have second thoughts about meeting him because she saw him getting hassled by a cop. All he wanted was a fair shot at getting his dog back.

♫

Elizabeth accepted Jillian's call. "We're almost there. Did you find out anything?"

"Good news. Captain Bryson's vehicle registration is expired, so I had a valid reason to run his license and record."

"And?" Elizabeth glanced in the rearview mirror at Bruce, his head out the window, enjoying the breeze.

"His hair looks longer than military regs length. Brown eyes. Nice looking."

"Not what I was asking." She already knew all that.

"He's six foot five."

He'd looked big in the picture with Bruce, but six-five? It's not like Bruce would be her protector against his former owner. *Take a breath. It'll be okay.*

"He has a clean record. Not even a speeding ticket. Though he's not happy with me right now and seems a bit on edge. I'm about to cut him loose. I'll stick around for a bit since they've had a few car break-ins recently at parks."

"Thanks. I'll see you in a minute." She looked back at Bruce again. "It's up to you, boy. If you don't want to go with him, just let me know." This sucked. Somebody was going to end up heartbroken. Probably her.

She exhaled as she drove past Bruce's towering owner and his truck to park several cars down. If the captain didn't take no for an answer, they might not have a choice, even though Jillian's police cruiser was parked in the shade at the end of the lot.

Bruce sniffed the air and barked excitedly twice. Then, he scrambled into the front seat to get out.

"Calm down. I'll come around and get you." She hadn't even exited the driver's seat before Bruce's oversized owner strode her way. Though she tried to block Bruce long enough to clip on his leash, the canine pushed past her, nearly knocking her down. By the time she regained her balance, Bruce had his paws on the man's chest, licking his face as the man hugged him.

As she watched their joyful reunion, her eyes got misty. When she closed in, she saw she wasn't the only one getting

emotional. Tears made the guy less intimidating, despite his size.

He kept Bruce off him long enough to extend a hand to her. "John Bryson." He firmly gripped her hand in his much larger one.

"Elizabeth Carroll."

"I don't know how to thank you." His voice cracked. "My ex-girlfriend was supposed to be taking care of him while I was deployed—"

"You left him with an ex?" She had to ask.

"She wasn't my ex when I left. Didn't know until I got in last night that things were over, and her current boyfriend didn't like having my dog around."

Ouch. The guy had come home to a double whammy.

"Things are over with her but seeing that Boss is okay . . ." His words broke off. He affectionately rubbed the dog's head.

"I thought his name was Bruce." Though he was clearly John's dog.

"His full name is Bruce 'The Boss' Springweiler. I call him Boss," he said with a grin.

"Okay," she laughed. That explained why the dog had responded better when Jillian jokingly called him Hoss.

"Do you have kids?" he asked with some hesitation and discreetly checked out her left hand.

"No." She swallowed the lump in her throat. She guessed why he was asking and wouldn't make him beg to have his dog back. "I'm glad you were able to track him down. I didn't think to bring his bed and toys. I can drop off his things tomorrow if you give me an address."

His eyes widened, and he swayed back slightly. "My priority was finding Boss. I didn't *exactly* think this through. I was living with the ex before I deployed, so I'm, uh, home-

less at the moment. I slept in my truck last night." He rubbed a hand over his face that was sporting a serious five o'clock shadow. "I planned to get a hotel room until I find a short-term place to rent, though hotels that allow pets usually have a size limit way under a hundred pounds. I can probably sneak him in."

"Sneak him in? What about leaving him all day when you go to work?"

"I've got leave for the next week, but you're right, I can't leave him in a hotel room or my truck while I'm looking for a place to live. Would it be an imposition for you to keep him for another day or two until I can find a place? I'll pay you back for adoption fees, food, and vet bills."

"It's not an imposition, and you don't need to pay me."

"I insist."

Jillian's cruiser rolled up on them. "Everything okay here?" she asked.

"Everything's fine," Elizabeth answered.

Jillian patted Boss's head when he approached the patrol car.

John's eyes narrowed. "You two know each other?"

Elizabeth hesitated. "We do," she admitted.

He waved a finger at Jillian. "You checked to see if I had a record."

"I wasn't going to let just anyone take her dog."

He gave the kind of throaty, good-natured chuckle that was downright sexy. "It wouldn't show I got busted for stealing two candy bars from a mini-mart when I was around twelve. But don't worry, I made full restitution and did my time. Grandmothers tend to impose stricter penalties than a court. I appreciate that you were looking out for my—her—dog."

"Take good care of him. Don't let me catch you stealing candy bars, or I'll lock you up and give her back that hoss."

"Yes, ma'am."

"Thanks," Elizabeth said before Jillian drove away, then shifted her guilty gaze to John.

"I'd love some time with Boss," said John, "but I don't want to inconvenience you or expect you to wait around. Would it be okay for me to drop him off or meet up with you a little later?"

It wasn't ideal, but they needed time together after months apart. "That's a good idea. He might not understand you leaving him right away. I'll text you my address. There's a gate at the drive. Press the button on the speaker, and I'll let you in."

"I won't be too late. Want to go for a ride, boy?"

Boss looked to Elizabeth before he turned toward John's truck.

John hesitated. "Thank you again. You—you don't know how much this means to me." His voice warbled, and she couldn't miss the moisture in his kind eyes.

She forced a smile and nodded. It wasn't the first time she'd given up an animal she loved. This time it was because someone loved the pet even more than she did.

♫

Shortly before sundown, John buzzed for her to open the gate. Instead of coming to the front door, he threw a ball for Bruce—no, Boss—to chase in the grassy field along the front of her property. As darkness settled, the game ended. John took a seat on one of the rockers on the front porch, talking to Boss in a soothing tone for several minutes before knocking.

FAKING IT WITH THE GREEN BERET

Elizabeth opened the door.

Rather than charge in, Boss remained at John's side. He extended a lovely, oversized bouquet of cheerful sunflowers, with yellow and white daisies, and purple statice to her. In his other hand, he held a bag from the pet store.

"You didn't have to do that." She had no real choice but to accept the flowers. Better than having to explain.

"A small thank you for all you've done for Boss. Many people wouldn't adopt dogs that are part Rottweiler. And feeding him isn't cheap. I tried to wear him out a little. Do you want me to get him settled for the night?"

Her mouth went dry at the idea of this oversized, powerful stranger coming into her home, despite Jillian running his license and tags. "Um, he usually watches TV with me before bed." With the dog bed in her bedroom, the front porch was as far as this stranger was getting.

"I understand. I just thought it might be easier for me to slip out. Here are some of his favorite treats." He handed her the bag from the pet store.

Boss's ears perked up.

John dropped to one knee while she opened the bag of treats. "You stay here, boy. I'll be back tomorrow. I promise." She held onto Boss's collar as John got to his feet and backed away. Boss pulled and barked as John walked to his truck. John waved, his reluctance to leave his best friend evident in the way he hesitated before driving away.

"It'll be okay, Boss." The name still sounded strange on her lips, but the idea of him being the boss of a big, badass soldier made her smile.

The flowers had been a nice gesture. At least they weren't a bouquet of red roses, but a man giving her flowers was still an emotional trigger for her. It seemed a waste to throw them out, so she divided them into two bundles and

put them in vases. She walked around the oversized rhodo-dendrons separating her house from The Oasis's tiny homes. She delivered one bouquet to Wren in Haven House and the other cluster to Ariana in Sanctuary Lodge. She didn't explain where the flowers came from since she didn't want to alarm Ariana or break the news that Boss would be leaving. She still needed a little time to process that herself.

Chapter Six

I'LL BE THERE – The Jackson Five

AFTER A SECOND DAY of trying to find a short-term rental that allowed big dogs and had a decent-sized yard, John picked up dinner and headed out to see Boss. He didn't want to drag this out or take advantage of Elizabeth's generosity—and definitely not give her reason to change her mind about giving up Boss. He didn't think she would, but they'd only spent a few minutes talking, mainly about Boss. Normally, he'd try turning up the charm with someone who looked like Elizabeth, except she hadn't sent any signal that she was interested.

He hadn't figured out if she was merely reserved or if the guarded look in her stunning blue eyes had to do with him reclaiming Boss. As attractive as she was, she came off as the no-nonsense type, from the cut of her simple, chin-length blond hair, her minimal make-up—not that she needed it—and her casual clothes. She drove a newer

model, mid-sized sedan. Flower baskets hung along the porch of her modest, farm-style ranch. The property was surrounded by several acres of woods. Nothing pretentious about any of that. It was the kind of place he'd love to have for him and Boss.

A gray sedan pulled up on his tail as soon as the gate opened. He'd thought it odd that Elizabeth had a security gate living on a rural road. Now, his internal alarm triggered. He pulled through far enough to let the gate close, preventing the sedan from following him. Though the male driver honked, John didn't budge.

Dude, you have to get buzzed in on your own.

He kept an eye on the vehicle as he parked in front of Elizabeth's house, about thirty yards past the gate. He didn't see the driver buzzed in, nor did the car back away. Boss scrambled down the steps. Elizabeth trailed, wearing tan pants and a blue blouse.

"You expecting someone else?" He pointed to the gray sedan behind the gate.

"No."

A scrawny, dark-haired male got out of the car. Elizabeth's eyes widened. "What do you want?" she called to the visitor.

"I need to talk to Ariana." Wearing ripped jeans and a baggy T-shirt, he looked rough. His words slurred as he shook the gate. "I saw her drive in there."

"She doesn't want to see you." Elizabeth's tone had gone drill sergeant serious. "Leave now, or I'll call the police."

Police? The security gate and this punk showing up pinged a danger signal to John's brain. He positioned his body between Elizabeth and the man at the gate.

"I'm not leaving until I talk to Ariana." He eyed the decorative white posts lining the front of the property,

telegraphing his intentions a split second before he climbed the fence.

Immediately, John was on him, blocking his way. The guy's eyes were shiny and rimmed with red.

"Ariana!" the man called past John.

"Stay inside," Elizabeth yelled over Boss's barking. She sounded nearer now.

The intruder slurred out more words. "I love you, baby. It won't happen again."

John kept his gaze trained on the guy's eyes and empty hands as he continued shouting to this Ariana woman, wherever she was.

"This is private property." Elizabeth held Boss's collar as he continued to bark. "If you don't leave, I'll release the dog and call the police."

"You heard the lady. It'd be best if you go." John went into full enforcer mode.

"This is none of your business." The guy came at him.

John planted his feet and leaned forward in anticipation. Though the kid struck John's chest with both hands, John didn't budge.

The impaired visitor didn't fare as well. He stumbled backward a few steps, barely staying upright.

"I'll give you that one, but if you touch me again or pull a weapon, I will put you on the ground, break your arm, and toss you over that fence. How's that going to look? Leave now and call after you sober up. If she wants to see you, you can have a conversation like two civilized adults."

The guy's right hand slowly reached toward his back pocket.

"I hope you're reaching for a phone because I'm a Green Beret. I've taken out way worse assholes than you,"

John warned, planning his defensive maneuver if the kid pulled a weapon.

The guy backed away, still unsteady on his feet. "You've made a big mistake." He waved a finger and scowled as if he could intimidate John.

John advanced in case the kid thought he could dart around him.

Once he'd climbed over the fence and into his car, John finally dared to look behind him. Nearly hidden behind a cluster of huge bushes covered with large pink blooms were three structures: one in a natural finish, a taller one with yellow siding, and a boxy blue one. They looked more like oversized kid's playhouses than sheds. He glimpsed movement of the blinds in the blue one closest to Elizabeth's house.

"I'm guessing you know who that was," he said when Elizabeth approached. She clutched Boss's collar with one hand and held her phone near her face with the other. "Good, boy." He patted Boss's head to calm him.

Elizabeth stepped closer to the fence as the sedan peeled away, sending gravel flying. "Did you see the make of his vehicle?"

"It was a gray Hyundai. Sonata, I think."

She nodded as if impressed. On assignment, details like that could mean the difference between life and death.

"He left driving a gray, four-door Hyundai, heading toward Fayetteville," Elizabeth relayed to someone on the other end of the line. Hopefully, the police.

A woman in her early twenties with long, black hair emerged tentatively from the little blue structure. She hugged herself as if she was cold, despite temperatures in the mid-eighties.

and worried her bottom lip.

"No. Jillian can have patrols cruise by." Her sigh was not a happy one as she stared from the fence to the woods

mined to get in.

whole property?" Not that it would keep out anyone deter-

John surveyed the area. "Does this fence surround the

the little blue house.

Ariana glanced down the road, then slipped back inside

the young woman.

may not even make the connection." He hoped to reassure

good thing. "If it happens a few miles away from here, he

"Trial? Interesting." J.R. getting arrested sounded like a

assured Ariana.

"That could keep him there until the trial," Elizabeth

him over, he may end up in jail," John pointed out.

"He was clearly high or drunk." Or both. "If they pull

things worse." Ariana's fear was palpable.

"If the police pull J.R. over, it will piss him off and make

"She's a personal friend."

necessary.

dial?" He was going to be seriously worried if that was

"The officer from the park? Do you have her on speed

She'll put out an alert for the authorities to look for him."

to John, then turned to Ariana. "I've called Officer Lewis.

"Thank you for not letting him through," Elizabeth said

to come through the gate.

several days since he appeared to be waiting for somebody

he knows where you work or your patterns." Maybe over

the gate opened," John said. "He probably followed you if

"He came up on my tail and tried to ride through when

"Yes. I swear I did not tell him I'm living here."

"Was that J.R.?"

"He's gone." Elizabeth walked toward the woman.

"What is this place?" John studied the row of three—he guessed they were houses.

"I call these tiny homes The Oasis. It's a place for women who've left abusive situations to help them get a fresh start."

"And that guy's her ex? What's he about to stand trial for? Battery? Or assault?"

Elizabeth nodded. "He's probably hoping to intimidate or sweet talk her out of testifying."

"Does he have a record?"

"Other than the battery charge he's facing, I think he's got a drunk and disorderly."

"Does she have a protection order?"

"Not yet."

"The police should have his address. I'll hang out here and eat with Boss until you hear from your officer friend."

"That's a good idea. Thank you. I'll check on Ariana."

Under the guise of playing with Boss, he scouted her property. The gate might keep a car out but keeping an individual out was another story, as J.R. demonstrated by hopping the fence. Or he could make a stealthy approach through the woods.

John would ask if Elizabeth had motion sensor lights or any security system—other than Boss. Her reason for adopting a big dog became a little clearer. Too bad Boss was likelier to knock someone over in his exuberance to play than to attack anyone. Still, it might be a good thing to leave Boss here a little longer if they didn't find this guy.

A faded-blue, older model sedan came through the gate and parked next to the little beige house. Boss bounded over to get love pats from a blond whose dark roots showed a good inch. Boss sniffed at the fast-food bag in her other hand. "No. This is my dinner." She raised it higher, which

was laughable since Boss could easily grab the bag and take off if he wanted.

"Come here, boy," John called.

"You must be Bruce's owner." The blonde smiled and checked him out. "We sure are going to miss him. He's a great dog."

"I'm glad he was loved on but happy that I found him."

John guessed the woman was in her late thirties or early forties. There were dark circles under her eyes and lines at the corners of her eyes and mouth. Her jeans hung loose on her thin frame.

She opened the door to the house, and a brown Doberman raced down the steps. The two dogs jumped on each other like puppies. A minute later, the blonde returned with a water bottle and her bag of food. "Would you like a drink?" she offered.

"I got one. Thanks." John tossed the tennis ball, and both dogs charged after it.

She took a seat on the far edge of the top step and opened her bag, glancing up at him in invitation. "How long have you had Bruce?"

"I found him about three years ago. Best thing that ever happened to me. His full name is Bruce "The Boss" Spring-weiler, and I call him Boss." He smiled, as always, when he explained the tribute to the legendary Bruce Springsteen.

"Must have been tough to leave him when you had to deploy."

"It was. The first time, some friends fostered him. This time, I left him with my live-in—now ex-girlfriend. That turned out to be a mistake." Though Britney seemed fine with it at the time.

"Wren, can you come over here for a few minutes?" Elizabeth called out.

The woman he'd been speaking to took another bite of her burger, then wrapped it up. "Excuse me."

John tossed the ball for the dogs a while longer. He refrained from peeking in the windows of one of the tiny homes and instead headed to Elizabeth's front porch to eat his meal and keep an eye on passing cars.

He finished eating and resumed tossing the ball for the dogs in the grassy area between the gravel drive and fence. When Elizabeth and Wren emerged from the tiny blue house. Wren checked out John again, then called to the Doberman and went into the home closest to the woods.

John strode over to Elizabeth. "Did you hear anything from your officer friend?"

"Unfortunately, they didn't find J.R. anywhere."

It'd been a long shot.

"Did you find a place to rent yet?" she asked.

"Not yet. I'm looking. I am. See, I own a house here, but I've got a renter in it. He's moving in two months, but I'm also transferring to a billet with SOCOM, which is Special Ops Command," he explained in civilian speak for her. "I'll be moving to Tampa in just under seven months. I'm trying not to sign a six-month lease somewhere because I was planning to move back into my house and do some major renovations. I haven't had any luck finding something short-term where I can have Boss. Looks like I'll have to piece things together with vacation rentals." Or shell out around seven thousand dollars for the next two months. So much for his plan to bank up rental income for his renovations.

"I have a proposition for you." Elizabeth drew the words out. "The yellow house in the middle, Hope Harbor, is vacant. If you'd like to rent here temporarily, Ariana and Wren said they'd feel safer with you here until J.R.'s trial."

"Seriously? That'd be awesome. I planned to ask if you

wanted to keep Boss around as protection. He looks and sounds a lot more intimidating than he is, but I'd feel better being here if that guy decides to try something worse. How long are you thinking?"

"She doesn't have a trial date yet. Best estimate is anywhere from four to twelve weeks. I can work with you."

"Perfect." With all this land for Boss to run, it beat any listing he'd looked at or pitching a tent somewhere.

"First, let me warn you, it's a tiny home. It's only a little over three hundred square feet."

John laughed. "I can see that. But I've spent six months bunking in a room about that size with nine other guys. That won't be a problem."

Elizabeth's expression was full-on we'll-see-about-that. "I charge rent based on income because—"

"I'm happy to pay the market rate."

"Well, you are doing us a favor."

"Not as big as the one you've done for Boss and me." He could never repay her for letting him have his dog back.

"A few caveats go with living in one of my properties. You've got the first covered."

Caveats? Interesting. "Okay. What's that?"

"I require tenants to have a pet."

"Done. For protection?" Not like *he* needed an animal for that.

"Emotional support, plus it gives them a sense of value and responsibility when they have something dependent on them for care."

"Makes sense," he agreed.

"The second rule might be a little harder. No alcohol or illegal drugs allowed on the property. I don't mind if you have a drink or two when you're out, but impaired decision-

making landed some of the residents here. It's better not to have it accessible."

"It won't be a problem. I go months without a drink on deployment."

"Good to know. Because if you show up drunk or get arrested for being under the influence, you'll be out."

"Yes, ma'am." Good thing she hadn't been at Jumpy's the night he got back.

"I also don't allow overnight guests. It's usually a safety thing for my tenants, but the same rule applies to you too."

"Again, not a problem." Since there was nobody in his life.

"Family is the exception, and I require ID."

"Sounds like trying to get on a military base, but I'm guessing there's a good reason."

"Yes." She didn't elaborate further. "Also, if you're interested in counseling, my colleagues have been great about working my tenants into their schedules."

"Counseling? You're a shrink?" A shiver ran through him just saying the word.

She gave a slight eyeroll and an amused smile. "Not a psychologist, but I have a master's in counseling."

"I'm protection detail. I don't need counseling."

"I'm just saying, many people find it helps to discuss problems or things they've experienced and need to process with an objective person. They want different results and need to change behaviors so they engage in healthy relationships."

"So, a guy doesn't end up homeless?" He got the hint.

"Well, I doubt you want that to happen, or Boss to end up at animal control again." She cocked her head a bit.

Dayam. He couldn't argue with that logic when she brought Boss into it. For Boss, he'd consider it. It wasn't as if

his buddies would know or it would go in his personnel record. "I'll think on it."

"If you just want to talk to a friend who has experience, I'm available as well. Let me show you the house."

"Let's do that when I get back. I want to run to the hotel, check out, and get back here before it gets too dark— just in case."

And, hopefully, the quick trip would be enough time for her to forget about psychoanalyzing him.

Chapter Seven

———————

When John returned with his things, Elizabeth let him through the gate and walked over with Boss to meet him at his temporary home. J.R.'s timing of showing up when he did and leading to John and Boss having a place to live was the best luck he'd had in a long time.

"This is for gate." She handed him a remote. "Hope Harbor was the first tiny house I bought. It belonged to the parents of one of my colleagues. They're Filipino and only about five feet tall," she explained. "It was custom-built for them to travel the country once they retired. It's on wheels, but it's connected to water, sewer, and electricity."

"Did they name it, or did you?" The name fit what she'd told him about the purpose.

"One of my tenants named them after I added the second house." Elizabeth unlocked the front door and handed him the key.

He mounted the steep step to follow her and Boss inside. "It's furnished. That's great."

"Most of the women who come to The Oasis don't have much, other than a car full of clothes and possessions."

"I don't have much more. Since my renter had furniture, I sold all my stuff to a new guy in our unit who lost most everything in a hurricane." And Britney's place was furnished in her style, so only Boss's bed made the cut.

With a window in the door and behind the sofa, and a skylight in the tall ceiling, the inside would get lots of sunlight and felt roomy. White shiplap covered the walls, and a gray love seat filled the area under the window. The yellow and blue floral accent pillows weren't his style, but this was temporary.

"There's storage under the sofa." She lifted a cushion for him to see. "The TV is on a swivel arm. You can watch here or angle it if you're in the kitchen or loft."

"Nice." There was a built-in bookcase below the TV and cabinets above. Three cubbies had blue cubes for storage. Light-gray flooring covered the entire first floor. This was definitely an upgrade over a tent with dirt floors.

"The oven is small but will hold a cookie sheet—probably not a full-sized turkey."

"Dang, there goes Sunday dinners, Boss."

Elizabeth gave him the kind of smile teachers used to give him when he cut up in class. Half charmed, half warning before he got out of hand. She was even prettier when she smiled. Not everyone got his sense of humor, but he'd learned it worked better to defuse tense situations than threats or weapons.

Since she was doing him a huge favor, he kept his mouth shut as she continued the tour. Besides, it'd been months since he'd spent any time with a woman. So what if

it was like some realtor trying to sell him on a property? He could enjoy the view of her appealing curves.

The large window over the sink bumped out and had a glass shelf, making the narrow galley kitchen feel bigger than the two-foot width. Floating shelves next to the sink held dishes, coffee cups, and glassware. A shelf held a microwave, and a coffee maker occupied the corner of the countertop.

"Below the utensil drawers are cans for trash, recycle, and compost, and a hidden compartment for Boss's water and food bowls to keep them out of the way." She pushed a panel with her toe and a drawer with the bowls slid out.

"Cool." He wouldn't have found that without her pointing it out.

"They maximized every inch of this place. I put the bag of dog food in here." She touched a large drawer next to the apartment-sized refrigerator. Beyond that was a stacked washer and dryer unit.

The ceiling dropped to about seven feet under the sleeping loft.

"Closet." She pointed. "And there's the bath."

Squeezing past her, he caught a whiff of a sweet smell like honeysuckle. He wanted to pause and breathe it in, but it might send the wrong signal. Especially with the way she'd flattened herself against the wall to let him pass. Though it'd been six months since he touched a woman, better not to get kneed in the groin or tossed out of his new home before he'd even moved in.

"The shower head might be a bit low for you."

"The last few months, *when* we got showers, it consisted of a bag of water hanging from a pole. This is fantastic. It's got everything."

Her serious blue eyes widened while she processed that,

and she tucked her blonde hair behind her ear. "Upstairs is a queen bed. I put fresh sheets on it for you. Watch your head," she warned as he mounted the steep steps. "If you have any questions just let me know."

"I need to know how much and how to pay you."

"I'll print off a lease agreement and get that to you tomorrow."

"I guess you don't have to do a background check since Jillian already did that for you," he joked.

"I don't require that. I know not everyone's background is squeaky clean and sometimes people do whatever it takes to survive." She avoided eye contact.

"Then I guess I'll bring my stuff in and get settled. Thanks for bringing over Boss's bed and food."

"I set the bed there. I wasn't sure where you had him sleep."

"Have you been letting my dog sleep in your bed?"

"No. *My* dog occasionally did, though."

"Touché," John laughed as she headed out. An image of her in bed flashed through his mind. *Boss, you lucky dog.*

He'd taken several boxes inside when Ariana approached.

"I appreciate you dealing with J.R. earlier and agreeing to stay here."

"No problem. John Bryson."

She tentatively shook the hand he extended to her. Even in the fading light, he made out the purple and green tinge of a bruise around her left eye.

"Kind of like it was meant to be since I needed a temporary place to stay. Do you have your phone with you?"

She nodded and pulled it out of her shorts pocket.

"Put me in your contacts and text me so I can add you."

If you hear anything outside or he shows up at your work and threatens you, let me know."

"You don't have to get involved."

"Too late. Did you hear what I said to him?"

"About being a Green Beret? I think that's what made him think twice about trying anything."

"I'm trained to deal with guys like him."

"He wasn't like this when we got together. He started doing drugs with friends and . . ."

"Yeah. It spirals."

"Can I carry a box in for you?"

"Sure." He tested the nearest two and handed her the lightest one. "Watch that first step," he warned. "You can set it on the sofa with the others." Needing a place to sit would motivate him to unpack.

Boss followed them in and squeezed past Ariana, nearly knocking her over.

"You and him in here? That's going to be interesting."

Ariana looked around.

"It's short term. Bigger and more amenities than a hotel room. We'll be fine."

"O-kay," Ariana didn't sound convinced.

"Does J.R. carry a weapon? That'd be good for him to know upfront.

"A knife, sometimes. He didn't have a gun. Who knows after these past few weeks, though." She dropped her gaze to the ground.

"How long have you lived here?"

"Two and a half weeks. It's been such a relief, until tonight."

"How'd you find out about this place?"

"Officer Lewis told me about it when she, uh," responded."

"Got it. Well, I'm almost always armed. I'm off this week, so don't hesitate to contact me if you need. I'd rather respond to a false alarm than you get hurt trying to handle him on your own."

"Thanks, I'll let you finish getting your stuff inside."

John brought in the rest of his belongings, unpacked three of the boxes, then took Boss outside to take care of business. He walked a surveillance pass around the houses. Now that this J.R. guy knew where Ariana stayed, he could come back anytime. "They need more security measures around here, Boss. Tonight, we're on guard duty. Let me know if you hear any humans."

The air was warm but cooler than an unairconditioned tent or outside in Africa this time of year. He opened the windows to catch the breeze and hear anything out of the norm—not that he knew the norm around here.

"Okay, boy. Bedtime."

Boss went to his bed, and John stripped down to his skivvies before he climbed up to the loft and crawled into bed. He placed his Sig Sauer on the nightstand and stretched out on the queen mattress.

The sheets were crisp and fresh. The ceiling, a few feet over his head, was about the same clearance as their bunks during deployment. Here he wouldn't have to listen to his teammates snoring in stereo. It was a great, temporary place to stay. He had his dog and a job he loved and was good at. He wasn't going to let the end of things with Britney bring him down.

He'd provide protection for Ariana, and once J.R. was behind bars, John would get *his* fresh start. He breathed in the scent of pine from the trees around them and closed his eyes.

An unfamiliar noise jolted John awake and upright. His

head bashed into the ceiling. "Ow! Shit!" He rubbed his head with his left hand and reached for his pistol with his right. Before he could identify the source of the sound, Boss's face peeked over the top step. "Dammit, Boss, I could have shot you."

At the sound of his name, Boss scrambled into the loft. Even Boss had to lower his head due to the low clearance.

John returned his weapon to the nightstand. He rubbed Boss's neck, and they settled down. Hearing only crickets and frogs quickly lulled his tired brain and body back to sleep.

Chapter Eight

HERE COMES THE SUN – The Beatles

JOHN WOKE to the sun streaming in through the skylight and window. His body spooned something warm. And soft. And furry. Damn. Still, better to wake up with Boss than Britney's cheating ass.

How could she have dumped him for Dicky? Was it his fault for not communicating more? Or was he not the kind of guy her parents wanted for her? He might not have a trust fund or a six-figure income, but he was educated and exceptionally good at a job he loved doing—most days.

He and Britney had a lot of fun together, and it'd felt like it could be love. Though, if he was honest about it, the breakup didn't hurt as much as he expected. Maybe because she let Dicky dump Boss at animal services, which proved she was clearly not the woman for him.

His head throbbed where he'd smacked it on the ceiling. Sitting up, he didn't make that mistake again. Hopefully,

the knot would be gone before reporting for work next week. If not, his team could ask, but he didn't have to tell what happened.

He stared at the steps, trying to figure out the best way to get down. He couldn't sit up straight, much less stand to walk down the steps. Scoot down on his butt like a baby? Back down? He could skip the steps. Turn and lower himself down over the loft's edge, but he didn't need Boss deciding to jump.

Boss watched him with big eyes rather than go first.

"Fine. I'll be the guinea pig." He bent over and went feet first. He was able to stand once he reached the fourth step. At least he only had to go up and come down once a day. Boss came down headfirst—probably after laughing at him—and went straight to the door to go out.

"Just a minute." He peeked through the door's window and let Boss outside. He pulled on shorts and a T before joining Boss. "Had to do that first thing, didn't ya?" He stared at the fresh pile of crap. "You know this is probably why Dicky took you to the shelter, don't ya? Though I'm glad you didn't take to Dicky and have them keep you."

Back inside, he filled the water and food bowls, then scoured under the cabinets and found a plastic grocery bag to use for clean-up. Once he'd disposed of that, he hit the bathroom.

He sank onto a toilet the size of ones found in elementary schools. It was barely a foot off the ground. With his knees spread, they had about an inch of clearance from the wall. He banged his elbow on the wall trying to reach the roll of toilet paper mounted behind him. Maybe he'd under-estimated the challenges of living in a tiny home. Still, it was a toilet that flushed, which beat the months of a make-shift outhouse or digging a hole and squatting. Once he

went back to work, though, he might wait to take a daily dump there.

♪

THE SOLID KNOCK on her front door made Elizabeth nearly jab the mascara wand in her eye. It had to be John. Neither Ariana nor Wren would be up at eight in the morning. She wiped the clump of mascara off her lashes.

Boss barked once as she crossed the gathering room's hardwood floor.

"Good morning." She opened the door to John. Boss greeted her with the ever-embarrassing muzzle to the crotch. "Is that a knot on your head?" she asked John as she patted Boss's head and pushed it back at the same time.

"Uh, yeah. Boss woke me in the middle of the night, and I kinda forgot where I was. Hit the ceiling. No biggie." John touched it gingerly. "Sorry to bother you this early, but I wanted to catch you before you left for work."

"I printed off the lease agreement for you." She stepped aside to retrieve the printout.

"I was thinking of picking up some motion-activated lights to put up around the perimeter of The Oasis. Since I'm off this week, I can put them up as a deterrent in case J.R. comes sneaking around."

"I had thought about putting some up, but there are so many animals out here, I'm afraid they'll be constantly turning on."

"I can try setting them so the smaller animals don't trigger them and adjust the positions if necessary. If they cause a problem, I can take them down."

"It's a good idea." Something happening to Ariana trumped the annoyance they might create. And John wasn't

telling her what she had to do; he was making a suggestion. "Get what you need, and bring me the receipt to reimburse you."

"I got it. Consider it payback for caring for Boss."

"You don't need to do that. Your labor is enough. Ariana works at a home improvement store. Why don't you see if she's working today and can get an employee discount on them?"

"I will. Thanks."

"There's a ladder in the storage shed you're welcome to use. Thank you for doing this for her."

"Security is kinda my thing." John said. "Better safe than sorry. Unless it's J.R. who's sorry. Based on the bruise I saw on Ariana's face, he's got a lot to be sorry for. A real man doesn't hit a woman—unless she's about to take a life. Or a bunch. Okay, on that depressing note, Boss and I are going for a run. I'll send the rent and bring the lease over tonight. Have a good one."

He ducked out before she could tell him where to find the trails. For a moment, she watched him jog back toward The Oasis with the lease in hand and Boss at his heels before she finished getting ready for work.

His comment about real men not hitting a woman still rolled around in her brain as she filled her insulated mug with coffee. Maybe she'd prejudged John and projected her father onto him because both served in the military. Only her father hadn't been honorable. He also wasn't the norm. She'd give John the benefit of the doubt—at least until she saw evidence otherwise.

Chapter Nine

YOU'LL THINK OF ME – Keith Urban

DURING HIS RUN, John scouted the property more thoroughly. Lights were a small deterrent, but there was too much acreage to secure on his own. He'd have to come up with a stronger first line of defense.

Back at Hope Harbor, Boss polished off his food while John drank coffee and ate the yogurt and bagel Elizabeth must have stocked for him. He unpacked two boxes, mostly clothes, though he found his favorite Special Forces logo coffee mug and beer glasses wrapped in T-shirts in the middle of a box. Those were special, but replaceable—unlike Boss.

He unfolded the garment bag crammed into a box and inspected his dress uniform before hanging it in the small closet. No telling when he'd have an occasion to wear it. He was proud of what it represented. One day he'd find a

woman who respected what he did and thought he was good enough.

He hung up the rest of his clothes, started a shopping list, then headed to the bathroom.

The water was hot in seconds, but when he stepped into the shower, the spray hit him in the neck. Angling it up only made it spray up his nose. He tried moving away and ducking his head, but even with his back pressed to the wall, there wasn't room in the confined space.

He evaluated his options: step out of the shower, bend his torso in, and get water all over the floor, or squat in the shower. He tried the wall squat. From that position, he could reach the inset in the tile to grab the shampoo. He'd get in some exercise and wash his hair. Double duty.

Next, he soaped up with the wild citrus body wash Eliz-abeth had provided. It smelled nice—though smelling it on a woman would be better. The hollow space in his chest expanded a bit.

Rejected again. It sucked, but experience taught him what was worth fighting for. You couldn't make someone love you or stay. Better to leave with his dignity dinged, but intact, than cling to a woman who didn't want him in her life. Even with his dangerous job and all the overseas deployments, he should have found something lasting by now. After Britney, he was back to ground zero. Maybe once he got to his new position at MacDill and didn't have to deploy as often, things would be different.

He toweled off, then lathered his face. The mirror wasn't high enough and cut off his head at his nose, so he bent over to shave, studying his reflection for a few seconds. He wasn't ugly, and women were typically attracted to his size and athletic build. He was educated and had common sense. He was fun to be around. Maybe a

little too over the top, making some women not take him seriously, but he'd dealt with too much bad shit to be serious all the time. He wouldn't change who he was. He needed to find the woman who'd accept him and his over-sized dog.

Time to re-activate his online dating profile—after he was done here. He'd taken on a mission and wasn't one to abandon his post. He looked at the tiny shower and sighed. Yeah.

His hands barely fit in the micro-sized sink to rinse his face. After hanging the towel, he turned and nearly tripped over Boss, who filled the narrow passage outside the bathroom.

"Boss, you gotta move."

Boss barely raised his head.

"She let you get lazy. The run wasn't that far. I'm seri-ous. I'm not jumping over you." He nudged the dog with his bare foot to no avail. Boss sprawled, blocking access to the closet. "You win. Let's get a treat."

Boss scrambled to his feet and moved the three feet to the kitchen.

John threw his hands up in defeat. "You get your treat after I'm dressed."

He gave Ariana a heads-up that he'd swing by the store later and clarified which location she worked at. When he arrived, John scanned the parking lot. An advantage of Ariana working at a big box store was they had security cameras everywhere. He made a surveillance pass before going to the lighting section and selecting solar-powered, motion-activated lights. They weren't anything pretty, but the range of coverage would do the job.

He picked up the tools he needed, then texted Ariana to meet him.

"I thought you were here to get lights," Ariana said as he checked out the grills.

"Already did." He motioned to the cart. "On our last tour, one of the guys had his wife ship him a little grill. We could only fit four burgers on it, but we used the heck out of that thing. This is a man's grill." He lowered his voice and grunted.

Ariana laughed.

He didn't need anything this big for him and Boss, though one day he could use one to feed his team, and, hopefully, his future family.

"Elizabeth puts on a monthly dinner where we all bring something. She fixed lasagna, and it was the best I'd ever eaten. I hope it won't disappoint everyone when it's my turn to do the main course. Maybe you can grill something when it's your turn."

"I'll think on that." He followed her to the checkout.

"Thanks for doing this, J.R. knowing where I'm living has me freaked out. I probably wouldn't have slept last night if you weren't next door. Just show your military ID, and you get ten percent off."

"Once I get these up, you'll feel even safer." He wasn't a big believer in coincidence. Elizabeth adopting his dog and him being at her place when J.R. showed up had to be divine intervention or good karma. Britney worked on the charity auction because that was her job; however, Eliza-beth clearly didn't help women like Wren and Ariana for recognition. Whatever her motivation, he found a woman like Elizabeth Carroll, rescuer of dogs and people, pretty damned appealing.

Chapter Ten

HOUND DOG – Elvis Presley

When Elizabeth got home that night, Boss loped over.

"Hey, boy. Did you have a good day with John?" She rubbed Boss's head. He flopped onto his back, legs up. "Are you not getting enough love and attention?" She dropped to one knee and rubbed his belly.

"Not enough attention from pretty ladies, maybe." John strolled up.

From her vantage point, he loomed over her. She froze. Couldn't draw in a breath.

John knelt next to them. "I suspect he's part hound dog because he can never get enough attention from beautiful ladies." He smiled at her, then dropped his gaze to Boss and rubbed his neck. "I'm surprised he hasn't ditched me for you entirely."

"He wouldn't do that." With John on her level, she could breathe again. She pushed to her feet anyway. "I

got the money transfer for the rent. You didn't have to pay for the whole month upfront." Everyone else paid her weekly.

"If you kick me out before a month, you can refund the overpayment. The Army gives me a monthly housing allowance, and it more than covers what you're charging. We're good."

"But you're doing security without being paid for your time."

He motioned to Boss. "Yeah, but you—"

"I know," she stopped him. "You think you have to pay me back, but if it wasn't Boss, I would have gotten another dog. I'm not out any money that I wouldn't have spent."

John hitched up both eyebrows.

"Okay, maybe a little more for food than a smaller dog, but I like big dogs too."

"And we're glad you do." He stood. Boss got to his feet at John's side. "Lights are up, and I'll test them after dark."

"Do you have the receipt?"

"He does," John pointed to Boss. "He ate it. Bad dog."

Boss hung his head.

"You expect me to believe that?"

"It was only thirty-eight and change."

"I don't believe you."

"I'm hurt." He didn't quite suppress that innocent grin. "They were on clearance, and I get a military discount. Anytime you want to feed me, I hear you make the best lasagna."

"Ariana told you about the dinners?" How had that come up?

He nodded. "I'm always up for food."

That wasn't surprising. "The dinners are to help instill confidence in social situations."

"A potluck dinner is a socialization exercise?" he asked with an amused chuckle.

"A lot of the women who come through here have been isolated by their partners. This is one way of interacting with others in a comfortable setting. They're responsible for bringing a dish and take a turn planning the meal and assign who brings what food item."

"I get it now. I'm not great in the kitchen, but I'm a barbecue master when it comes to roasting meat over flame. After picking up the lights, I was checking out grills. I'm thinking I might get one and bring it over, if that's okay."

"As long as you keep it away from the houses. You can take it with you when you move."

"I meant for here. Thought it'd be a nice addition for your residents. You can think on that and decide whether you want to invite Boss and me to your next potluck."

"The dinners are Friday nights. I thought you might have plans."

"At the moment, my social calendar is wide open. And right after I get home from overseas, I prefer smaller get-togethers to reintegrate."

"I've heard crowds can overwhelm soldiers returning from deployments."

"The dinner sounds like the kind of therapy I need." He gave an easy smile.

"Food therapy as opposed to females' tendency to do retail therapy?" It didn't surprise her that he objected to the idea of counseling. The stigma attached to getting help still prevailed, especially in the military. "I do want to caution you, however, that it's not a good idea to be alone with Wren or Ariana." He needed to take her at her word because she wouldn't disclose their stories and issues.

"I understand. Order acknowledged, ma'am."

"Thanks." She'd been prepared to encounter resistance. Hopefully, he'd follow orders from a civilian. Her father hadn't always followed orders from his superiors, much less civilians. So far, John acted nothing like her father.

Instead of scary and domineering, John was fun and thoughtful and had a way of endearing himself and putting people at ease—even her. Despite denying it to Jillian, Elizabeth did find John's appearance appealing. His build, his eyes, his smile. And he got better looking every time she saw him. It was a good thing he was only going to be here a short time, or she might regret giving up men.

Chapter Eleven

I WILL SURVIVE – Gloria Gaynor

AFTER DINNER, Elizabeth sat reading on her front porch when John's truck drove past.

Minutes later, Boss lumbered over to join Elizabeth. He raised his face for her to scratch.

"Sorry. He took off for here before I could stop him. I guess he got used to roaming free at your house."

"No worries. He's welcome anytime."

"I see the 'no alcohol' rule doesn't apply to you." John grinned from the base of the steps.

"I own the property. I get to make the rules." She took a sip of her wine and held onto the glass. "Burnout is high for counselors, especially ones trained to deal with trauma. A glass of wine, reading, watching my hummingbirds, and listening to the leaves rustle in the breeze helps me unwind and separate." She rarely drank more than a glass or two now that she didn't need it as a coping mechanism.

"I can only imagine."

"I'm guessing you've seen your share of traumas too."

"I have." His pause before answering was telling. He also didn't elaborate as he glanced around her property.

"I'm jealous of this place. I'd love to find something like this when I move to Florida."

"The family who owned this land raised tobacco, pigs, other crops, and timber around here. This was part of the timberland. I liked that there was a house already, even though it needed a lot of work. It still does."

"I hear ya. I had big plans to renovate my house when I bought it. The kitchen needs to be gutted and completely redone to bring it into this century. The carpet's like twenty years old, so it needs new floor covering throughout. One of the bedrooms is painted a bright yellow that has to go. But every time I go look at options, I get overwhelmed. Décor and design are not my thing. Now, I'm getting down to the wire with moving. I need to get it done to flip it or keep it as a rental property."

"My realtor friend, Rachel, has a great eye for design and loves picking out cabinets, counters, flooring, lights, paint, hardware. She helped me pick out everything for Sanctuary Lodge. I can get you her contact information. She charges a reasonable fee, or if you decide to sell and need a realtor, she'll do it for the listing."

"That would be great. Will she help you with your house too?"

"She will, after I put aside the money to do it."

"Which you don't have because you keep sinking your money into buying tiny homes." He eyed her knowingly.

"Guilty. But I got great deals on them."

John clicked to Boss, then tossed a tennis ball for him to

chase. "Isn't providing housing to your clients going above and beyond?"

"They aren't my clients. Just women who needed a safe place to stay. My friend, Jillian—"

"The police officer?"

"Yes. She told me about a domestic abuse call she responded to. It wasn't the first time she'd been to that house. She and her partner tried to get the woman to leave previously, but she didn't have any family and wouldn't go to a shelter. There aren't a lot of resources in rural areas for single women in need of shelter, so she'd stayed with her abusive spouse. Only this time things had escalated. It sounded a lot like my mother and father's relationship."

"Oh." His pitch dropped, and he dragged the two-letter word out.

"Yeah." She wasn't going into her dysfunctional family story now. "Anyway, a short while later, I heard a coworker talking about her parents wanting to sell their tiny home. I made a kind of impulsive decision and bought it."

"Was the woman Jillian told you about the first one to stay?"

"No." She'd first tried her damnedest to get her mother to leave her dad and come stay with her, but Mom had insisted he'd mellowed with age and things were better. That remained to be seen, not that she visited. "It was a later call that Jillian responded to that resulted in my first tenant, Mable. A sweet woman in her sixties who'd seen her share of abuse over the years. Different men, same story." She'd finally found the courage to leave, unlike Elizabeth's mother. "This was the first place she felt safe. I got her into counseling, hoping to prevent her from getting into another abusive relationship."

63

"And it worked?" John asked.

"Yes. Though it was tough. There's a difference between being independent and being lonely. I ended up hiring a builder for Sanctuary Lodge, thinking the emotional support and inspiration of seeing someone with a similar situation move forward would be beneficial."

"How long after did you add the third home?"

"Only about six months after the second. The owner of the company that built Sanctuary Lodge had a model he wanted to sell and offered me a great deal to support what I was doing. It was clear that having a community helped both Mabel and Rhonda, so I added Haven House."

"Nice. You going to clear land and build more?"

"I'm sure there'd be enough women in need to fill two dozen homes if I advertised to social services or law enforcement, but I'm not looking to start a non-profit. Just helping a little where I can."

"I understand. You're doing way more than most people to address the problem."

"It's not that much."

"Don't be modest. How many women have come through here?"

She understood his interest due to staying here. For safety and to protect the women's dignity, she didn't talk about The Oasis to many people. His compliment was an unexpected affirmation of what she did. "Not counting the ones who only stayed a week or two, seventeen. And now one man."

John chuckled. "I figured I'm not your typical rescue." He took a few seconds to rub Boss's head before tossing the ball again.

"There are abused men too, but I focus on the women."

And typically steer clear of most men. She tried to relax. They were having a conversation about her work, but she didn't have to sound so clinical and formal.

"How long do they stay?"

"It varies. Sometimes only a couple of weeks."

"That's quick."

"Those are usually the ones who go back to a bad situation."

"They bounce back here?"

"Not anymore. I tried that a few times before I implemented the rule that you can remain here as long as needed, but after leaving, you can't come back to stay. It makes them think hard about going back to a bad situation if they know they don't have a fallback."

"But you'd take them back if you had a spot." He winked and tossed the ball again.

"Yes, but don't advertise that." She wasn't sure if it was the way he winked or how his shirt stretched across his broad shoulders when he effortlessly threw the ball nearly to the fence that stirred something nearly forgotten in her. "Most women are here four to six months. Wren's been here the longest. She got COVID shortly after she moved in. She was out of work for nearly two months. Then she had a relapse after about six weeks and missed another month of work."

"That's gotta suck."

"Her luck always seems to run bad. She's been through a lot."

"Thanks for the history. I wanted to offer to cover some self-defense basics with Ariana. Actually, it'd be good for all of you. Not only to protect yourself from attacks but situations that get out of hand."

Chill bumps broke out on Elizabeth's arms as his meaning came through. Her throat tightened at the memories she still couldn't forget. "That'd be good. I don't want them to ever be victims again."

She wasn't going to be either.

Chapter Twelve

A short, loud bark woke John from a deep sleep. Motion sensor lights lit up the loft enough for John to see Boss on his feet, his head up, listening.

John bolted upright and struck the top of his head on the low ceiling—again.

"Shit!" Hunched over, he rubbed the spot to lessen the pain. He grabbed his pistol off the nightstand and edged to the steps. Boss scrambled down behind him.

Looking out the living room window, he saw nothing. Not that he expected J.R. to be standing in plain sight. He donned his helmet and stuffed his bare feet into his tactical boots without bothering to lace them.

"You stay," he said to Boss. He waited until the sensor lights went off, then lowered his helmet's enhanced night-vision goggles and slipped outside. He scanned the area but saw no human or animal heat signatures. Still, something

had triggered the lights, so he listened. Cigarette smoke tainted the air. Footsteps on gravel by Wren's place interrupted the comforting concert of crickets and frogs.

Hair on his bare arms stood on end. He raised his weapon and peered around the front of Hope Harbor. Sticking close to the side, he crept across the front. Smoke wafted toward him, stronger now. John had hoped J.R. would take his chances in court rather than force a showdown, but even if J.R. brought someone with him, with John's training, J.R. was outmanned.

John peeked around the corner just as Wren's Doberman, Coco, whipped his head around and barked, killing any element of surprise.

Wren shrieked and jumped away from the side of her car as John stepped into sight. The cigarette fell from her fingers. "'What the hell? You nearly gave me a heart attack.'" She pressed a hand to her chest.

"'Boss heard something, and the lights came on in the middle of the night. I thought it could be J.R. What the hell time is it?'"

"'Around two thirty.'" Wren's words were a bit rushed.

"'What are you doing out here?'" Had she heard something too?

"'I just got home. I let Coco out and was finishing a cigarette since I'm not allowed to smoke inside.'" She crushed out the cigarette with the sole of a dressy, high-heeled sandal.

He flipped up the NVGs and removed his helmet.

"'Sorry to get you geared up for nothing.'" She grinned and stepped toward him. "'Though it's kind of hot. You should have come out with me and my friends. It's more fun dancing at the club than the Veterans of Foreign Wars Post.

It's all no-touchy line dancing at the VFW. And my girl-friends would love you." She looked him up and down.

"Sorry I scared you. Goodnight." He didn't say anything to encourage her and shuffled back home. It'd been a long time since he'd been with a woman, however, Elizabeth had warned him about Wren's issues, and he didn't need to add to them or risk disappointing Elizabeth—especially when she was the woman he'd been thinking about when he'd gone to bed alone.

Since he'd gotten stateside, the only women he had contact with, other than those taking his food orders, were Ariana, Wren, and Elizabeth. The best he could tell, Elizabeth was in her early thirties, so close to his age. She had a natural, no-fuss kind of beauty and curves that could fill a man's hands. Except she hadn't given any signs of romantic interest in him. His dog was welcome at her house anytime, but her guard was up when it came to him. Or it could have to do with what she'd shared about her father abusing her mother.

Boss waited at the door.

"You might as well come take care of business."

Boss came out and sniffed his usual spot, lifting a leg for a few seconds, then tromped back inside while John stowed his boots and helmet by the door again.

John felt the knot on his head. Great. At least this time it wouldn't show. Maybe he'd attach some foam to the ceiling over the mattress—just in case.

Chapter Thirteen

"HIT ME WITH YOUR BEST SHOT" – Pat Benatar

JOHN PARKED at The Oasis with supplies he'd picked up at the training compound at Fort Bragg and the PX. Yesterday, he'd checked the doors and windows on Sanctuary Lodge—the name Elizabeth had given to the little blue home where Ariana was living—and replaced the short screws used for the door's strike plates with longer ones.

He wasn't going to go overboard and freak the women out, but he wanted to give them self-defense basics in case J.F. showed up again. It wouldn't hurt to teach them how to protect themselves should the need arise after what they had likely been through before ending up here.

He tapped on the truck's horn, then went to let Boss out. When Wren stepped out of her house, her Doberman, Coco, shot out too. The two dogs romped and chased each other in the clearing.

Ariana appeared, and Elizabeth joined them a minute

later. Wren eyed the bags in his hand as he looked around for the best place to set up his training exercises.

"I have a gift for each of you." He handed them each a package.

Ariana took out the two canisters. "What is this, breath or air freshener?"

"No! It's pepper spray. Put the one with a ring on your key chain and keep the second within reach in your car, just in case."

"I carry a Taser in my purse," Wren said.

"That's fine." And didn't surprise him. "I'm going to share some self-defense tactics." He taped a paper target to a tree trunk, then demonstrated the proper technique to hold and dispense the pepper spray.

He let each of the women take a turn aiming at the target from about five feet away. With no breeze, even in the open air, the brief squirt was enough to make them cough as their throats burned and eyes stung.

He moved them to an area with fresher air and taped a new target to a different tree to try again at twice the distance. "Remember, aim at their eyes and mouth. It's harder to hit the further away you get, so spray back and forth. As you can tell, a little taste should encourage them not to get closer."

After they each took another turn, he tucked the pepper spray in his pants pocket. "It's fairly easy to hit a stationary target, but someone coming at you can be a different story. So, this time, you're going to target me."

"With pepper spray?" Elizabeth protested.

"No, not with the pepper spray. I don't want to cry in front of you ladies. Besides, they were out of the mint flavor."

"Mint?" Elizabeth repeated before rolling her eyes.

"We'll use this." He produced a can of Silly String and handed it to Ariana first.

"So, we won't get to Taser you either?" Wren asked.

"Not today. Go for the eyes and mouth." He jogged back about ten yards, then spun to face them. "Pretend I'm J.R." He didn't give Ariana a countdown before he charged toward her. Before she could spray him, he reached her and knocked the can from her hand.

"Dammit." She cowered as he loomed over her.

"J.R.—or any bad guy—is not going to give you time to get prepared. Be aware of your surroundings at all times, and be prepared to act. I also recommend that you have a coworker walk you to your car after work. Look under the car as you approach and check the back seat before getting in. J.R. already knows where you live, but it's still a good idea to change up your route and not stop in isolated or dark areas. Let's try this again."

This time, Ariana hit him in the ear and shoulder with the Silly String. "Better. We'll let Wren and Elizabeth have a turn, then you can try again."

After depleting the can of Silly String, he moved to phase two, motioning for Elizabeth to stand in front of him.

"Our next lesson is what to do in the event someone gets too close. Grab my wrist." He held out his arm, then let out a high-pitched shriek in Elizabeth's face a second after she took hold.

She released him and reared back. Ariana and Wren both laughed. John grinned back at Elizabeth's sheepish smile.

"It's simple, but it works. They don't expect it. They let go. You run."

"After we kick him in the groin," Wren stated.

"Better to just run. Put as much distance between you

and the perp as possible. If they're high or drunk, they have a higher threshold for pain. Without a solid strike, you may just piss them the hell off."

"That could apply to J.R.," Ariana mumbled.

"If yelling doesn't get them to release you or summon help, you need another way to get free." He took hold of Elizabeth's wrist.

Without hesitating, she pulled free.

"Perfect," he said, though she looked shocked at his proclamation. "The thumb is the weak point. If you pull in the direction of their thumb, you're most likely to break free. However, if he gets you in a choke hold . . ." He took a step toward Elizabeth and raised his arms.

Her eyes widened, and she stepped back.

"Wouldn't it be better for Ariana to practice this since she's most at risk?" Elizabeth deflected breathlessly.

His blood froze. "Good idea." Damn. He should have consulted her first. He'd picked Elizabeth to run through scenarios, thinking it might be traumatic for Wren and Ariana, but he hadn't connected the dots that this mission of hers might have come about because she was a survivor of domestic abuse. If her father abused her mother, it wouldn't be a stretch for him to abuse his kids too. *Son of . . .* "Tell you what—you put *me* in a choke hold, Ariana."

She switched places with Elizabeth and hesitantly put her hands to his throat.

"If I pound on her arms, it pits strength against strength. That might work for me, but a better technique is for you to dip your chin as low as you can and take advantage of the thumbs being the weak point. Hold tighter."

In a flash he was free.

"Whoa," Ariana gasped.

73

"Yeah, but you're three times stronger than her," Wren said.

"Doesn't matter. You okay to try?" he asked Ariana. He waited for her consent before lightly gripping her throat. "What I did was step back on my strong side and simply bow down using my whole body to break the hold." She followed the instructions in a practice run-through.

"Now, let's try it for real." He placed his hand around her neck again, tight enough to simulate an actual threat. And she slipped right through his hands. "I did it!" He chuckled at her exuberant smile. "Told you. You can try it on each other." He waved a hand toward Elizabeth and Wren.

Lastly, Wren helped him demonstrate what to do if an attacker grabbed both arms to shake or pin them against a wall. "You have two options," he explained. "Pushing your arms out against their hands doesn't work as well as pulling up against their thumbs."

Wren pulled free to prove his point.

"Or you can bring them closer and grab their arms. Now, you're in a position to knee him in the groin."

"Can I try?"

"O-kay," He released one of Wren's arms and covered his junk before letting her try.

"Don't trust me?" Wren raised an eyebrow.

"I'm really sorry about the security lights going off last night."

"Three times!" Wren scowled.

"I readjusted them this morning." He put both hands on her arms, hoping for mercy and that her instincts didn't kick in like Elizabeth's or he'd be singing alto.

"I wouldn't do that to you—because if that adjustment still isn't right, they'll keep waking me up if I kill you."

She executed the maneuver and got free from his grip, simulating, but not actually, kneeing him.

"Thank you." He released the breath he'd been holding. Elizabeth hid a smile behind her hand, but amusement shone in her pretty blue eyes.

"Now, I'd hit him with the Taser," Wren said.

"In the time it takes to dig your Taser out of your purse, an assailant may pull out a weapon. It's best to get away. The goal is not to inflict pain or vengeance. The goal is to not be a victim."

"I guess you're right," Wren agreed.

"That's enough for today. Don't feel like you need to remember everything we covered. We'll review again in a few days. If there are any situations you want instructions on how to handle, let me know and we'll cover those too. What kind of animal do you have?" he asked Ariana since he hadn't seen her walking or playing with a dog.

"A cat. But now I'm kind of wishing I had a dog."

"Yeah, even yappy little dogs can be good because of all the barking. Something for you to think about," John said.

"Though after you testify against J.R. in court in a few weeks, you'll be safe with him in jail," Elizabeth said.

"Thanks for the lessons and the pepper spray. I already feel more empowered." Ariana gave a confident smile before she headed inside her house.

Wren whistled to Coco, which brought both her and Boss over for some head rubs.

"How'd I do?" He asked Elizabeth once they were alone with Boss.

"Very helpful. Good information without it being an overload or making Ariana feel singled out—other than me making her do the choke hold with you."

"Sorry. I should have checked before I laid a hand on

you. I hadn't stopped to consider you might not appreciate that either." He tried to word it diplomatically.

"You caught me by surprise, is all."

"Really? Then you have excellent self-preservation instincts."

"Thank you." She downplayed it.

Since she didn't volunteer information, he didn't pry. Whatever had happened to hurt her seemed to be in her rearview mirror. And she was doing all right now.

Chapter Fourteen

WE WILL ROCK YOU – Queen

JOHN HADN'T EVEN GOTTEN out of his truck from work before Coco raced over. He petted the dog on the head as Wren approached.

"Those lights went off again last night," she said through gritted teeth.

"Sorry about that."

"You sneaking around outside is just as bad since Coco starts barking."

"I've got to do a perimeter check in case it's J.R. I'll adjust the angles to see if that eliminates the false alarms."

"It'd better. You owe me, and I need a favor."

"Sure."

"Can we go inside? I don't want Elizabeth to see or hear us."

Oh crap. Bushes hid them from view, and he didn't know what the chances were of Elizabeth wandering over.

How did he tactfully get out of this? "Why is that?" He gave his best innocent grin.

"Because we're planning a surprise party for her birth-day, and we could use your help."

"Okay. Got you. But if you don't want to arouse suspi-cion, we should hang right here. Give me a second." That was innocent enough. He opened the door to Hope Harbor and let Boss out. "How can I help?"

"Elizabeth makes a big deal to celebrate our birthdays with a cake and gift, but she won't tell anyone her birth date. I had to use one of those 'what would your historical romance heroine name be' games to get the month and day. We totally missed it last year, so we're doing a surprise party. I've invited as many of the women who've stayed here as we could get in touch with. I thought it would be less suspicious if *you* asked what kind of gifts she might like."

"When's the big day?"

"Two weeks from Saturday."

"Mission accepted. I'll do my best to get gift suggestions ASAP."

"Thanks so much. You rock!"

"We will, we will rock you."

Wren burst into song with him. Even Boss howled along to the familiar tune.

"Are you going to the VFW for line dancing with us next Friday?" she asked, once they finished the chorus.

"Is that what you mentioned the other night?"

"It's something Elizabeth invited us to. It's not a requirement or anything. There's no alcohol, but it's fun if you want to come." She batted her lashes, her hazel-eyed gaze locked on him.

"I'll think about it," he deflected. He'd check with Eliza-beth after he formulated a plan to dig for intel.

TWO DAYS LATER, Wren was already asking if he'd gotten ideas for gifts. He'd come up with a valid reason to talk to Elizabeth and a way to work getting an idea about gifts into the conversation. "Let's go see Elizabeth," John called to Boss, who quickly took the lead.

As usual, she sat on the front porch in one of the rocking chairs, a wine glass on the side table and her e-reader in her hands.

"Evening, I wanted to thank you for getting me in touch with Rachel. My friend that's renting gave us the okay to show her my house, so I can order stuff and start the renovations as soon as he's out. Rachel took me to the design place she likes and helped me pick out cabinets and flooring and paint colors and tile for a walk-in shower. She's a natural and had great ideas." He took a seat on the porch swing after Boss sprawled at Elizabeth's feet.

"I'm glad it worked out."

"She wouldn't let me pay her, but I want to get her a thank you gift for her time. Do you have any suggestions?"

"I'm sure she's hoping you'll decide to list it with her."

"That won't be for a while. I'd like to do something now."

"I'm not the best person to ask. Gifts aren't my love language."

"You're not helping me here. There's got to be something you'd like to get. Hanging planters, shrubs, candles. Knickknacks you collect. Gift certificate to a fancy restaurant you like."

"I don't collect anything, and I don't know her well enough to guess on that. Fancy restaurants aren't my thing

because I don't like to eat out alone. You could pick any, and I'm sure she'd appreciate it."

It wasn't in his DNA to concede defeat, but he was getting nowhere. "Okay, what if a friend wanted to give you a gift to say thank you for all you've done for him and his dog?"

"I'd say it's not necessary."

"I wasn't asking if it's necessary."

"I've got everything I need. Except a dog. And I can't take yours."

"Good. I don't want to test his loyalty. There has to be something you want that you don't have or something you've always wanted to do," he persisted. "Skydiving or—"

"Pass." She held up both hands and laughed.

Man, he loved her laugh. "White water rafting?"

"That'd be fun, though it'd be better to go with a friend. I think that's beyond what you're asking though."

He wouldn't mind going with her. He'd been thinking about a rafting trip since seeing his buddy Nate's adventure on *Say Yes to the Rose*. "Do you ever take trips with the women here at The Oasis?"

"No. They can't afford it, and while they deserve a break and would enjoy a trip, it's not a good idea for me to pay their way because it sets an expectation of somebody paying for their companionship."

"I wouldn't have thought of that." He was totally striking out getting gift suggestions but didn't want to push and make her suspicious of why he was asking. "Guess I can always get her and you flowers."

"Um," Elizabeth slid the silver knot charm on her necklace back and forth. "I'm not the typical woman who likes getting a bouquet of flowers—long story. Just save your money."

FAKING IT WITH THE GREEN BERET

"Okay," That sounded like something other than aller-gies, but he wasn't going to ask. "Come on, Boss. Dinner time." At that, Boss got to his feet. After getting a stroke from Elizabeth behind his ear, the dog tagged after him.

Her mention of love languages sent him on an internet search. He found a book by that title, bought it, and down-loaded a copy. Giving up on a mission was not in his blood.

Before turning in for the night, he started reading the chapter on physical touch. He ruled out massages and pedi-cures as gifts Elizabeth would appreciate. She was big on giving words of affirmation to others and certainly gave of her time. Acts of service would likely appeal to her, but he hadn't put his finger on one specific idea. He turned out the bedside lamp, hoping the outdoor lights were better posi-tioned after even more tweaking so Wren didn't kill him in his sleep.

Chapter Fifteen

GOTT'A BE SOMEBODY – Nickelback

When his phone rang, it only took John two steps to get from the kitchen to the sitting area in Hope Harbor and check the name on the screen.

"No, Boss. No. That's my dinner." He waved a finger in warning. Boss sat and turned sad eyes from him to the steak on the counter as John answered. "Nate! How you doing?" He edged into the kitchen, crowding Boss back.

"Better after getting your text. Welcome home."

"Good to be back in the USA." John broke into song. Nate laughed. "I was a little worried about timing since you hadn't officially RSVP'd for you and Britney from the wedding invite."

"Yeah, about that. Britney and I aren't together anymore."

"I'm sorry to hear that. That happen while you were deployed?"

FAKING IT WITH THE GREEN BERET

"Yeah. She got back with her ex. Had packed my stuff and they took Boss to the animal shelter."

"She didn't."

"They did."

"What a bit—. Sorry."

"Don't be. You wouldn't be the first to say it." Or even the fourth. "I was able to get Boss back. However, I don't have a permanent address yet. Long story. I'll tell you about it at the bachelor party. Snap a picture of the invite and send me details of what I need to do and wear, and you know I'll be there."

"I'll count that as an RSVP with no plus one. Shelby might be happy to hear that. She asked about you at the reunion show."

"She did, huh?"

"If you want to show Britney you're over her, we can pair you with Shelby at the wedding reception. I'm sure a few pictures of you two on the dance floor would make it into some social media posts or even an entertainment magazine."

"Britney won't care. Things with Shelby might be fun for a little while, but long term? I can't see it. You and Cecilia doing good? She hasn't turned into a Bridezilla, has she?"

Nate gave a low laugh. "Not even close. She wanted to go down to Costa Rica with just our families, revisit the nature center, and get married at the waterfall rather than do this big to-do for TV. She's about the marriage more than the wedding. But the studio wanted the live show."

"They're footing the bill?"

"Oh, yeah. Wedding venue, reception with a fancy dinner, DJ for dancing, and an open bar. Your suit and hotel room are even covered."

"Sweet. It's like a fairy tale. Meet. Fall in love. Boom. Happy ending. Who's your fairy godmother?" He needed some magic for his love life.

"Parks, the host on *Say Yes to the Rose*, was my fairy *godfather*. Want me to tell him that you're available to be the next lead? Twenty-five women vying to win your heart."

"Right. I don't think that would jibe with my life. Especially with the new job and move coming up."

"Congrats on making the promo list, Major. That's impressive."

"I didn't think I was in the promotion zone, so it was not expected. I hate leaving my team, but the training job at SOCOM is right up my alley. Not constantly deploying might give me a chance to make a relationship work too."

"If you want what Cecilia and I have, you'll have to put yourself back out there. Shelby wasn't the only one disappointed when I said you were seeing someone. You might have to fend them off."

"I don't know that I want to try long-distance dating. Deployments are hard enough. Maybe I should bring a date to the wedding to avoid temptation." He didn't have any idea who, though. There had to be somebody out there for him. Somewhere.

"Let me know. I'll keep you down with a plus one. Snapping a picture of the invite now. I'm looking forward to seeing you for the bachelor party, but, hey, no strip clubs. I've still got media hounding me, and I don't want my mom or Cecilia to see my picture on social media or in grocery store tabloids."

"Roger that. Now that I'm back, I'll get up with Linc to plan something epic—even without strippers."

He had an idea to run past Linc that would make for a unique bachelor party. What did most guys like almost as

much as women? Fast cars, shooting guns, and blowing things up.

Nate had mentioned a DJ and dancing. With John's rusty dance moves and size fourteen-and-a-half feet, he might hurt somebody. Maybe he needed to ask Elizabeth about the dancing at the VFW that Wren had mentioned. The idea of dancing with Elizabeth brought a smile to his face and an idea to mind.

Chapter Sixteen

STAYIN' ALIVE – Bee Gees

As was becoming their ritual, Boss loped over to get love pats from Elizabeth before she climbed her porch steps after work. "Hey, Boss. You have a good day?" As she expected, John followed close behind. He'd changed out of his uniform already into a pair of black athletic shorts and simple gray T-shirt and she couldn't keep from checking out his muscular thighs and calves.

"I'm starting to think my dog likes you better than me."

"I don't know about that. I'm generous with treats, is all." And seeing the two of them was a treat for her.

"He is a sucker for treats and pretty girls." John's smile lingered on her.

She broke eye contact, but not before heat started to build in her. "I don't have treats on me, Boss."

"Wren told me I'm supposed to go line dancing at the

"VFW with you ladies on Friday. Is this another one of your requirements for renting?"

"No. It's just something I've invited them to do with me."

"But I can come if I want to show off my dance moves?"

John rolled his hands in a circle, then struck the iconic Saturday Night Fever pose.

Was he teasing her? She couldn't always tell when he was serious. "All the ladies would probably love that since you're under sixty. Do you have a white polyester suit?" She played along.

"I'll check my closet. If not, will jeans and a T-shirt work?"

"You're serious?"

"About the suit or coming?"

She laughed. With his looks and build, he could get any woman to dance with him—even dressed in a seventy's era white suit.

"Unless you count picking our way through fields riddled with landmines, I can't remember the last time I went dancing. It could be fun, and I've got a friend's wedding coming up. Why do *you* go?" He turned the tables on her.

"The VFW Hall doesn't have the 'pick up' atmosphere of a club. It's a way for a woman who may have issues due to abuse to get used to interacting with men in a non-threatening manner." Though Wren sometimes still misinterpreted a smile from the older men as flirting. "You're not a dancer?"

"I usually stick to singing. Which, believe it or not, is better than my dancing."

"Then you might need a lesson or two—or three." Eliza-beth teased. She'd heard his off-tune renditions of classic

rock and country songs when playing with Boss while she was cooking or sitting on her porch. "Darrin teaches the popular line dances."

"Sign me up. Hey, do they have a trial date for Ariana's ex yet?"

"Still no firm date."

"I'm in a friend's wedding next month on the seventeenth. I'm gonna be out of town at least two days and nights. I'll leave Boss here, if you don't mind looking after him for the weekend."

"I'd be happy to. Or maybe Boss can stay with Ariana those nights."

"Good idea. What time do we leave for the VFW?"

"Seven-forty. I'm hoping Ariana comes with us, so I'll drive."

"I'll meet you here on the porch."

She wouldn't get her hopes up that he'd really come. John wasn't like any man she'd known in a long time. Maybe ever. There was something refreshing about him that kept her anxiety from spiking when he crashed her safety bubble of solitude. Maybe it was the way he loved Boss and treated her and the other women here with respect. He also hadn't pushed anything too far. That might be because he didn't yet have a place to live.

Chapter Seventeen

NEVER REALLY OVER – Katy Perry

ARIANA DROVE past while John gave Boss his nightly workout. He attempted to head Boss off as he trotted toward the blue house with the ball in his mouth.

By the time John reached them, Ariana held her arms up, clutching a bouquet of flowers as she tried to move past Boss.

"Boss, she doesn't want to play with you. Sorry."

"No problem." She scooted around them as he held Boss by the collar.

"Nice flowers." A new guy in her life could be a good thing. Except she avoided making eye contact. Crap.

"Ariana?"

She stopped, her head down as if studying the ground intently. She sighed heavily, her shoulders slumping even more. "They're from J.R. He came by while I was at work."

"Ariana," he repeated, his voice dropping as he drew out each syllable.

"He said he was sorry for what happened and asked if I'd give him a second chance."

John rolled his eyes.

"I know, it's just . . ."

"What?"

"I agreed to meet him for dinner. Tonight."

"You think that's a good idea?" Because he could think of a dozen better ones off the top of his head. Tell him hell no. Show up with a date. Stand him up.

"I don't know," she confessed.

Fantastic. "Then don't go."

"But what if he's sincere? Pink roses are my favorite flowers, and the note with them was really sweet. I know he's made some mistakes, but it sounds like he's trying to get his life together."

"What if he's just trying to get you to drop the charges?"

"I'll be able to tell. I think."

"You said you're meeting him there?"

"I thought that would be better. Besides, I think he's scared to come here." She eyed John.

"There's no reason for him to be scared of me unless he hurts you again." His voice deepened. "Promise me just dinner. That you won't go anywhere with him after."

"But if things are going well . . ."

A grumble escaped, despite John's attempt to be supportive.

"I'm thinking I'll ask a friend to be at the restaurant."

"I volunteer."

"I didn't mean *you*."

"That's what I'm here for."

"It'd be awkward if you're there alone, staring at us," Ariana explained in protest.

"A girlfriend won't provide protection if J.R. tries some-thing. I could get a friend to meet me for dinner."

"One of your Army buddies? Right, like two of you being there would be less obvious." She laughed. "But if you brought Elizabeth, like you were on a date and got there before us . . ."

"That could work." To help Ariana, Elizabeth would go. And it wasn't like he'd mind having dinner with Elizabeth. Not at all. She intrigued him.

"We all do things we wish we could undo, so I want to give him a chance. I don't want to be stupid, though. I'm meeting him at seven."

"Plan to be there about ten minutes early. Text me the restaurant name and address. I'll talk to Elizabeth when she gets home."

♫

John threw a ball for Boss in the front clearing when Elizabeth arrived home. Boss bounded over and dropped a slobbery tennis ball at her feet. She tossed it in John's direc-tion as he ambled toward her. Her other tenants usually respected her space. John, not so much.

"Evening. Hate to ambush you, but thought you'd want to know when Ariana got home a little while ago, she had a bouquet of flowers. I was hoping they were from a new love interest, but—"

"No, please. Not J.R."

"Yup. And she's meeting him for dinner."

Why? Why? Why? She sighed. "She's an adult . . ." Which didn't guarantee making the wisest decisions.

"I asked her not to go anywhere with him afterward, and she mentioned being open to having a friend at the restaurant."

"Okay." At least that was something.

"I volunteered."

"Oh. Good." Maybe John would scare J.R. into leaving her alone.

"She wants you to come too and pretend we're on a date. I don't think she trusts me not to make it super awkward if I'm alone."

"We're supposed to pretend we're on a date? Like he'd believe that we happened to be at the same restaurant."

"It's what she wants. If you have plans or don't want to, I'll still go." He rubbed Boss's head and waited.

She looked for an out. "Did you see if you can even get a reservation?"

"Don't need to. He's just taking her to Mi Casita. You won't need to put on heels and diamonds. I'll change into something nicer for our date, though."

"It's not a date."

"Throw me a bone. I came back from deployment to get dumped." He winked at her. "I'll change and feed Boss. Pick you up in twenty minutes, if that'll give you enough time. I want to get a table where I can keep an eye on them."

Something told her John looked forward to this mission, maybe a little too much. "I'll be ready." But it wasn't a date. *He* hadn't asked her out. Elizabeth would do it for Ariana, who wanted her to go. And to make sure John didn't end up in trouble.

Chapter Eighteen

JOHN COUGAR, JOHN DEERE, JOHN 3:16 – Keith
Urban

John was already out of his truck when Elizabeth stepped out on her porch.

"You look nice," he said, and spun to open the truck door for her. "Sorry about the dog hair." John brushed a hand over the seat before she climbed in his truck.

"No worries. I'm in Boss's spot. You look nice too."

He'd changed out of his uniform and wore khaki cargo pants and a polo shirt instead of his usual jeans, graphic T-shirt, and ball cap. With his short, dark hair smoothed into place, he looked dressed for a date more than a reconnaissance mission. Only this was not a date.

She turned her gaze away from his all-consuming one before he closed the door and went around to get in the driver's seat. "I appreciate you looking out for Ariana tonight."

"'That's why I'm here. Though I don't get why she'd go to dinner with him. You're a counselor. What's your take on why she'd consider getting back with a guy who hit her?'

"'There are lots of reasons people go back to or stay with partners who abuse them. They think they're in love and that they can change them. Or their partner makes them think no one else would love them. Sometimes, the abuser manipulates their target into blaming themselves for events.'

"'Seriously?'

"'That was my dad's favorite. It was never his fault. If someone else had done or hadn't done—whatever—he wouldn't have lost his temper and yelled, thrown something, or hit someone.'

"'Sounds like a swell guy. Want me to have a friendly chat with him?'

"'It probably wouldn't be very friendly. Dad has anger issues and does not like being told he's in the wrong. You might have a size advantage, but he's an ex-Marine and—'

"'Once a Marine, always a Marine.'

"'Not if you're dishonorably discharged.'

"'You're right there.' He cut his gaze from the road to her.

"'His temper got worse after he got kicked out.'

"'So, she left?'

"'No. She stayed with him for a combination of the reasons I mentioned. If she left, she felt she couldn't support herself and three kids.'

"'But you're all grown and on your own now.'

"'True, but he's made her believe she can't provide for herself and no one else would want her.' Elizabeth had offered to assist financially, but she suspected her mother was more afraid of being on her own than her father's anger.

Mom hadn't learned to love herself and pointed to Elizabeth's own inability to establish another romantic relationship after Adam to back up her fears she'd never find anyone else to love her.

"After a fight, he brings her flowers and apologizes. He says he loves her, and she forgives him—usually blaming herself for setting him off." Elizabeth hadn't planned to follow in her mother's footsteps. On the surface, Adam was so different from her father. Now she saw that abuse came in many forms.

"That's why you told me not to get you flowers."

"I'd get so angry seeing them sitting on the table, like they made up for hurting her. She thought it meant he loved her."

"Makes sense."

They stayed silent for over a minute. On the radio, a country singer crooned about everyone having a story to tell, having a hallelujah, and going through a little hell. She slid her necklace's Path of Life charm back and forth on the chain as the chorus repeated.

"You mentioned siblings. Do they live nearby?"

"Not anymore. My younger sister, Jennifer, lived here when I was in school, but now she and her husband are near Tacoma, Washington. We talk a lot, but I don't see her much. We lost track of our older brother years ago."

"Lost track? How?"

"He moved away the day after his high school graduation. The last time I heard from him he was working for a natural gas company in Louisiana but planning to go to South America to get even further away from our father."

"Did you follow your brother in getting the heck out of Dodge?"

"Not right away. Jennifer was still in high school, so I

stayed. A friend's father was the manager at an upscale restaurant, and I worked there and took community college classes. I acted as a mediator at home while I saved money for a car and rental deposit. When Jennifer turned eighteen, we moved into an apartment with two other girls."

Those had been the best times of her life, other than being so broke they ate ramen noodles and peanut butter and jelly most days. But she'd been free from her father's dominance. That only lasted until she'd married Adam.

"What about you? Do you have siblings?" Elizabeth transitioned before she fell further down into that dark hole.

"I have step and half siblings, but I don't really know them."

The catch in his voice made her go into counselor mode.

"That's got to be hard."

"It is what it is," he said quite matter-of-factly. "My parents met at a pizza joint where they both worked in high school. After they broke up, she quit working there. Then a coworker from her high school told my dad she was being homeschooled her last semester, and there were rumors it was because she was pregnant. He showed up at her house and found out it was true."

"And she hadn't told him?"

"Nope. She didn't want to have an abortion because of her religious beliefs. Going off to college with an infant didn't fit too well with attending class and her plans to join a sorority. Her parents didn't want to raise another kid when they had five and their youngest was in high school. So, she'd already picked a couple to adopt me after she gave birth."

"Without telling him? Isn't that illegal?" And unfair to not allow the baby's father a say.

"Yup. My dad and his parents decided they wanted

custody. At the time, I think my dad hoped they'd get back together. That didn't happen. And caring for an infant screwed up his plans to enlist in the Army. We lived with my grandparents for a few years. My grandmother quit her job to help Dad out, but they hadn't planned on raising another kid at that point in their lives either. I interfered with a lot of their plans."

Sitting side-by-side while he drove, he didn't have to look her in the face. Lack of eye contact often encouraged people to open up.

"You know none of that was your fault. It's not like you had a choice about being conceived, whether you were born, and whether you were adopted or raised by your birth parents."

He shrugged. "As for siblings, my dad married his first wife, Lynda, when I was in elementary school. They were married about three years. Her kids only lived with us half the time, and we haven't kept in touch. Dad got married again a few years ago. Emily is great. I've spent some time with her and her two adult kids on holidays, but I don't have a strong connection to them."

He sighed and cut his gaze to her. "You don't have a counseling file on me, right?"

"No. We're just two friends talking."

He nodded but didn't speak right away. "My birth mom married a guy she met at college, and they had three kids. She'd given my dad sole custody, so I was never a part of her family. Just a past mistake. I only met those siblings a couple of times."

"She may have considered getting pregnant a mistake, but *you* aren't a mistake." She wasn't his counselor, but she couldn't help but give him her professional perspective.

"She and her folks definitely thought I was. When my

dad was dating his first wife, Lynda, she wanted him to go to church with her. I was about eight at the time, and they dropped me off in a Sunday School class at this big church. They told the story of Jonah and the whale that day. I'd never heard it and wasn't buying a guy being swallowed by a whale and living. When my dad and Lynda came to pick me up, the teacher lady tells Lynda how I was asking lots of questions and didn't know any Bible stories. My dad stepped up and looked her in the eye, and I still remember him saying, 'Well ma'am, I'd be happy to bring John by and you can spend a little time with your grandson and teach him Bible stories if that's important to you.'"

"Oh, my." What were the chances of him ending up in the Sunday School class taught by his grandparents?

"Yeah. She made some face, and she said real quietly, 'don't bring him back here.' But my dad wouldn't let it go. He got louder when he said, 'What? You don't want your church friends to know that your daughter had my baby in high school and that you were going to put him up for adoption without even telling me? Is that what Jesus would do?'

I'm not making this up."

His father must have as big a personality as John to say that.

"Needless to say, they didn't invite me over to tell me Bible stories, and we didn't go back to that church." John made eye contact as if expecting a reaction.

"I can see why." Churches were full of imperfect people and hypocrites, but to turn away their grandchild? Maybe they needed to be in church and learn about grace and compassion as much as anyone.

"Not long after that, my dad took me to a park to meet my birth mom. She bought me ice cream and asked me questions. Told me about her baby girl and showed me

pictures. I was on my best behavior, thinking I'd have a mom and get to spend time with her. It didn't go like I pictured. No hugging me, saying she was sorry or made a mistake not raising me. Instead, it became a once-a-year thing. Usually at a park. She'd bring a gift—something nice to lessen her guilt." He turned into the restaurant parking lot.

"Wow, that's a lot." Elizabeth's heart ached, picturing a young John desperate for his mother's love. At least she'd had that. This could definitely give him abandonment issues and explained his desperate need to find Boss.

"She started bringing her kids—a boy and another girl. Guess she figured they'd find out about me someday. But it's not like they thought of me as their brother. I've got my dad and that set of grandparents, and my Army family, though. Now you know my life story. You can analyze me later. Let's focus on Ariana."

Chapter Nineteen

SHAKE IT OFF – Taylor Swift

"Table for two?" The young hostess picked up menus.

"Yes, I'd like that booth in the back."

With John in full mission mode, Elizabeth let him take lead following the hostess.

John stopped in the middle of the dining room. "Excuse me." He tapped an empty table. "There's someone coming in a few minutes we need to keep an eye on. Female, early twenties with long, dark hair. A guy her age will be joining her. I need you to put them at this table." He handed the hostess a folded bill.

"If you're planning on spying on your daughter and her date, I think she'll notice you." The girl craned her neck to look up at him.

"Daughter? No. She's just a friend, and she asked us to be here."

"Ah, an internet date. I get it." The hostess palmed the bill.

John took the seat giving him a full view of the dining area. Their server brought them water and bowls of chips and salsa.

As Elizabeth looked over the menu, John gave a hand signal. She turned to see the hostess seat Ariana. Ariana's ruffled, off-the-shoulder, navy dress definitely sent a this-is-a-date vibe. So much for Elizabeth's hope this was to simply give Ariana closure.

"He's here," John said a few minutes later. He held the menu so it covered most of his face.

Elizabeth peeked over her shoulder. J.R. didn't glance their way as he gave a seated Ariana a side hug and kissed her cheek. Though J.R. was dressed and groomed respectably, compared to when he'd shown up on her property, a knot still formed in Elizabeth's stomach.

The server returned. They ordered, then Elizabeth peered in Ariana's direction again.

"How was your day?" John asked to distract her.

"Sorry. Work was fine."

"But you can't tell me specifics since everything is confidential."

"That's correct."

"This is where you ask about *my* day," he drawled, aiming a grin at her. "Which was great. We're breaking in a newbie to the team, so we practiced running live-fire exercises in the shooting house."

"Isn't that dangerous?"

"Compared to a deployment? Naw."

She hadn't figured John out yet, but learning about his mother gave her a good bit of insight. His mother had only been a teen, probably with little say in her decision, but

she'd likely never told John her side of it, or how hard and heartbreaking that decision had been. Did she regret giving him up? Is that why she wanted to see him every year? It seemed more like torturing herself *and* John.

He gave a wave to someone in the dining area and flashed a smile. "J.R. knows we're here."

John pulled her from her counselor mindset, which was a good thing. She was not his counselor, and he hadn't asked her for her take on his parents' and grandparents' decisions.

"And based on J.R.'s body language, he's not thrilled. Ariana looks like she's explaining. Why don't you wave to them?"

Really? She feigned surprise and lifted her hand in greeting. Once she had settled back, she said, "You're enjoying this, aren't you?"

"After what you said earlier, I want her to know she's not alone. And if we throw him off his game, all the better."

"Ariana is so young and vulnerable. And trusting." Like she'd once been.

"Need a real drink?"

"I'd better pass. I'm a lightweight and get chatty after more than one glass of wine. I don't want to say anything to her or him I might regret." Especially with the places her mind was going tonight with Ariana agreeing to go on a date with J.R.

"What kind of music do you like?" John dragged her attention away from her past and back to him. "I'm guessing some soft rock, pop country, easy listening, oldies."

"How old?"

"Seventies and eighties. The nineties only had about fifty decent songs and forty of those were country."

"I'm sure there's more than fifty."

"I don't know. That's when screamo took off. And gangsta rap and all that grunge crap."

"Not a fan?" She did like that John spoke his mind rather than tell people what they wanted to hear.

"Everyone's entitled to their opinion. I prefer classic rock or country. After a beer or two, I'll listen to some pop. I bet you know all the words to Taylor Swift's songs."

"I don't know all, but I could at least do the chorus for a few."

"We should do a karaoke night at The Oasis."

"Pass on the karaoke," she said with a laugh as the server delivered their food.

"Come on. It'd be fun. Though Taylor's got a song called 'Dear John.' I don't like it. But I do like 'Shake it Off.'" John sang and danced in his seat with a big grin, obviously not caring that he drew looks from half the people in the dining room.

"You're losing your intimidation factor." She cut her gaze toward J.R. and Ariana, who now had a large margarita sitting in front of her.

"Good. Let him drop his guard."

A chill shot through her. John might come off like an overgrown kid at times, but he also projected that same confidence that had drawn her to Adam. She missed any signs of Adam's darker side in the early days. She'd paid the price for falling for him. Better not to be lulled by John's easy-going charm since she'd learned how deceptive that could be. She didn't want to be in Ariana's shoes. Not again.

"Why did you join the military?" she asked to keep from thinking about her past and give her more insights into John.

"My dad was still a kid when I was born. In some ways, our relationship was more like brothers. We used to play

army men together. He couldn't afford college tuition, and I wanted him to have his own life after giving up so much of his for me. Maybe I wanted to fulfill his dreams that he didn't get to live out. Figured I'd enlist, then use the GI Bill to cover my tuition and get my degree, which I did. I thought about doing international business or law school, but I liked military life—the feeling of family, not by blood but forged under fire—so I joined back up as an officer. And here I am."

"You seem to enjoy what you do."

"For the most part. There's a term, 'embrace the suck,' that applies to a lot of things we do. Horrible living conditions, pointless missions, wasted time. It's dangerous work, but when you see the difference you make, bringing hope to people, it makes it worthwhile."

"Like stepping in with J.R."

"It's not that different than what you do."

"I've never been shot at."

"Good. Let's keep it that way." His gaze cut in J.R.'s direction.

"Jillian constantly warns me of potential dangers in dealing with domestic situations. That's why I put up the gate—and now have you on a temporary basis. Did you know you wanted to be a Green Beret when you joined?"

"I started thinking about it during my first enlistment, but I knew if I made it into the unit prior to getting my degree, I probably wouldn't leave. I got tapped for selection pretty much right after I became an officer. Another instance where my size worked for me. Tribal leaders tend to listen when they have to look up to you."

"I've heard it's tough to make it through the process to join Special Forces."

"The Q Course isn't for sissies, that's for sure."

Unlike Adam who touted his successes whenever possible, John didn't brag. If it weren't for him warning J.R., she wouldn't even know he was a Green Beret. She was impressed with a lot of what he'd told her. "It seems you've done a good job of setting goals and meeting them."

"Despite what Britney and Richard did with Boss, I don't need counseling." He scrunched his features into a classic I-told-you-so expression.

"No past disappointments or areas where you haven't accomplished your goals?" she couldn't resist challenging him.

John laughed. "You know, I've told you more about myself tonight than I've probably told anyone in my entire life, except my buddy, Nate. Either you're magic or have a gift for making people talk about themselves."

"Training and experience." But she didn't want to push, especially since he wasn't a client.

"Looks like we're going to have to order some dessert since I don't want to leave before they do. Should we say it's your birthday or mine?"

"What? We can just order dessert."

"If they sing to one of us, J.R. is more likely to believe us being here is a coincidence."

He had a point. "Yours." Unlike her, he didn't mind attracting attention.

"Do you want your own dessert, or are we sharing?"

"What makes you think I share my dessert?"

"It's your giving nature. Unless you're a germaphobe, which you're not since we shared salsa. You would have asked for your own or made a no double-dipping rule."

"I'll just say it depends on the dessert as to whether I share."

"*Hmm*, I'm seeing a different side of Miz Elizabeth

Carroll," he teased, aiming his charming smile at her. "If we share, I won't have to do extra PT." He patted his stomach.

"I'm full, but I can manage a few bites if you're offering to share." Considering his shape, one dessert wouldn't require him to do more PT. It took effort not to stare at his muscular arms leading up to his broad shoulders.

"Can I get y'all some dessert or coffee?" The server picked up their dirty plates.

"We're going to get some dessert for the birthday boy," Elizabeth interjected, just in case John tried to say it was her birthday.

"Happy birthday. We do a complimentary mini-serving of the brownie a la mode."

"I don't really do mini, and we're going to share. Bring us the full size, and just put it on the bill."

The server chuckled, her gaze roving over John. "Do you still want a candle and us to sing?"

"Sure. I was deployed on my real birthday, and it wasn't real fun."

"I'll put in the order." The waitress carried off the dishes.

"Sorry you were deployed on your birthday. And holi-days," Elizabeth added.

"Being with my team beats being alone. Once I have a family, it'll be harder to be away, though. That's a big reason I'm looking forward to the new position. I won't have to deploy every eighteen months."

"Have you ever been married?" she asked cautiously.

"No. I didn't get serious with anyone in high school. There was one woman when I was first enlisted. That didn't work out. I decided I wanted to get my college degree before I got married, probably due to my parents. Working and taking online courses to get prerequisites out of the way

didn't give me a lot of time to put into a relationship. I was deployed half that time too."

His answer surprised her. In her experience, many military members married young, and from what he had told her about enlisting right out of high school, serving four years, then college, he had to be in his early thirties.

"What about you?"

She should have figured he'd ask. "For a little over two years. I was in my early twenties."

"Sorry it didn't work out."

That was an understatement. "How many times have you been deployed?" She shifted the conversation to a safer topic—at least for her—and managed to keep the conversation off her past until three servers approached.

The server in front handed John a ridiculously oversized, embellished black sombrero that he plopped on his head before another set the dessert on the table and lit the candle.

"Get a picture." John slid her his phone.

She took his photo while one server banged a tambourine near her ear. Another shook maracas as they sang their version of "Happy Birthday."

"I'll take a picture of the two of you," the server offered.

"That's okay."

"Come over here." John motioned with his hand and made room for her on the bench seat.

"Really?"

He smiled and waited for her to slide in next to him, then leaned his head close to hers for the picture before blowing out the candle. He handed back the sombrero and took his phone from the server.

Elizabeth returned to her side of the booth. "Happy belated birthday."

"Thanks for helping me celebrate." He handed her one of the spoons, then dug in, his focus locked on J.R. and Ariana.

"What's going on?" Elizabeth asked rather than turn to look.

"J.R. asked for their check. I want to see if he pays for both of them since he invited Ariana out. I might be willing to cut him some slack if, in addition to apologizing to her, he was man enough to come over here and apologize to you for showing up high or drunk at your place."

John ate another big spoonful of brownie and ice cream, then mouthed something and pointed to the back. Less than a minute later, Ariana wove through the tables. John had his phone out, tapping on the screen before she disappeared into the hallway to the bathrooms.

"I told her to take her time." He pulled out his money clip and flagged down their server.

Elizabeth fished out her wallet as John asked for the check. She extended a twenty to the server.

"I got this." John waved a hand at her and gave the server his credit card.

"You don't need to pay for my dinner." She tried again to give the server cash.

"You didn't even drink. You're a cheap date." He sent the server away with a nod.

"This isn't a date."

"Dinner out and engaging conversation with a lovely lady. It's the closest thing I've had to a date in over six months."

Try over six years. Not that she disclosed that and risked having to explain. She pushed the money at him.

"Your dinner was like twelve bucks. Bring me over a plate of any dinner you fix, and we'll call it even."

"Fine." She wasn't going to make a scene by arguing. A trade kept things in the friend zone. Since there was no chance of things going anywhere, especially with him living at The Oasis before moving out of state, friends is all it could be between them. Besides, he was looking for someone who was relationship material. Even if she couldn't deny her attraction to a guy that looked like John and had a heart as big as his, thanks to her ex, her brain shut down her body's instinctive response within seconds at the thought of intimacy.

Chapter Twenty

When J.R. and Ariana headed to the front door, John took one last bite of dessert. "Time to move out." He slipped from the booth. Elizabeth followed. "Hold up." He halted at the entrance and peeked through the glass in the door.

"We're flat-out spying on them now?" Elizabeth asked.

"I prefer to call it covert surveillance, but yeah. I'm worried she might go somewhere else with him, where anything could happen. Based on her crossed arms, though, I'd say she's holding her ground on something."

When Elizabeth leaned in to get a glimpse, her shoulder rested against his bicep. The contact and her honeysuckle scent distracted him until J.R. threw his hands up and out. John startled and Elizabeth let out a gasp.

"She's fine," he assured Elizabeth. "I think he's surrendering on something, and that's good."

When J.R. walked away without getting a hug or a kiss, John let out a breath.

"Please don't follow him," Elizabeth murmured under her breath, watching intently as Ariana got in her car.

"Let's go," John said as soon as J.R.'s car pulled out. Ariana got out of her car when she saw them exit.

"How are you?" Elizabeth asked.

"Still confused," Ariana answered. "Things started off good. Then he recognized you."

John shrugged. She shouldn't know he couldn't exactly hide.

"I tried to play it off as coincidence, but he accused me of not trusting him. I told him that I don't after what happened."

"Good for you," Elizabeth said.

"He kept swearing it wouldn't happen again and talking about second chances." She sighed. "He tried to get me to come back to his place to talk more, but I said I wasn't comfortable with that. I also passed when he suggested going to a movie. I did agree to unblock him so he can text and call me," she said in an apologetic way.

John had to admit the guy was persistent.

"The only thing I've got to say is make good choices. We're here for you. Whatever you need," Elizabeth voiced John's same sentiments.

"Did he mention dropping the charges?" John asked.

"Not directly. Though he brought up that one of his supervisors is leaving and he might get a promotion at work if things work out—like he was hinting about that."

At least she picked up on that. John gave an affirmative nod but kept his mouth shut.

"I missed him, but now I'm thinking I missed who I was before him even more." She gave them a weak smile.

"Thank you both for coming. I'll see you back at The Oasis."

John opened Ariana's car door for her, then escorted Elizabeth to his truck.

"I was hoping that she'd get the closure she mentioned, but at least she's not going home or anywhere with him tonight," John still watched to be sure she turned toward The Oasis.

"Agreed," Elizabeth sank into the seat. "I appreciate you giving up your time to come out."

"It is what I signed on for." He didn't mind playing protective big brother to Ariana, especially since he'd never had that kind of relationship with his half-sisters. "My only plans were to eat a sandwich and hang out with Boss. It might not have gone like we hoped, but it was still a treat."

Despite the fact that Elizabeth had been quick and adamant this wasn't a date, he'd do dinner with her any time. She was easy to be with, but she was a different person when she dropped her guard. That fun side, her laugh, her smile . . . She deserved to be like that all the time.

What she'd shared of her not-so-picture-perfect past could explain her reserve. However, she'd sure been quick and smooth about segueing to a new subject after he asked if she'd been married.

He couldn't blame her for not wanting to delve into painful memories. He still couldn't believe how much he'd run his mouth to her earlier about things he rarely talked about. Like his mother. What kid didn't need to feel wanted? While he tried to act like it wasn't a big deal, the hollowed out feeling lingered in his gut. In his chest too.

It's not like he'd told Elizabeth everything. How he'd never been invited for a holiday with his mother's family or to his half siblings' birthday parties. Or how his mom sent a

check, but she hadn't come to his high school graduation. Or his boot camp graduation.

Before he graduated with honors from college, he'd called to invite her and the family to the ceremony. After a few attempts to reach her, he left a message. Good old mom texted back—texted—that her daughter—not his sister—was also graduating that weekend and they had family coming in, so they couldn't make it. And she didn't invite him. Instead, she sent a card and another check—which he never cashed.

Rising to the rank of major might earn his mother's respect. It'd probably take more like full-bird colonel. His promotion was a big step in that direction. He hadn't told her yet. It wasn't like they talked.

He was balanced and well-adjusted—all things considered. But he did want more in his life than work. He wanted to share his life with someone special. Someone who'd say their life was better because he was in it. Why couldn't he find it? Some professional insight could be beneficial.

The truck's stereo filled the silence. They were halfway back to The Oasis. If he was going to ask her input, now was the time.

"You know what you were saying earlier, about talking with a friend who happened to be a counselor and trained to help people figure out their problems?"

"Yes." Elizabeth shifted in her seat.

"And you asked about any goals I haven't accomplished? I thought I'd be married and have a family by now."

"And that's something you want?"

"Of course." Someone there to welcome him home from a long day or deployment. Someone who wouldn't walk away—or let *him* walk away. Boss gave him a taste of that

kind of unconditional love he ached for, but it wasn't enough.

"Why do you think you haven't settled down?"

"I was hoping you could tell me."

She laughed lightly. "I'm a counselor not a dating guru. I help my clients identify unhealthy patterns of behavior to break or change them."

"How do you do that?"

"You want my perspective. As a friend?"

"Yeah. Because what I've been doing clearly isn't working. And don't they say doing the same thing over and over expecting different results is the definition of insanity? I could use some sage advice."

"Okay. Approximately how many romantic relationships have you had?"

Oh, crap. "What's your definition of a relationship?" he hedged.

"How about we say since high school, at least four dates, and you were exclusive for over a month."

Whew. That ruled out a lot of non-starters and other things he'd rather not disclose to Elizabeth. "Maybe six or seven."

"That's pretty normal. Everyone has to learn what they do and don't want in a relationship." She gave a disgruntled sounding half chuckle and gave a slight shake of her head that seemed directed at herself rather than him. "You don't want to settle. How long did those relationships typically last?" She shifted her focus back to him with an overly bright smile that made him wonder what had gone through her mind.

He thought back over the relationships for a minute. "Average? Around three or four months."

"Thinking back on even the short-term relationships, do

you see any commonalities on why they didn't go anywhere or ended? Sorry, that came out in counselor speak. I can't help it."

"No worries. It's like me going into military mode." For the next few minutes, he gave her a rundown of his past relationships which ended for various reasons. She asked pointed questions without sounding judgmental. Still, reliving his failures was about as fun as running out of ammo in a firefight.

"Is any of this helping?"

"Somewhat," Elizabeth's mouth shifted. "Not everyone is a match, even if you do want the same things. It sounds like you weren't compatible with any of those women. Why do you think Britney cheated?"

"She used me to get back at her cheating ex but didn't think I wasn't good enough for her family." It slipped out, and he began to see a pattern. They wanted someone with a similar, affluent background. "You think I have mommy issues?"

"The mother-child relationship is a key factor in our development, though it sounds like your dad was very involved in your upbringing, as were your grandparents. And I'm in counselor mode again. Sorry, I can usually do better at turning it off, but you said 'mommy issues' and . . ."

"It's my fault," he laughed. He'd been kind of joking when he said it. "But . . .?"

"Not everything stems from parenting issues. There's no handbook and most people do the best they can by their kids, but her not being around could affect your ability to make emotional connections."

Dayum. Was she right?

"Look, you're educated, employed, compassionate, fun, nice-looking, good to animals. All admirable and appealing

115

qualities. But you could still harbor feelings of inadequacy. And it's possible that in your personal life you walk away from conflict rather than try to work things out or fight for what you want to protect yourself from rejection. Nobody likes being rejected."

"True. So, what do I do about that?" He felt as naked as a newborn.

"You can't change the past, but you can do things differently going forward."

"For instance . . ."

"How do you meet the women you date? Dating sites, social groups, bars, friends?"

"Different ways," John shifted in the leather seat. "Britney was at a bar called Jumpy's. You ever been there?"

"No."

Didn't think so. "It's popular with the Spec Ops community. Where do you meet the men you date?" He turned the tables on her.

"I don't."

"You don't . . . date men? You and the police officer . . . ?"

That could explain some things.

"No. I'm straight," she clarified patiently. "She and I are friends. I don't date."

"You don't date. At all?"

"Not anymore."

Dang, that was disappointing. "Why?"

She hesitated. "I . . . like my independence."

"But don't you want someone in your life. And to have kids?"

She sighed and her hand went to the silver charm on her necklace. "I thought we were talking about *you* and *your* dating life."

"Sorry. You just surprised me."

"Back to Britney," she redirected him. "Is that a typical start to your romantic relationships?"

"Not always." How lame was that? "I've done online dating and exchanged messages before meeting to hang out. You know a lot of those people lie? Use old pictures, fake names."

"It's often for their security. You should appreciate that. Did you see better success there than say a bar?"

"Not really. I connected with about a dozen. Mostly a date or two."

"Then maybe it's not how you meet, but what happens afterward."

That uncomfortable sensation of being in the super-hot seat returned. "Britney came to Jumpy's with friends to drown her sorrows and have some fun after a bad breakup. It's possible she and I didn't have a strong foundation to build on." He tried to put a respectable spin on it.

"We can stop if this is making you uncomfortable."

He expected a snarky smile to counter her serious tone, but one glance at the sympathetic expression on her pretty face gave him the courage to continue. "No. Go ahead and give it to me with both barrels."

"I'm not here to judge. Just to help. Physical attraction is an important element of a romantic relationship."

"But?" He knew it was coming.

"But you need more than that for the kind of long-term relationship you say you want. Finding out if you enjoy being with the person first and if you want the same things could save you time and heartache. And I am speaking from experience."

"Around how many dates do you think that takes?"

"Depends on how much time you spend *actually* talking and getting to know each other. Hanging out and

doing things together—outside the bedroom. I'm not saying you can't have a good time now. After all, you did just get home from a long deployment. Since you're about to move, now probably isn't the best time to start a serious relation-ship. It might be better to take care of your needs. Then, when you're ready, maybe try slowing things down and see if you get different results."

He nodded, thankful to be driving through the gate.

He parked in front of Elizabeth's house and unfastened his seatbelt.

"You don't need to walk me to my door." She edged out of the truck.

"Habit. My grandma taught me a gentleman always picked up a lady at the door and sees her to it. 'None of that honking from the driveway,'" he mimicked an older woman's voice.

"'This wasn't a date, and I think I can make it safely the ten feet to my porch. Sorry, that I detoured out of the friend lane into counselor territory."

"Quit apologizing," I pressed. "Thanks for the, uh, advice. And thank you again for going with me." And another reminder this wasn't a date. He probably shouldn't take it personally.

While he liked sex, he wanted more. A little more deprivation might be worth the sacrifice in the long run.

Chapter Twenty-One

I'M A BELIEVER – The Monkees

After refilling the feeders, Elizabeth watched the hummingbirds flit about while she waited for the others to arrive to head to the VFW post. John strolled into view, alone.

He and Boss hadn't made their usual appearance last night. His truck had rolled in about ten. Not as late as she expected, after deducing he went out. She couldn't blame him. She'd practically encouraged him to get laid. He had needs. And it was better to take care of them with a willing partner.

"Wow. You look amazing. Am I underdressed?" he asked.

His unexpected compliment sent heat through her. "No. What you're wearing works, since you don't have the white, seventies-era suit." He could probably pull off the suit if he could find one his size, but his well-worn jeans

showcased his long legs, and the navy T-shirt highlighted his muscular arms and chest in a very appealing way.

"Wanted to let you know that I'll be tied up with Nate's bachelor party the weekend after next."

"Thanks for telling me. I don't expect you to give up activities to be here on full-time guard duty. How long will you be out of town?" She tore her gaze from him to pick dead blossoms from the hanging basket of petunias.

"We're doing it here."

"In Fayetteville?" *Well, there were a lot of bars and strip clubs.*

"His buddy, Linc, and I met up last night to plan." John broke into a huge smile. "Nate was an engineer doing construction, so he didn't get to play with the cool toys that Linc and I do. We're gonna let him, his brothers-in-law, and other groomsmen run through some training exercises and shoot guns. Linc even managed to line up time in a flight simulator through a teammate's wife who flies Black Hawks."

She'd guessed wrong. On both accounts. John continued to surprise her—in good ways. "That sounds memorable."

"It will be. There's something I'd like to run past you. That big step to get in Hope Harbor isn't a problem for me or Boss, but I thought it'd be nice for your future tenants if I built a front porch for an outside living area."

"I can't ask you to do that."

"You aren't asking. I offered, and it's self-serving. Boss and I don't like being cooped up inside. Unless you don't mind us continuing to crash your peaceful evenings here."

She eyed him as he grinned at her.

"It's not a big deal. My team does construction projects all the time. Quarters for us or to make inroads with the

locals. I'll do up a sketch to show you what I have in mind. I've got the time."

"Include an estimate on cost."

"I got it."

"*I'll* cover the materials." She sprinkled the spent blossoms onto the mulch around the shrubs as Ariana and Wren approached. "I'll be ready in a minute." She ducked inside to wash her hands.

John kept on surprising her. Identifying a need and offering to do something generous. Not telling her what he was doing. She shook the water from her hands but couldn't dispel the off-balance effect he had on her. Of course, he was probably on his best behavior. If he were sticking around longer rather than moving out of The Oasis and to Florida, she'd get a glimpse of what was hidden beneath his attractive exterior. If something or someone seemed too good to be true, they usually were.

She slung her purse over her shoulder, determined not to let John dominate her thoughts. However, after Wren and Ariana ceded the front seat to him, it was hard to ignore his looming presence in the passenger seat of her car for the drive to the VFW Hall.

Butterflies in her stomach were barely noticeable this time when they pulled into the parking lot. None of the older veterans she had met here reminded her of her father, and line dancing did not involve any physical contact with anyone, other than the occasional bump when somebody missed a step.

The lot was half full with trucks and sedans, many sporting a variety of military decals or bumper stickers. She parked a few spaces over from where the instructor, Darrin, unloaded his equipment.

John exited her car and hustled over to Darrin. "Let me give you a hand." He picked up the speakers.

"Thanks. I can grab one, though," Darrin said.

"No worries. I'm balanced this way."

"You're invited back anytime." Darrin pulled the cart with his other equipment to the building as Elizabeth followed with Ariana and Wren.

"Sorry I'm running late, folks. Ran into traffic from an accident," Darrin announced once inside. "You guys flirt with the pretty ladies to give me a minute to set up."

Tables were pushed to the left side of the room. Elizabeth led Ariana and Wren to an empty table next to where veterans crowded around two adjoining tables.

Wearing the bored expression akin to a teen dragged to an event by her parents, Ariana shifted on the wooden chair and eyed the men at the next table, most of whom were two or three decades older. Once the dancing started, hopefully Ariana would have fun. Elizabeth had been nervous to the point of nausea her first time here until the dancing started. She'd forgotten how fun and freeing it was, at least when no touching was involved.

John set the speakers on the small stage, then joined the table of veterans next to theirs, shaking their hands or clasping them on the shoulder. Within a minute, he was seated and laughing while Darrin set up and did a sound check. From what she could hear of the neighboring conversation, John thanked the older vets rather than espouse on his own service.

Two of the regular couples in their fifties came in, trailed by Air Force veteran Buck Holland, who was alone. He beamed at Elizabeth and Wren and headed straight for them.

"You ladies look lovely tonight. Got a first timer with you, I see. Welcome. I'm Buck." He smiled at Ariana.

"I'm Ariana."

"You're new too." He eyed John, who introduced himself.

"Buck is quite the dancer," Elizabeth said.

"Had to be. When you're my size, you need to stand out another way to win the ladies. At the USO dances, I was more popular than the big handsome guys who just sat there." Buck wasn't more than five-foot three, but he still grinned at John as if issuing a challenge.

"Where is Jean?" Elizabeth asked.

"She's at Myrtle Beach for a ladies' golf tournament. I wasn't invited. Did I tell you my wife uses the promise of sex as a way to get little jobs done around the house."

Ariana's mouth hung open as she stared at Buck.

"She does not," Elizabeth chuckled.

"She does too. The plumber told me."

Behind her, John snickered.

From the first night she met Buck, Elizabeth hadn't expected slightly ribald jokes from the sweet-looking man. She'd believed he was telling her the truth until he delivered the punch line. Every time she came, he had a new joke or two.

"My wife found all the letters I was hiding and accused me of cheating on her," Buck paused. "She got mad. Now, she says she's never playing Scrabble with me again!"

John leaned in. "I thought my girlfriend was joking when she said she'd leave me if I didn't stop singing 'I'm a Believer.' Then I saw her face..."

Buck hooted. "You trying to give me competition?"

"Well, I have no moves on the dance floor. Maybe you can give me a lesson to impress the ladies," John said.

"I doubt you need help there." Buck looked John over.

"Not true. My life is like a country song. I came home from deployment and nearly ruined my girlfriend's black-tie affair when I showed up and found her with her not-so-ex-anymore ex. And she gave away my dog."

Buck waited. "What's the punch line?" he finally asked.

"No punch line. Just a punch in the gut. My next mission was to find my dog—at least that was successful. And he was well cared for since Elizabeth had adopted him."

"That's how you two got together?"

"Oh, we're not together," Elizabeth said quickly. Probably too quickly, as heat raced up her face.

"No?" Buck shifted his gaze from her to John. "If I weren't married, I'd be filling up her dance card."

"And I'd let you. You know I adore you," she deflected. She wished her father had been more like Buck. The only dance she'd partaken in with her father had been to dance out of his reach when he was drunk or angry.

"I'll give you a dance lesson—maybe two," he said to John. "You're on your own for the jokes."

"He might give you a run there too," Wren warned.

"Naw, he's got me beat," John admitted.

"I think I like you." Buck squeezed another chair up to the table with the vets and John.

John clearly had a knack for fitting in and putting people at ease. Adam had too, though. And he'd taught her to be cautious.

Chapter Twenty-Two

CUPID SHUFFLE – Cupid

"Look who made it." Elizabeth waved to Jessica and Brooke. She'd texted earlier in the week, hoping they'd come since they were closer to Ariana's age. Both women had successfully escaped from toxic and dangerous relationships.

While hugs were exchanged, John slid his chair to their table.

"Thank you," Brooke acknowledged the gesture and took the seat.

"This is Ariana. She's living in Sanctuary Lodge now," Elizabeth introduced them.

"That's where I lived." Jessica gave an understanding smile.

"And I was in Hope Harbor," Brooke said. "We moved into an apartment together last month."

"How are things going?" Elizabeth asked.

"Good. We're still getting things to make the apartment feel like home."

Wren leaned closer to Jessica. "How are things with Connor going since you're on your own?"

"Really good." Jessica broke into a shy smile. Her gaze flicked from Wren to Elizabeth. "He was going to come with us tonight but switched shifts with another nurse to get a long weekend. He's taking me to meet his family. I hope they like me."

"Just be yourself. Introducing you to his family is a promising sign," Elizabeth reassured her.

She wished she'd had the foresight to at least meet Adam's family before they eloped, but she'd believed him when he said it didn't matter what his kids or siblings would say about their age difference and didn't need their approval. It wasn't as if she wanted to introduce him to her parents—not that they'd necessarily have disapproved or cared. It was only after they were married that she realized Adam was afraid his control issues might somehow come up. She'd been too naïve to recognize the attention he'd lavished on her and him getting jealous over silly things, like cuddling the dog, as red flags. Instead, she'd learned the hard way. As had Jessica with her controlling ex-husband. It was great to see her happy and moving on.

Brooke's gaze lingered on John. Elizabeth shook off the niggle that rose as the women chatted. It wasn't any of her business if the two connected. Brooke wasn't living at The Oasis anymore, where it might create awkward situations or problems, and John wasn't a monk.

Darrin summoned them to the dance floor. Everyone quickly got to their feet. The nearly three dozen dancers formed four lines on the small dance floor.

A veteran wearing a red hat emblazoned with USMC

in bright yellow letters waved a hand at the women around John. "Is your plan to hoard all the pretty ladies and not share with us old timers?"

"My only plan is to hide here in the back where no one sees me stumble over my combat boots," John said.

"There's no hiding on my dance floor." Darrin donned his headset. "We'll have you dancing like a semi-pro by the end of the night."

"I'm in a wedding in a few weeks, and I don't want to embarrass myself. At least more than usual."

"If your sense of rhythm is anything like your ability to carry a tune, you'll need more than one lesson," Wren said from her spot next to John. "Just listen and watch Darrin, or me. We got your back."

Elizabeth ended up in the middle row, over one spot from John and between the Marine and Buck.

Darrin started his lineup, walking them through "Boot Scootin' Boogie" as a warm-up. By the end of the song, John was singing along. Then Darrin played "Copperhead Road."

"No. Just in front with this song."

Elizabeth resisted the urge to look when Wren corrected John. When they did a quarter of a turn, Elizabeth watched him out of the corner of her eye. Her early attempts had been full of missteps too. That John wore the same easy-going smile, even when Wren corrected him again, was an unexpected, but pleasant, surprise. Adam had absolutely hated being corrected in front of others. She'd learned that lesson all too well.

Darrin rolled through another country song, then gave them a break. When everyone returned to the floor, he changed things up with hip-hop and the easy "Cupid Shuffle."

"I thought you didn't know these songs and dances," Wren grimaced, ducking John's arm.

"I said I wasn't good. I don't live under a rock—totally. Mostly in the desert."

Wren rolled her eyes and took a step further away.

Next, Darrin played another crowd favorite, the "Cha Cha Slide." Dancing to those songs reminded Elizabeth of the happy, nearly carefree days when she and Jennifer had lived with friends, out of their father's reach, and before she'd met Adam. She moved in step, only to find herself knocked off-balance by John. His arm slipped around her and pulled her to his side to keep her from crashing to the floor.

"Sorry, sorry, sorry. The reverse got me." He righted and released her nearly as quickly as he had rescued her.

His sudden touch triggered memories of Adam's fingers digging into her and left her fighting for breath. Even as non-threatening as John's actions were, the normalcy of seconds ago had completely dissipated.

She joined in the dance again, determined not to let her past control her. It took several moments to match her steps to the music while she acknowledged the feelings and let them pass. The past was the past. It couldn't be changed. *Focus on now.* That was the only thing she could control. Would she ever move on? Not withdraw and shut down at a man's touch?

She made it through the rest of the song and the next. Darrin gave them another short break.

John grabbed a cup of lemonade and two cookies off the snack table.

Buck picked up a cookie. "Nice catch back there. I was afraid Elizabeth was going to land on the floor."

"You and me both. I might have ended up homeless—

again." John grinned and handed her the cup of lemonade, then got another for himself.

"Wait. She said you weren't—together. And . . ." Buck looked from one to the other.

Elizabeth shot John a semi-mock glare. "He and his dog are living in one of my tiny homes."

"Wait," Buck hooted. "*You're* living in a tiny home?" He chuckled between each word and ended up nearly doubled over.

"It's temporary, and not so bad." John absently rubbed the top of his head.

"You're living in Hope Harbor? Sleeping in the loft? And with that tiny shower?" Brooke asked wide-eyed. "Haven House at least has a bedroom and a decent sized bath."

"It does?" John drawled, shifting his gaze from Brooke to Wren who gave an embarrassed shrug.

"I wasn't going to ask her to move twice when you're only there a few weeks." Elizabeth took the blame. She had hinted to Wren about switching to give John the house better suited to his size, except Wren hadn't offered.

"Naw, it's all good. I've got my dog. Nobody's shooting at me. It's tight quarters, but better than a submarine. Anyway, I'll be fixing up my house when my renter moves out. It has a bedroom where I can stand and plenty of space for the two of us."

"After we wrap the last set, how about I give a lesson on partner dances so he can sweep the ladies off their feet at that wedding?" Buck suggested.

"Great idea," Darrin agreed. "Now it's time to hit the floor. I'm going to teach you all a new dance so you can impress your friends, being all fancy-like."

Everyone laughed as they danced. John sang with a

definitive country twang to the fun song while Darrin broke down the steps. One of the older women blushed when John pointed to her during the chorus. John then ignored the dance steps and reached out a hand to the woman.

"I'm so going to have this song stuck in my head all night," Brooke said, watching John spin the older woman.

Elizabeth was impressed with John's timing, gracefully moving so that no dancers had to maneuver out of the way. She'd already noticed he was a quick study, memorizing the dances by the second run-through. Maybe it was due in part to his military training, or that, despite his good-ole-boy persona, the man was keenly intelligent.

He wasn't perfect, yet he really was the "whole package." He loved his dog. Handsome, with a well-built physique. An endearing, not cutting, sense of humor. A protector, yet he didn't run over people with his alpha nature.

She turned her attention back to Darrin before anyone caught her staring at John or her memories took her to a dark place. She rubbed a fingertip over the Path of Life charm on the necklace she wore most days. Maybe it'd been her lot in life to go through hell in order to help others. Usually, she was okay with that. Her life was better than she'd thought it would turn out when in the midst of purgatory, but watching the couples dancing side-by-side and having fun together, the void in her life hit her—hard. Once John and Boss left The Oasis, she definitely needed to get herself another dog to ease the loneliness of coming home to an empty house.

After Darrin closed out the set, Buck took center stage and invited anyone interested in a ballroom dance lesson to stay. Either they were hardcore dancers or wanted to keep

John from being singled out, because only about five people left.

Everyone quickly mastered the basic box step.

"Elizabeth, will you come demonstrate the waltz?" Though Buck phrased it as a question, he extended a hand and pulled her from the front line.

Buck placed a hand on her shoulder blade and lightly gripped her hand.

She froze.

This is Buck. It's a room full of people. Everything's fine.

The few seconds of him explaining gave her time to regain her composure and perform the steps with him.

"Everybody partner up and give it a try," he said.

Brooke headed toward John, but the man in the USMC hat intercepted her. Ariana quickly paired off with John. Two men watched rather than pair up with each other.

"Not too many of you young people do the waltz anymore, so we'll move on to the three-step." Buck released Elizabeth but motioned for her to stay beside him. "With it, you can do several dances, including the polka."

"I may have to make a special request to get the wedding DJ to play a polka," John cracked.

"The polka is versatile. It can be done to songs other than the traditional German accordion drinking songs, which can be fun too," Buck conceded, counting aloud as he demonstrated the steps.

This time, when Buck reached out to her, Elizabeth was ready. She didn't react when he took her hand and placed his other on her back. She moved with him to the music Darrin played.

"You can jazz it up with some hip action," said Buck.

"What about spins and dips?" John asked.

"Come back again, and we'll work on that. Change part-

ners. Are you up for it, missy?" Buck crooked a finger at Ariana and placed Elizabeth's hand in John's.

Great. Just when she felt safe with Buck and had her anxiety in check. She inhaled before cautiously meeting John's gaze.

"So, no spins or dips. You got this," he said. "Just one, two, three. Quick, quick, slow." He led her through the steps. "This was a lot of fun. Talking with the vets and the dancing. It's good for me to do things outside my comfort zone, and you're making me look like I know what I'm doing."

"I think you know exactly what you're doing." And she was grateful for the way he put her at ease, talking to her like a friend and not demanding anything from her. At least she could have that.

Chapter Twenty-Three

I'VE GOT A ROCK AND ROLL HEART – Eric Clapton

WREN TURNED down the volume on John's Bluetooth speaker as he recorded the measurements on his sketch. He kept right on singing, "I've Got a Rock and Roll Heart."

She moved closer. "What are you doing?"

"Going to build a porch for me and Boss to sit out here and serenade y'all."

"What evil thing have we done to you to deserve that?"

He hooted. "I'm not that bad."

"So, you figured out the perfect gift to give Elizabeth. What about Ariana and me?"

"You want to stain the porch?"

"No. I want something she can unwrap."

"I struck out twice getting her to tell me anything. Short of rooting through her trash to see what kind of wine she drinks, the best I got is a gift certificate to buy digital books

since she enjoys reading, but I don't know what kind of books she's into. Though I read this book she mentioned, and words of affirmation and acts of service are things she appreciates. Maybe make her dinner or take her out since cooking for one gets old."

"I'll think on it. Do you have a plan to get her out of the house?"

"Excuse me?"

"We need you to get her out of her house and off the property for at least an hour to decorate and for people to get in to surprise her."

"Wait. You're doing the party *in her house*?"

"It'd be totally suspicious if we wanted to go somewhere on her birthday, and the tiny houses are too small to host a party for more than three people."

"True that, but . . ." It seemed like an invasion of her privacy.

"Invites are out with that as the location."

"How are you getting in?"

"Can't you pick the lock, Mr. Green Beret?"

"I can, but I won't." Was she serious about breaking in?

That was definitely crossing the line.

She laughed. "I have a key. I'd let Boss out for her when she had to work late. He couldn't fit through the doggie door."

"No surprise there." Elizabeth might take that key back after this. "I'll take her with me to pick up the supplies for the porch. If she says she has plans, I'll let you know."

"Make sure she doesn't."

"That'll be up to you to figure out if she does."

Wren posed with her hands on her hips, as if she could intimidate him. "Let me know if we need a plan B ASAP."

"I'll ask her today." He went back to work as Wren got in her car.

He finished the sketch, double-checked the measurements, then went inside and sent a picture of the sketch to Nate for him to review.

"I think we need a grill, don't you?" he said to Boss as he put four beef franks in the microwave. "Nuking meat is a sacrilege." He split the buns, then took out the franks to heat up the chili. He cut up two and put them in Boss's bowl.

After topping his dogs, he turned to put the containers away and tripped over Boss. The chili slipped from his hand as he grabbed for the counter to keep from landing on Boss.

"Dammit!"

Chili covered Boss's back and splattered the front of the lower cabinets and the floor. John sighed and wolfed down a hot dog while Boss started licking chili off the cabinet doors. "Yeah, thanks buddy. You are so going to need a bath." That had not been on his to-do list today. He ate the rest of his lunch then herded Boss to the bathroom.

"Okay, this is gonna be fun." He started the water, then stripped off his clothes. Boss didn't fit much better than John in the tiny space. Trying to reach in and rub the chili off before shampooing required the flexibility of a contortionist—which he was not. Why hadn't he installed a handheld sprayer? That would have made his life easier. Instead, water hit him in the face, filling his ear and blinding his left eye.

"Turn around."

Boss didn't budge.

"Come on. I need a little help." Boss nuzzled John's face. "That's not helping. Turn." For a dog that took any opportunity to stick his head out the window of a moving vehicle or wade in a creek, water hitting him in the face

shouldn't have been a big deal. He pressed Boss's rump until he shifted and tried to escape. John landed on his ass with his wet dog looming over him, chili still streaking his coat.

"That's it. Plan B." He struggled to his feet. What was Plan B?

He changed into dry briefs and pulled back on his shorts, then grabbed a towel and the shampoo. Gripping Boss's collar to keep him on course, he led him out of the bathroom.

After circling all three of the houses in The Oasis and not finding a hose, he headed to Elizabeth's. She had to have a hose, or at least a bucket. He wasn't going to let Boss drip chili all over her floors.

As he had hoped, there was a hose on a decorative reel on the side of her house. He scouted a spot before turning on the water and nearly had the chili scrubbed off before he spotted Elizabeth watching from a few yards away.

"What's going on?" she asked.

"Had a little mishap in the kitchen. Ended up with chili on all the dogs. I tried cleaning him in the shower, and that didn't go well." Understatement. "I didn't see a hose down there. I didn't think you'd mind."

"It's fine." She raised her gaze from Boss up John's body to his face. "You're soaked."

"Yeah. Still got water in my ear and my eyeball. I should have come here first." He started shampooing Boss, who was suddenly on his best behavior. "You think you're going to get a treat, don't you? Well, it was my fault. Kind of. I'm sorry." Boss licked John's face. Either accepting his apology or cleaning off chili. "What?" He eyed Elizabeth.

"Y'all are too cute."

"You hear that, Boss? She's calling us cute." As if on cue,

Boss barked. "He said he prefers *ruggedly handsome*." Though John would take cute coming from Elizabeth, who gave a delicate laugh as she dropped her gaze, before it flitted back to his face. He could swear her cheeks turned a bit pink. Women often gave him a second glance due to him being unusually tall and in great shape, but Elizabeth Carroll was not most women.

"Oh, wait, before you run off, I've sketched out plans for the deck and sent them to my engineer buddy to look over. Are you free on Saturday to go with me to pick out the supplies? You can make it pretty for your future tenants."

"And I need to pay. Can we make it after ten?"

"I was gonna say after lunch. Best not to shop hungry so we don't buy stuff we don't need."

She gave that cute laugh, shaking her head. "That's when you go grocery shopping."

"Ah, that makes sense. I've got plans in the morning, so about one works." He held his breath and shifted his attention to Boss as if the matter was settled.

"All right."

John watched as she sashayed away. She didn't date, so she wasn't playing hard to get, but he liked a challenge—and every little thing he learned about her. He liked that she was smart, independent, good to dogs, didn't expect perfection, and had a sense of humor. Even better, she was able to keep a confidence and was not all about herself. It didn't hurt she was easy on the eyes. The kind of beauty that grew on a guy.

Chapter Twenty Four

S.O.S. – Abba

WHEN ABBA's "S.O.S." started playing, John whipped his phone from his side pocket. "Top, cover. I've got to take this," he instructed his first sergeant and stepped away from where his team practiced running an urban insertion drill. "John Bryson."

His greeting was met with a sob.

"Ariana, are you okay?"

"No." More crying. "I came out of work and my car has two flat tires."

Two? Shit. "Are you hurt?" he asked.

"No, but I don't know what to do." She sniffled.

"Is somebody with you?"

"My co-worker, Janae."

"Take a look at the tires and see if you see a nail or slice in them."

"Just a second."

John waited for what felt like minutes.

"I don't see anything, but the caps for the air valves are both missing."

That was the better alternative. "Here's what I want you to do. Have Janae walk you back into the store. Go to your security team and ask them to let you view the camera footage from the parking lot. See if you recognize J.R.'s car or somebody going to yours. If you do, call the police. Wait inside. I'll be there in twenty-five minutes." Hopefully sooner.

He quickly explained the situation to First Sergeant Rodriguez and turned the team over to him.

John ducked into the unit's maintenance building and grabbed a portable air pump. He eyed the used tires stacked in the corner. Two flats? Possible, but not likely an accident. What an asshole. Hopefully, J.R. wasn't a total asshole and only let air out and didn't slash them.

John made good time and parked near Ariana's car. He got out and inspected the tires. They were noticeably, but not completely, flat. He ran the pump for a few minutes, then turned it off and listened. No hissing. Fingers crossed, he filled the back tire too.

He texted Ariana. *Here. Fixed flats. Where can I find you?*

Security office. By bathrooms. Back right corner near appliances.

He made his way to the back of the store and knocked. Ariana opened the door and let him into the office where a man in his forties sat at a bank of screens. His eyes roved over John's uniform.

"Did you find out anything?"

"Some guy with a ball cap pulled low knelt down next

to her car. He stayed there for a minute then moved near the back tire, so I'm sure he did it."

"It wasn't J.R., though. We never saw him or his car." Someone would only need seconds to slash a tire versus taking the time to let air out. What was J.R.'s end game here? Send a warning to intimidate her to drop the battery charge but make sure he didn't get in trouble with the law?

"Did you see any suspicious cars cruising the lot earlier?"

"Hadn't looked for any. What unit are you with?" the store's security guy asked.

"Third Group."

The man's head bobbed in acknowledgment despite John leaving out the Special Forces part. "I was in the 82nd Airborne. Having police cars sitting in front of the store isn't good for business and the cops won't be able to do anything, but your attorney might be able to use anything we find," he said to Ariana.

He printed off the clearest and the most incriminating pictures, then they watched as he rewound the parking lot footage until John picked out a car that cruised the aisles and never parked. It disappeared off screen. A minute later, the guy in the baseball cap wove through the lot to Ariana's car. When he jogged off, he got in the passenger seat of the car John had picked out, which waited two rows over.

The security guy scrolled back to see if he could get a clear shot of the car's license plate. The best he got was the last two numbers. He printed that off too.

"Can you fast forward?" he requested. "Ariana, look for J.R.'s car."

A minute later, Ariana tapped a finger to one of the displays. "There. That looks like J.R.'s car."

"What time was your shift today?"

"Nine to three. But one of the girls in my department was running late. I didn't leave until almost three-twenty.

"Your shift typically end on the hour?"

"Usually, unless I'm helping a customer."

J.R.'s car lapped the lot several times, then disappeared. A few minutes later Ariana came out.

No sign of J.R., but John tried to think like J.R. might. He checked the time. "He might have been guessing about when you would be off. Decided you're working 'til four. He might show up in a few minutes. Let's get out there and see if he comes back."

"Are you serious?"

"Heck, yeah. We need to be out there before he sees I already put air in your tires. Can we get a picture of that car?"

He thanked the security guy and added the printout to the stack before leaving with Ariana. "Wait by the exit. Let me do a surveillance pass. I'll let you know when it's safe to come out."

"If he's out there, he's going to see you."

"Naw, I'm in camouflage."

Ariana rolled her eyes at him.

John headed down to Lawn and Garden and exited there, peeking through the shrubs before dodging between vehicles to his truck. He backed out and made a pass through the parking lot, then chose a discreet space where he had a clear line of sight to Ariana's car.

He parked then called Ariana.

"Come out alone this time and walk slowly to your car. Reenact checking your tires and getting on your phone."

Ariana barely got to her car before John picked out J.R.'s sedan as it edged out of a parking space by the office

supply store down the strip. *Nailed it.* Now it was time to nail this asshole.

J.R.'s car stopped when it rolled up on Ariana. John exited his truck and kept out of sight as he snuck nearer. He couldn't make out all J.R. said to her through the open window, but something about dinner and talking.

"Really? That's why you're here?" Ariana didn't move closer.

"What's wrong, baby?"

John crossed the lane in a few long strides while J.R. was focused on Ariana. He slapped the roof of J.R.'s car.

J.R. jumped in his seat. "What the hell, man?"

"You coming by to play hero? Too late. I already put air back in her tires."

"I don't know what you're talkin' about." J.R.'s gaze darted away.

"No?" John flashed the first print out in J.R.'s face. "This is the guy who let the air out of two of her tires. And this is a picture of you cruising through the parking lot about the time she was supposed to be coming out. Coincidence? I don't think so."

"That wasn't me. I just got off work. I've been there all day."

"I know it wasn't you—and I hope to hell you are smart enough to have an alibi. However, this is the car he got into. When we run the plate, is the car going to come back registered to one of your friends?" He waved the paper so J.R. couldn't get a clear look. "Cut your losses. Admit what you've done and throw yourself on the mercy of the court, rather than dig yourself a hole you can't get out of. Capiche?"

"It's not your business, man."

"That bruise on her face made it my business."

"J.R., we're over," Ariana spoke up. "He's right. You need to get yourself together before hanging out with your druggie friends lands you in prison."

"You're the one trying to put me in prison," he snarled.

"Dude, that was all you." John pointed a finger at J.R. "If anything else happens to her, or her car, or her friends, you're gonna wish you'd walked away. Get out of here, but remember, we've got evidence you were here."

J.R. peeled out, nearly running over John's boot.

"Good job," John commended Ariana.

"I didn't do anything. It's all you. Thank you."

"You okay to drive home? I'll be right behind you."

"I am now. Thank you for taking care of my tires. I may have overreacted."

"Naw, you did the right thing." Though he hoped she didn't mistake his intervention for romantic interest.

"Let me text Elizabeth. I asked if she thought I should call the police, and she hasn't texted back. I want to let her know everything is okay."

It only took her a few seconds to type a message with both thumbs. John jogged to his truck and pulled out behind Ariana's car. He needed to talk to Elizabeth too.

Chapter Twenty-Five

ELIZABETH READ the second text from Ariana again. What did *John handled it* mean? Like her father might have handled it, with violence? This protection plan would totally backfire if John ended up arrested instead of J.R.

She pulled up her contacts. Her phone rang and displayed John's name before she found his number. "I got a text from Ariana and was just about to call you. Is she okay?"

"A little shook up. Physically, she's fine."

"What happened?"

"Someone let the air out of two of her tires."

"J.R."

"It wasn't *him*. We saw video footage of the guy, but I'm sure he's behind it. He cruised through the lot about the time she was supposed to get off work and then again

an hour later. We had a little chat. He didn't get to say much."

"You didn't do anything, did you?"

"Just instilled a healthy dose of fear. I think he wanted to swoop in and act like a hero. Instead, she's told him they're through. I'm going to put my dash cam in her car, just in case we need evidence if someone tries something else. I don't think they will, but J.R. and his friends don't seem to be the brightest characters. You should invite me to the Friday night dinner, just to be safe."

While he sounded completely serious, Elizabeth pictured John's face with that slow, sexy grin. "We'd love to have you join us at the dinner," she conceded. "Ariana's in charge of the menu. Ask her what she wants you to bring." And if Elizabeth had a lasagna in the freezer, he'd get that for dinner tonight. He'd earned it.

"I'll ask her. Oh, and Ariana did the right thing calling me, but I don't want her getting the wrong idea. I'm just doing my job."

If Ariana was over J.R., Elizabeth could see her crushing on John. While he was at least ten years older, that didn't rule out anything. Adam had been eighteen years older than Elizabeth. He'd seemed like her hero then too—nice looking, with a stable job and financial security. He'd showered her with attention and gifts. He hadn't shown his true colors when they were dating, or maybe she had blinders on then. She'd learned her lesson about men putting on a good front to get what they wanted and feeling entitled to continue to take it—even when you said no.

Would she ever shake Adam's hold on her? Even after all these years, he still had control over her and repressed her joy. Hopefully, Ariana could escape without the same invisible scars.

♪

John gave his reflection in the rearview mirror a naughty grin. Getting an invite to the dinner had become a personal challenge. There was something fun about teasing Elizabeth. She wasn't like any of the women he'd known, much less dated. That was probably a good thing. Her beauty wasn't the showy, everybody-notice-me kind. From what he'd observed, she shied away from drawing attention to herself. While he liked feeling needed, there was also something about an easy-going, independent, low-maintenance woman like Elizabeth that matched his lifestyle.

He quit daydreaming and kept an eye out, not that he expected J.R. or the sedan from the video to try and tail Ariana home. Her tires seemed to be holding air just fine.

Once they were parked back at The Oasis, he asked for her keys. "I'm going to put my dash camera in your car." Ariana dropped the keys into his outstretched hand.

"Thank you, again." Her eyes got a little misty.

"No problem. Looks like Elizabeth is coming to check on you. Why don't you talk with her, and I'll show you how it works when you get back." He let Boss out to do his business while Ariana headed to meet up with Elizabeth.

Boss played while John dismounted the security camera. After he installed it in Ariana's car, he did a last check on her tires. All good there. He carried the air pump around to check Wren's tires, which he had noted looked low.

From inside Haven House, Coco started barking the moment he came around the corner. Wren popped out a minute later. "What are you doing?"

"I'm checking the pressure. Your tires are bald. They won't pass inspection."

"You're not telling me anything I don't know. I also need an oil change and to pay insurance and get my meds and buy some groceries and food for Coco."

Properly maintained vehicles were key when John and his team were on a mission. Their lives depended on it. Wren's wasn't safe simply driving down the road, much less in wet conditions. However, Wren was a prime example of *if it weren't for bad luck, she'd have no luck at all.* Every day, she was livin' on a prayer.

Her car door wasn't locked, not that anyone would want to steal it. He popped the hood. "Please get me a paper towel or rag," he requested while she stood there watching.

Wren went inside, then came back and handed him a paper towel. He wiped the oil stick clean, then dipped it back in the reservoir. "How long has the check oil light been on?"

"I don't remember. A while."

"Like two weeks a while or two months?"

"Longer."

He inspected the smear of black oil on the stick. "You're on the verge of destroying your engine, which will cost a fortune to fix or replace."

"I had to refill my meds. I'll get a jug to add after I get paid next week."

"Pick up three quarts of motor oil and an oil filter, and I'll change it for you. I won't charge for the labor. We'll take it out in trade." Her eyebrows dipped as she eyed him. "You give Boss his next bath, and we'll call it even." He'd thought about asking Ariana, only she was too scared of the big lug.

"How much will that all cost?"

"Less than thirty bucks."

"Any way you can spot me that until next week? I was supposed to go out with my friends tomorrow night."

He shook his head instead. "It's your decision. Go out with your friends, or get your car taken care of. I can do it Saturday, but I'm tied up next weekend."

She huffed a sigh. "What kind of oil?"

"Might want to write it down or make a note in your phone," he suggested before reading it off the reservoir cap. When she took the oil-stained paper towel inside, he checked the size of her tires.

He was tossing a tennis ball for Boss when Ariana and Elizabeth strolled up from the wooded path. Ariana's eyes were red and puffy, but a more peaceful countenance showed in her tentative smile. She even stroked Boss's neck when he went to stand in front of Elizabeth and tried to give her an intimate nuzzle. Couldn't blame the dog for trying. Funny that Boss only did that with Elizabeth.

"Let me show you how the camera operates." After tossing the tennis ball as far as he could to send Boss off in chase, he led Ariana around Hope Harbor to her vehicle. He fished her keys from his pocket and had her climb in.

"I can't reach the pedals," she fussed, sliding the driver's seat forward.

"Sorry. I had to get out." Which wasn't happening if he'd returned it to her driving position. He moved the passenger seat all the way back before climbing in next to her and giving her a complete run-through on how to operate the camera and flip it in the event she was followed.

"Now, if anyone messes with your car, we'll have evidence to give the cops," he said and got out of the car.

Ariana thanked him and went inside.

John's attention shifted to Elizabeth as Boss trotted back with the ball that she'd been tossing to keep him occupied. She caught John staring. "I'll bring you dinner in about thirty minutes," she said as she walked his way.

"You serious?"

She nodded. "Unless you have other plans. I still owe you from paying for dinner at Mi Casita."

"Nope. I didn't get to pick anything up after work, then came straight here with Ariana. You're not uninviting me to the Friday night dinner, are you?"

"No. I had a pan of lasagna in the freezer, and I really appreciate you leaving work to help Ariana out."

"No problem. We were close to wrapping up for the day."

"Still, not many men would drop everything to help a friend."

"Really, it wasn't a big deal. It's not like you're asking me to stake out a Taliban stronghold for a week." That had turned into two weeks: surviving on two MREs a day and knowing that if one of the forty Taliban fighters found his team, they'd love nothing more than to slice off their heads. That wasn't even their most dangerous mission.

"I hope you were someplace safe."

"Darlin', no place is safe over there. It's relative. First time you get mortared, you're diving under bunks or behind sandbags. But you get desensitized to it. Still, you never let your guard down. That's when bad shit happens."

Her eyes widened. "I can imagine."

No, she really couldn't, which was the way it should be. "Sorry to bring the mood down. You don't need to hear all that. Let me get Boss fed so he doesn't try and steal my lasagna."

He usually didn't talk about deployments. Some women got turned on by the danger aspect, others got turned off—for multiple reasons. Elizabeth, however, regarded him for a few seconds as if psychoanalyzing him. There was defi- nitely something appealing about her. He watched the

subtle movement of her hips as she walked gracefully away.

The woman had class, and a great ass, and fantastic legs.

He wished he knew who had hurt her to make her fearful and so closed off that she wouldn't date. He'd like to get his hands on that guy's neck even more than J.R. or the tribal leader assholes who thought it was okay to kidnap young women and force them to be wives—more like sex slaves—to their fighters. His team had rescued some girls, but it would happen again. Sadly, it was a tale as old as time. Virgin girls considered as spoils of war.

His stomach roiled with anger more than hunger. He needed to compartmentalize for now. He went inside and changed out of his uniform and into shorts and a T-shirt and flops, trying to get out of a mission mindset. Their last mission had been turned over to Charlie Company for the next six months. Constant turnover made it hard to gain inroads with the locals, but longer deployments over and over took a toll on his men and their lives. He wasn't the only one to come home and find his girl with someone else. Someone who wouldn't disappear for six months, be home a year, then bounce out for another six months. It was why the position with SOCOM appealed to him, though he would miss his team. And life as an operator. But life involved trade-offs.

In the bathroom, he scrubbed the grime from his hands and combed his hair. He'd shaved his beard before coming home from Africa, planning to show up in his dress uniform at Britney's big event. Since guys in Special Forces didn't have to adhere to normal Army regulations about facial hair and length, his hair was long enough for a woman to run her fingers through. The way Britney had liked it.

She turned out to be another love lesson in what not to do. Don't settle for being the rebound guy. She was

educated, with a good job, and came from money. He hadn't realized how much she'd been like his birth mother. Right down to thinking she was too good for him.

Elizabeth didn't act like that. She appreciated the things he did.

He checked the time. With over twenty minutes before dinner would be ready, it gave him time to peruse another chapter in the *Five Love Languages* book. Maybe he should reread the chapter on acts of service to try and come up with a birthday gift idea. Yeah, like that was his main purpose in wanting to know more about Elizabeth. Something about her shy smiles, the way she blushed when Boss got too friendly, and the sound of her laughing with—not at—him, made him want to get to know her better. Peek behind the wall she had up.

Not quite through the chapter on quality time, he decided to finish it. An idea brewed. Maybe he could experiment to see which was Elizabeth's love language.

He breathed into a cupped hand. Not horrible, but he went and brushed his teeth anyway. Not that he'd get close enough to Elizabeth for her to smell his breath. Done with his dinner, Boss cocked his head and watched him.

"How do I look, boy? Presentable?"

Maybe too casual. He rethought the shorts, but, hell, he had muscular legs. They were tan from wearing shorts during downtime at their combat outpost. He was going as is.

"No, boy. You need to stay," John left Boss to pout.

Time to experiment.

Chapter Twenty-Six

FIGHTER – Keith Urban & Carrie Underwood

ELIZABETH RETURNED the lasagna to the oven after adding the top layer of cheese. She opened a bottle of wine and poured herself a glass. As she covered one of the salads with plastic wrap, John knocked on the front door.

He stood on the porch without Boss. "The lasagna won't be ready for a few minutes. I was going to bring it over to you."

"Thought I'd save you a trip and see if I can help with anything. Fix some salad or garlic bread. Open a bottle of wine for you."

"Done, done, and done," It was thoughtful of him, though. "Would you like a glass of wine?"

"If it's not against the rules." He winked at her.

She felt her face flush. "No. It's fine."

John wasn't like any of her prior tenants—at all—but she hadn't wanted to risk him coming home with a case of beer

and anything happening that would make her tenants uncomfortable or require her to kick him out.

He opened the screen door before she could offer to bring his glass to him on the porch. Panic washed over her, but she let it pass, trusting he didn't have sinister intentions. It was merely her issues causing her to overreact.

"Man, it smells good in here."

She got out a wine glass as he admired the view out the kitchen's bay window.

"This is the life. I kinda hate that I'm going to move back into my neighborhood without all this free space and nature. I'm getting spoiled here. Other than the tight quarters."

"It's not for everyone. Wren doesn't like that it's so remote. But you can't have tiny houses in most neighborhoods."

"I read how some cities are building tiny home communities for homeless vets. They offer resources to get them jobs and mental health services. A lot like what you do—except for vets. Not a place where these ladies would feel comfortable though. Have you ever had residents with kids?"

"I tried that at first. It was hard. Not only the location for getting them to school or daycare, but I'd get attached to the children."

"And eventually they'd leave."

"Exactly." Opening the wound of not having kids of her own. She'd thought of adopting. Instead, she'd somehow ended up with a rescue dog and then The Oasis. The oven timer went off before she got too emotional.

John stood out of the way as she took the lasagna out, the cheese melted to the perfect golden hue.

He grabbed napkins from the metal holder on the counter and set two on the kitchen table. "Forks?"

"You're eating here?"

"If that's okay with you. Boss already ate, and he's not the best conversationalist. Sometimes I don't have any idea what he's saying." John flashed that endearing grin.

She couldn't help but laugh. He had a way of making her feel relaxed. It felt good, like who she'd been years ago, before Adam.

"Sure," she said. It'd be rude to wrap up a plate and send him on his way now. She scooped a piece of lasagna onto her plate. "I wish I could tell if J.R. wants Ariana back or just not to testify."

"That's what I was wondering. And since today's plan backfired, he could escalate. I want the punk punished for hurting Ariana, but she doesn't have any long-term injuries—not physically anyway. If she's definitely over him, maybe it's better to call a truce rather than give him reasons to continue coming after her and to eff with her head."

"I've been thinking about what's best long term too. According to Jillian, if Ariana dropped the charges, it'd still go on his record, but he wouldn't do time. Her attorney could request a restraining order." She served up a double serving of lasagna on the second plate.

"Do you have a preferred seat?" John asked when she handed him his plate.

"I usually sit facing the window, but it doesn't matter." She discreetly took the plastic wrap off John's salad bowl while he wasn't looking, then set both on the table.

"More wine?" He picked up the bottle and held it over her glass.

"That'd be good." Typically, she only drank one glass, but a second might help her relax enough to get through

154

dinner with John. Three lowered her inhibitions too much. Who knew what she'd say? She didn't need to lead John on.

John took a bite of lasagna, closed his eyes, and made happy noises. "I can see why they rave about your lasagna. This is delicious." He took another large bite. "Does Ariana have any family she could stay with? Someplace far from J.R.?"

"Unfortunately, no. She and her younger sister were in foster care, then aged out. It's a tough transition, and it made her vulnerable, which can be what guys like J.R. look for. Make the woman dependent on them. Even compliant."

"I figured she may not have family, with her being here, but . . ." John's mouth pursed. "Do you think she'll be okay?"

"I think so. She's smart and mentally strong. She got out of that relationship before things got too bad. She hadn't been trafficked or fallen into a pattern of one bad relationship after another. Long term, any kind of abuse can wreck a person's self-confidence and keep them trapped. Sometimes, living with different men to keep from being homeless."

John's solemn expression deepened. "What about Wren? She mentioned having a daughter. She can't help her?"

"Wren has a daughter and son. Neither would take her in after she finally left her second husband. He helped raise the kids, so divided loyalty came into play. She's estranged from her mother and wouldn't ask her for help. A lot of the women who've stayed here have families, but relations are usually strained. Each woman's story is different. Stories that aren't pretty and they're usually complicated." At least the side she heard.

"The two women at the VFW last week lived here the same time as Wren?"

"Yes. They all got along, but with their age and personality differences, living together wouldn't be ideal."

He nodded. "What's it going to take for Wren to move out?" He took another bite of lasagna.

"I'm not sure," she admitted. "Maybe getting a better offer? She has friends she goes out with, but she hasn't mentioned moving in with any of them. She's not crazy about my restrictions and thinks I don't know she smokes outside the house. My intention was for this to be short term—a better option than a woman's shelter to help them get a fresh start, but I don't have a time limit in the contract. With tiny homes, I've never needed one before."

John laughed. "I get that. If she does want a place, I can keep an ear out for anyone looking to sublet when they deploy. She'd have to understand there's a time limit though. When my first sergeant was based in Hawaii, he came back from a deployment and couldn't get the people out. He ended up bunking on a friend's couch for months. He still tells the story about those squatters. They trashed his place before they finally moved out too."

"That's awful. I can't believe someone would do that to someone serving our country."

"That's not the worst I've heard. Houses robbed, credit card fraud, infidelity." He raised his eyebrows. "At least I wasn't married, or even engaged. And I'm here—and hoping it's okay if I get more lasagna."

"Of course."

John stood before she could get up to serve him. It was nice to have a man appreciate her cooking, and, considering all he'd been through and done for her and Ariana, at least she could offer him that.

"Would you like more?" he asked before serving himself.

"I'm good. You can finish it off." What she wanted was more of this. Enjoying a meal with a man who made her feel things she hadn't felt in a decade.

"Come on. Just a little bit more so I don't feel like a mooch." He approached with the foil pan and spatula.

"Like a quarter of that is plenty."

He served her. "Soak the pan or toss it?"

"Toss it." She waited until he sat again to take the conversation in a new direction. "Did you have a dog growing up?"

"No. My grandparents had a cat. My dad had his hands full with me, so we never had pets. I wasn't looking to get a dog because, in my line of work, it's not real practical. When Boss showed up though . . ." He shook his head. "I was in the Georgia mountains with my buddy, Nate, decompressing after a deployment. Boss wasn't afraid of people, but he hadn't been fed in a while. I don't know if he was abandoned or lost. He wasn't chipped. I brought him home at the end of our week, thinking that any day someone would see the posters I put up and call to claim him. Lucky for me, no one called. What about you? Did you have pets growing up?"

Now it made sense why he had Boss, despite having to leave him behind on deployments. It supported her assumption about John not wanting Boss to feel abandoned again.

"No. My dad claimed to be allergic. He said if we had a dog it'd have to be an outside dog, and we never had a yard for it. We had goldfish for a year or two."

"Not the same, is it? Though you don't have to bathe them. I'm guessing Boss wasn't your first dog."

"No. My first, Ginger, was a rescue. Well, I tried to

rescue her. I wasn't working and thought a dog would be good company, but my ex wasn't a fan. And he won." As Adam always did. He hadn't liked competing for her attention.

"What do you mean, 'he won'?" John asked in a low, ominous manner that made her swallow before answering.

"I took Ginger back to the no-kill shelter out of fear of what Adam might do to her." Based on the way John looked at her, Elizabeth wasn't sure if he was judging her for returning Ginger to the shelter or considering the possibility Britney took Boss there to protect him from her boyfriend. "Right after I bought this house and property, I adopted Barkley and had him for eight years."

He nodded, finished off his lasagna, and carried their plates to the sink. "Act of defiance?"

"More like independence." She got up to do the dishes. "I loved the freedom to do what I wanted."

John began rinsing plates.

"You don't have to do that."

"Rule at my house was the cook didn't have to clean up. I got this."

"Okay." That was unexpected. Adam had never done dishes or served her food. Did John do something nice because he expected something in return? She stepped away and put a stopper in the wine bottle.

After loading the dishwasher, John wiped down the counter and table. He even rinsed the cloth and spread it to dry. "Thank you for the wonderful dinner and conversation."

"Thank you for coming to Ariana's rescue."

"Gotta earn my keep. Feel free to invite me over anytime you have extra food and want someone else to do KP duty."

"Good night." She didn't make any promises. Even though he hadn't made reference to tonight being a date, it was better to keep things friendly, not romantic. Once John moved out of The Oasis, she'd be out of his sights and off his mind as he went on with his life. A life that didn't include a woman with a past that left her too scarred and scared to love again.

Chapter Twenty-Seven

HUNGRY LIKE THE WOLF – Duran Duran

After freshening her face, Elizabeth stood in her closet, debating what to wear. They typically dressed up for the Friday night dinners, but she hadn't mentioned that to John. Maybe she should wear something casual so he'd feel comfortable since Ariana had gone with a low-key Mexican food menu. Only this dinner wasn't about him. It was about the women. Better not to change things up on them.

She changed into a simple purple dress with a sweetheart neckline, a silver bangle bracelet to go with her necklace, and low, strappy nude heels, then gave herself a once over in the full-length mirror. There was something empowering about knowing she looked her best, especially when it was her decision, not going all out because Adam, or any man, wanted to show her off to make himself look good.

Shaking off the memories, she went to the dining room

and set the china, crystal, and silver chest on the table, along with cloth placemats and napkins. Before she could head into the kitchen, a knock sounded on the frame of the screen door. It had to be John.

"Come in," she called. "You're early."

When dressed in his usual jeans and T-shirt or uniform, John exuded a rugged sexiness. Tonight, he wore dress slacks and a crisp, white button down that accentuated his muscular build in a way that nearly made her sigh aloud.

He carried in two plastic grocery bags. "You said seven o'clock. And it's six fifty-seven. That's late, according to Army time."

"I guess you're right." She was used to Wren and others showing up fashionably late. "You look very nice."

"Wren said it was business attire. I figured that didn't mean my business attire of camouflage and weapons, though. I was afraid she was punking me, but based on the way you look, I'm underdressed. I can go put on a tie."

She laughed at his pained expression when he said tie and hoped she didn't blush noticeably at the way his gaze roved over her. "You're fine." It'd be a shame to button up and cover the swath of tanned chest currently showing. "The dinner is an opportunity to get made up and feel like it's a special occasion. I should have mentioned that, though it doesn't really apply to you."

"I don't mind following orders. I need to put the ice cream in the freezer. Can I do anything to help?"

"I usually have the first timer set the table. Everything is already out."

He followed her to the kitchen. She put away the ice cream while he unloaded the other bag. "Those brownies smell delicious." She inhaled the chocolatey aroma.

"They're still warm if you want to sneak one." He pulled jars of chocolate and caramel syrup and a can of whipped cream from the bag, then went to the dining room. "Whoa, fancy." He picked up the placemats and set one in front of each chair.

"These dinners are a way of showing the women they're worthy of breaking out the good stuff."

"I see." He opened the silver chest and took out four place settings. "Was this your wedding china and silver?"

"Uh, no. I got married by a Justice of the Peace. No wedding or registry or gifts." No fancy white dress. No guests to witness the biggest mistake of her life.

"Sorry. Thought the monogrammed C on the silver was for your last name."

"Carroll was not my married name, which I changed after the divorce."

"Back to your maiden name?"

"Actually, I didn't want to be associated with that part of my past either. So, I picked a name." New name. New Elizabeth.

"You can do that?"

"You can." Her parents had been shocked, and her dad had acted all offended, but it was his doing.

"Why'd you pick Carroll?"

What were the chances Wren or Ariana would show up right now to save her from having to answer? No rescuing knock or entry.

"It's complicated, but there was a woman who helped me come up with a plan to help me leave my husband. Her name was Loula Carroll."

"You couldn't just leave?"

"It wasn't that easy. Like a lot of the women here, I was in a bad situation with no resources and nowhere to go."

162

"I understand why you didn't want to go to your parents, but what about alimony or a settlement?"

"Adam took a big financial hit when he divorced his first wife, so he had me sign a prenup. I had no job, no income, and no access to savings or credit cards. When I first left home, I had run up credit card debt and got behind on payments. He used that as an excuse not to add me to his credit cards—or his bank accounts."

"That's nuts. You were his wife. How did he expect you to pay for things like clothes and groceries?" John clearly recognized that wasn't how things should be in a marriage.

"If I needed things, he'd take me shopping." And buy her the clothes he wanted her to wear. "He gave me cash to buy groceries or go to lunch, but I had to give him the receipts. He said it was to enter the amounts for our budget, but he'd question expenses."

"Was he a control freak?"

"It was about keeping *me* under his control. He didn't want me taking college classes or working. Said he was going to take care of me." She had wanted to get an education, though she'd hoped to stay home once they had children.

"Was he older than you?"

"Eighteen years older."

"Was he afraid you'd meet someone in class, or if you got a job, and leave him?" The way John said it sounded as though he was trying to figure out Adam's thinking rather in defense of the way he'd treated her.

"That could be *part* of why he isolated me. Though, as an only child, Adam never learned to share and thought the world revolved around him and his wants."

"We're here." Thankfully, Ariana breezed in carrying a glass baking dish with potholders, saving Elizabeth from

sharing more of her past. "Sorry I'm late. I made a double batch of the enchiladas since John was coming, and it took longer than I thought."

Wren followed with a drink pitcher in one hand and a small baking dish in the other.

"What's in the pitcher?" John asked.

"Sangria," Wren sang the word. "Friday night dinners are an exception to the no alcohol rule. Does everyone want some?" She set the dish with refried beans on the table, then filled her glass.

"Please." Though part of the purpose was to encourage drinking in moderation, Elizabeth could already use a glass. "I'll get the rice and salad."

John waited for her to sit before taking his seat next to her.

"Is it okay if we bless the food?" Ariana asked.

"You're the hostess," Elizabeth answered.

"Okay." Ariana swallowed and extended her hands to John and Wren.

John's hand covered Elizabeth's with a light grip. Not quite intimate but not in a controlling manner either. They bowed their heads while Ariana gave thanks. John's thumb rubbed over Elizabeth's knuckles when Ariana mentioned The Oasis and bringing John there at the right time. It wasn't until she finished and John gave a sign-off squeeze that Elizabeth realized her fingers had curled around his. When he released her hand, she chanced raising her gaze. The warm smile on his handsome face sent a forgotten kind of heat through her.

She took a generous drink of the sangria while they filled their plates.

"This looks and smells amazing," John took a bite. "Mmm. Delicious."

"Thank you," Ariana beamed. "I was afraid I'd forget, so I, um, wrote some questions down on a notecard. I hope that's okay."

"Perfectly acceptable," Elizabeth encouraged her.

"Smart," Wren chimed in. "My first time, I had a couple of conversation questions in mind, and I completely forgot them."

John's brows scrunched and his gaze shifted. He wasn't clued in on the purpose of conversation prompts during Friday night dinners, but he'd insisted on coming. His participation would likely put an interesting spin on things.

"I thought it'd be fun to start with everyone sharing what was the first concert you ever attended? I saw Selena Gomez with my friend, Haley. We both loved her and had posters of her up in our rooms."

"Afraid I don't know any of her songs to sing," John gave a shake of his head and took a bite of food.

"Thank goodness," Wren said. "Now I'm afraid to say that I saw Duran Duran with my boyfriend who even wore his hair long and feathered like Simon Le Bon."

"They were a great band," John nodded his approval. "Better than the boy bands that followed. They even did the single for the James Bond movie. A view to a kill," he sang. "I think 'Hungry like the Wolf' was my favorite of their songs."

"I think you were born a decade too late," Wren said. "Probably. You can credit my eclectic tastes on listening to my grandmother's musicals and dad's country and rock songs from the eighties."

"And who was your first concert?" Ariana asked him.

"Joey and the Tims."

"Who?"

"Not The Who. You walked right into that one." John

165

laughed. "Though they were great too. My dad used to take me to this local restaurant that had live music. He knew one of the guys in the trio. Joey and two guys both named Tim. They were in their fifties and just loved performing. There was another guy, David Porter, who played guitar and sang there weekly. He'd put out song lists, and you could make requests. Most weeks, there was this group of women who'd bring their daughters after dance class and without fail they'd ask for 'Sweet Home Alabama,' 'Yellow Submarine,' and 'Friends in Low Places.' Didn't know that was going to be my life story."

"Except no whiskey flows at this Oasis." Wren took a drink of her sangria.

"'It's whiskey drowns,' but you ladies do help chase my blues away. I have to say that the best concert I ever went to was Bruce Springsteen. Both times I've seen him. I also got to see Toby Keith and Rodney Atkins when they did tours with the USO in Afghanistan. Got my picture taken with Rodney. That was pretty cool."

"I bet so," Elizabeth said.

"You look a lot like Rodney in his early videos." Wren shook a finger in his direction.

"Except I'm taller, and he's richer."

"And he can carry a tune."

"Well, I'm happy being an American soldier," he sang.

"What about you, Elizabeth?"

"The first concert I remember going to was Kenny Chesney with my boyfriend who loved country music. I think I recognized two of the songs. The first concert I picked was the Backstreet Boys."

"Really? I had you pegged as a New Kids on the Block groupie," John eyed her.

"No, the Wahlberg brothers didn't do it for me. I was totally in love with Kevin Richardson." That felt like a lifetime ago. "That was a great question, Ariana."

"What is the most interesting or beautiful place you've ever visited?" Ariana asked as Wren poured sangria.

"Refill?" Wren held the pitcher over Elizabeth's glass.

She nodded, debating whether to answer truthfully or make something up. John went first, telling them about the animal safari he and his team had done.

"You were in Chad? I didn't know we had any troops there," Elizabeth said, buying herself a little more time.

"*Shhh.* Can't really talk about it." John held a finger to his lips, giving a coy smile. "What about you?"

"Maui."

"I'm jealous. Hawaii is on my bucket list," Wren said. "Was it totally beautiful?"

"It was. I'd never seen anything like the clear blue water and palm trees."

Ariana sighed. "Who did you go with?"

"I'd just started dating my ex when he earned an incentive trip for being top in sales. It was all expenses paid for two people. I was twenty years old, and, other than the occasional trip to Atlantic City with my family, had never really traveled. It was an opportunity I couldn't pass up."

"Work trips with my ex meant stays in cheap hotels." Wren rolled her eyes. "Usually, we were at remote places where the fanciest restaurant to spend our food per diem was something like Polly's Diner. I'd love to have gotten to sit on the beach sipping fruity drinks instead,"

"It was definitely a taste of life like I'd never experienced," Elizabeth admitted. "The company hosted a sunset dinner cruise. Dolphins swam alongside the yacht as we

went out. Another night they had a private luau. For one of the day trip options, we sailed out to a coral reef where we snorkeled with fish and sea turtles. It was all pretty perfect."

Even with Adam. Which was why she had accepted when he impulsively proposed. That perfection sure had not lasted. "What about you, Wren?" Elizabeth picked up her glass of sangria and shifted the focus as memories escaped.

"I got to see the Black Hills and Mount Rushmore. That was cool, but it's not tropical paradise. Maybe someday my prince will come."

Elizabeth shivered involuntarily. This wasn't the time to explain about Adam not being her Prince Charming—or even close. She forced herself to focus on every word of Ariana's details of a trip to Puerto Rico to shut out the memories.

"You mentioned your bucket list, what's something on everyone's bucket list?" Ariana transitioned.

"Mine is Hawaii, or any place with a beach and palm trees and drinks." Wren lifted her glass like a toast.

"I want to get married and have kids," John said without a hint of joking, affirming what he'd said the night they'd gone to Mi Casita.

Wren laughed. "That's not a bucket list item."

"It's something I want to do before I die. Bucket list." He held up his hands, one still holding a fork.

"That's just life. Bucket list are things like trips and experiences," Wren insisted.

"Okay, I want to come home from a deployment and have my wife and kids there to meet me." He threw out a challenging stare.

"Can't argue with that," Elizabeth interceded. "I want to see the Northern Lights." She forced cheerfulness into

her voice, despite the ache in her soul, pulsing painfully at John declaring exactly the things she'd once wanted most in life. She drained the last of her sangria, trying to avoid his lingering stare.

Chapter Twenty-Eight

BROKEN WING – Martina McBride

AFTER ONE MORE OF Ariana's dinner conversation questions, everyone had empty plates.

John stood. "You ladies stay put. I'm bringing dessert." He stacked their dinner plates and carried them into the kitchen.

He rinsed the plates and loaded them in the dishwasher before cutting up the brownies and topping them with ice cream. Dinner had been eye-opening. Everything Elizabeth did for the women had a purpose.

He'd gotten part of her story, but Wren and Ariana showed up before he'd gotten full disclosure. Certain things made more sense now. In addition to a physically abusive father, her husband was emotionally abusive—or more, considering she had to escape from him.

The questions and dinner conversation kept him from dwelling on what she'd been through. With the way Wren

kept pouring the sangria, Elizabeth was chattier than usual. After dessert might be a good time to see if she'd tell him the rest. It was a good thing her asshole ex was out of her life and not showing up like J.R. now that John knew how he'd treated Elizabeth.

He compartmentalized again and served up dessert with a smile. Ariana's question about talking with an accent had everyone laughing as they ate and polished off the sangria. He, naturally, had the good ole Southern boy accent down but could pull off a decent Bostonian accent and kept up with the Boston Red Sox enough to fool most people. He showed off a little, proving his ability to speak French and Arabic. Elizabeth admitted to turning up her Southern accent and faking an Australian accent to get better tips back in the days when she worked at an upscale restaurant. It surprised him, but he could see how it'd worked since she'd sounded down-right sexy speaking with both.

Once dessert wrapped up, John carried the bowls into the kitchen. He stayed behind scrubbing the serving dishes when Wren and Ariana headed out. "You didn't finish telling your story. Did this Carroll woman inspire what you do now by offering you a place to stay?"

"No. Loula was the front-end manager at the grocery store I went to. See, I was doing anything I could do to earn enough cash to pay for an attorney and a place to live. I started buying expensive bottles of wine at the grocery each week. After Adam logged in the receipt, I'd return the wine for cash, buy cheap wine, and refill an empty bottle I'd kept."

"That's inventive."

"Well, Loula noticed that I returned the same brand of wine more than once. I thought she was going to block my

account or something, but she asked questions and picked up on what was going on. She invited me to lunch and got the brunt of me unloading. I hadn't told anyone how bad things were with Adam."

The wine had loosened Elizabeth's tongue.

"She told me about legal aid lawyers who take cases at affordable rates. I had no idea that kind of help was available, and I hit the jackpot with a lawyer, Denice, who had a passion for helping women and children. I just wanted out, but Denice was adamant that I was due some type of settlement, despite the prenup. The settlement we eventually negotiated was enough to cover tuition and living expenses for me to get my degree."

"Good for her. And you. Did you know you wanted to be a counselor?" He tried not to imagine what shit her ex had done to negate the prenup.

"Not initially. I was thinking of becoming a nurse. I could help people and always find a job wherever I decided to live, but when I was taking my second psychology class, I had one of those *ah-ha* moments about how I'd left my abusive father, only to end up in a different abusive relationship. Being a counselor had different benefits."

"Like not dealing with puke and crap." Not that she'd ever complained about caring for Boss.

"There's that, and less physical contact. And being my own boss."

"Was it hard going back to school, being older than the other students?" He put a large brownie on a plate for her for later.

"There wasn't a huge age gap, though my life experiences made me feel a lot older."

"I know what you mean. I was only four years older, but I'd been in combat. I was not going to live in a dorm with a

bunch of kids. Some guys tried to get me to join their fraternity. I already had brothers I could trust to have my back. I just wanted to get through school and back in as an officer, so I kind of missed out on the college life experience. What about you? Did you party or date much?" He was fishing, but maybe she wouldn't pick up on that.

"I dated a little my first year. But like you, I pretty much stuck to classes."

"Were the guys too immature for you?"

"Most were. I went out with a senior a few times, but he was kind of the typical frat guy only interested in drinking, partying, and . . . Anyway, that didn't go anywhere."

"Anyone else?" Might as well keep asking while her inhibitions were lowered. He'd already told her his dating history, and wanted—no, needed—to know more about her.

"A grad student in my psych program. I thought he'd be different."

"What do you mean?"

"I'd rather not talk about it." She closed up the dishwasher. "I think tonight went well. I thought adding you to the mix might be too soon for Ariana, but she did great, and you were fun."

She softened her redirect with a compliment and a smile that did things to his ego and his body. "I think Ariana sees me as an overprotective big brother." That was what he kept reinforcing with her. "Sorry for pushing for you to invite me when you weren't planning to. I didn't really get what you were doing. Showing them they have value. Boosting their confidence and teaching them about entertaining, not just chowing down. You're a good woman with a big heart."

"I do what I can and encourage them to get counseling."

"Why don't *you* counsel them?"

173

"Ethical issues could arise with them living here and paying rent. I could be sued or lose my license to practice."

"I can't see anyone you've helped doing that."

"Even though I'm trying to help, it could happen if the relationship goes south. Even offering advice as a friend, I have to be careful, especially when it's not what they want to hear. You also can't be totally objective when it's family or friends." She dropped her gaze from his face and dipped her head.

"Guess that's what we get for asking."

"Not everyone takes it well. I've probably crossed the line with Wren—okay, I have—but she's been through a lot. Yet somehow, she's survived and not given up hope. Some of the ladies that leave, I never hear from again. Usually the short-timers."

"That could also be because they want to put the hard times behind them. Soldiers can be that way. Some you have a brother-like bond with for life. Others don't want the reminders of what they did or went through."

"I can understand that."

"It's hard, but you have to accept it and not take it personally."

He sure hoped The Oasis' former residents showed up for the surprise birthday party tomorrow, or it was going to be a bust.

Chapter Twenty-Nine

COUNT ON ME – Bruno Mars

JOHN WOKE Wren to get her keys and work on her car. Hopefully, she'd forgive him after a cup of coffee or two.

After he changed the oil, he covertly ducked around to his truck and hauled out two of the discarded tires he'd gotten from the shop at work. As he finished replacing the second tire, Coco bounded out of Haven House and sniffed around him. Wren emerged seconds later.

Her eyes widened. "What are you doing?" She paused between each word and her pitch dropped on the last word.

"Replacing your tires. These aren't new, but they've got a good bit of life in them. Should keep you on the road a year or longer."

"Really? How much do I owe you?" Worry lines creased her forehead.

"Nothing. My unit does a lot of defensive driving training. We change tires out early for safety. They get used for

barriers or just sit around. Figured this was a great use for them. I've got the other two in the back of my truck."

Tears welled up in Wren's eyes. "Thank you. I'll bathe Boss, trim his nails, brush his teeth. Whatever you need. And dinner. I'll make barbecue and slaw and potato salad and green beans and banana pudding. Do you like real bananas in it? Some people don't."

He chuckled as she rattled on. "However you make it is fine. I'm not picky when it comes to someone feeding me."

She sat on the step, watching him work and petting Coco.

"I'll let Boss out so they can play. Just keep them away from the car." The service jack he'd borrowed from the shop at work was stable, but Boss slamming into the car at full speed was not something to experiment with. He hefted an old tire in each hand, carried them to his truck, then let Boss out.

The dogs romped and chased each other. Wren stood a few feet away while he swapped out the back tires.

"What's all this?" Elizabeth appeared, holding a glass casserole dish while he wrestled off one of the rear tires.

"He's got some new—well, used—tires for my car. He's my hero." Wren's voice cracked a little.

"It's no big deal." He felt Elizabeth's gaze on him as he kept working. It's not like he was doing it to score points. He had the means and skills to help someone who hadn't had many breaks in life, so he did it.

"I forgot to give you the leftover enchiladas last night."

"Would you mind putting them in my fridge?"

"Sure. Did you still want to get the deck supplies today because I—"

"Yup. I'll pick you up around one."

"Okay then." Elizabeth went inside John's house.

FAKING IT WITH THE GREEN BERET

"She has no idea about the party," Wren whispered.

"Thank you for taking her with you—and for this. Is there a way we can keep you around longer?"

"You've got me around a couple more weeks until the trial. I won't disappear forever after that." Not if he could help it. He had another five months until he headed to Florida. He tightened the lug nuts with an eye on Elizabeth as she exited Hope Harbor and headed back home.

Every time he watched her go, it got harder to see her walk away.

Chapter Thirty

YOU GIVE LOVE A BAD NAME – Bon Jovi

WREN GAVE John a thumbs up when he came outside. "Make sure you keep her away for at least an hour, but we need you back by two-thirty. I know how men can be when shopping in a home improvement store."

"Yes, ma'am." He acknowledged the order rather than give her a hard time.

He stopped his truck in front of Elizabeth's house. She didn't come out right away, so after a minute he went to the front door. "Ready to go?" he asked when she appeared.

"Are you sure you need me?"

Crap. He could not fail at this mission. "You don't have to come. I might not pick out the railings you would, but I don't have to fight you over who's paying."

She grumbled a sigh. "I'll get my purse."

Who said reverse psychology didn't work on those with a degree in the field?

"It won't take long, and I do appreciate you coming with me," he said as he drove away from her property. "I want this to appeal to the ladies. I could use someone with an eye for design."

When they got to the store, he tasked her with looking at the railing options while he went to lumber for the decking.

"That looks like a lot of wood." She studied the cart when he joined her. "You know what you're doing, right?"

"It's best to get extra in case I make a bad cut. What did you decide?"

"I want your opinion." She showed him the two railings she'd picked.

"Both will work just fine. The composite is lower maintenance, and I think the white will look best with the white trim on Hope Harbor."

"I agree on the white, and I like low maintenance."

"It's decided then. Now, which post caps? I recommend ones with solar lights." He pulled out three white ones. Once she'd decided, he slipped in a reject with two of the ones she picked.

After loading the railings, he calculated how much time he needed to kill while selecting tools.

"I'm paying for the tools since I'll be using them in the future," he said when he caught Elizabeth eyeing prices on the circular and jig saws. "They'll get a lot of use when I move back in to fix up my place. Building the deck is practice."

He selected what he needed and reviewed the list of supplies Nate had sent him. Once he had everything, John pushed the cart to checkout. He got in line behind a woman whose cart was filled with pots and flats of flowers. Eliza-beth reached into her purse and palmed her credit card. He

put the two saws, the drill, and the hammer on the conveyor.

"Dang, I got one of the wrong post caps." He handed it to Elizabeth. "Can you run back and swap it out for the right one?"

She eyed him with a hint of suspicion before taking it and hustling off.

"Can you ring up the railing and lumber first?" he asked the cashier. After she scanned the first item, he stuck his credit card in the machine and signed his signature before Elizabeth returned. "Thanks." He added the cap post to the cart.

Elizabeth slid her credit card into the chip reader and stared at the screen.

"I rang up one of the caps twice, and he already paid," the middle-aged cashier said cheerfully.

Elizabeth gave him the stink-eye. "You did that on purpose. You said you were going to let me pay for the supplies."

"Actually, you said you were, but I never agreed to that. Man, I'm looking forward to more lasagna and other meals." He winked at her.

"Your boyfriend's a keeper." The cashier handed him the receipt but directed her comment to Elizabeth.

"He's not my boyfriend." Elizabeth said, awfully damn quickly.

Ouch. He didn't want to take it personally. After all, she didn't date. Still, it was like a shot right through the heart. It's like he gave love a bad name. At least he didn't sing that out loud.

"You need to let me cover the materials," she tried again. "It's less than what it cost you to feed my dog while I was deployed."

"I doubt that. Consider it doing my part to support the troops."

"And this is my way of supporting your mission," he deflected. "I admire what you do."

Their gazes remained locked—not in a showdown over who'd pay, but in a kind of mutual admiration until Eliza-beth finally swallowed. "Just when I thought you would take orders from a civilian."

"I get a ten percent military discount." John wasn't going to cave. "I didn't think it was an order. Sometimes you got to let somebody do something nice for you for a change."

"Okay," she conceded, not breaking eye contact as her reluctant smile grew ever so slowly.

He got it was hard for her to give up control, but the guardedness in her eyes dropped a level. She gave up the standoff to help him load the back of the truck. After he closed the tailgate, he checked his text messages.

All set, read the message from Wren. *ETA 15 min,* he texted back, which gave him a small window of time to go through with the big ask he had in mind.

Chapter Thirty-One

FALLIN' FOR YOU – Colbie Caillat

Ever since Adam, Elizabeth hated feeling like she owed a man for anything. She'd only agreed to John building the deck with her paying for the supplies. Then John aimed that grin her way and lulled her into lowering her defenses.

There was no way she could pay him for this in lasagna, or even filet mignon and lobster, and she wasn't about to offer to do his laundry and handle his boxers or briefs. What the hell was she doing wondering which he wore when him not taking no for an answer raised a red flag that put her on edge?

"You know that wedding I'm going to?" He pulled out of the parking lot.

"Yes."

"What I didn't mention is that my buddy, Nate, was the lead on *Say Yes to the Rose*."

"The TV show?"

"Yeah. Do you watch it?"

"No, but I've seen enough commercials and tabloid headlines to get the gist of it. Is the wedding off?"

"Oh, it's on. Nate and Cecilia are perfect for each other. But I was on one of the episodes with two of his other buddies to vet the women."

"That didn't out your Green Beret secret identity?" she teased.

"Since Nate was engineer, we never mentioned what I do. Anyway, one of the women posted on social media that she's looking forward to seeing me and giving me some singing lessons."

A chuckle escaped Elizabeth.

"I know I need them, but I don't think she means singing lessons. I kind of flirted with her back then, or tried to, to see if she was really there for Nate. Anyway, Nate mentioned at the *Say Yes to the Rose* reunion show I was seeing somebody. In light of what I was recently told, I need to be careful so I don't fall back into old habits. I thought it would be better if I didn't show up alone."

What was he hinting at? "Keep your distance, and you should be fine. It shouldn't be hard with a lot of people there."

"She's pretty persistent." He glanced at Elizabeth while waiting for the light to change. "It looks like the producers are trying to *ship* us too. So, I wondered if you'd be willing to go if you don't have plans that weekend."

"Me? That's—that's not a good idea." Why would he ask her? "Don't you have a friend you can take?"

"Besides you? No single ones who are strictly friends. I'm not asking one of my buddies' wives, and I don't have cousins."

He gave her puppy dog eyes that rivaled Boss's begging

look. Was the whole deck part of his plan to have her indebted to him before asking her to go? Just when she was starting to trust he was different. "What about taking Jillian?"

"Officer Price? Am I her *type*?" he drew out the word, making his innuendo clear.

"No, you're definitely not the type she goes for. It doesn't matter if you're just faking it. She's attractive and in a line of work that matches up with your career. People would buy you being a couple to keep other women at bay."

"It could work."

His disappointment jabbed at her, but it wasn't a good idea for her to go. She'd never be able to convince people they were involved romantically. "I'll see if she's free for lunch and give her a heads-up that you'll be asking."

Why was she even going along with this? Was it because he was actually trying to change his pattern of behavior like she'd suggested? Or did the idea of him potentially hooking up with some woman bother her, even though she wanted him to find the love and happiness he deserved?

Chapter Thirty-Two

I'LL BE THERE FOR YOU – The Rembrandts

DAYAM. That hadn't gone as he hoped. Instead of getting in Elizabeth's good graces by doing something nice for her and her residents, he managed to annoy her, at best, with his insistence on paying for the supplies. He didn't totally get that, but she wasn't like most women he knew. He liked that about her. But he wasn't going to make her feel like she owed it to him to attend the wedding.

He did his best to keep her distracted as he waited for the gate to open in case a guest had parked where she might see their car. No vehicles were in sight, and he hoped he wasn't early. It would suck if nobody showed up.

"I can help you unload," she said when he stopped in front of her house.

"I've got it from here. I've taken up enough of your time." He engaged in his own silent showdown when she didn't immediately get out of the truck. "You can start fixing

some of that delicious lasagna." He tried to keep it light so she wouldn't feel too bad about turning down the wedding invite.

"You really are incorrigible."

"I've been called a lot worse. No rush. I've got the enchiladas."

She got out of the truck. To avoid making her suspicious, John didn't wait for her to go in.

He smiled, seeing all the cars parked around the tiny houses and even one peeking out from behind. They'd taken his spot and where he planned to unload the lumber, so he parked at the edge of the woods.

When he let Boss out, the dog sniffed the air and looked for the people he heard. His barking probably startled a few of the party guests.

A few minutes after going inside, there was a knock at his door. Wren opened the door without waiting for him to answer. "Aren't you coming to the party?"

"I didn't know I was invited." Since she'd never said anything about him coming, he figured it was women-only.

"Of course, you are. Bring any ice you've got. We might need it."

"I'll be right there. How'd she react to the surprise?"

"She was surprised, all right."

"In a good way?" He grabbed the ice trays and a baggie.

"Mostly. We scared her, but when she saw everyone who came, her reaction made it all worth it."

"Then it sounds like that's the gift she appreciates."

"I guess you're right. Come on. The women want to meet you."

"What? How would they even know about me?"

"When we mentioned you were bringing her back, they

asked who you were. We told them you were the Green Beret who's living here in Hope Harbor."

"You're not supposed to tell people I'm a Green Beret," he reminded her—too late. "Let me change my shirt." He took the three steps to the closet and grabbed a clean polo.

She didn't look away as he quickly changed.

"Wait. Do you have a bow?" he asked.

"For what?"

"My grandma taught me not to show up for a birthday party without a gift."

"And what are you going to put the bow on?" Wren eyed him with a suggestive smirk.

"Not what you think." He shooed her out the door and went to the back of his truck where he grabbed a post for the deck. "For this."

"I've got some ribbon we can wrap around it." She ducked inside Haven House and came out a minute later with a spool of red ribbon. It didn't exactly scream happy birthday, but it was better than nothing. He formed a bow and cut the end. The guests might not get it, but it was a decent gift, all things considered.

The women must have carpooled. Inside Elizabeth's house, over a dozen women milled around. He stood out, not only because of his size, but because he was the only man in the room. He recognized Brooke and Jessica from the VFW and nodded to the eclectic mix of women of every age and ethnicity. They all stared at him.

"Here. I'll put that with the other gifts. I don't think she'll need a tag to know who it's from." Wren took the post from his hands and put it on the coffee table.

Seeing the spread of food on the dining room table, he ducked in there and found a wide array of options. He filled his plate with a sampling of everything.

Two women picked up plates as he admired the lavish birthday cake that had yet to be cut.

"Good afternoon. Did you ladies bring all this food?"

"We each brought a dish. I made the ham rolls." The attractive woman looked to be in her thirties and wore turquoise glasses that matched the flowers in her dress. She gave him a shy smile.

John took a bite. "Delicious. I'll have to get another."

"I made the cake." A woman with a strong resemblance to a young Paula Abdul said.

"It's beautiful. Almost too pretty to eat."

"Thank you. Because of Elizabeth's help, I have my own specialty cake business."

"Do you do kids' cakes?"

"I do all kinds. Birthday, gender reveals, wedding, cake pops, cupcakes."

"If you've got business cards, make sure you get me some to share with my unit. I'll try to send some business your way."

"I appreciate that. I'm Neecy," she introduced herself as Jillian joined them.

"And I'm Valerie," the woman in the floral dress said.

"John."

"We know." Valerie glanced away with a slight smile

Yeah. What all did they know? "Officer Lewis. Nice to see you again." He should have expected Jillian to be here, but he wasn't going to invite her to the wedding in front of everyone. For her sake, and his.

"Elizabeth said you gave the women some security training and set up motion-activated lights," Jillian commented.

"I did. I think I've got them situated now. But if you find my dead body, it's because they were going off in the middle

of the night again and Wren killed me." He followed the women into the living room.

Jillian chuckled. "I usually don't investigate murders, but if that happens, I'll pass that tip along to homicide," she promised, with a smile and nod.

"How did you and Elizabeth meet?" Neecy asked when they joined the circle of women.

"She stole my dog."

"I did not *steal* Boss!" Elizabeth protested.

"I came back from deployment, and you had my dog." He fought not to laugh at the stern look she fixed on him. "All right. I'm kidding. She rescued my dog. And I owe her big for that. See, I left him with my girlfriend when I deployed. Only she got back together with her ex who didn't much like Boss, and Boss didn't much like him. Instead of finding somebody to foster him, my now-ex took my dog to the animal shelter."

"Oh, my," said Neecy. "What a—"

"You don't have to say it. We all know and agree."

"So, how did you end up fostering him?" Neecy asked Elizabeth.

"Actually, I adopted him. About a month after Barkley passed away, I looked at the shelter's website. I went out to see two pitties. One had already been adopted and something didn't feel right about the other. I walked past Boss on my way out. He looked so dejected in that tiny enclosure. I gave him a little love, but when I said goodbye, he gave me that look, like *where are you going?* And his whimper did me in. I took him out in the yard, thinking he'd be too rambunctious or wouldn't obey. That wasn't the case, and there was just something lovable about him. So, I started the paperwork and brought him home."

"I came back from overseas and found out what my ex

189

had done and made it my mission to find my dog. Sorry." He'd watched Elizabeth's serene face and listened to her tone of voice as she told how she came to be Boss's guardian angel. Boss had come to mean so much to her too. He'd never want to hurt her, but she'd made the decision to let him have Boss back, regardless of how much it hurt her.

"No apologies needed," Elizabeth said.

"I gotta say, you're my hero for rescuing my dog and giving us a temporary place to stay." Damn it, he was getting emotional in front of a whole room full of women. He loved Elizabeth's heart and compassion. A tingle started in his arms and spread through him realizing how much he loved about her.

"Aw. It's like it was meant to be," Neecy said.

"Things worked out how they were supposed to with John getting his dog back," Elizabeth added quickly.

"You should bring him over," one of the women said.

"With all this food and all these people, I don't think that's a good idea. He's one hundred and five pounds of stepping on toes and begging for food."

"He sounds huge!" one of the women said.

"Compared to Barkley, he is. My old dog was a fifteen-pound poodle," Elizabeth told John.

"Wow. At least he wasn't a chihuahua."

"What kind of dog is he?" Neecy asked.

"I think he's part springer spaniel, half Rottweiler, and something else. Maybe Clydesdale." His joke made some of the women laugh. "His full name is Bruce 'The Boss' Springweiler."

"He loves telling people that." Wren rolled her eyes.

He pulled out his phone, opened to his favorite picture, and showed it to Neecy, who passed his phone around to the other women.

"Are you sure he's Rottweiler and spaniel?" Valerie asked.

"Not one hundred percent. I found him, or he found me, after being abandoned, so I don't know his pedigree. Not that it matters."

"He just looks big even for those breeds."

"Like I said, he might be part Clydesdale."

"I'm guessing you're the comic relief around here." Neecy gave a tinkling giggle.

"Definitely," Wren interjected.

"I'm going to get more food." After filling his plate with another round, he took up post on the fringes and studied the guests. A slender woman in her forties with a distinctive accent chatted with a woman with shoulder-length, bright blonde hair. When he edged closer trying to identify the woman's accent, they both stopped talking to look at him. "I like your accent," he explained. "Scottish?"

"Yes. Most people guess Irish."

"How do you ladies know Elizabeth?" Something about these two was different than the former Oasis residents.

"Paula and I work with Elizabeth. I'm Charis," she said in that delightful brogue. "So, you're the soldier whose dog she adopted?"

He nodded. Did everybody know about him? Was that good or bad?

"I thought she was a little daft adopting a dog that size, until I heard what happened with you coming home. Things often happen for a reason. I can see you having a dog that big and energetic."

"Yeah, little dogs can't keep up with me on my runs." John turned instinctively when the front door opened.

"Rhonda. Oh my." Elizabeth moved to greet the new arrivals coming through the door and embraced the woman.

The man who entered behind them gripped a baby carrier at his side. "You had the baby already?"

"She was nearly two weeks early. Sorry we're late. We're still trying to figure out schedules," Rhonda said as women gathered around.

"She looks so perfect," Elizabeth cooed.

"She is." Unconditional love played out in Rhonda's voice. Her husband set the carrier on the coffee table and stepped back, allowing the women to get a better view.

"What's her name?" Wren asked.

"Elizabeth Rose." Rhonda smiled at Elizabeth. "After you."

"You didn't need to that," Elizabeth's voice faltered.

"You're the one who didn't need to do everything you did for me."

"For a lot of us," Neecy chimed in.

Rhonda's husband parked himself next to John. "I'm Matthew." He stuck out his hand.

"John."

"Which one is your wife?"

John choked on the meatball in his mouth. "No. I'm just a friend," he said as Wren and Ariana neared.

"He's more than that. He's a resident here," Wren smirked.

Matthew looked John up and down. "You're staying here?"

"Because my ex-boyfriend was causing trouble," Ariana explained. "John is a Green Beret. He's staying here in case my ex shows up again."

"You're no fun," Wren retorted to Ariana. "At least I didn't tell people he's the birthday stripper-gram." John choked again as Wren turned to Matthew. "Congratulations. Rhonda said you have the letter."

Matthew nodded and discreetly pulled an envelope from the diaper bag. Wren took it and disappeared into the kitchen.

"I'm going to get something to eat," Matthew said when the women started asking his wife about labor and delivery.

"Everything's great." John followed.

"A Green Beret. That's impressive. Thank you for your service." Matthew loaded up his plate.

"What do you do?" John took another ham roll.

"I'm a loan officer at a bank. I couldn't do what you do."

"I just analyze different kinds of risks than you. There are days I wonder why I do it, but most days, I can't imagine doing anything else."

Wren breezed through the room with a gift bag. "We're going to do gifts now." She summoned them with a wave of her hand.

"You all didn't need to do gifts," Elizabeth insisted.

"We knew you'd say that." Neecy smiled adoringly at Elizabeth.

"I didn't get to go shopping. But you can hold your namesake when she wakes up," Rhonda said.

"That's a perfect gift." One by one, Elizabeth opened small gifts: scented lotion, a new hummingbird feeder, a pair of silver bracelets with something written on it that made her emotional.

"It's almost the same as yours that you gave me. Plus, a spare for the next time you give it away," Valerie said as Elizabeth slipped it on.

Elizabeth laughed when Wren handed her the post with a ribbon.

"What's that for?" Elizabeth's co-worker, Paula, asked.

"I'm building a deck on Hope Harbor," John explained.

"Considering I nearly broke my ankle more than once

because of that step, it's a fantastic idea," a petite woman with streaks of royal blue in her jet-black hair said.

"Your presence here and seeing you all happy is the only gift I need," Elizabeth said. "And getting to hold the baby later."

"Along those lines, we need everybody to get together so we can take a group picture," Ariana requested.

"I can take it for you," Jillian volunteered.

"You should all be in it. I'll take it," John offered.

"You both need to be in it too." Ariana nudged Jillian and John toward the group. "Matthew, can you take the picture?"

"Of course."

"Come on. I'm not part of this group that way," John protested.

"You need to be in at least one. You'll see why in a minute," Ariana implored softly, batting her eyelashes.

"Fine. One. Don't be posting it on social media, though."

"I promise."

After Matthew took numerous shots, Wren handed Elizabeth the large gift bag, from which she pulled a binder with roses decorating the cover.

"Look inside," Wren urged. "We'll put one of the pictures we just took on that first page."

Elizabeth turned the blank page. From what John could see, there was a letter mounted on colorful, printed paper. Elizabeth's head shifted as she scanned the words. Her hand went to her mouth.

"There are letters from all of us and some of the women who couldn't make it here today," Wren said.

"I'm going to read them later, because I can already tell

they're going to make me cry—in a good way. This is a gift I'll treasure," Elizabeth's voice cracked.

"You can thank John for the inspiration," Wren admitted.

"Really?" Elizabeth's gaze shifted to John.

"I tasked him with getting gift ideas. He mentioned something about affirmation words from a book you liked. I used to scrapbook, so I came up with the idea of a book thanking you for what you've done for us."

"You read the *Five Love Languages* book?" Elizabeth stared at him with an impressed, yet slightly bewildered, smile that made him feel ten feet tall.

"I had a mission to complete. It was insightful."

The focus shifted to Rhonda taking the baby out of the carrier.

"Way to score major points," Matthew whispered.

"That's not why I . . ."

"No? Too bad. My wife thinks the world of Elizabeth."

"I'm not disagreeing with you. But I don't think she sees me that way." It'd be too much to hope for when she gave no indication of wanting a man in her life. But the utter longing on her face when Rhonda put her baby in Elizabeth's arms told him what she did want—even if she wouldn't admit it.

"How's it going living in a tiny house?" Matthew asked, snapping John's attention from staring at Elizabeth holding the infant.

"Oh, just fine and dandy," John rubbed his head where he bonked it. "I'll be moving out in a few weeks." It was for the best, but there were things he was going to miss about living here. Not the tiny house but spending time with Elizabeth and that smile of hers. He may have to resort to saying

Boss missed her as an excuse to come visit. Or was that a good idea with him relocating to Florida in a few months?

Though he'd planned to duck out after making an appearance, he got caught up talking with the women while observing Elizabeth's interaction with them. Ariana fixed him two plates of food before the guests departed.

"You were in on this." Elizabeth cornered him as he took down the streamer decorations, since he didn't need a step ladder to reach them. "Asking about gifts. The trip to the home improvement store today."

"I got drafted, and it was under duress." He jerked his head toward Wren.

"I figured she was behind it. She was fishing for my birthday a few months ago. Normally, I hate surprises, but this was . . . It meant a lot." Her eyes got misty again.

"You've earned every bit of that love and respect." That wasn't why she did what she did. He understood that. Other than their love of Boss, in most ways they were opposites. But the adage about how opposites attract was becoming more and more true—at least on his end.

Chapter Thirty-Three

I CAN SEE CLEARLY NOW – Johnny Nash

Elizabeth placed her and Jillian's lunch order at the kiosk, then found a table on the outdoor patio. Jillian slid into the seat across from her, her uniform and gun drawing attention from tables of nearby diners.

"Thanks for ordering for me. How much do I owe you?"

"This is on me."

"You don't need to do that." Jillian gave a dismissive wave of her hand.

"Well, I have a favor to ask."

"Ariana having more problems with J.R.?"

"No, fortunately. It has to do with John. He's looking for a date for a wedding where he's a groomsman next weekend."

"What does that have to do with me?" Jillian's brows dipped cautiously.

While Elizabeth finished giving her a rundown of

John's situation with the reality show contestant, the server brought their food. "I told him he should ask you."

"Sounds like he was asking *you* to go."

"That's not going to happen."

"Why not?"

"It's just not. Besides crossing lines since he asked for relationship advice—"

"Wait. You're counseling him?"

"Not counseling, though I did suggest he might see someone after what happened with his ex, but he asked me for advice as a friend."

"Okay. Whatever. But how does that preclude you going to the wedding with him?"

"It could make things awkward."

"Because you *like* him?"

"No. I mean as a friend, yes, but that's all. And all it can ever be. I'm not giving up control of my life to a man again."

"From the little I've seen of John, and what you told me, he might be pretty alpha with giving orders, that's not the same as the controlling type. You're talking about attending one event together, not any kind of commitment." She leaned back in her chair and studied Elizabeth.

"He's probably on his best behavior. He still needs a place to live. I didn't see any warning signs with Adam while we were dating either. Afterward was an entirely different story. John has military training. With his size and strength, he could do what he wants and . . ."

"Not every man is like your father or your ex. John comes off much more like a protector, not an abuser."

"I'm still not interested." That sounded weak, even to her. "I don't need, and am not looking for, a man in my life. Besides, he's moving out of The Oasis soon and then to

Florida in a few months. So will you go with him to the wedding?"

"No. I started seeing someone."

"And you hadn't told me?"

"I was going to tell you today, but you asked me to be your tenant's fake date before I could." Jillian laughed and broke into a huge smile. "Her name's Cayla, and she's beautiful, funny, and sweet. We like to do the same things. I'm not going to do anything to make her jealous, since I don't owe your friend any favors."

"I don't either. I took care of his dog."

"You didn't do that for him." She leaned forward and drilled Elizabeth with her stare. "You adopted that dog for yourself."

"I'm just saying that I don't owe him. And Ariana going wouldn't be a great idea."

"Why not?" Jillian challenged.

"Just, you know. Her age and with what she's been through, she may see him as her white knight saving her from J.R. If he asks her to the wedding, even explaining his circumstance, she might get the wrong idea and develop romantic feelings for him."

"So, you're protecting her?"

"Well, if he doesn't reciprocate, it could be awkward with them living at The Oasis right now. It might push her into making bad choices. I can't forbid them from dating, but I'm certainly not doing anything to encourage it while they're both there."

"Make the same kind of mistake you made? Isn't that a stretch?"

She'd anticipated Jillian having reservations but being in the hot seat was not how she'd expected this to go. "I thought you were my friend."

"I am, so quit trying to guilt trip me. If he asks, I'll tell him yes and cancel at the last minute so you have to step in." Jillian aimed a mischievous smile at her while she shot down Elizabeth's fleeting moment of hope. "You might as well say yes."

"No. He's going to have to come up with another option or go stag and deal with her for the wedding. How bad can it be? Maybe he misinterpreted her posts."

"Have you seen what she posted about him?"

"No." And John could be exaggerating, though why?

"What's her name?" Jillian pulled out her phone.

"I don't know. He only said something about flirting with her and her posting about them singing." She ate while Jillian searched on her phone.

"This could be her. Shelby Perkins from Nate Crenshaw's season. Former Miss South Carolina. There are videos of her singing."

"That was fast. You'll make a great detective."

"I hope so, but anyone can check the internet."

"Do you see any posts related to John?"

"I'm checking. She posts several times a day and only one picture at a time."

"Her breakfast, lunch, and dinner?"

"Not food. Mostly her." Jillian kept scrolling. "She's posted screen captures from the show. Says she's looking forward to the wedding and the reunion with her friends. Here's one of her with John. She's definitely the one."

"How can you tell?" Elizabeth asked.

"She wrote something about giving him singing lessons so they can 'make beautiful music together' or 'they can just make joyful noises.'"

"Did he respond to her?" It wasn't up to her to judge if he took Shelby up on what she was clearly offering. Some-

thing Elizabeth couldn't. John had needs and the poor guy had come home from his deployment to get dumped.

"No. And she didn't, or couldn't, tag him. He likely doesn't have a social media presence, or at least a public account, for security reasons."

That made sense. She didn't have accounts either. There wasn't anything newsworthy in her life to share. "You sure you won't go to run interference for him?"

"I'm sure. Besides, I think you should go with him. You've got some unresolved issues to deal with, my friend, and going with him might be a step in the right direction. Even if it's just a short-term, no-strings, it's-been-way-too-long, get-back-in-the-saddle experiment."

Chapter Thirty-Four

YOU BROKE UP WITH ME – Walker Hayes

Boss NEARLY KNOCKED John down Hope Harbor's steps with his exuberant greeting. "Hey, buddy. Did you miss me?" He rubbed Boss's head. "Go on. I'll be out in a minute."

He'd changed out of his uniform and started tossing a ball to burn off some of Boss's energy when his phone sang. He recognized the ringtone. Damn. Had he left Britney in his contacts? She'd sure ruined "I Want Crazy" for him forever.

Question was, did he answer or not? What the hell?

"Hello." He kept his voice neutral as if he didn't know who was calling.

"It's Britney." Her voice was sugary sweet.

He didn't immediately respond, but Boss must have recognized her voice because he barked—and not in a friendly way.

"Is that Boss? I'm so glad you got him back."

"Me too." No thanks to you.

"Was he still at the shelter?"

"No, a kind-hearted woman adopted him but was willing to let him go when she heard of the circumstances of how he came to be at the shelter."

"That was Richard's doing." Hurt leached through her voice. "I should have told you." It wasn't exactly an apology. She still hadn't said why she was calling, and he wasn't asking. He picked up Boss's tug toy and let his playful growl fill the silence.

"I called because a reminder popped up on my calendar about your friend Nate's wedding."

"No worries. I figured with Richard moving in with you, you weren't planning on going."

"Richard and I—we're, uh, not together anymore."

What was he supposed to say? Sorry?

"He, um, cheated on me. Again."

"I'm sure that hurts." He didn't point out that he spoke from experience. Karma's a bitch sometimes.

"I got to thinking about you and the fun we had. I thought we could get together for a drink, or you could come over here to talk things out."

Talk things out sounded like Britney's code for sex. Maybe she was lonely or horny or hoping for revenge sex as payback for Richard sleeping with someone else. Or was she angling for an invite to the wedding in hopes of connecting with reality show celebrities? "There isn't any point."

"I'm sorry about everything. It just was so hard not being able to talk with you while you were gone."

"I told you communication would be limited. Then you went and posted things on social media after I specifically

told you it was confidential. You put me and my team in danger."

"I took them down as soon as you asked. How did you even know?"

"That's not the point." He deserved better.

"You don't have to get all serious. Just have a little fun. If you need a date for the wedding . . ."

"I'm good. I'm trying to make better choices. Maybe you should do the same, because I'm not the right guy for you, Britney. I hope you find a guy who is." He ended the call rather than give her a chance to play him.

After tossing the ball again, he pulled up his contacts to block her. He probably didn't need to do that; however, he was changing her ringtone. The question was, what did he change it to? "Heard it Through the Grapevine?" Nah, she wasn't worth crying over. There was some song about a cheating heart, but after that call, "You Broke Up with Me?" fit perfectly.

Though there was no way he was taking Britney to the wedding, he wanted a date more than ever. Elizabeth planned to have lunch with Jillian today. Maybe his luck would change to keep him from singing the blues.

John played with Boss while waiting for Elizabeth to get home. He gave her a few seconds to park. "Take it to Elizabeth." He sent the ball sailing toward her house.

Only Boss didn't follow orders as he trotted back in John's direction. "Come on, boy. It's a simple command. I bet Elizabeth has treats. Take it to her." He tossed it again, trying not to appear obvious or desperate. Having heard the magic word, Boss chased the ball, then disappeared from view. Good boy. John ambled that way too.

Boss had done his job, effectively delaying Elizabeth, who rubbed his head. He took in the sight.

"How did your lunch with Jillian go?"

"Lunch was fine, but I'm afraid she said no to go being your date to the wedding. She doesn't want to risk making her new girlfriend jealous."

"I didn't know she had a girlfriend. I would never have had you ask her," he stammered. Why had Elizabeth even suggested it?

"I didn't know until today either."

Part of him was relieved, but he wasn't going to put Elizabeth on the spot and ask her again. "I've faced terrorists. I'm sure I can figure out how to evade a singing beauty queen for a few hours."

Or maybe he wouldn't dodge Shelby. They were adults. They could hook up. Hell, Elizabeth had even suggested he get laid. He'd be upfront with Shelby. They'd have fun in the sack. He wouldn't expect more, so he wouldn't get emotionally invested, or get hurt when Shelby pulled a Britney and moved on with someone more in her league.

Why didn't it feel right? Maybe because it crossed his mind while standing in front of Elizabeth?

"Not to change the subject, but we heard from the prosecutor for Ariana's case. We have a confirmed court date."

"She's not going to drop the charges?"

"Not exactly. The prosecutor said most likely J.R. would get a max sentence of thirty days and a fine of one thousand dollars, which isn't much. However, it could still piss him off enough to create problems in the future. But if she dropped the charges, the judge might not grant a restraining order. She suggested we wait until the trial date and offer to drop the charges if he admits his guilt. At that time, she could ask for the restraining order as part of the agreement."

"Makes sense. And if he doesn't agree to plead guilty,

then she still has to testify and hope the jury finds him guilty?"

"Right. He may roll the dice in hopes of keeping it off his record, since the sentence is minimal and may not involve jail time."

"When is the court hearing?" John asked.

"Next Wednesday."

"You're going, right?"

"Yes. She's going to need moral support."

"Text me the time and courtroom information. I'll be there too."

"You don't have to go."

"I want to be there. It'll be a reminder to J.R. that Ariana is not alone. Hopefully, she can put this in her rearview mirror after next week." It also meant that he'd be moving on soon, though he had another mission to finish the deck. Even if Elizabeth wasn't going to the wedding with him, he wasn't going to bail and leave her with an unfinished project. He had a couple hours of daylight left with nothing else to do.

He headed back toward Hope Harbor, but Boss whimpered and raised his snout to Elizabeth. Oh yeah, treat. Boss had the memory of an elephant, if not quite the size.

"Come on, boy." He snapped his fingers, hoping Elizabeth didn't deduce he'd resorted to bribing his dog to have an excuse to see her. "I'll get you a treat at our place."

Chapter Thirty-Five

COURTESY OF THE RED, WHITE AND BLUE –
Toby Keith

By LATE MORNING, John had nearly completed attaching the deck's support beams to the base anchors. His phone dinged. "Nate's here, Boss." He picked up the remote and strolled toward the gate with Boss at his side.

Boss pranced around while Nate parked where John directed.

"Hey, boy. Remember me?" Nate knelt on one knee.

"Of course, he does."

"Good to see you, buddy." The two exchanged a bro hug. "I heard you when you said we were building this deck on a tiny house, but I didn't think you actually meant a tiny home. Are these bed and breakfast rentals?" He waved an arm at the other two.

"Not exactly. The woman who owns this place is a counselor. She offers transitional housing for women, typi-

cally, getting out of abusive relationships and needing an affordable place to stay."

Nate nodded. "How'd you end up offering to help her?"

"Elizabeth is the one who adopted Boss—and gave him back to me."

"Ah, so, you figure you owe her?"

"I definitely owe her. Turns out one of her tenants was being stalked by her ex. Since I was homeless and they had an empty place, I'm living here as security until her ex goes to trial."

"You and Boss are living in there? This I gotta see."

"Won't take long. It's only about three hundred square feet."

Nate walked around, checking the foundations John had poured. "You do good work. You may have to join me when you retire."

"That'll be a while. But I'd love to get your help over at my house. I can do the demo of the kitchen, but installing all the cabinets is at least a two-man job."

"I can do that—after the wedding and the honeymoon. We're spending two weeks in Europe. Any chance we can get in so I can get a feel for what we'll be doing?"

"Yeah. My renter is a guy on another team in Third Group. They let me take Elizabeth and the women living here in last week to see it. I wanted their input on a few remodel ideas—and I think they were afraid I'd use a camouflage motif and make it too masculine for resale."

Nate laughed. "Show me this house first. I see what you mean about the front step." He took in the high ceiling. "The height makes it feel bigger." He picked up a floral throw pillow. "It's, uh, cute."

"It's temporary. There'll be another woman in here after I

leave, so . . . I did put up a flag. The colors kind of match." John sang, "Courtesy of the Red, White and Blue." and pointed to the American flag he'd hung on the wall facing the sleeping loft.

Nate climbed up the steps to see the loft. "Bed's not made to Army regs." He grinned down at John.

John flipped him off. "You go ahead and try it."

Nate's laughter rumbled through the tiny home as he backed down the stairs. "Guessing you don't bring women up here."

"Hardly." He didn't get into Elizabeth's rules.

"Sorry about things with Britney. I still can't believe she dumped Boss at the shelter."

"She says it was her boyfriend, but she knew and didn't stop him. She most definitely was not *the one*. But, hey, I've got my dog. I'm not paying alimony. And I'm trying to make better decisions."

"No plus-one for the wedding, then?"

"Not looking like it." He wasn't going to pick up some stranger or hire someone just to have a date. "Let's knock out this deck." That sounded like more fun than talking about his non-existent love life.

♫

SOMEONE POUNDED on Elizabeth's front door. Before she could open it, Wren rushed in.

"We need you at The Oasis right now," a panicked Wren called, already heading back out.

"What's wrong? Is it J.R.?"

"It's John. Ariana is with him. She called 911, but we need you."

Elizabeth dashed after Wren. "What happened?"

"I don't know. One minute he was working on the deck and the next he was just there."

Wren wasn't making any sense. Elizabeth's heart pounded as she rounded the corner, stealing herself for blood or broken limbs or—not John rocking on the new deck with Boss at his side.

"You're all right?"

"Yeah. Why?"

"I thought—" Elizabeth looked at Wren, her hammering heart slowing slightly. "She implied you were hurt."

"Aw, you care." He rocked back. "Or were you thinking if something happened to me you could keep my dog?"

"No." Exasperation crept into her voice, yet his easy smile and humor took the edge off. The panic came from her not wanting anything to happen to him—except she couldn't come out and tell him that because of how he'd likely take it.

"He asked me to get you down here to surprise you that it was finished, but it was my idea to trick you. Sorry. I forgot you hate surprises," Wren said.

"No, but I, uh—" she broke off when the door to Hope Harbor opened, and a vaguely familiar-looking, bearded, dark-haired man joined them.

"You must be Elizabeth." He gave her a genuine smile that instantly made her feel like a friend as he shook her hand. "John's told me all about you. I'm Nate."

"From the TV show. I saw you in the commercials."

"And probably on magazine covers," John added.

"That was me." Nate ran a hand through his mussed hair.

"Nate came up early to help me knock this out before his bachelor party weekend."

"That's very generous of you. This is amazing." She

took in the deck that ran the length of the home. They'd added a built-in bench seat that wasn't in the original plans.

"John told me about what you do here. I was happy to help out in a small way."

"Small? It's twice the size of the plans you showed me." She eyed John.

John gave his usual shrug. "I watched some show about tiny home Airbnbs and the host kept going on and on about one's spacious outdoor living area. Made sense to have enough room not to trip over Boss and for two chairs. We added the bench in case all you ladies want to hang out here rather than on your front porch." He winked at her. "The retractable awning is manual, and it'll shade about half the space."

"Wow. You went above and beyond."

"I had help," he motioned to Nate.

"I only looked at the plans and did a few hours of labor." Nate also downplayed his efforts. "This guy never does things halfway. Go big or go home."

That was John. She knew better than to ask about additional expenses, especially in front of his friend. She'd have to find some way to pay him for the additional cost and his hours of labor—other than attend the wedding or other things she couldn't do.

Chapter Thirty-Six

Outside the courtroom, Elizabeth sat next to Ariana, who clasped and unclasped her hands as she bit on her lower lip. If not for Jillian standing by in uniform and John's camouflage-clad, looming presence, Ariana might have caved already.

"Oh, seriously?" Ariana muttered. "He's dressed like a frat boy."

Elizabeth studied J.R. as he strolled down the court-house hallway in a suit and tie, freshly shaven, with his hair in a short, conservative cut, like a clone of the attorney with him.

John kept his body between Ariana and J.R., his head pivoting as if daring J.R. to make eye contact with him.

"Just ignore him. The judge will see through appear-ances," Jillian's prosecutor attorney friend, Cindy, assured Ariana.

"What if the judge won't grant a restraining order?" Ariana asked once the pair disappeared around the corner.

"I don't think that's going to happen, especially with Judge Fraley. But, if it does, at least it's on file that you requested one if he proves to be a threat again. And the arrest stays on his record even if you don't press charges. Though he wouldn't do time, it would be a bad move to threaten you again, and any premeditation would weigh heavily at sentencing."

"Doing the smart thing isn't exactly J.R.'s forte."

"He's not totally stupid, and he's going to know what he's dealing with." John pointed down the hallway to a group of men in camouflage uniforms heading directly for them. "Ladies, I'd like you to meet my team. They're also *your* team," he said to Ariana.

"Oh my." Ariana's eyes misted and she gave a relieved smile.

"It's not overkill, is it?" he asked Cindy.

Elizabeth doubted he'd care if it was. He hadn't said a word to her about bringing his entire team. This went over and above the call of duty not only for him, but his men.

"As long as you all sit there quietly and respectfully," Cindy warned. "That means no gestures. No sounds. Not even eye rolls."

"Yes, ma'am." John acknowledged the orders.

Elizabeth gave a grateful nod to the men, several of whom seemed to discreetly study her. What had John told them about his current living arrangements? About her?

When the bailiff summoned them into the courtroom a short while later, Ariana made the sign of the cross, took a deep breath, and rose to her feet.

"Wait and let J.R. and his attorney enter first," Cindy advised. Based on the wide-eyed, concerned expressions

when J.R. and his attorney filed past John and his team, her strategy worked. "All right then. Let's go kick some ass the legal way."

Ariana and Cindy took seats at the table near the empty jury box.

Elizabeth sat between Jillian and John, while his team filled two rows behind them. Upon entering the courtroom and taking the bench, the robed judge raised her eyebrows at their silent presence. Everyone sat as court was called to order.

"Mr. Elliott, you're being charged with misdemeanor assault on a female. How do you plead?" Judge Fraley asked.

"Your honor, we're willing to offer a plea deal," Cindy spoke before J.R. answered. "If Mr. Elliott agrees to plead guilty and to the issuance of a restraining order for the protection of Miss Mercado, we'll drop the charges, allowing Mr. Elliott to avoid jail time."

"Your honor, may I have a moment to confer with my client?" J.R.'s attorney requested.

The two bowed their heads and conversed in whispered tones. J.R. cast a glance Ariana's way. They stood after only a few moments.

"We agree to the plea agreement."

"Mr. Elliott, do you understand that a guilty plea will go on your permanent record? A restraining order will be issued prohibiting you from contacting Miss Mercado in any manner and you'll be required to keep a distance of fifty feet for a period of three years. Any violation of the restraining order may result in charges and up to five months in jail for the first offense."

"I do," J.R. answered.

"For the record, how do you plea to the charge of misdemeanor assault?"

"Guilty," J.R. said.

Ariana's relieved sigh sounded in the silence. Elizabeth could relate. Tears sprang to her eyes.

"Yesss," John said under his breath.

"Thank you." Elizabeth placed a hand over his and squeezed.

"You're welcome." He leaned his head closer to hers. "It was a joint effort. Mostly you and Ariana."

She didn't totally believe that. It took several seconds for her to tear her gaze away and remove her fingers, which he'd trapped with his.

Everyone remained seated in the courtroom while the judge issued instructions on the restraining order. Elizabeth watched J.R.'s face once the case was closed. He gave a solemn nod to Ariana and the look in his eyes was one of relief, not the kind of vengeful parting look Adam had drilled Elizabeth with upon agreeing to their settlement. She shivered at the memory. Even though she hadn't seen him since that day, triggers occasionally still popped up. More things had triggered her in the weeks since John moved into The Oasis than the previous year or two combined. If that didn't abate once he moved on, she'd make an appointment with her counselor.

The courtroom cleared out. Their party waited for J.R. and his attorney to disappear into the elevator before exchanging a few victory high-fives.

"Thank you. Thank you so much." Ariana gave hugs, then thanked John's team.

Elizabeth was aware that Special Ops teams' members typically stayed together longer than in regular Army units. The camaraderie amongst the men was obvious. As was

their respect for John, who was all seriousness today. Leaving his team for the new training position in Florida was going to be a huge change, especially for someone who considered his team his family. He didn't have a lot of other family and clearly longed for it.

"Are you all free for a celebratory lunch?" she asked.

"Thanks, but we need to get back to work," John answered for the group. "I'll see you tonight for some celebratory lasagna or enchiladas." He winked.

"You got it," Ariana said quickly.

"And I'm sending in cookies for everyone with John tomorrow," Elizabeth added.

"Great. Tomorrow is Rodriguez's day to lead PT. We already call it groan day. He'll be even tougher to make us work off those cookies," John grumbled good-naturedly.

"I've got a decade on most of you, and if you can't keep up with me, I get your cookies." The soldier with kind eyes and a mustache rallied the troops toward the elevators.

John spoke to his team but made eye contact with Elizabeth before the doors closed. Somehow, his departure felt premature, like there was something still unfinished between them.

♫

JOHN'S TRUCK rumbled past two hours later than usual that evening. Elizabeth carried the containers of cookies she'd baked to Hope Harbor, praying she wouldn't lose her nerve.

At the familiar sound of Boss and John's nightly reunion, it hit her how much she was going to miss them when they moved out. He'd given up a lot for the military and hadn't complained once about putting his life on hold to help them here at The Oasis. He deserved to have a full

life—more than she could give him—but there was one thing she could do.

John caught her discreetly watching them play.

"Your cookies, as promised," she greeted him.

"You didn't have to, but I won't say no. Promise you won't snitch to First Sergeant Rodriguez that I'm sneaking some tonight?" He opened the top and helped himself to a cookie. "*Mmm.* These are awesome. Do you ship overseas to soldiers on deployment?"

"I'll be happy to send you care packages the next time you deploy. And, after all you've done, I'll go to the wedding with you—as friends."

"What?" He coughed out, choking on the cookie.

"If you still need a date, that is. If you already found someone, that's—that's great," she stammered. Of course, he had no reason to tell her if he'd found someone to go after she had turned him down.

"No." He coughed again, clearing his throat. "I was going alone."

"Well, if it's not too late. I don't want to complicate things last minute." She gave him an out in case he'd changed his mind about dodging the beauty queen.

"Absolutely not. I'll let Nate know tonight. I was going to give him an update on Ariana's case anyway."

His happy smile gave her butterflies, despite the fact they weren't going as a real couple.

"Will you be able to come to the rehearsal dinner Friday night?" he asked, pausing between words.

She hadn't even thought about that. "Where's the wedding and rehearsal?"

"Outside of Charlotte."

About three hours away. Her insides clenched at the thought of what that meant in the way of an overnight stay.

"I don't have time to reschedule my clients on short notice. How about I meet you at the wedding on Saturday?"

"That'd be fine." A hint of disappointment leaked through his voice. "The wedding is in the afternoon, and the reception will probably run late. I'll get you a hotel room so you don't have to drive home afterward and can enjoy yourself."

His offer made her feel better about this whole thing. "If it's afternoon, I'm guessing this isn't formal? I want to make a good impression, even if I am just your fake date."

"Wedding's at four, if that tells you what you need to know for dress. I'm not worried about you making a great impression. I'll be the envy of every man. Except maybe Nate."

"You're laying it on kind of thick. I already agreed to go." Still, her face heated and a pleasant tingling from his compliment reminded her she wasn't totally frigid.

"Not at all. There's no one I'd rather go with. We're going to show off our dance moves, right?"

She couldn't help but smile. "Yes, we'll dance." This could be a lot of fun. Going with a friend. No pressure— well, maybe a little. "Text me the information on the wedding."

"I will. And I'll get Wren or Ariana to take care of Boss."

She was committed now, and for John's sake, she was going to have to be convincing.

Chapter Thirty-Seven

NEARLY ALL THE sofas and chairs in the hotel lobby were filled when John walked up to the registration desk.

"I'm with the Crenshaw-Ryan wedding. Registration is under Bryson," he told the man. "I called the other day to add—"

"John!" The voice calling his name had a strong southern accent.

He'd done enough covert surveillance to know Shelby appearing at this moment was no coincidence.

"It's so great to see you." She came at him with open arms.

While he couldn't completely avert Shelby's hug, he managed to limit her to hugging him from the side. She kept one hand low on his back.

"You wanted to add another night?" the clerk started.

"I won't need to after all."

"Everything's covered, but we'll need a credit card for any incidentals," the clerk said.

John reached for his credit card, forcing Shelby to remove her hand.

"Some of us have been catching up in the bar, but we're about to head out to the pool. Why don't you join us?" Shelby batted her long lashes at John in invitation.

"You're in room fourteen twenty-six." The clerk slid him a card holding his room key.

"I'm down the hall. Room fourteen fifty-three. I'll ride up with you. The elevators are this way."

Dayam, she was hardly subtle. Old John would have taken her up on that offer without thinking twice. New John was trying to make better choices. He'd rather have a lonely heart than a broken one. And with Elizabeth coming tomorrow—as a friend—he couldn't let her down.

With no tactful way to extract himself, John took hold of his suitcase and draped the suit bag over his other arm to follow her.

"I heard your song on the radio." He tried to make small talk after Shelby punched the button for the fourteenth floor.

"I've got another song coming out next month."

"I'm glad your career is taking off. Have you got plans to go on tour?"

"Not yet. I need another release or two to take off to create a bigger following, but I'm hopeful that will happen soon."

"I bet being on the show was great exposure."

"It was a good start," Shelby said as they exited the elevator. She paused outside his door. "I'll stop by after I change, and we can go back down together."

"I didn't pack swim trunks."

"Shorts will be fine. Or we can get a drink and hang out poolside."

"I want to call Elizabeth first."

"Elizabeth?" Shelby broke the name into bite size portions, and her brows dipped.

"Yeah, she had too many clients scheduled to make it down for the rehearsal. I'll introduce you to her tomorrow."

"Oh." Disappointment laced that lone word.

He tapped his key card to the lock and a green light flashed.

Shelby peeked in when he opened the door. "Looks like the wedding party got upgraded rooms. Are you the best man?"

"Ben won that honor." John left his suitcase to block Shelby from entering while he hung the suit in the closet. "He's known Nate the longest." He'd also picked Cecilia over Diana for the final rose. Considering John's track record with women, he'd done exceptionally well to pick the right final two, though he'd thought it would be Diana. "I'll see you downstairs."

Shelby backed out of the room. John kept his door from closing completely and listened until a door closed down the hall. When the coast was clear, he headed to the lobby.

He waited for the ginger-haired desk clerk who helped him earlier to finish with his current guest. "I tried to book a second room for tomorrow online, but you were full. I'm on a wait list. Can you check the status?"

"Once word got out that the *Say Yes to the Rose* cast was staying here, everything booked up."

"Nothing? Not even a penthouse suite?"

"The studio booked all those when they reserved the block."

"You'll have cancelations tomorrow, right?" He'd promised Elizabeth her own room.

"Since you're in the wedding party, I'll put you at the top of the list, but the chances still aren't good. I can reserve you a room in our sister hotel with complimentary shuttle service."

"Yeah. Put that reservation in my name." He'd stay here tonight and use that as a backup if he couldn't get another room here tomorrow. Though he didn't need Shelby showing up at his door—or Elizabeth's, if he gave her his room. "I need to change to a different room."

"Is there a problem?"

"You gave away my room number in front of someone I'd rather not know it."

"I thought you were friends."

"We are acquainted, but I need to keep it in the friend zone."

"I understand. I am so sorry." He tapped on the keyboard.

Maybe the vision of a drunk or tipsy Shelby knocking on his door wasn't realistic, but there were too many ways that could blow up with a picture turning up on social media or in some tabloid.

The clerk frowned. "I don't have another deluxe room available."

"It doesn't have to be deluxe."

"The only thing I've got clean at the moment is a standard double."

"I'll take anything as long as it's on a different floor."

He handed John a new keycard. "We've got your number in the system to text if we get a cancelation."

"Thanks. And can you make a note not to put calls through to my room?"

After collecting his luggage, he did a surveillance pass before exiting his original room and hustling to the elevator in his escape-and-evade-Shelby mission. It wasn't that Shelby was the enemy or the deadly kind of dangerous, but with Elizabeth conceding to come, he didn't want Shelby tanking any chance he might have with Elizabeth.

Chapter Thirty-Eight

LOOK WHAT GOD GAVE HER – Thomas Rhett

THE GPS DIRECTED Elizabeth down a rural road lined with soybean fields. She hadn't expected an actual working farm to serve as the wedding venue, though the barn was clearly new and modern. A huge white tent was set up in the grassy field to her right. An attendant directed her to park in the field on the left. As she got out of her car, an open-air, six-passenger shuttle came down the row. She joined two couples for the short ride across the field to the barn. It was a nice touch, so the women didn't have to walk through soft grass in heels.

Upon entering the barn, a groomsman extended his arm to the woman ahead of her. Before the next groomsman stepped forward, John put a hand to the man's chest.

"I've got this one," he proclaimed. "Wow. You look fabulous."

She tried to calm the butterflies in her stomach from his

compliment and the way his gaze lingered on her for several long seconds before he offered her his arm. This wasn't real. It was all for show, and he wasn't used to seeing her in a cocktail dress.

"You look very handsome, yourself." Did he ever in the well-fitting navy-blue suit. "I thought you might be in uniform."

"Nate's now out of the Army, and not everyone in the wedding party served. I'll find you after the ceremony." John's smile lingered on her before he pivoted on a heel and proceeded back down the aisle.

A few rows up and across the aisle, Elizabeth picked out Shelby from the pictures she'd looked up online. The redhead bent toward the blond seated next to her as they talked.

Elizabeth had attended plenty of events alone over the past decade. Sitting by herself today was different. Was it fear that people would see through their ruse and make John look bad, or that she felt—lonely? It had to be the wedding and everyone else seemed to be the part of a couple—a real couple—or with friends.

She'd get through it. It certainly wouldn't be the hardest thing she'd ever done.

She drew in a deep breath and studied the décor. The white tule bows around the wooden chair backs were accented with greenery and mini red roses. Inside the barn, the wall boards had been given a weathered look. Chande-liers of wrought iron in a scroll-and-heart pattern hung from the vaulted ceiling and arched stained-glass windows gave the interior an upscale elegance.

Professional camera stations were set up to film on both sides and at the back of the venue.

Minutes later, the music grew louder as the family members were seated.

When the groomsmen took their places next to Nate, Elizabeth caught John staring at her. He winked and gave her that sexy grin of his. It made her feel less alone. It also sent that ripple of sexual attraction through her. The kind that she'd feared she'd never experience again after Adam.

How did something as simple as a wink and smile manage to have that effect on her? No. It was John. John who had that effect on her. And that physical attraction was growing stronger, despite her efforts to keep things strictly in the friend zone—for his sake even more than hers.

She tore her gaze from John's. He was just playing up the role, though Shelby turned and looked in her general direction.

Despite the unconventional process that started with Nate dating twenty-five women, his beaming smile and the joy Cecilia radiated appeared totally authentic. Their personalized vows included humorous things about their journey to find love yet were also heartfelt. The officiant didn't ask if anyone objected to their union, which was smart considering there could be a dozen women here who might wish they were standing in Cecilia's spot. By the time they were pronounced man and wife and Nate placed his hands on either side of Cecilia's face and kissed her, Elizabeth was a believer in this happily-ever-after ending.

Her gaze settled back on John who watched his friend. As if aware she was watching him, John's head angled her way. His eyes locked on hers, and he broke into a slow, consuming smile that made her smile back.

She wanted John to find that epic love story he deserved. The kind she once thought she could have.

Chapter Thirty-Nine

OPPOSITES ATTRACT – Paula Abdul

AFTER THE CEREMONY, John waited outside the barn for Elizabeth. Hopefully, no one could tell he'd teared up when Nate exchanged vows with Cecilia. Between the bachelor party weekend and the rehearsal dinner party last night, he had no doubts about his best friend being in love. That's what *he* wanted too. Not to just be married or with someone but that special connection that made other people want the kind of relationship he had.

Elizabeth had challenged him to change his patterns, to become friends with a woman first. And he had. With her.

Over the past few weeks, he realized it didn't have to be instant fireworks or passion that was great for a night. It was the small, day-to-day things. That smile that popped up just seeing the person or their smile when you cracked a joke. Rocking side by side on the front porch with a dog at their

feet, though cuddling together on the swing would be even better.

The way she sometimes looked at him, he wanted to believe the attraction could be mutual, despite her insistence she didn't date and didn't want to cross lines with him living at The Oasis. But there was something more, something she hadn't shared that went beyond her father's physical abuse and related to her controlling ex-husband. Could she move past it? Maybe with help. Not unlike what she did for others.

Elizabeth made her way out of the barn, surrounded by groups and couples. She glanced around. Her gaze landing on him. Everyone else faded into the background as he watched her come to him. Next to Nate, he felt like the luckiest man here. And he wasn't faking it. Time to move to Mission Make-it-Real.

"Shall we?" He offered his arm.

"Don't you have to do pictures first?"

"We did them before the wedding. They weren't totally traditional about not seeing each other before the ceremony."

He escorted her to the tent for cocktail hour where the studio had even more cameras. He recognized contestants congregated in groups around tall tables. Some women greeted him. Others positioned themselves near the cameras.

John directed Elizabeth to Nate and Cecilia, who circulated and greeted guests.

"Congratulations. Everything was beautiful," Elizabeth said.

Cecilia leaned in closer, and her voice dropped to a conspiratorial level. "It's actually a little over the top. Maybe a lot." She rolled her eyes. "The studio wanted to

make a big show. Fortunately, the Biltmore Estate wasn't available, nor was some castle, so we compromised."

"Kind of." Nate chuckled. "You'll see later. We're glad you both could come."

John picked out Shelby and her posse and steered Eliza-beth to a table on the far side of the tent with several of the other *Say Yes to the Rose* contestants. "Good to see you ladies again. Can we join you?"

"Of course," the group welcomed them.

"This is Elizabeth." He kept it simple with a touch to her lower back and aimed an adoring smile at her to make it look real, not that he had to fake it. "And let's see if I get this right. You're Lauren." She nodded, and he gave her a side hug, careful not to crush the woman half his size. "Diana, and Imani." They were easy to remember too since he'd had them in the top three with Cecilia. "And . . . I'm sorry, I . . ."

"Beth. We didn't meet since I wasn't there long, but I did connect with Cecilia."

"And this is Trent." Wearing a bashful smile, Imani introduced the man next to her.

"How long have you been back from your deployment?" Lauren asked.

"Around a month. Nate mentioned you're starting grad school."

"Yes! I'll be studying Clinical Psychology at UNC."

"You two should talk. Elizabeth is a counselor in Fayet-teville."

"We definitely should." Lauren said.

"What are you drinking?" John asked. All the women had what looked like the same drinks in martini glasses.

"I think the bartender called it a Flirtini. It's got pineapple juice and whatever else goes in a martini." Diana took a sip.

"Want me to get you one or would you like a glass of wine?" John asked Elizabeth.

"I'll try the Flirtini."

She and Lauren were talking about psychology when John returned with their drinks. He caught the eye of a server circulating with trays of hors d'oeuvres.

His stomach growled, but he waited for the women to each help themselves.

"These avocado egg rolls are amazing," Lauren popped the remaining half of the pastry in her mouth.

"Go ahead," Elizabeth offered him the last one.

"We'll split it." He couldn't resist holding it near her mouth, challenging and tempting her until she caved and took a small bite.

"You two are adorable together," Lauren said.

"Thanks. I think so," John said, while Elizabeth choked.

"Is it too spicy, sweetheart?"

"Just went down the wrong way." She gave him that narrow-eyed, teacher-reprimand look that only made him smile bigger.

"Here comes Reginald," Imani warned out of the side of her mouth.

"Who's that?" John scanned the crowd for a threat.

"Keeping it Real Reginald. He's a reality TV show vlogger. He was on *Say Yes to the Rose* for an episode," Diana explained.

A bald man in a trendy, tailored purple suit showed his bare ankles sashayed up to their table. His white shirt had purple stripes in a check pattern and a folded pocket square.

"I've been trying to get over here to get the scoop from you ladies, but I keep getting stopped by my fans. Sorry to keep you waiting." He exchanged air kisses with Imani,

then lifted Diana's hand to his mouth. "No ring. But that doesn't mean anything, does it? What scoop can you give me on your season, darling?"

"You know I can't divulge any spoilers."

"But you can drop an exclusive hint. In exchange, I promise to make you look good in my coverage."

"Sorry. They've got me locked up with confidentiality clauses." Diana smiled sweetly.

Reginald implored her with his eyes and a pout. Getting nothing, he turned to Imani and took her hand. "No ring either, but you're here at a wedding together. That's promising."

"Things are good, but we're taking it slow." Imani beamed at Trent.

"I know you two bonded in a bowling alley, but you need to step up your game and pick someplace more upscale if you're going to propose." Reginald waggled a finger in Trent's face.

Trent just smiled.

"And you," Reginald shifted his gaze to John and Elizabeth. "So, the rumors about you and Shelby aren't true?"

"What rumors? Ones you started?" He took a guess. "I didn't *start* any. So, what do you like about the big guy?" Reginald eyed Elizabeth.

"What's not to like? He's kind. Makes me laugh. He's good to his dog." Elizabeth smiled up at John.

He'd take that. It was a start anyway.

"He's also tall, with muscles, and handsome in a rugged kind of way. How about a picture of the three of us?" Reginald flicked on his phone's camera app.

"Pass." John squelched the request. Reginald extended the phone anyway, forcing John to strategically block the shot.

"Really?" Reginald sighed and pouted as if unaccustomed to being told no but covered a bit under John's I-can-kill-you-if-I-have-to gaze. Reginald gave Lauren a quick once-over. "Weren't you the Harry Potter girl?"

"Yep," Lauren said cheerfully. "I'm a Gryffindor. I'll be in grad school and am still single."

"Oh honey," Reginald patted Lauren's hand and gave Beth a dismissive glance before he moved on to mingle with other guests.

Elizabeth was still hitting it off with Lauren and the others when the wedding director came around and invited everybody to the barn for dinner.

"I've got to make my entrance with the wedding party. I'll join you at the table," John walked her out, then he watched as she headed to the barn with the women. He'd never seen her in heels. They accentuated her great legs. The urge to kiss her had nothing to do with putting on a show for Shelby and everything to do with his growing and undeniable attraction to Elizabeth. As opposite as they were, it seemed she was made for him and he for her, even if she didn't fully know it yet.

He hummed "Opposites Attract" while waiting for the rest of the bridal party to assemble but was not about to admit he knew the words to the Paula Abdul song.

Chapter Forty

(I'VE HAD) THE TIME OF MY LIFE – Bill Medley &
Jennifer Warren

ELIZABETH ENTERED the tent with Lauren and her friends from *Say Yes to the Rose*.

Diana offered her a pen after the women stopped to sign one of the pages for the guest book.

"I'll let John sign for us." She was just the plus one. A fake date for the day. At least everyone seemed to be believing their act. Not that it was hard to pretend with John, and they knew each other well enough to be convincing as a couple.

Elizabeth studied the seating chart and moved to their assigned table, saying hello to a woman and man already seated at the head table. The DJ turned down the music after everyone was seated and announced the wedding party's entrance. The pairings each danced their way in. John held hands with a pretty bridesmaid and gracefully

twirled her. Unexpected tightness in Elizabeth's chest finally eased when they made their way to the table and the brunette sat next to the man at the other end of the table and kissed him.

John didn't kiss Elizabeth as he slid into his seat, but he did drape an arm around the back of her chair with his fingers lightly brushing her shoulder as the other couples entered. Watching Nate and Cecilia dance together as husband and wife for the first time, Elizabeth swallowed the sensation of missing out, similar to how she'd felt holding Rhonda's baby at the birthday party.

She chanced a glance at John. He watched his friend, then he shifted his smile to her. While his touch didn't feel possessive, the way they held each other's gaze should convince anyone watching they were a couple, especially since it took effort to tear her gaze from his and accept the champagne glasses the waitstaff brought everyone.

After Cecilia's father gave the first toast, the best man followed, then the maid of honor. John got to his feet.

Nate's, "Oh, boy!" brought ripples of laughter from several people.

"Naw, I'm not going to tell a bunch of embarrassing stories about Nate. Just remember that at my wedding because there are definitely stories you could tell about me."

Elizabeth didn't doubt that was true.

"Cecilia, today you married one of the best men I've ever known. And that is saying a lot, because I've served with a lot of honorable men. I always thought Nate was one of the smartest men I knew, but I did rethink that when I heard he was going on a reality dating show. But after he became the lead and had twenty-five women throwing themselves at him—"

"'Twenty-four," Nate called out. "Someone played hard to get." He looked at Cecilia, who bashfully shrugged.

"I knew how much he wanted to find love, but I was afraid he was in for a lot of drama."

"So much drama," the host of the show confirmed.

"While I had my doubts, I've never seen Nate happier, and that's because he found the right woman. I wish you both a lifetime of happiness. Cheers." He raised his glass. "Elizabeth and I will be singing 'I've Had the Time of My Life' while Nate and Cecilia perform the closing dance from Dirty Dancing after dinner."

"Oh no, we won't." Elizabeth hid her face behind her hand.

"That's not happening. But thanks for the thought."

Cecilia laughed, and Nate motioned for him to sit.

Elizabeth shook her head at John.

"No duet?"

"I think we'd need to practice for something like that."

"Next time."

With him moving out of The Oasis, then to Florida, there wouldn't be a next time. That made her more than a little sad.

Chapter Forty-One

CAN'T FIGHT THIS FEELING – REO Speedwagon

AFTER THE DINNER, Cecilia danced with her father, and Nate danced with his mother. Then the DJ invited the bridal party to the dance floor.

John held out a hand to Elizabeth. "That's us." He couldn't take his eyes off the smile on Elizabeth's face as they let loose, dancing to "Walking on Sunshine." Nate and Cecilia sang to each other, laughing with love shining in their eyes. Damn, that's what he wanted.

Once the song ended, the DJ tapped on the microphone. "I thought this was a party!" he proclaimed loudly. "Let's dance!"

Guests swarmed the floor, taking turns showing off their moves as the theme from *Footloose* played.

"Can we sit this one out?" John asked when a group of the contestants shrieked as "Girls Just Want to Have Fun"

236

started up. Elizabeth nodded, and they slipped back to the table.

When the next song started, Shelby came up and laid a hand on his shoulder. "Can I borrow Big John for a dance?"

"Uh—"

"Sure," Elizabeth answered over him. "You can have him—for one dance."

The proviso tempered Shelby's smile.

"I'll be back." He leaned in and brushed a kiss to Elizabeth's cheek. "Thanks a lot," he muttered before being dragged away.

"We missed you last night. I thought you were coming down to the pool." Shelby leaned close as they danced.

"Figured I should save my energy for tonight."

"Did you know about the thing between Nate and Cecilia?"

"Thing? You mean Nate trying to get out of the contract because he liked her and the producers tricking her into going on? He didn't say a word about it beforehand, but he did give us the scoop over the bachelor party weekend. We all had Cecilia in our top three. Ben claims he could tell she was the one from her answers to his questions and the way Nate watched her on the home build date. They are perfect together."

"Everyone was surprised, but I'm so happy for them both." Shelby almost sounded convincing.

"How many of the women from Nate's season came?"

He scanned the room.

"About half. Some that weren't invited to the wedding still came to party last night. One crashed the cocktail party here, but a producer escorted her out. I think she was hoping for a shot at being on Second Chance Island.

Speaking of that, fans were posting how they'd love to see you, Ben, and Linc on the island."

"Not happening."

"Why not? You'd get paid to hang out on the beach, drink, and go on dates for three weeks."

"Don't think I can get leave for that long. And Ben's married." Going on one episode for Nate and being minor players was one thing, but there was no way in hell he or Linc would risk their careers.

"Not everyone comes in the beginning. You could come the last week."

"When people are already paired off? I'd just get sent home." Like a loser.

"Not if I were there."

"Isn't the point to have people who are available? Not in a relationship?" He stretched the truth and nodded toward Elizabeth who was talking in a group that included Lauren and the other women they'd chatted with during the cocktail hour.

"The point is to find love. Explore your options. That's why I'll go on if asked. I want to find love and get married. Have kids with the man I sing love songs about." She batted her lashes at him.

And get airtime to further her career. She claimed to want the same things he did, while Elizabeth didn't even want to date—anyone. Was he wasting his time hoping she'd suddenly change her mind?

The song ended, transitioning into an old REO Speedwagon love ballad.

"Oh, I love this song," Shelby draped an arm over his shoulder, her body swaying and brushing against his.

"It is a great one. And I'm going to go dance to it with my date." He removed her arm and gave her hand a

squeeze. "Thanks for the dance." He beelined toward Elizabeth.

"May I have this dance?"

"You may." She put her hand in his.

He held her close but kept a few inches between their bodies. "You were supposed to play the jealous girlfriend and tell Shelby I couldn't dance with her."

"Then I'd look insecure in our relationship."

"You're secure with us, then? Good. Because I can't fight this feeling anymore," he sang along. The words rang true. What started out with Elizabeth as friendship had turned into so much more. Because of her, he had a new clarity and direction. He wanted a wife and family more than ever. But not with just any woman. It was deep, unconditional love he wanted. That crashing-through-the-door, crawl-through-a-minefield-to-get-to-her kind of love.

They both needed to feel the same. And he was willing to fight for it.

Chapter Forty-Two

ELIZABETH DANCED with John and in groups for at least half an hour before John linked his fingers through hers and joined their hands at the small of her back. He leaned close.

"I need a drink."

His body heat and hot breath near her ear dialed up her arousal another notch.

He led her to the bar. "Two waters and one of those Flirtini cocktails." He downed most of his water and handed it back for a refill when the bartender placed the cocktail on the counter.

Elizabeth took a sip of the Flirtini. "Whoa."

John chuckled at the face she made. "Too strong?"

"A bit. And I need to drive to the hotel later."

"I'll help you out." John took a long sip from her cup. "Can you top this off with some more pineapple juice?" He handed it to the bartender." I rode up on the shuttle bus but

240

planned for us to ride to the hotel together. How about I drive your car back?"

Other than a glass of champagne at dinner and a swig of her drink, John had stuck with water. Not what she expected, considering the open bar. Even if she didn't have to drive, she still needed to stay sober to keep from saying anything that would out their relationship as fake. Or to keep from stepping over the line with John in selling them as a couple.

They'd only sat out one song when Elizabeth noticed the teen who had been the junior bridesmaid slowly approach their table. The girl's gaze locked on John. "I think someone wants to dance with you."

"Again?" His eyes widened in alarm until he looked over his shoulder. He broke into a big smile and motioned the girl to join them. "This is Cecilia's younger sister, Katie. You did great today. This is my friend, Elizabeth."

"Nice to meet you, Katie." Elizabeth held out her hand. The girl made fleeting eye contact and gave a weak handshake.

"Will you dance with me, Katie?"

Her face lit up. "Uh, huh." Katie took John's hand and pulled him to the dance floor.

Despite her developmental delays, Katie didn't appear afraid of John or his size. Elizabeth's heart melted, and she couldn't keep her eyes off them as John held Katie's hands and they danced in a circle.

Why hadn't she met a guy like him years ago? How different would her life be today if she'd known someone like John, who would have stood up to her father back in her high school days? Or before Adam had scarred her so badly.

John and Katie stayed on the dance floor through the

next song. After Linc cut in, John made his way back to the table wearing a dopey grin.

"What's with that look?" He sat and slid his chair closer to Elizabeth's side.

"It was sweet watching you dance with her."

"Took a little while for Katie to warm up to me last night. She hid behind her mom when she first met me at the rehearsal."

"Because of your size?"

"I'm not that big."

She chuckled lightly. "The women keep referring to you as Big John."

"It's how Nate introduced me on the show. Army nickname. Come on, we know this dance."

They joined the crowd. Somehow, Shelby and her blonde friend ended up on the other side of John. After a series of line dances, the DJ slowed things down with another love song.

John pivoted to face Elizabeth and slid a hand to her lower back. He squeezed her hand and stared into her eyes as he softly sang along with Ed Sheeran about how a touch of a hand could make people fall in love.

Desire like she hadn't experienced in nearly a decade had been building. Now it flowed, unchecked, through her. She couldn't let him see it, so she broke eye contact. "Do you not know the lyrics, or do you just not care?" She forced a lightheartedness into her voice.

"A little of both. It's not in my favorites playlist, but I like it." He kept smiling at her.

Near the end of the song, he dipped her. She froze. His face hovered just inches from hers. Strangling powerlessness made her chest ache.

full-blown panic attack.

thing as innocent as a dance move had her on the verge of a

reminding her of what she couldn't have. Not when some-

dance. The pair stared adoringly into each other's eyes,

into tears, she diverted her gaze to watch Nate and Cecilia

She nodded and faked a smile. To keep from breaking

"You sure?" His eyes narrowed, but he swayed with her.

shoulder.

"I'm fine," she lied, putting her free hand back on his

lower back and loosened his grip on her hand.

"Do you need to sit?" He removed his fingers from her

enough to draw in a ragged breath.

"It's okay. You just surprised me." The tightness eased

her. "I'm sorry. I wasn't thinking."

"Shit," he whispered under his breath, quickly righting

Chapter Forty Three

UNFORGETTABLE – Nat King Cole

AFTER CUTTING the cake and lots more dancing, including every line dance Elizabeth had ever learned, the party wound down. The DJ interrupted the music and called all the couples to the dance floor for the anniversary dance.

"What's that?" John asked.

"It's a newer tradition to replace the bouquet and garter toss. All the couples start the dance, and it's whittled down until the pair together longest are left and give marital advice. It's sweet."

"I don't know whether to be relieved or disappointed that I don't get to watch these women fight for the bouquet."

He held out a hand. "Come on. We're a couple."

The dance floor quickly filled up and John held her close as "Everything I Do" played. Maybe it was the alcohol that had lowered her body's instinct to view him as a threat,

but she relaxed as he effortlessly took small steps to keep from bumping into other people.

"Any couples that have been together less than a year, take a seat," the DJ prompted.

"Dang," John sighed and nodded back toward their table.

The crowd quickly thinned as the DJ sent couples of less than two, five, ten, and twenty years off by the end of the second song. A handful of couples danced and John crooned along to "Unforgettable."

After the song concluded, only Nate's and Cecilia's grandparents remained with fifty-plus years of marriage. The DJ asked them to share their best marital tips.

"Considering how things started with all those women, don't ever call her the wrong name," Nate's grandfather started, eliciting laughter throughout the room.

"He never did that, though he did have lots of girl-friends before me. He still makes me laugh, and typically listens to me. He occasionally needs a reminder." Nate's grandmother looked at her husband, who gave a sheepish shrug. "Good communication is a key to success."

"I'll remember that, Gram," Nate said.

"Don't criticize her cooking unless you're willing to fix dinner yourself," Cecilia's grandfather added.

"Or order takeout," a woman in a sequined gown more appropriate for a red-carpet event called out from a nearby table. The former contestants seated with her laughed, and the newlyweds whispered to each other before Cecilia's grandmother shared her advice.

Then the bride and groom took turns dancing with their grandparents before the floor opened up to others again.

♫

After the last dance, Katie and a young boy passed out sparklers to guests who formed a path leading from the tent to a limo SUV. John and the other groomsmen lit the sparklers as fireworks shot into the air and gave the guests a show.

A cameraman filmed Nate and Cecilia as they passed between the two lines of guests.

"That's something you don't see at every wedding."

John watched the wedding couple kiss with fireworks exploding in the background.

Elizabeth could clearly see Nate and Cecilia's faces. The two had their own fireworks going off between them. Nate paused before opening the door. "Promise me no crying in the limo."

Cecilia gave a delightful laugh. "Definitely no crying."

She kissed Nate again.

The fireworks died out as the limo pulled away. Elizabeth trailed at John's side as he walked around, lighting more sparklers for the kids and gathering the spent ones in a bucket. Bridesmaids passed out shimmering drawstring bags. John set the bucket down and opened his bag. He held up two cookies shaped and decorated like rosebuds. The first red iced cookie had "She said Yes" written on it, and the second cookie had "They said I Do" in white icing.

"Which do you want?" John held them out.

Elizabeth accepted the "I Do" cookie.

John took a bite of the other, his gaze fixed on her face. He picked up the bucket and completed his pass, collecting sparklers and saying goodbye to Katie and the groomsmen. Most of the guests had already headed to their cars. However, a large group she guessed was associated with *Say Yes to the Rose* congregated near a limousine passenger bus.

"John, are you riding back with us?" Shelby's blonde

sidekick asked.

"Naw, I'm set." He wrapped an arm around Elizabeth. "Where'd you park?" He didn't miss a step or look back, and his hand remained on her hip all the way to her car. "Keys." He held out a hand, and walked her to the passenger side, opening and closing the door like a true gentleman.

It was nice to slip her shoes off her aching feet as he slid the driver's seat all the way back before getting in. After adjusting his seat and setting the mirrors, she handed him her USB cable to connect his phone and display directions.

Rather than put the car into gear, John stared at her like he wanted to say something, or maybe, kiss her.

And in that moment, she wanted him to kiss her. Probably more than she'd ever wanted to kiss a man before, even though it would be a really, really bad idea. She refrained from leaning toward him—but barely—and only because she knew her reaction wouldn't match up with any romantic fantasies. His or hers.

On the drive to the hotel, John told her how he and Nate met early in their careers through Officer Candidate school. Though they served in different units, they had been deployed together in Afghanistan, which strengthened their brother-like bond.

"Nate and I went to the mountains together after that deployment. It was his idea, so I kind of have him to thank for finding Boss."

"You two didn't fight over him?"

"Nate was based in Germany, so getting the dog shipped over there wasn't practical. I got Boss. Now he's got Cecilia."

His gaze lingered on her again in a way that made her wish things could be different. More than platonic. That she could be the woman she'd once been.

Chapter Forty-Four

SWEET DREAMS (ARE MADE OF THIS) –
Eurythmics

Elizabeth slipped her shoes on as John navigated into the parking lot of the hotel in Uptown Charlotte. Despite stressing out prior to the wedding, everything had gone smoothly and been a lot of fun. Now that it was over, they could drop the act. After a good night's sleep and some needed distance from John, tomorrow morning, they'd be back to status quo—friends.

John took her bag from the trunk and pulled it behind him. When they entered the lobby, she stayed at his side as he headed to the reception desk.

"I got a text that you had a cancelation and you're holding another room for me," he told the agent. "Last name's Bryson."

Cancelation? A chill swept through Elizabeth.

The clerk typed on the keyboard. "Yes. We did have a

cancelation."

Whew. Elizabeth breathed an internal sigh.

"It's an executive suite," the clerk paused between each word. "It's three hundred ninety-eight for the night. Do you want that on the credit card on file?"

John hesitated a moment before reaching for his wallet. "Let me give you a different card."

"No. Don't do that. I can drive back home." Elizabeth couldn't let him pay that much.

"Not this late and after drinking."

"I'm fine," she insisted.

"I promised you your own room. What are the rates at the overflow hotel? They were holding a room for me there," he asked the woman.

"I'm pretty sure we canceled that when the suite opened up. Let me see. They did cancel that, and they're full now. I can check our other brands and see if I can find you a standard room."

"That'd be great. While you do that, I'll take her up and get my bag from the room. I'll check back in a few minutes."

"I'm sorry I'm making things difficult," Elizabeth told him once they were in the elevator.

"No worries. I just didn't anticipate all the celebrity-seekers."

"I wouldn't have either."

When they got to the room, John set her bag on the bed closest to the window.

"You didn't mention there were two beds."

"Because I told you that you'd have your own room. I slept in the other bed last night." He went to the closet and removed a suit bag.

His chivalry was impressive. Two beds. This wasn't worst-case. He was sober, and if he did anything stupid, he'd

be homeless and put his career at risk. "I think we can manage to share a hotel room for one night rather than spend that much for separate rooms."

"Are you sure?" He cocked his head as he hung his suit jacket on the hanger from the bag.

"We're two adults," she said, despite the beads of sweat breaking out on the back of her neck.

He stood with the suit bag in his hand for several long moments. "She can find something half that rate with all the hotels around here. I'll—"

"John . . . It's okay. Just stay here." She forced the words out.

"Okay. But if I start snoring, just throw a pillow at me, and I'll go sleep in my truck." He picked up the hotel phone and called down to tell them they were set after all.

That he started humming "Unforgettable" calmed her racing heart, for the most part.

"Do you want to use the bathroom first?" she offered.

"After all that dancing, I kind of need a shower."

"That's fine."

Once she heard the water running, she changed into her pajama set and got out her toiletries. In less than five minutes, John emerged wearing a pair of sleep pants with a towel over his shoulder.

"Bathroom's all yours."

She tried not to stare as he laid his suit pants and shirt on his bed. Water dripped from his short hair to glisten on his bare back. Veins stood out on his corded arms as he rubbed the towel over his hair again.

Grabbing her cosmetics case, she hustled into the bathroom to keep from staring at the thin trail of dark hair from his belly button to where it disappeared. She closed the bathroom door and locked it behind her, sucking in a deep

breath, and willed her heart to slow. There was no condensation on the mirror, and the water she splashed on her face wasn't even warm yet. Maybe she should take a cold shower too.

Instead, she took her time removing her makeup and preparing for bed. The bedside lamp was still on when she exited the bathroom. John wore a T-shirt and leaned against the headboard. He hummed along to Ed Sheeran's "Perfect" and scrolled on his phone, letting out an occasional chuckle.

"I thought that song wasn't in your playlist."

His head jerked up, and he cleared his throat. "I like it. Sometimes, you hear a song in a situation that makes you see it a different way."

His gaze remained locked on her as she moved past his bed.

"Pictures from the wedding are already all over social media," he said.

That didn't surprise her, considering there had been a sign at the reception with a hash tag for the wedding, along with ones for the show. "You're on social media?" That did surprise her after what Jillian had said.

"I am, but not as me." He flipped his phone around.

The name on the account was Michael, with a last name she couldn't even begin to pronounce, and a profile graphic of a music note and CD.

"You know how people create fake accounts claiming to be military generals or doctors?"

"I'm not on social media. Wren's commented about getting messages from fake accounts all the time, though."

"I'm an actual military guy—though I'm not a general, at least yet—pretending I'm a DJ. Just like these influencers here want followers, the same's true in every country. Start

following some DJ or model wannabe, expand your network, and you start gathering intel."

"I see." Elizabeth handed back his phone and sat down on her bed.

"When I'm not on a mission, I may come off like life is all fun and games. Not to sound cocky, but my team and I are very good at what we do. Which means dealing with some very bad people. J.R.? He's a punk. Easy enough to deal with. But you get someone with the evil mindset to round up twenty impressionable guys and promise them women, money, and favor in heaven, then arm them, and you have a recipe to create terrorists. Those guys have nothing to live for, and everything to die for. Sorry, this might be getting too heavy."

He diverted his gaze back to the phone's screen.

"Looks like that Reginald guy managed to get a picture with us. Guess he bought us being a couple." He showed her a selfie of Reginald where, in the background, she was in John's arms. "Thanks again for coming and being the perfect date. We'll have to do it again sometime."

"Sure." She said with a light laugh, though wishing it were a possibility. "I doubt there'll be another wedding and reception quite like that."

"Probably not. I want a more intimate wedding, but with a great DJ and music and dance partner." He stared at his phone's screen again before setting it on the nightstand.

"Good night."

"Sweet dreams."

"Are made of this," he sang, as if unable to help himself.

She walked right into that. "You aren't going to sere-nade me to sleep, are you?" She talked over him.

He stopped abruptly. "Not with that one."

Thank goodness. The old Eurythmics song had earned

an immediate skip-to-another-station when it came on because of the line about some people wanting to be abused.

"How about 'Unforgettable,' since that's what you are?" He turned off the lamp and hummed the soothing tune in the darkness.

Only the other lyrics still played in her head. She might not have seen Adam's need for control as a warning sign initially, but she had not *wanted* to be abused. And when he'd crossed from emotional to sexual abuse, she'd done what she had to do to move out and on.

Only she hadn't been able to move on completely. When she'd tried kissing or being the least bit intimate with a man she dated, panic attacks had ensued. That's why she'd given up hope after years of meeting with a trauma counselor, and she simply stopped dating.

Yet, over the past few weeks, she gotten comfortable enough with John—a big, alpha, military guy, of all people— that she didn't jump at his touch. Dancing with him, she'd felt almost normal. Almost healed. Until he'd dipped her, and her vulnerability triggered her fight or flight instinct. But it passed. She didn't have to fight. Or flee. Just breathe. And trust. Trust John *and* herself. For the first time in years, she had a spark of hope.

As they lay in separate beds in the dark hotel room, the need to protect herself warred with her physical attraction to John. Could she enjoy a physical relationship with a man again?

She imagined kissing John. It felt good. Her thoughts leveled up—his hands on her, her body pressed to his. There was barely a ripple of anxiety, and good memories returned.

He stopped humming. What was he thinking? What would he say or do if he knew what *she* was thinking?

She didn't move a muscle as the minutes ticked past and

his breathing slowed and deepened. Then she pushed her imagination forward—to them taking off their clothes. Memories flooded back. Sweat broke out all over her body. Her heart raced, and an invisible band constricted around her chest. She countered the anxiety by breathing slow and deep and grounding herself that she was safe here in this hotel room.

Hot tears burned her eyes and trickled down her cheek as reality set in. It wouldn't be fair to use John to see how far she'd get in real life before panic enveloped her. With what she'd learned from their talks, he'd see that as another rejection of him, rather than her inability to function when it came to sex. She could push him right back into a sex-based relationship instead of building the kind of healthy one he needed to get what he wanted most—love and marriage.

He deserved those things. If it weren't for his abandonment issues making him walk away rather than risk rejection, a woman would have locked him down for sure. Her life, her work, and The Oasis were here in Fayetteville. With his upcoming promotion and move, he didn't need her holding him back. If he could move forward, he could have everything he wanted.

Chapter Forty-Five

I WANT TO KNOW WHAT LOVE IS – Foreigner

JOHN'S PHONE chimed from an incoming text message. Elizabeth opened one sleepy eye as he grabbed the phone.

"Ben says he and his wife are going down to breakfast in thirty minutes if we want to join them."

"Sure." Elizabeth's voice was thick and dreamy from sleep.

He couldn't remember the last time he woke up with a woman where she'd slept in a different bed. While he would have liked for her to share his, this felt nice, not the morning-after awkward—unless he got up now and she saw his morning erection. It'd gotten harder just thinking of her being in his bed. "You get first dibs on the bathroom. I'll text him back."

They entered the hotel breakfast area a half hour later. John groaned as he spotted Linc, Ben, and his wife seated at

a long table with several contestants from Nate's season, including Shelby.

"Sorry," he whispered to Elizabeth. "I didn't know they'd be here too."

"No worries. We'll just fake it a little longer."

With them leaving soon, there wasn't a need to keep up the charade any longer, other than how he felt being with her as a couple. She might be faking it. Him? Nope. Not anymore.

One day at a time, between their dinner at the restaurant and this weekend, his feelings had become undeniably real. Different than he'd ever felt about a woman. Was there any possibility she felt the same? She didn't flirt. Didn't seek him out. But she'd never turned him away when he crashed her evenings on the porch. She laughed with him, not at him.

She also didn't date.

The only way things were going to change was to come clean. He'd hinted at it, singing to her last night, but clearly, he needed to come right out and tell her he was falling for her. Even if it was like standing in the open with a target painted over his heart and handing her a loaded automatic weapon.

When though? After the incident on the dance floor, it hadn't felt right. Sharing a room could have been a good time, or the absolute worst.

Now wasn't the time either. They took empty seats across from Shelby and Hannah.

"Weren't the wedding and reception perfect? Well, near perfect. The DJ didn't have my song to play." Shelby gave a little pout.

"Don't get me wrong, I love your song, but a heartbreak song is not exactly dance music at a wedding," Hannah said.

"I'll have to add it to my playlist so I can sing along," John commented before thinking that through.

Shelby blushed. "You know he can't carry a tune, and he changes the words?" She spoke in conspiratorial tones to Elizabeth as if trying to prove she knew him, despite their time together being two afternoons of filming.

"Trust me, I'm aware." Elizabeth smiled at him, totally nonplussed. He wasn't sure if that was a good or bad thing. "Nobody's perfect, but he excels in many other areas that more than make up for it."

"We weren't introduced yesterday. I'm Shelby."

"And I'm Hannah. It's nice to meet you, Britney."

Crap. John's body went into battle mode. That slip was no accident. The inflection and slight quirk of Hannah's mouth confirmed it.

"Britney's his ex. I'm Elizabeth. We've been together since right after he got back from his last deployment." Elizabeth smiled at John, handling Hannah like a pro.

"Oh, I'm sorry about that. I saw a post and . . . My bad." Hannah raised a manicured hand to her mouth feigning embarrassment.

"A post?" Likely the very one that led to the demise of his and Britney's relationship. "Were you stalking me?" This felt as dangerous as being watched by enemy fighters.

"No, I wasn't stalking you, silly. She posted a picture with you saying her boyfriend had been on *Say Yes to the Rose* and tagged the show. It showed up in my feed. I commented, and then she followed me. I don't always remember faces, but I'm good with names," Hannah said, as if to justify her mistake.

Yeah, right. Britney and Elizabeth looked nothing alike.

The server took their orders. While they waited, Hannah dropped in mentions of them following her on

social media. John wasn't certain if her disappointment that Elizabeth didn't have accounts came from not getting a follow or not being able to dig up more information on their relationship for Shelby.

"We need to pack and catch a shuttle to the airport, unless one of you are going that way." Shelby's gaze roved over them, settling on him.

"We're booked on the noon shuttle," Ben said.

"Nate arranged late checkout, so we're gonna hang out a while longer," John lied to get himself off the hook since she knew he and Elizabeth hadn't arrived together.

Shelby gave an understanding nod. "Y'all stay safe when you're deployed. I appreciate your service. And if you ever want concert tickets where I'm performing, contact me via my website, and I'll take care of you."

Chapter Forty-Six

OPEN YOUR HEART – Madonna

Elizabeth tried not to sigh aloud when the two women left. She couldn't blame Shelby for dropping not-so subtle hints to John, especially since she hadn't expected him to be there with a date and figured out John and Elizabeth hadn't been *together* long.

That she wished she were more like Shelby amplified the ache in Elizabeth's chest that hadn't abated since last night. This fake relationship was about to end, and things would be back to normal—at least *her* normal. It wouldn't be long before John would be in his own home, then off to Florida. Based on this elaborate ruse, he did seem intent on making better decisions for his love life, but he'd be free to move on however he wanted.

They hung out in the hotel restaurant a little longer. While there were no cameramen around, many of the

show's former contestants took selfies together or posed for pictures with other guests.

A pair of older women wearing T-shirts with "Say Yes to the Rose" printed on them approached their table after the server cleared their plates.

"Sorry to interrupt, but we wanted to say that we loved you guys on the episode with the home build. And it was clear you were there to help Nate, not just to get on TV. They barely showed your face," the taller woman with glasses said to Linc. "We have a group that does watch parties, and we all agreed it was the best season in a long time."

"Maybe ever," the woman's red-headed friend added. "We were kind of hoping one of you might go on Diana's season or become the next bachelor on the show."

"I'm married." Ben flashed his ring and put his other arm around his wife's shoulders.

"I've got a good thing here." John smiled at Elizabeth, keeping up pretenses.

"I'm a no drama guy. Hard pass," Linc rounded out the nos.

"Too bad. But it was nice to see a real happy ending. Thank you both for your service and stay safe."

They lingered rather than walk away.

"Did you want a picture with us for your watch-party group?" John asked.

"We'd love that." The ladies beamed and pulled out their phones.

"I'll take the picture," Elizabeth offered.

The woman with glasses craned her neck, looking up at John when he stood between them. Ben and Linc flanked them on either side. "Wow. You are big."

FAKING IT WITH THE GREEN BERET

Elizabeth mouthed Big John and got a mock scowl from him before she snapped several pictures.

"Can we get one with you ladies in it too?" The redhead asked when Elizabeth handed back her phone.

"Okay." She and Ben's wife traded places with the women, who both took pictures.

"Looks like we better retreat before we are overrun."

Linc cut his gaze to nearby tables of women.

"Normally I'm not one to retreat, but I'm with you on this." John picked up their check.

Taking John's picture with two middle-aged women was one thing, but what did it say that Elizabeth would rather not take pictures of him posing with a dozen other adoring women? Pretty young ones who'd smile when he put his strong arm around their shoulders for a picture.

In the elevator, Linc pushed the number fourteen on the panel. John jabbed the button for their floor.

"It was great seeing y'all again. When do you deploy?" John asked Linc.

"Next month. Let's get together." They exchanged a fist bump as the elevator doors opened.

"Well, hi again." Shelby and Hannah stood there with their oversized suitcases. "It's like divine forces keep bringing us all together," Shelby proclaimed in her smooth, southern accent, aiming her brilliant smile at John.

Next to Elizabeth, John let out a faint grumble at the coincidence.

When Linc stepped out, Hannah threw herself at him for a goodbye hug, then moved on to Ben and his wife like they were old friends.

Shelby also gave them hugs after blocking the doors from closing with her suitcase. "Aren't you getting off?" She batted her lashes at John.

"We're going up to say goodbye to Nate's family."

Elizabeth caught how John hesitated, then toed Shelby's suitcase off so the door could close. "What was that about?"

"Shelby ambushed me when I checked in Friday night. Then she tagged along when I went up to my room, which was on her floor. When I went back down to add your room —unsuccessfully—I changed rooms so she wouldn't know where to find me." He let Elizabeth off the elevator first.

"Are you regretting pressuring me to come?"

"Not at all. You were the perfect date for this. For me. I had a great time with you. Besides, Shelby's too high maintenance."

"How would you know that?"

He tapped his card key to the lock and held the door open for her. "We worked together building a playset. Only about every thirty minutes, Shelby disappeared to 'go tinkle.' She'd come back with her hair and make-up all touched up for the cameras. I prefer a woman not so concerned about appearances. A natural beauty, like you."

"Thank you for the compliment." She reached for her dress in the closet.

"I think the reason everyone bought us being a couple is because they see how good we are together. For real." Instead of packing, he stood there with his gaze locked on her. "I don't want to go back to Fayetteville and the way things were—just being friends. Because what I feel for you is—" He took a step toward her.

Though her heart did a little jig, her brain fired off warning shots. This was exactly why she shouldn't have come. "John, stop. You—"

"Dancing with you yesterday, the lyrics kept hitting me. I've been falling in love with you."

Love? "No. You're—you're just . . ."

"Just what?"

"I don't know. Caught up in the weekend?"

"That's not it. This has been building since—since the night we met. You loved Boss enough to have Jillian check me out, and you still let me have him back. You said I should get to know a woman to see if I like being with her. You were right. Every time I'm with you, everything you do . . . you're everything I want."

He was breaking her heart because she couldn't give him what he wanted. "We can't be together."

"I won't ask you to give up your independence. In my line of work, that's a needed quality in a partner."

"It's more than that." More that she didn't want to get into. Not now. Not ever.

"Every time I see you, I smile. When I'm away from you, I want to see you again. I send Boss over so I have an excuse to come sit on the front porch with you," he admitted.

A ball of emotions caught in her throat. She wished she could tell him she felt the same—because she did.

With all he'd done, she owed him the truth so that he'd see it wasn't him. It was her. All her.

Chapter Forty-Seven

WARRIOR – Demi Lovato

"I APPRECIATE all you've done and enjoy spending time with you." She started with the easier truth, summoning her courage to continue. "But trying to be more than friends wouldn't be fair to you. You deserve more. Someone who can give you what you need—in the way of a physical relationship."

"Is this because of things with your father?" John's tone was even and guarded.

"He was physically abusive, but . . ."

"Your ex? You said he was controlling, but there's more. What did he do to you?" Now, John's voice dropped to an ominous threat.

She swallowed. There were only a handful of people who knew all the details. Adam. Her. Their attorneys. Nurses and police officers. Her therapist. She'd disclosed pieces to help build trust with clients. Even Jillian didn't

know the whole story. As impulsive as it was for John to think he might be falling in love, it left her limited options, with the ugly truth being best.

She drew in a deep, shaky breath and sank onto the side of the bed. "In the beginning, our marriage was happy and normal. We'd been married about a year and a half and were trying to start a family." Or so she thought. "Adam's son and daughter had been with us for the weekend, but he had to go out of town on Sunday afternoon. When I took the kids home, I mentioned to his ex-wife that we wanted to take them to New York City to see a musical and celebrate his daughter's sixteenth birthday. Lorraine commented that just because I wouldn't have kids, hers would never see me as more than Adam's second wife."

"That was vicious."

"She didn't want to see him happy. I just didn't know why she'd come at me since I didn't meet Adam until after they were divorced. I told her I wasn't trying to be their mother, but I would want the kids to be on good terms with their half-siblings when we had children. She laughed and said I didn't know Adam if I thought he would agree to adopt." She shivered at the memory of Lorraine's cruel, cutting laugh. "When I said Adam and I were trying to have children, she told me Adam had a vasectomy."

"Was she making that up or . . ." John's mouth hung open.

"That's what I thought—or hoped—at first. But why would she lie about that? I confronted him when he got home."—three agonizing days later—"and Adam confessed he'd had the vasectomy after their son was born. In his defense, we had not talked about having kids before we got married. In my naïveté, I thought it'd been a given we'd have at least one child."

"'There's ways around that, or you could adopt.'

"Except Adam blamed the stress and demands of parenthood for the rift that led to their divorce. He said he'd already raised his kids and our marriage would be stronger if it was just the two of us.' Classic narcissistic behavior. Adam wanted to be the center of her world.' After learning he'd kept that from me and let me think we were trying for me to get pregnant, things changed in our relationship.'

John gave a mirthless laugh. "No doubt, after him lying about something so important to you.'

"'I felt betrayed and went into a depressive cycle. I wasn't interested in sex, only he didn't take no for an answer." She couldn't look John in the face when she said it. His hands fisted at his sides, but he didn't interrupt. "I finally recognized our relationship was about Adam's need for control and to have everything revolve around him, not him loving me or wanting to protect me. I had to leave. Only, as I've already told you, I had nothing. And nowhere to go. I started saving and planning. When I met with the legal aid lawyer, I told her everything. Denice explained that, without evidence, spousal rape is hard to prove.'

John inhaled sharply, fixing his gaze on the ceiling. Rage played out on his features.

"'I used my escape money to buy motion-activated spy cameras.' Her voice went flat as she recalled hiding them while he was out of town for business—in the kitchen, the bedroom, the bathroom, the living room. He returned the next evening and wanted to celebrate the deal he'd landed. 'The next morning, after he left for work, I went to the hospital for them to perform a rape kit.' Only I was afraid it wouldn't be enough to show a pattern, so I didn't press charges. Not yet.'

"You went back?" He sounded more distraught than disgusted like she'd feared.

"Until I had enough evidence to prove it wasn't a one-time thing." As shocked as Denice had been when Eliza-beth gave her the three recordings and rape kit reports, it had to be enough that Adam couldn't deny it. "In New Jersey, you don't have to go through a separation period in a case where there's fault, so we filed for divorce and asked for a settlement. Enough to get me into housing and to live on until I found a job." The amount was less than Adam made in two months. "He refused, citing the prenup I'd stupidly signed."

"I hope you pressed criminal charges."

"That was our next step. Denice figured he wouldn't want to explain the charges. Except he countered that he'd testify that I had rape fantasies, and we were role-playing. Say I liked it that way, which was why I'd recorded us. Or that I'd set him up to blackmail him. That either way, it would ruin my reputation."

"The son of a bitch." John's voice was filled with anger as he finally sat on the opposite bed. "He wouldn't chance that."

"Adam thought he was smarter than everyone else. Except, by that point, he'd isolated me from all my friends. I had no reputation to protect. Though it would be my word against his to convince a jury, until his ex-wife agreed to testify in a civil trial. That's when he agreed to settle."

"Why civil?"

"He could keep his job and keep paying her alimony and child support. I still wonder if I did the right thing letting him avoid jail time. If he learned anything or moved on to another naive young woman." The numbness that started in her hands traveled up her arms, to her face and

267

chest. "Denice pointed out I couldn't protect other women forever. We negotiated a settlement that covered living expenses and college tuition."

"He's why you became a counselor." John's voice was raw and sympathetic.

"It was definitely a factor." They sat in silence as she let him process what she'd been through. What she'd done and allowed Adam to continue to do to her.

"I'm sorry. For everything you went through. I'd kill him if—"

"No! That is *not* why I told you." Tears burned her eyes. "You cannot—"

"I'm not. I just— want to. You know?"

Oh, she knew. But it would destroy her if John landed in jail or was kicked out of the military because of anything to do with her.

"I get why your past would make you react the way you have, but you don't know that you can't have a normal physical relationship now."

But she did. "When I was in college, I tried dating. Every time it ended with the guy frustrated and me having a full-blown panic attack."

"That was a while ago. You've been in therapy since then. How do you know you'd still react the same? Yesterday, when we danced, you were in my arms, and—"

"And I nearly had a panic attack when you dipped me."

And again, trying to imagine doing more than kissing him.

"Nearly? But you didn't. You don't want to go through life letting your ex continue to rob you of the things you want, like love and a family." He leaned forward, extending an open hand to her.

Instead of panic, an overwhelming sadness prevented her from putting her hand in his. "Except, it's not as easy as

wanting them. It wouldn't be fair to you." John deserved that love and family. When he found the right woman, together they'd sing a happy love song instead of the heart-broken, country song of his past.

"Let me decide what's fair for me. Don't you think you owe it to yourself to try again rather than stay stuck? Is that what you let your clients do? Because you aren't practicing what you preach if you tell them they can move past their traumas and have a full life when you aren't willing to do it yourself."

His words sliced through her like a scalpel. "I have tried. I underwent counseling for years. You don't know where I am in the healing process. Or how long it can take to work through trauma." John didn't understand there were no guarantees she would be comfortable being intimate with him or anyone *ever* again.

"I'm a patient man."

It took more than patience. The few men she'd dated in college had called her a tease or frigid. The last, another student in her counseling program, claimed to understand, then pushed too far trying to "help her become desensitized" and unraveled much of her progress.

Despite what she'd seen of John's big heart, he was also damned persistent and didn't always take no for an answer. That's what scared her. What made it hard to breathe.

"I can't. It's me. I'm not ready." She couldn't keep him waiting, especially when they had so little time before he'd move on. "I need you to accept that." Her voice broke, and her throat burned. She didn't want to cry. She did not want to cry.

Tears escaped the second she closed her eyes.

"Okay. I appreciate your honesty, and I'll respect your decision." He got to his feet and disappeared into the bath-

room before she could retreat there for the box of tissues. It took longer than it should have for him to return with his shaving kit, which he placed in his suitcase without looking at her. "I'm ready to leave whenever you are."

The raw edge of his voice tore at her already hurting heart. "I need a few minutes. You can go on."

He stayed in place next to the bed for several long seconds before sighing. "I'll see you back at The Oasis."

"I'm sorry," she whispered, uncertain if he heard her as he opened the door and let it click closed behind him.

Why? Why had she agreed to come when she'd known he might read more into it? She'd hurt him. Failed him as a friend. Worse, she might have destroyed any progress he'd made when it came to establishing a healthy romantic relationship just because he picked the wrong woman.

Her.

Chapter Forty-Eight

IF YOU'RE GOING THROUGH HELL – Rodney
Atkins

IN THE PARKING GARAGE, John sat in his truck, willing his
rage to abate. He couldn't be mad at Elizabeth. He'd known
there was more to her story, but he never imagined it was as
dark as what she'd been through. After what she shared, he
hadn't dared touch her to offer comfort.

He'd refrained from punching a hole in the hotel wall.
That wouldn't have won points with her, but he still wanted
to hit something. Himself for making her relive it, or prefer-
ably, her asshole ex-husband. He didn't know Adam's last
name, but with a little digging, he could find out. Except
beating the crap out of her ex wouldn't make things better
for Elizabeth.

He loosened his white-knuckled grip on the steering
wheel, pounding on it with both forearms so hard the horn
blared and echoed off the cement walls. He'd crossed the

line, calling her a hypocrite. Maybe the reason she worked so hard to help other women was to get them to a point she hadn't reached in healing. Was there any way to salvage this?

A car driving past jarred him into motion. After starting the ignition, he immediately turned off the radio. For once in his life, he wasn't in the mood for music. Not some sappy love song, and he didn't want some heavy metal rock to add to the pounding in his head.

He made it about an hour into the trip home before he queued up Rodney Atkins' "If You're Going Through Hell." Playing it for the third time straight, he finally sang along. Despite Elizabeth's rules, he resolved to pick up a bottle of Jim Beam and get drunk tonight. If she kicked him out, at least he and Boss had a place to go to now that his renter had moved out. While his house might not be furnished, it was no emptier than his life.

At least he still had Boss.

♫

John didn't stop at the liquor store—a decision he might regret tonight but not in the morning when he had to report for duty. He drove past Elizabeth's home and empty porch. There'd be no sitting there with her tonight. Or ever again.

Wren let Boss out. He raced around the truck to greet John.

"How did everything go?" Wren asked.

"The wedding was great." He ruffled the fur on the back of Boss's neck.

"I meant with you and Elizabeth." Her innuendo made it clear she'd picked up on his attraction.

"Not so great." His rage had collapsed into a hollowness in his chest.

"What happened?" She sounded truly surprised.

"I told her how I felt about her—"

"Romantically?"

"Yes, and she is not interested in a relationship."

"Did she actually say that?"

"Yeah. There's no other way to interpret it."

"I can't believe that. Since you've been here, she's changed—lightened up. She's smiled and laughed more in the weeks since you came than in the entire year and a half before."

That should have made him feel better, not worse. "I don't know what she's told you about her past . . ."

"A good bit. When I first came here, I didn't want to tell her what I'd been through because most other people don't believe me. Or help. But Elizabeth said she understood—that she'd been afraid people wouldn't believe her story either. She shared, and I trusted her enough to finally tell her what I'd been through and done."

He'd go with that and not divulge anything Elizabeth had told him in confidence. "Because of what happened, she's still not ready for a relationship. I don't know what to do. I'm open to ideas."

"I wish I knew what to tell you. Even though we've been through similar—abuse—everyone's story is different. So is how we react. Some women, they, um, devalue?—I can't remember the term Elizabeth used. They act like sex is no big deal. For others, sex brings back what they went through, and restarts the trauma cycle. They may shut down and avoid relationships and sex."

That sounded like Elizabeth. "Forever?"

"I can't say. I went through a lot of bad shit, and I

learned a lot from Elizabeth. First, I had to be ready. You can't force a person to speed up the healing process. People would say 'just get over it.' That's not helpful. Seriously, I would if I could, but it's not that easy. It was like they were invalidating what I felt."

He let Wren's warning settle in. Elizabeth had made him see his pattern of walking away in the face of rejection. Since he couldn't get his mother to love him and be a part of his life, he'd learned to protect himself rather than fight a battle he couldn't win. While you couldn't force a person to love you, sometimes you did have to fight for a relationship. Show the person you loved that you wouldn't abandon them. Only from what Wren said, the very thing Elizabeth had encouraged him to do in a romantic relationship could hurt her and push her away forever. He was damned if he did, and damned if he didn't.

He didn't know what else to say or do. He conceded this might be a battle he couldn't win. "Thanks for the insight and for taking care of Boss while I was gone."

"I owed you. Still do."

"Let me grab his bed and food from you."

Back in Hope Harbor, Boss plucked a ball from the basket of toys. "Not now, boy. I gotta figure things out." He doubted Elizabeth wanted to come home to him and his dog in her front yard since Boss would inevitably head over for some love. He couldn't blame him.

It wasn't just tonight though. What about tomorrow? And the next day?

She hadn't asked for this. She'd warned him going to the wedding with him wasn't a good idea. It's not like she'd ever flirted or come on to him, though the way she looked at him made him hope she felt the same. He'd been attracted to her from the moment he saw her with Boss. Staying here, being

around her, seeing her beauty, both inside and out, had him feeling different than he ever had about a woman. It went beyond sexual attraction. But damn, that did need to be a part of a romantic relationship at some point.

She wasn't ready and asked him to accept that. The way she'd whispered she was sorry—at least he believed she did care. That it hurt her to reject him. The way she wished things could be different. *That* was different from his mom. Different from Britney. Different from pretty much anyone he'd dated. Because of Elizabeth, he felt like a different man now. More self-aware. Even worthy of love. Which could be why it hurt that Elizabeth wouldn't even give them a chance.

What she'd said about her ex not taking no for an answer stuck in his brain. Did she think he was the same way? Maybe he hadn't let her pay for the deck supplies, but that was a totally different situation. He needed to prove he was different from her ex. He needed to do what she wanted, even if it was the last thing *he* wanted. The end.

"It's time to move on, Boss."

♪

JOHN'S TRUCK stopped in front of her house. That he left the engine running was telling. Elizabeth understood he may not want to see her. In the hours since she'd gotten back from Charlotte, she'd been on a closet-cleaning binge. She couldn't explain why that suddenly seemed important, other than it gave her a reason not to crawl into bed and cry some more. It'd taken over half an hour to get herself together enough to leave the hotel room and drive home.

Boss's nails clicked on the wood coming up the porch steps. She wouldn't be hearing that again soon. Maybe ever.

She swallowed the lump making it hard to breathe, thinking how John's truck wouldn't rumble past, crunching the gravel. She wouldn't hear his singing. Wouldn't blush when he winked or complimented her.

It wouldn't be right to ignore his knock on her door, especially since her car made it clear she was home.

Boss pressed his nose to the screen while John stood back, his shoulders slumped. His head hung uncharacteristically low. Because of her.

"I'm glad you made it back safely." He studied her as she opened the screen door and stepped onto the porch.

While she'd held it mostly together until he'd left, she couldn't hide her red-rimmed eyes. Crying that wasn't from a panic attack or depression, though that might come. It was pure heartache. "Wren texted that you were packing and moving out."

"With the trial over, y'all don't need me anymore. You'll have Hope Harbor free for someone else."

"You haven't started the renovations and don't have furniture or a bed at your house."

"It's got four walls and a roof. Electricity and running water. It'll save time if I'm there versus traveling back and forth. It's for the best," he added.

She sniffed back tears. It was.

"Here's the key and remote for the gate." He held them out to her. "I told Wren to help herself to the food in the fridge, so the house isn't locked. I got all my stuff and did some clean-up, though it's not move-in ready. Wren said she'd—"

"Don't worry about that."

He gave a nod, his eyes and mouth looking tortured. "I already said goodbye to Wren and Ariana. Y'all have my

number if you need anything. Thought you'd want to say goodbye to Boss."

Goodbye, not see you later. She hadn't wanted or expected things to end this way.

She dropped to one knee, fighting the suffocating effect of her chest constricting. "I'm going to miss you." Boss licked her cheek as she rubbed his neck. "I'm glad you were part of my life." And that Boss brought John here when they needed him to protect Ariana from J.R. John showed Wren there were honorable men who'd help without expecting sex as payment and challenged her to make responsible decisions. He'd made Elizabeth feel like the young woman she'd been a decade ago and awoken feelings she hadn't experienced in nearly that long.

Now he needed to be free to live his life and find a woman who could give him all the love he deserved. That was clearly what he wanted—not a friend.

"If you ever need someone to take care of Boss, let me know." It was the one tenuous connection she could offer.

"I won't deploy as much in the new position, but down the road, I may need to take you up on that. I promise I won't ever leave him in a situation like before. I appreciate all you've done for him and me. Even though—you had to give him up." He swallowed, still looking at her with a pained expression before walking down her porch steps and out of her life.

Chapter Forty-Nine

SOMEBODY LIKE YOU – Keith Urban

JOHN GROANED AND STRETCHED. Light streamed through the bedroom blinds. Between the hard floor and thinking about Elizabeth, he'd barely slept. His neck hurt. His back hurt. His heart hurt most of all. He sat up. At least he didn't have a hangover.

"Mattress shopping is mission one today. Thanks for sharing your bed as a pillow."

Boss touched his nose to John's neck.

He needed a long, hot shower to loosen his muscles. While he had food for Boss, he had no coffee maker or anything for him to eat. Obviously, he hadn't thought that through when packing or picking up dinner. Course, he hadn't been hungry then.

"Come on, boy. I'll let you out."

♫

John checked his shopping list. He debated whether to swing through flooring and see if Ariana was working. Instead, he headed to the checkout. He wasn't sure he could put on a smile and say he was fine.

It had been three days since leaving Hope Harbor, and he hadn't heard anything from Elizabeth, not that he expected to—at least anytime soon. He'd been tempted to text and ask if she'd found Boss's stuffed bear, which hadn't turned up with his other toys. Rather than bother her over an eight-dollar toy, he'd ordered a replacement.

They hadn't been in a relationship. Circumstances, and Boss, brought them together, but they had never been more than friends. So, why did this hurt more than the end of any real romantic relationship he'd had?

Boss hung his head out the window as John loaded the supplies. It'd only been a few weeks since he'd been here with Elizabeth and asked her to go to the wedding. Big mistake.

He'd keep busy doing renovations so he wouldn't have time to think about Elizabeth. Though there was a possibility of moving back to Fort Bragg with his next promotion, he'd decided to list the house rather than keep it as a rental. Cut the ties, hassles, and temptation that would come with returning here to take care of things when renters turned over.

Before starting his truck, he scratched Boss behind the ears. "I'm gonna change my dating profile write-up to start with 'Must love big dogs.' They gotta love you, or it isn't gonna work out." Like none of his prior relationships. He needed to revamp his whole profile. Go in a different direction. What else should he say? "Military guy' lookin' for love,'" he broke into song, then stopped. He was done looking in all the wrong places. "Maybe 'You don't have to

be a beauty queen but have a beautiful smile and heart.' Is that too wussy?"

Boss didn't respond.

"I'll think on that part. 'Interested in an independent woman ready to settle down. Someone who likes sitting on a porch swing.' Should I add and 'dancing in the moonlight?'" He hummed the tune. "'Must like classic rock and country music, tolerate off-key singing, and have a sense of humor. Ability to cook a plus.'" All the traits he'd mentioned were ones Elizabeth exemplified, all except ready to settle down.

There had to be more women like her out there.

Eh. The dating profile could wait. He wasn't ready to jump into a relationship. Better to wait until after he moved.

♩

AFTER SECURING the gate to keep Boss out of the bathroom and at a safe distance, John put in his earbuds and started up his demolition playlist of hard rock. He rolled his neck and did some stretches before putting on his safety goggles.

"It's smash time."

Despite the warning, Boss howled at the first strike. After a few more, he retreated to another part of the small house. By the time John finished swinging the sledge-hammer and prying off the tiles, he'd worked up a sweat and burned off a lot of frustration.

His playlist ended while hauling trash to the dumpster, so he punched up country and sang along to "If You're Going Through Hell," which, for good reason, topped his current most recently played list. A pop-country love song started. Before he could get to his phone to skip to the next song, the words about loving somebody and forgiving himself stopped him. He listened closely to the words. The

line about her teaching him to be a better man drudged up a slug of emotion.

He replayed the Keith Urban song, thinking about Eliz-abeth and how she made him feel. Phone in hand, he pulled up the pictures of her with Boss. He could text her a picture of Boss to let her know he was thinking of her without the pressure of saying he missed her.

No. She had to see him as a safe place. With Elizabeth, pushing, or not accepting her decision, might be the surest way to lose this war.

If he hadn't heard from her after thirty days, then he'd text. If she didn't respond, he'd regroup and come up with another plan of attack or strategy. Maybe drop by with Boss to see them all. He was not ready to concede the war.

Chapter Fifty

MISSING YOU – John Waite

When Elizabeth got home Friday night, she changed out of her work clothes, then took the key and headed to Hope Harbor. She admired the work John and Nate had done building the deck that John barely had time to use. When he'd showed them his house, he mentioned plans to add a porch or deck, promising to invite the women over for a Friday night dinner at his place when he was finished with the kitchen.

Tears burned her eyes again when she realized that wasn't going to happen now. She'd managed to cut John out of Ariana and Wren's lives too. She hadn't heard from him since he and Boss had moved out five days ago. Sitting on her front porch seemed lonely rather than the relaxing end-of-day treat it had once been. Everything was so quiet without Boss and his evening play sessions and John's happy, though off-key, versions of songs to entertain her.

Inside Hope Harbor, she recalled giving John the tour. No big deal living in a tiny home he'd said. Right. She straightened the pillows on the little sofa. She hadn't spent time with John in here, but when she'd come over one evening with a toy for Boss, she'd seen him through the door. He'd been stretched out, with his long legs crossed and propped on the coffee table. Boss crowded him, his head in John's lap.

Climbing the stairs, she pictured him crawling into the loft. He'd bumped his head on the low ceiling twice—that she knew of.

Stripping off the sheets, she found the plush bear Boss liked to sleep with next to the mattress. Should she let John know? Use it as an excuse to reach out? No. She shouldn't send mixed signals after asking him to accept her decision. Let him move on.

Still, she inhaled his scent that lingered on the sheets. A masculine, woodsy aroma. Maybe sandalwood. She didn't know fragrances to identify them, though she remembered the designer cologne Adam had worn too well. That smell was burned into her subconscious. Anything close to it triggered her to the point of nausea. Even now, a chill gripped her at the memory of his scent. Kneeling on the mattress, she let the memory pass. She lifted the sheets balled in her lap to her nose and breathed in John's scent again, letting it calm her body's fight-or-flight reaction.

She carried the sheets down and dumped them in the washer, despite the urge to keep back a pillowcase. The fridge was empty, and the dishes were clean. It only took a few minutes to sweep the floor. Boss never shed a lot. She'd look for the same laid-back temperament and loyalty in her next dog. Maybe that would help keep her busy so she wouldn't have time to think about Boss. And John.

Scrubbing the walls in the tiny shower made her wonder how John even fit in there. Somehow, their presence still loomed in the tiny house. Maybe that would dissipate once she moved in another tenant.

Step one of moving forward completed, she texted Jillian to put the word out that Hope Harbor was available.

♫

While eating dinner, Elizabeth scrolled through the pictures of available dogs on the animal shelter's website. Almost all the dogs were pit bull terriers or mixes and half the size of Boss. She skipped over puppies and clicked on the picture of a tan and white female. That she didn't play well with other dogs ruled her out. Next, she clicked on a recently arrived fawn-colored male, except his bio mentioned separation anxiety and needing to be with his human in the home, which didn't mesh with her work schedule. On the fourth page, Beldar, another male, white with large brown patches on his body and face, smiled at her.

There were no red flags in the details, though she noticed the dog's front leg wrapped in a bandage in one picture and a scar on that leg in another. Watching the posted video, Beldar had a slight limp as he ran to get a toy, but his tail wagged as he brought it back and placed it at the handler's feet. He also took treats gently from the handler.

Elizabeth wrote down Beldar's identification number with a lightheartedness that she'd lacked all week. She continued her search and clicked on two other dogs but came back to Beldar.

♫

When Elizabeth opened her car door in the lot at the Animal Control Center, high-pitched yelping, plaintive whines, and barking filled the air.

She got in the adoptions line behind a family with a young child and a man holding the leash of a brindled pit bull terrier with a raw wound near its eye. The dog wouldn't look up, and its owner stared straight ahead. Had Boss had a clue what was going on when John's ex brought him here? She stepped up when it was her turn. "I'd like to see Beldar." She handed over the paper with his id number on it.

The woman tapped on the keyboard. "I have good news for Beldar, but bad news for you."

Elizabeth's tentative joy leaked out of her like a sieve.

"A family is in the process of being approved to adopt him. You can still meet him and be put on the list as a backup in case it falls through."

"That's okay." She didn't want to get her hopes up only to be disappointed.

"Are there any other animals that you wanted to see?" the volunteer asked hopefully.

"None in particular. I'll go take a look, though." Maybe she would feel an unexpected connection with one like she had with Boss.

Elizabeth walked past the enclosures. Each animal tugged at her heartstrings, but she couldn't take them all home. At the far end, she paused to observe a volunteer, sitting in front of a kennel talking to a black and white Pitbull in low, soothing tones.

There was no name on the plaque. "What's his or her name?"

"Missy, but she's not available for adoption yet," the

older man said. "She's a sweet girl, but apparently someone had been abusing her and made her afraid of men."

Elizabeth could relate.

"She got adopted once, but the woman brought her back because Missy tried to attack a man who came to her house to do some work. We're trying some desensitization exercises so that hopefully she can find a home."

Elizabeth mulled it over for a minute. With John gone, there were no males at The Oasis, but she would still get the occasional workman or delivery man. "I hope she is able to be adopted."

"It may take time, and it's up to Missy."

Elizabeth made her way past the enclosures, looking at the animals through the eyes of a counselor, noting the animals' different responses. The majority still had hope and sat or stood by their gate, their eyes pleading for a second chance at love. Others slept, as if resigned to their fate. Worst-case dogs, like Missy, cowered in corners, trembling at the sight of humans. The volunteer hadn't given up on her, but had she given up on herself?

As painful as what John had said at the hotel, was he right? Was she stuck? She was free from Adam, but he still had power over her because she let him. She hadn't fully healed. She played it safe to avoid flashbacks and potential panic attacks. Had she given up on what she wanted in life?

What did she really, really want?

The ache in her chest grew and robbed her of breath. She wanted real freedom. Freedom to laugh and love and let a man touch her without fear. And not just any man. As much as she missed Boss, she missed John even more. Tears moistened her eyes as it became harder to breathe.

"Let me know if there's any animal you want to take out

to the yard," one of the volunteers offered as Elizabeth hurried past.

"I don't think I'm quite ready." None of these dogs would fill the gap in her heart. John had been right.

And she wasn't going to be the one who cowered in a corner any longer.

♫

AFTER ESCORTING her last patient of the day back to the lobby, Elizabeth detoured to Charis's office. The door was open, affording Elizabeth a view of the gorgeous landscape of purple heather-covered hills along a loch in the Scottish Highlands.

"I love that photograph," she commented to get her colleague's attention. "I would love to visit Scotland someday."

"You'll love it. You should go in August when it's the warmest and the heather's in bloom." Charis's lovely brogue made Elizabeth want to visit even more.

Elizabeth closed the door behind her. "I know your schedule is full, but I was hoping you might be able to squeeze in a patient you're familiar with from your old practice."

"One of your patients?"

"One of yours. Me."

"Oh."

"I know it's frowned on with us being in the same practice now." A slight understatement, as Charis's expression confirmed. "It wouldn't be counseling, but EMDR therapy. I'd like to give it a try again. With you this time."

"I can give you recommendations outside our group who are certified as well."

"Then I'd have to start from scratch to establish trust for it to be effective. You know my history, and we'd made a lot of progress before you went out on maternity leave and took a break."

"But not quite enough progress?"

"I got to a good place, but . . ."

"Not where you want to be?"

"Not anymore. Right now, I'm questioning if I'm even qualified to counsel others when I can't get past my own issues to have the life I want." She didn't know what she'd do if she quit practicing. It wasn't what she wanted, but John's challenge had shaken her.

"We can't have you doubting yourself and the excellent work you do," Charis agreed. "If you're certain, I'll find a time to work you in. We can start this week."

"I'm certain." To keep from losing the little security she had left in her life, she needed help to slay these demons.

Chapter Fifty One

KISS A GIRL – Keith Urban

DESPITE THE BREAKTHROUGHS in therapy the past three weeks, Elizabeth's heart pounded harder and sweat broke out when she turned into John's neighborhood. She slowed her car to a crawl, willing her body to calm down. She hadn't experienced this much anxiety since plotting to leave Adam. She also hadn't had this much at stake since then.

This time she needed every ounce of resolve not to face a monster but to face a giant. A gentle giant with a ginormous heart. Not to leave, but to stay. If he'd have her.

A white pickup truck rolled up behind her. The female driver didn't tailgate her car, but Elizabeth sped up to the speed limit. The truck also turned onto John's cul-de-sac, like a nudge to keep her from pulling over or backing out. She had to do this.

A construction dumpster took up one side of John's driveway. His truck was backed in on the other side. She

drove past and circled the cul-de-sac, only to see the white truck stopped in front of his house.

What the . . .

She pulled over and watched a woman in jeans and a pink shirt carry plastic bags in through John's open garage. Into his house.

This wasn't some delivery. Nope. John was already dating. And not just dating. The way the woman breezed in, it was like they were a couple.

Damn, that was fast. It hurt. She couldn't fault him, though. Not when she'd pushed him away.

If she stayed parked here for a good cry, she risked a neighbor coming across her. She let out a long breath and took her foot off the brake. A flash of gray and black fur dashed past John's truck to the end of the driveway and into the street. Boss's deep bark reverberated in her heart. Could she drive right past him? No, because now John strode out and called to Boss, who didn't budge. John glanced down the street and did a double-take.

No way was she getting past without him seeing her now.

He shoved his hands in his front pockets, took a cautious step into the street, and then another step toward her. She had no choice but to pull to the curb and park. She rolled down the window when he approached.

"Were you not going to stop?" His tone lacked its usual playfulness. He gripped Boss's collar, as Boss strained toward her car.

"I found one of Boss's toys. I—didn't want to interrupt and make things awkward with your guest, so . . ."

"You wouldn't be interrupting. Cecilia just brought dinner and Nate and I were taking—"

"That was Cecilia?" Thank you, Lord.

"You saw her?" John's eyes narrowed. He broke into that irresistible grin. "Were you jealous, or did you think I slipped back to my old ways of rushing into things?"

"Both," she admitted.

His smile grew bigger as Boss pulled harder against his grip, his front paws lifting off the pavement. "Naw. I want to get to know a woman before starting anything romantic. Why don't you get out of that car before Boss here hurts both of you jumping through the window onto your lap." He opened the driver's side door.

She turned off the engine and handed John the bag of toys and treats before dropping to a knee. Boss nuzzled her so hard that she fell back against the car, laughing and hugging him.

"I've missed you too, boy. Okay, okay." She pushed Boss's face away. John tugged him back. She wiped the wet spot on her cheek while John stared down at her with a smile that made her heart race again. This time, in a good way.

He offered her a hand, and she took it. After helping her up, he rubbed his thumb over her knuckles. It sent electricity coursing up her arm and through her, igniting the kind of internal fire she'd feared she would never experience again. She stared into his eyes as the heat built.

"Do you need help getting Boss or . . ." Seeing them, Cecilia stopped short and broke into a big smile. "Hi."

"I've got him. He must have dashed out because he heard Elizabeth's car or caught her scent. I'm glad he did," John added softly. "Come on in." He released her hand to lightly touch her back and steer her toward the house.

"John didn't mention you were coming by. I just picked up dinner. I'm sure there's enough for you too." Cecilia kept smiling in an I've-got-a-secret kind of way.

"I just came to drop off some toys for Boss."

"She's staying. I'll share."

He didn't give her a choice, but this time she was okay with him not taking no for an answer. Though this wasn't going how she planned when she wanted desperately to talk to him, it wasn't all bad. Not with the way he was smiling and touching her. His touches felt damn good. With Nate and Cecilia here, it'd be less pressure, and she could ease into things.

"Did you get Boss?" Nate drew out the S's and broke into a smile similar to his wife's when he caught sight of John and Elizabeth walking into the kitchen-turned-construction zone. "Good to see you again, Elizabeth." He wiped both hands on his dusty jeans, then turned dirty palms up. "Sorry. It's kind of a mess in here."

"It looks entirely different already." All the cabinets and dated vinyl flooring had been torn out and over half of the new upper cabinets were hung.

"Taking the cabinets to the ceiling was a good call on Rachel's part. Provides more storage and makes the ceiling appear higher, which works for me." John didn't take his eyes off her as he talked about the renovations.

"Why don't you guys wash up, and I'll set dinner out," Cecilia said.

"I'm afraid it's standing room only at Chez Bryson at the moment." John indicated the square card table resting atop the tall boxes of kitchen cabinets where Cecilia started unloading the food. "Will you feed Boss for me?"

John flashed a signal to Cecilia.

"Sure."

"Come here. I'll show you the master bath." He crooked a finger and jerked his head for Elizabeth to follow him. Nate went in the opposite direction.

John closed the door after ushering her into the bedroom. His camouflage ballcap sat on the dresser and a book was laying on the nightstand. The walls were bare. Though the king-sized bed was neatly made, an image of him there, his bare shoulder and arm exposed, flashed through her mind.

She admired the glass walk-in shower with bench seat while he washed his hands. "Wow. I'm envious. This looks great."

"And it's big enough I can wash Boss in there."

It was definitely big enough for two, though now, she pictured him in the spacious shower. Naked. She liked the way her body heated and tingled at that image. "Did you do the tile yourself?"

"My first sergeant helped. How are you doing?" He dried his hands and laid down the towel.

"Better, I think."

He cocked an eyebrow at her and leaned against the counter.

"After what you said at the hotel, I resumed therapy."

Pain flickered across his face. "I shouldn't have said what I did. It was insensitive and out of line." He didn't make excuses.

"Actually, you weren't. It hurt and made me doubt myself and my effectiveness as a counselor. But I went to the shelter to adopt a dog the next weekend and kind of had an epiphany. You were right about me being stuck. I told you I had been in counseling."

He nodded.

"I started right after the divorce. Talking to process what I'd been through helped, but not enough. My counselor suggested I try a technique called EMDR therapy that helps to resolve unprocessed traumatic memories. However,

she had complications with her pregnancy and was put on bedrest before we could start. I did several sessions with a colleague she referred me to, and I had a breakthrough. After the next session, he said it had done all it was going to do.

"It became obvious when I dated that I was still suffering PTSD. I thought that was as good as it was going to get for me. Even after I became a counselor, I simply accepted his diagnosis. Except it's kept me from living the life I want."

He nodded as he listened without interrupting.

"I restarted EMDR therapy with my original counselor who knew my complete story."

"Good. How will you know if it works this time?" Hesitation laced his words.

"I have to put myself out there. Open myself up to physical contact in intimate situations."

"I see. How do you plan to experiment? Do you need a test subject?" He tried to sound nonchalant, though now a smile tugged at the corners of his sexy mouth.

"I hadn't thought of you as a 'test subject,' but if you're not seeing someone . . ."

"Nope, like I said, this counselor friend suggested getting to know a woman, and I, uh, haven't been ready to meet someone. I was giving it thirty days before I reached out and sent you pictures of Boss to see what happened. I've been making him pose so I'd have some good ones ready."

Based on the vulnerability in his eyes, he wasn't making that up. Tears built that he'd given her time and space but hadn't given up on her—or hope for them.

"Will there be other test subjects?" he hedged.

"You're the only one I want to experiment with. But"—

now came the hard part—"I can't promise you that I'll ever be able to have a normal physical relationship."

"We won't know until we try. We can take things as slow as you need."

"There's also the matter of your move. We don't have a lot of time, and the last thing I want is to hurt you, if . . ."

"It wouldn't be the riskiest thing I've ever done." He grinned and held out a hand to her.

It might be the riskiest thing she'd ever done, but she stepped closer and put her hand in his. Their gazes locked.

"When would we start?"

She moved to stand mere inches from him. Close enough to feel his body's heat. To inhale his scent. "We could start now. With a kiss, to see if I've made progress."

"I like that idea." His hands rested on her hips. He dipped his head until his mouth nearly touched hers.

Her heart pounded—in anticipation, not fear—as she ran her fingertips up his hard-muscled arms like she'd dreamed of doing. She closed her eyes and lifted her face, eliminating the scant distance until her lips met his. A tentative meeting at first that ignited a craving she hadn't experienced in years.

He took his cues from her. Lingering kisses led to the parting of lips and the gentle brush of tongues. She nipped his lip, and he groaned. His grip tightened on her hips. He pressed a firm kiss to her mouth before pulling back and resting his forehead on hers.

"As much as I want to continue this experiment, I promised we'd take this slow." Desire deepened his voice. "Nate and Cecilia are also out there, so we're going to stop before you make me totally forget all that."

She nodded. "You're right." She trailed her fingers

down his arms. It was better not to rush and risk ruining the amazing way she felt and the hope it inspired.

He linked his fingers through hers. "We're going to have to tell Nate and Cecilia something, because when they asked about you, and us, I told them it wasn't happening. They're going to realize that changed. I don't want to explain that I'm your test subject and why, so can I tell them we're dating?"

"That sounds like an accurate description." Her gaze cut to his bed before as they passed going to the kitchen. She wasn't ready for that yet, but thoughts of being there didn't induce any signs of a panic attack. Another sign of progress.

John cleared his throat. "Don't mind us."

Nate and Cecilia moved apart.

"Newlyweds. They're kissing every time I turn my back," John grumbled.

"Didn't want to eat without you." Nate smiled adoringly at his wife.

"I thought you two might need a few minutes to talk. The subs and chips could wait." Cecilia's gaze flitted from John to Elizabeth and back to John again.

"I have an announcement," John stated matter-of-factly. "Elizabeth and I are dating. Not fake dating for the wedding. This is for real."

"Told ya." Cecilia nudged Nate with her shoulder.

They gathered around the makeshift table. Elizabeth had been too nervous to eat earlier, but her appetite returned, and she accepted half of the meatball sub that John placed in front of her. "How was the honeymoon?" she asked Nate and Cecilia.

"Fabulous. First, we went to Scotland and did all the

dates Cecilia originally planned for the show that we didn't get to do. Then we went to Greece for another week."

"And I didn't have to plan dates for anybody but us."

Cecilia laughed.

"I have a confession to make," Elizabeth said. "After the wedding, I binge-watched your season of *Say Yes to the Rose*. I was curious after meeting everyone at the wedding. It was interesting how they edited it to keep viewers on edge. Knowing how it ended, I picked up on the way Nate would scan the room and break into a smile when he saw you."

"Really?" Cecilia smiled at her husband.

"Of course. I still do."

"Aww." Cecilia brushed a kiss to Nate's cheek. "I haven't watched. I don't want to see him kissing other women."

"I can understand that," Elizabeth said, because he had definitely kissed more than Cecilia. "I watched your body language for clues. Like how his tension slid away when he was with you too."

"Other than when I was trying to tell her I wasn't faking my feelings for her."

"Scary, isn't it?" John cracked, giving her the side-eye.

"You weren't supposed to . . ." Elizabeth started.

"Fall for you?" he finished. "Says who? Because it seems like it's a good thing. What do you think, Boss? You approve? Me and Elizabeth, your two favorite humans together? You're probably gonna take credit."

"We need a group photo to commemorate the occasion," Cecilia proclaimed. "Here, you have the longest arms." She handed John the phone with the camera engaged.

"Everybody get close. Come here, Boss." He slipped an

arm around Elizabeth's waist, pulling her to his side. "Okay, kissing pic." He pressed a kiss to her cheek for the next shot. When he didn't turn his face away or lower the camera, she angled to kiss him, first on the mouth, then a grateful kiss to his cheek. Everything about it felt right.

"Send those to me." He handed Cecilia back her phone. "I'll forward them to you." He winked at Elizabeth. "Now, as much as it pains me to say this, we need to get back to work. I only have Nate for the weekend and these cabinets need to be installed for the guy to measure for countertops."

"Is there anything I can do to help?" Elizabeth wasn't ready to leave yet.

"We've got an extra roller if you're up for painting. It's taking two coats to cover the bright yellow. Though you aren't dressed for painting." Cecilia pointed to the splotches on her shirt and arms.

"That's more my speed than hanging cabinets." Though she'd worn her favorite top for tonight. "Do you have a T-shirt I can wear that you won't mind getting paint on?" she asked John.

"We've been dating all of thirty minutes and you're already stealing my clothes? You know that takes our relationship to the next level."

"If you'd rather I not . . ."

"I'm not saying that at all. I've got plenty of old Army PT shirts you can wear."

This time it wasn't a panic attack making it hard to breathe. More like the heat inside her sucking up all the oxygen as his gaze roved lazily over her.

Chapter Fifty-Two

JUST A KISS – Lady A

ELIZABETH FELT ridiculous in John's oversized shirt until Cecilia knotted it in the back for her. That she was wearing her boyfriend's shirt made her happier than she'd been in a decade.

Cecilia asked about her work with the women at The Oasis, having heard about it from Nate and John. Conversation flowed as they finished painting the bedroom a calming blue-gray color. The buzz of electric tools died out and was soon replaced with the deep timbre of the men talking and the pop of cans opening.

"Looking good, ladies," John stood in the doorframe, staring at Elizabeth while holding a beer can. "It'll be nice not having to squint against the bright yellow when I walk into this room. Should have painted it when I first bought the house."

John strolled over to stand at the base of the ladder as

Elizabeth carefully touched up the line along the window frame. It was the first time she'd stood taller than him and inspired thoughts of him holding her against the wall in a romantic clinch. The naughty thoughts brought on the good kind of heart palpitations.

"Thanks for letting me borrow your shirt." She showed him the spot near her hip where she'd accidentally leaned into the wall.

"No worries I've got a dozen PT shirts and can always get more. You can keep that one if you want." He grinned up at her. "Do you ladies want a beer when you finish?"

"I'm a sissy drinker," Cecilia said. "I only like the fruity, sweet drinks."

"I never acquired a taste for beer either." Elizabeth found another thing in common with Cecilia. "I just need to finish around this window. You got the upper cabinets all in?"

"We did. We'll put up the molding and knock out the lower cabinets tomorrow."

"I'll wrap the rollers and take a closer look in daylight to see if we missed any spots. Are you coming back tomorrow?" Cecilia cast a semi-innocent smile at Elizabeth.

"I'm free if you need some help."

"If you've got an eye for landscaping, I'm going to the nursery to get some plants for the front beds."

"I can do that," she agreed to the low-key way to spend time with John and his friends.

After they finished painting, they joined Nate and John who lounged in two sports chairs with a TV tray between them, admiring their work.

"I'm glad Rachel suggested the blue-gray cabinets. They brighten the room and won't show the dirt or dog hair like white." John rubbed a hand down Boss's back.

"I'm not a design guy, but I agree. From the before pictures you sent me, you'll make back every penny you're spending when you sell. I'm going to want pictures for my portfolio." Nate toasted John with his beer.

"I'm happy to leave you a good review and send pictures," John said, his tone subdued as he cast a glance at Elizabeth.

Nate's comment served as an unwelcome reminder of the major obstacle they still faced. Even if John restored her ability to have a healthy relationship, what would happen in a few months when he moved to Florida? Her practice was here. Even with the rise of telemedicine, she'd risk losing the majority of her clients and have to rebuild. But it wasn't about the money. She knew firsthand the frustration of having to find a new counselor when circumstances ended a good therapeutic relationship. It had stalled her healing for years.

Could she walk away from the women at The Oasis? Ariana would be okay, and Wren, well, she might need a push out of the nest, but Mayala had only moved in a week ago. It was impossible to predict where she'd be in a few months.

Nate got to his feet.

Cecilia picked up her purse and scratched Boss's head.

"We'll see you in the morning."

When Elizabeth followed suit, John gave her a hard stare. She set her bag back down and got an approving nod. After saying goodbye to his friends at the front door, John smiled at her for several tantalizing seconds.

"You didn't see me come peek at you while you were painting, did you?"

"No," she drawled.

"I wasn't being creepy. Just wanted to make sure I

wasn't imagining things. Looked like you and Cecilia hit it off."

"We did."

"That's always a good sign."

"True." Her sister hadn't liked Adam. John had already won over Ariana, Wren, and Jillian.

"Are you free Monday night so I can take you on a real date? I like you being here, but working on my house isn't a date, and I want to do this right. How about a fancy dinner out?"

"How about someplace not fancy and pretentious? Someplace casual, with good food, where we can sit and talk as long as we want."

"If that's what you want, that's what we'll do."

"It is." He didn't need to impress her. Expensive meals had never been her thing. She was impressed with how he listened to what she wanted. That was a quality she could get used to. "I'll still wear something nice." She winked.

The way he raised his eyebrows made her laugh. He moved in to kiss her. Surprisingly, he tasted like mint. It clicked that only Nate had a beer when they'd joined the guys in the kitchen. John had brushed his teeth after she said she didn't like the taste of beer. This man constantly surprised her. She tested herself, pressing her body to his.

He kissed her harder. His highly aroused state could be a reaction to any woman, but it felt good, though still more than a little scary. Therapy was working, but John played a big role. It was better not to take things too far too fast, for her sake and in fairness to him.

He kept his hands on her hips rather than grab or grind or grope as they continued to kiss. Her body aroused like it hadn't been in years. Her heart rate climbed, and her breathing faltered.

Almost immediately, John ended the kiss and put a sliver of space between their bodies. "You okay?"

She nodded. "Better than okay, but . . ."

"We need to slow this roll a little?"

She fanned her face. "I forgot how fantastic kissing could feel." Especially the way John kissed her. She doubted his talents ended there.

"Amen to that. Your kind of kisses are addictive. But I'm going to send you on your way wanting more, not giving you second thoughts. I do not want to screw this up."

She definitely wanted more. "What time?" They headed to the door.

"Around nine. Nate's a civilian now. I also don't want to piss off my neighbors by waking them up at oh-six hundred with construction noise. Boss, you need to go out?" Boss scrambled over. "Thanks for bringing his toy and coming here. I was giving you time and space so I didn't push you away for good, but I hadn't given up on us. I knew it had to be your decision to face your past and choose what you want for your future." He raised a hand to her face, his thumb stroking her cheek. "I'm so freaking glad you're here and taking a chance."

His face blurred due to the tears in her eyes. "Me too. Thank you for waiting." For understanding. They needed to take this one slow step at a time, but she now had hope of restoring a piece of her she'd feared she'd never get back.

Chapter Fifty-Three

WHO YOU LOVE – John Mayer

"You know where we're going, don't ya, boy?" They weren't quite to Elizabeth's house, but Boss recognized the route or familiar smells from the neighboring farm and couldn't sit still. John was as excited to see her as Boss.

They'd had time together Sunday when Elizabeth helped Cecilia with landscaping. Monday had been their first real date, and they'd talked for nearly two-and-a-half hours over dinner. He couldn't recall ever spending that much time talking with a woman. His buddies, sure, but this had been girlfriend-to-boyfriend talk with romantic under-tones, looks and touches, and some making out in the parking lot. Taking it slow.

Tuesday night, after the guy came to measure and make the template for his countertops, John spent the rest of the evening digging holes for new shrubs. He'd called Elizabeth, and they'd talked for nearly an hour again.

Wednesday, he'd offered to pick up some ice cream and come over for a bit, except Elizabeth had been helping The Oasis's newest resident apply for jobs. Two days apart was akin to torture, though he doubted it violated any of the protocols of the Geneva Convention. They'd had dinner again Thursday night. Though he didn't get an invite to join the ladies for last night's monthly potluck, things were progressing even better than he'd hoped.

Today, he looked forward to an afternoon and evening with his girl and his dog. And seeing if they could make it another step further after Elizabeth's EMDR session this week. Meeting at the restaurants kept things safe, but it had been her idea for him to come to her house tonight for privacy.

Before John's feet hit the dirt, Boss bolted out of the truck and was at Elizabeth's front door, forcing John to wait for a kiss. "He's jealous I saw you this week without him." John moved in for his turn. He slipped an arm around her, pulling her close and inhaling her sweet floral scent. He wanted to find out where all she'd dabbed it. "I missed you. How'd the group dinner go last night?"

"It was a little rough."

"Oh?" After the dinner he'd experienced, her answer wasn't what he expected.

"It didn't occur to me that when I told Mayala the dinner was a potluck and asked her to bring an appetizer that she thought she was there to serve us. When I asked her to join us at the table, she started crying. In the two years she was with the family that sponsored her to come to the US, they never once had her join them for a family meal. She ate with the kids as she was feeding them breakfast or lunch, but she'd fix dinner and eat in the kitchen alone."

"'They saw her as a servant, not part of the family," he deduced.

"'Definitely. They worked her thirteen-hour days, cook-ing, cleaning, and caring for three kids and a grandparent with dementia. They didn't technically 'buy' her, but they covered her way here and only paid her about two bucks an hour. She shared a bedroom with the grandmother and had no money and no family or friends here. She had no self-worth or hope for anything better. Last night, seeing that flicker of life turn on . . .' Elizabeth brushed away a tear.

"'You'll have to introduce me to her.'

"'We'll stop by The Oasis when we go for a walk.'

"'Do Wren and Ariana know about us yet?'

"'No. I didn't want that to become the focus of last night's dinner conversation.'

"'Gotcha. But we can tell them?'

"'Of course. I doubt we'll be able to hide it. And there's no reason to keep it secret.'

The way she smiled when she said that kicked the ass of the voice whispering in his ear that he wasn't good enough. Unlike his mother or her family or Britney and her parents, Elizabeth saw the worth in people, and it had nothing to do with education or money or status.

"'We'll take Boss for a walk in the woods, then come back here and have lasagna for dinner. I can cook other things, but I know you like it, and I never make it just for myself.'

"'I'd eat it every night of the week with you.'

"'You don't need to kiss up.'

"'But I like kissing you. A lot.' He lowered his mouth to her willing one to prove his point.

His lips caressed hers, taking his time, despite nearly two days apart. His tongue teased her lips apart to slide in

and touch hers, liking how hers sought his when he retreated. He probed deeper.

She leaned into him, pressing her breasts against his chest. He dropped his hand just below the waistband of her pants. His fingers drifted lower, testing her reaction as they kissed. They began inching even lower when Boss's wet nose nudged his hand. Elizabeth flinched and laughed. His grip kept her from stumbling and falling on Boss.

"Thanks a lot, Boss. Next time, I'm gonna put you outside," he grumbled. "I guess he wants to take that walk."

"We'll resume this later. I picked a movie for after dinner, but nothing that we really *want* to watch."

It took a second for his brain to interpret her implication. "Gonna use me as your test subject?"

"You agreed."

Oh, did he ever.

As soon as they headed to The Oasis, Boss loped toward their old home without waiting. John smiled at the sight of him making the rounds to get love from the three women on the new deck at Hope Harbor.

"How are you ladies doing?"

"Really good—thanks to you and Elizabeth making sure I don't have to worry about J.R. anymore. It's so good to see you." Ariana moved in for a hug.

Mayala stared at him with the wide-eyed, mouth slightly open expression he often got meeting someone half his size.

"We've missed Boss and your comedic relief." Wren's gaze shifted from him to Elizabeth with a curious smile.

"And my singing?" he teased.

"Maybe a little," Wren conceded.

John laughed.

Elizabeth handled introductions. "Mayala, this is John Bryson. He lived in Hope Harbor for a while before you."

"How did you fit?" Mayala asked with a heavy accent. She looked from him to the tiny home.

"Not very well."

Elizabeth chortled. The other women laughed, as well.

Mayala smiled and met his gaze for a second before diverting her gaze downward to play with the end of her jet-black braid that nearly reached her waist. John took a seat on the bench so he wouldn't tower over her. The petite woman didn't even look to be in her twenties. She gave Boss a tentative pat.

"Sit, Boss." The dog sat nearly on Mayala's feet. "Here boy." He snapped his fingers and motioned to him. "Have you gotten a pet yet?"

"No." Her eyes widened as she looked at Boss.

"You can't have Boss. Elizabeth already tried to take my dog."

She shook her head and rolled her eyes in that amused way that made him want to kiss her. Not that it took much for him to want to do that.

"I was thinking of getting a rabbit or a cat."

"What brings you out here today?" Wren eyed him, then Elizabeth.

"I invited him to come for dinner and a movie date." Elizabeth stepped closer and rested her hand on his shoulder.

"Date?" Wren asked with a triumphant smile.

"Yes. John and I are dating."

His chest swelled hearing her proclamation. He kissed Elizabeth's hand and continued to hold it.

"That's so great." Ariana clapped.

"How loooonggg has this been going on?" Wren sang.

He recognized the lyrics from a song on the oldies station. "You're stealing my shtick."

"And doing it better." Wren laughed.

"I went to see him last Saturday. So, a week."

"A week! And you didn't tell us?" Ariana scolded.

"That explains your unusually good mood," Wren said.

"Good mood?" John smiled up at Elizabeth.

"Yep, like when it's been a long time and you finally get—"

"Kissed!" John and Elizabeth said in unison.

"That's what I was going to say." Wren acted all innocent.

John pushed to his feet and stared into Elizabeth's eyes. He kissed her lightly to sell it. "We're going to take Boss on a walk now. Mayala, it was a pleasure to meet you. I'm sure I'll see you again soon." He took Elizabeth's hand as they walked down the porch steps. "You know that's not what she was going to say, right?" he whispered.

Elizabeth made an adorable noise and blushed. What did it mean that she wouldn't look him in the eye?

Chapter Fifty Four

UNCONDITIONALLY – Katy Perry

"This is even better than last time." John finished off his second helping of lasagna and laid his silverware on his empty plate.

"It's the same recipe."

"Yeah, but this time I'm eating it with my *girlfriend.*"

He aimed a scorching grin at her.

"And I like having my boyfriend here for dinner." Though she was anxious in a different way than tonight last time.

"If you're free tomorrow, would you go shopping with me? I need to outfit my kitchen. I don't have plates, cups, silverware, pots, utensils. Basically, I need everything. I figure you have a good idea what and where to find what I need since you've done it for your house and all three at The Oasis. Plus, you'd make it more fun."

"I'm happy to help. I'll meet you at your house to save

time." Unless he ended up spending the night here. She'd see how things went first.

"Thanks. Now, I'll do the dishes since you cooked."

She knew better than to argue about it. Besides, there was something sexy about a hot guy doing the dishes in real life. She studied his butt. Why not? They were dating now. It wasn't Captain America's ass, but it was darn nice. She'd always been attracted to the swimmer's build: broad shoulders, strong back and arms, muscular legs. Add in John's handsome face and generous nature, and it was truly a miracle he hadn't married. That he stood in *her* kitchen loading dirty dishes into the dishwasher was possibly a bigger miracle.

She hummed the chorus of *The Sound of Music*'s "Something Good."

John started humming along while drying his hands.

"Really?" Though he was constantly surprising her, this was totally unexpected.

"*The Sound of Music* was my grandmother's favorite movie. She had the soundtrack. At one time, I knew the words to almost all the songs."

Elizabeth loved that he admitted that. "And did you change the words?"

"Me? Nah. Well, I couldn't relate to the favorite things in the song. I mean whose favorite thing is a copper kettle? That might have been why I started changing the lyrics to what fit better."

"What were your favorite things?"

"I don't remember. I was like six or nine. Probably hot dogs and baseball. I can do a new version with dogs named Boss and . . ." he paused, his mouth and hand moving as he tried out lyrics in his head, ". . . counselors with blue eyes and sexy asses."

311

She laughed. He had a knack for conjuring lyrics on the fly.

"It rhymed with the original." He swaggered over and extended a hand, smiling as she rose into his arms. "If you want, we can switch to *The Sound of Music* for our movie and sing 'Something Good' as a duet. It'd be very romantic."

"Maybe next time."

"Okay, 'Do-Re-Mi?' Don't mind me."

While John hadn't put any pressure on her and certainly put her at ease with his teasing, she did want to try getting romantic. Getting to the next stage of physical intimacy was no laughing matter. If she couldn't get there, she was going to have to end things before she fell completely in love with John.

And she was more than halfway there already.

♫

"What movie are we watching?" John ushered Boss inside from doing his doggie business.

"*Top Gun.* The original."

"Seriously? Navy jet jockeys?"

"*Top Gun* has good music, action, some comedy, and romance."

"Fine. But we're making out during the volleyball scene."

"Okay."

He looked surprised at her instant answer. "I was thinking, if it's all right with you, I could angle the couch. Instead of sitting next to each other to watch, I can lean back." He demonstrated, stretching his left leg nearly the length of the couch, his right foot on the floor. "And you sit here." He

patted the space between his legs. "I'll put my arms around you, and if there's any place you want my hands, you can place them strategically—or move them if they wander someplace you aren't ready for. How does that sound?"

"Very good." Perfect in fact. Her body tingled at the thought of his touch.

"There's another thing we need to address." He cleared his throat and shifted on the sofa. "I think we need a plan that will give you control. That said, we are not having sex of any kind tonight."

She could tell that pained him to say, but the pressure in her chest immediately lifted.

"I don't know what's going to work best leading up to our first time. Here at your house, where if things get uncomfortable, you can tell me to go. Or is that the worst place to try because if things don't go well, then something about that room becomes a trigger for you? Maybe my place is better so you know that you can get in your car and leave, though I hope to hell that doesn't happen. Maybe you want us to go away for a weekend to a hotel or rent someplace. Or will that make you feel trapped unless we drive separately?" He spread his hands helplessly.

That he'd thought so much about her needs made her feel valued, even loved, like never before. "I honestly don't know at this moment."

"That's why I want you to do—what did you call it?— visualization. Think about where and what exactly you want to go down." He licked his lips, and his gaze drifted down her body.

She swallowed, already visualizing one scenario that sent a wave of heat and desire through her.

"Once you decide, we'll talk and come up with a signal for when you're ready to try. No pressure."

"That sounds like a well-thought-out plan." And a way to avoid what happened when she'd gotten into potentially intimate situations after her divorce. "Are you this good at planning when it comes to your job?"

John flinched, and his jaw tightened. "I have to be." His easy-going persona went MIA. "The places I go? There are always people who want to kill us. My life and the lives of my teammates depend on me anticipating all outcomes."

She shuddered. "I see."

"My new position will involve training. There are still risks, but I won't deploy to dangerous places with enemies— at least for a while. I don't want to bring the mood down, but we should address the elephant in the room. And I don't mean Boss."

"Your move?"

"Yeah."

"Can we take this one step at a time? We've only been dating a week, and we should see if this is going to work before we have to figure out logistics. I don't want potential complications to hold us back."

"Okay, I like the way you phrased that." Though slightly subdued, his smile returned. "I was kicking myself for even bringing that up now."

"No, you were right to. Actually, you'd make a good counselor."

"Me? A counselor?" He laughed. "Yeah, right."

"I'm serious. Often, a counselor's role is to challenge people to go to a place they aren't comfortable going. Make the suggestion. If they aren't ready, you don't push. You work to develop trust and try again. Like you did with me."

"Wren explained that after I came back from the wedding. I don't think your clients would open up to me like they do you."

"No, but with your combat experience, other vets would."

"We do that in a bar or around a fire with a few beers. I don't think that'll work for you."

"Probably not." However, it was time to take one of those steps forward to see if she'd be able to conquer her past. "Are you ready to be my test subject?"

"Hell, yes," he said, his voice low and sexy.

Chapter Fifty Five

DANGER ZONE – Kenny Loggins

As soon as John plopped down on the couch, Boss tried to climb up to join him. "No, Boss. You're down there." He pushed Boss back and pointed to the floor.

Boss turned his pleading gaze to Elizabeth.

"That's my spot." She patted Boss on the head, started the movie, and settled into place, immediately cognizant of John's erection pressing into her.

"Ignore that. I'm a guy that's gone without and you're gorgeous, so I can't control the effect you have on me."

It was impossible to ignore, but she liked the effect she had on him. The contact made her feel empowered instead of fearful.

"I'm guessing you didn't think about the songs in this movie when you picked it."

"No. why?"

He cleared his throat. "You'll see." His fingertips tapped

her outer thigh as the music transitioned to "Danger Zone." As he sang the line about touch-and-go, his hand mimicked flying—into the danger zone as it hovered over her breast.

"I see your point." She took his hand in hers and placed them atop her thigh.

"You probably thought this song was about flying, not sex."

"It is—about flying."

"If you say so."

She angled her face to catch his mischievous grin.

"We watch a lot of movies while deployed. Typically, we read innuendo into everything. For this song, I'm pretty sure it was intentional to mirror the love story." He nuzzled the side of her neck, heating her up more.

"I like that."

"Good to know." He pressed several open-mouthed kisses down to her collarbone, slipping his fingers free from hers to trail them up her hip to her belly. His thumb rubbed right under her breast. She didn't even flinch.

By the time the first flight scene ended, she visualized his hands invading more than one danger zone.

John grabbed the remote when they reached the bar scene. "We're fast-forwarding through this song."

"Good call," she agreed when she realized which song it was. She was intent on *getting back* that loving feeling.

"Did you crush on Maverick or Iceman?" he asked when the volleyball scene started.

"Slider. I've always liked my men tall."

"I'm taller than he is."

She laughed and John rolled her to her side, keeping his back against the sofa, probably aware she'd feel trapped there. "You are. And your abs are just as nice." She ran a hand over his firm abs to his pecs.

"You can touch me there as much as you want," he whispered, then claimed her mouth with his.

She pressed her hips against him. Damn, that felt good. Based on his throaty rumble, he agreed. His hand slipped down, resting lightly, as if to gauge her reaction before cupping her butt. Their kisses deepened, and their bodies sought pleasure from the contact.

A low growl erupted from John, and he broke the kiss. He pulled back as much as he could and repositioned his hand to her lower back. "As much as I don't want to stop this . . . "

"We need to?" she answered breathlessly, not wanting to stop either, but even he had limits.

"For now." He pressed a kiss to her forehead.

They lay together a little longer, then he patted her hip. "I need you to let me up. Pause the movie and give me a minute."

"If you want to watch the rest with me, I was kind of visualizing something I'd like to try if you're still up for being my test subject."

He let out a long breath. "If you promise to go easy on me."

Once he disappeared into the bathroom, she went to the kitchen, poured glasses of milk, and got the container of chocolate chip cookies.

He grabbed a cookie when he returned. Her protective walls were coming down, and she wanted to take another step forward. "You good with assuming our original seating position?"

"Yes, ma'am." He took a swig of milk and snatched another cookie.

Once they were situated again, she resumed the movie. She didn't wait long before laying her hands over his and

FAKING IT WITH THE GREEN BERET

leading them up to her breasts. His warm hands covered and caressed, his fingers and thumbs rolling over her nipples. John crooned "Take My Breath Away" in her ear, then trailed kisses from her ear down her neck. His right hand traveled upward.

When his fingers touched her throat, she lurched forward and off the couch.

"Whoa." His arms flew out, and he froze.

Boss also scrambled to his feet and stood, watching her.

She crossed her hands over the center of her chest, trying to drag air into her stalled lungs. Sweat erupted all over her shaking body. "I—" Dammit. Tears choked her.

"*Shh. I'm sorry.* I was going to ask about the charm on your necklace. Do you need to sit?" He shifted to make room.

She released a steadying breath and sat near him. Boss edged closer and rested his chin on the cushion, not quite touching her. "I'm sorry. I wanted tonight to be perfect."

"It doesn't have to be perfect, though it's been damn close. We made good progress tonight. I learned I can kiss your neck, but I'll do my damnedest to remember not to put my hand on your throat."

She nodded to acknowledge that was what had triggered her: memories of Adam choking her to pin her down. "I didn't know I'd react like that." Or if she'd be able to move past it.

"What do you need right now? Do you want me to stay or . . ."

She took several deep breaths. "It's best if you go. I need to decompress. I'm sorry." It would also give him time to process her reaction and what it meant for them.

"Okay." He still didn't touch her. "Do you want me to

leave Boss here tonight? You can bring him when you meet me to go shopping."

"I'd appreciate that." That he wanted to keep them on track for tomorrow, despite what just happened, released the tension wrapping tightly around her. She could use Boss for emotional support too.

"Come over whenever you're ready." John stood in place, clearly uncertain what to do.

She summoned her energy and went to him. "I hope I didn't freak you out."

He shook his head. "I'm sorry I made you react that way."

"You didn't do anything wrong. Okay? I've got some more things to work through." Her reaction called for another EMDR session this week.

"I'm still here as your willing test subject, because, despite one little misstep, everything else was damn good tonight." He tilted her chin up and pressed a gentle kiss to her lips.

She walked him to the door, and Boss clambered over. "Sit. Stay with the pretty girl tonight, Boss. I'll see you in the morning." John kissed her again. She held Boss's collar as John headed to his truck.

She turned off the TV, then went to the bathroom and washed her face. Boss stuck close, like he sensed her distress. Her heart rate had slowed to normal, but she felt drained from the crash of adrenaline.

"You want to sleep in my bed tonight? You can't tell John." She patted the bed, shaking her head at how she was now talking to Boss the way John did. Boss snuggled up next to her, resting his head on his paws and staring at her. "You're cute, but this wasn't the ending I wanted for tonight."

Things had been going so well. While John had handled it with grace and tact, how many more triggers lay dormant just waiting for the right, or wrong, moment to attack? What if, even with EMDR therapy, she could never entirely shake her past?

Chapter Fifty Six

NOTHING'S GONNA STOP US NOW – Starship

ELIZABETH PARKED in the lot next to John's truck at the café near her downtown office. Her confidence wavered. Maybe they should go somewhere that served alcohol and wait until she had a little liquid courage. No. They were here, and she needed to do this. If she couldn't even tell him her plan, how was she going to summon the nerve to go through with it?

He'd made his way to her car by the time she got out.

"You look professional but still sexy." He placed both hands on her hips.

"Back at ya. What do they call this?" She pinched the front of his shirt a few inches over his waistband.

"A combat shirt."

"I like the way it fits. Much sexier than the jacket top."

"That's what the Army was going for. They thought it would up our recruitment," he deadpanned. His face

closed in, and he kissed her senseless. "I missed you last night."

"About that, I needed some alone time to think. Can we take a little walk before dinner? There's something I need to talk with you about."

John's face went devoid of emotion. "Sure."

"It's nothing bad." She took his hand. "I've been visualizing scenarios for our first time, and I'd rather not lay out my plan in a public restaurant."

"Oh." John's cautious demeanor gave way to a huge smile. "Let's go then."

Butterflies swarmed in her stomach.

He gripped her hand as they made their way along the path that led to a fountain.

"I'm thinking what would work best is your house." Then, if things did not go well, she wouldn't be reminded whenever she was in that spot. She waited for two women pushing baby strollers to pass them on the walk. "The scenario I'm most comfortable with for starters involves oral sex."

"Okay. And how will I know when you're ready for me to go down on you?" His voice dropped to a sexy timbre.

Her entire body heated at the way his smile did not waver an iota at her suggestion of something Adam never would do, or for, her. She fanned her face. "I'll bring an overnight bag, and we'll go from there."

"Pack enough for two days in case you decide to stay more than one night. Are all our dates going to be at my house going forward?"

"I'm not sure how long it's going to be until I'm ready," she warned. "I've got another EMDR session with Charis tomorrow. You could bring Boss over for dinner at my place on Thursday."

"'I don't get to see you tomorrow?" He pouted in an adorable fashion for someone who was six-foot-five.

"'I'm afraid not. I promised Mayala I'd help her with more job applications. I spoke to Cindy, the attorney who represented Ariana, and she thinks there's a good chance she can get enough compensation from the family Mayala was working for to get her a decent used car and some savings for a place of her own."

"'That'd be great. She earned it. It's good to see everyone moving forward. You ready for dinner or do you have more dirty talk for me? You weren't very detailed in your instructions."

She elbowed him in the ribs.

He laughed.

"'I may need to signal you to do more or less of something. Or to slow down so I feel safe, but I think you probably have a good idea of what to do."

"'Trust me, I do. And darlin', I'm going to rock your world." He sang softly and in tune, "I will, I will rock you."

"'I have one more request. As endearing as your singing is, not while we're . . ."

"'Ever?" His voice squeaked.

"'I'm not saying ever. Just not the first time. Or dozen."

"'I guess that's not a deal breaker."

She loved how unfazed he was by her insecurities, how he neutralized their power over her and made her laugh. More than ever, she wanted to get to the point where they had a shot at a future together.

♫

Boss served as the welcoming committee for Elizabeth's arrival. She took a deep breath and a moment to collect her

thoughts and pray this past week's dates with John and her last EMDR therapy were enough.

Shopping with John last Sunday served as a good transition after her panic attack the night before. Being in his house together, organizing his kitchen that night, had been safe and comfortable. Them, doing life together.

Then there'd been dinner on Tuesday after she'd laid out her plan. She'd expected him to drop innuendos throughout dinner. Instead, he suggested getting an electric bike or moped for Mayala to provide transportation and open up more job possibilities. Last night, he'd casually inquired if her therapy had gone well. He'd been on his best behavior for dinner.

Tonight would be different. Hopefully.

She got a treat for Boss and her bag out of the back seat.

"Hi." John stared at the bag in her hand. He swallowed.

"I see you brought a, um ..."

"A treat for Boss." Boss nosed the bag in her hand. "It's an elk antler."

"That's not what I was gonna say. You brought what looks like an overnight bag."

"I did."

"Do you want to set it down"—he paused between each word—"or do you want me to put it in the bedroom?"

"I thought we'd give Boss the antler to keep him busy while we go to the bedroom."

She gave Boss the bone. John reached for her bag and took her hand. Once he closed the door behind them, she sang, "Nothing's gonna stop us now."

He laughed. "And I was being so good." He set her bag on the floor, moved close, and ran a finger along her cheek and under her chin, careful to avoid her throat. "No matter

how much I want this, if you need to stop, just say the word."

"Okay." And even though "Stop in the Name of Love" went through her mind, she was not about to sing and ruin the mood or stop them from getting started.

Open the bedroom door.
[https://bookhip.com/LFWLHPF]

Chapter Fifty-Seven

I COULD NOT ASK FOR MORE – Sara Evans

JOHN TURNED from the stove to see Elizabeth leaning against the door jamb. With Boss around, the sensation of being watched while he cooked bacon, or any kind of meat, was nothing new. While he wanted to think last night created some special connection between him and Elizabeth, more likely a movement from Boss signaled him to her presence. "Good morning, gorgeous."

"Good morning."

"Come here." He switched the tongs to his left hand and extended his arm. Holding her to his side, he kissed her tousled hair. "I see you helped yourself to one of my shirts."

"I didn't think you'd mind, and you weren't wearing it." She cast a smoldering smile up at him and trailed a finger down his bare chest.

He didn't mind in the least. "It gets hot when I'm cook-

ing." And it was getting hotter with her here looking at him that way. He was getting harder by the second too.

After their successful initial experiment last night, she'd completely dressed before joining him while he cooked the steaks. Kind of a bummer, though she'd given him that sexy, disapproving teacher look and reminded him they were taking Boss for a walk. But she'd gotten naked again later. And so had he. Then she'd rocked *his* world.

After Boss woke him to go out this morning, it'd been so tempting to crawl back in bed. Though lying in bed, staring at her while she slept, could be seen as needy or creepy, and he hadn't wanted to wake her when she probably needed more sleep. He'd decided fixing breakfast was a better idea, but her looking at him like this definitely had him wanting to take her back to bed.

"A steak dinner better than an upscale restaurant and now breakfast. You're spoiling me."

"It's chipotle bacon." He offered her a piece of the batch he'd already cooked.

"Yum. Cooked just how I like it."

"Grilling meat and breakfast are my specialties—in the kitchen," he added. "How do you like your eggs?"

"Are you sure those are your only specialties in the kitchen? Because I have to say that the way you're wearing these sleep pants low on your hips is making me visualize a new scenario. Especially when there's a drawstring." She gave it a gentle tug.

"I thought you'd be hungry."

"Eh." She gave an adorable shrug. "Are you?"

"Boss and I each had a piece of bacon. Okay, two each, but there's plenty for you." He turned off the burner and moved the pan. "I'm ready and willing to continue as your test subject."

Elizabeth walked him to his new kitchen table and turned a chair around. She laid a hand on his shoulder, indicating for him to sit. He licked his lips as she straddled him, lowering herself to his lap. She was quickly dispelling any notion that her past inhibited her when it came to sex.

"I have to be honest"—she draped her arms over his shoulders and ran her fingernails along his scalp with her heavenly touch—"I don't like calling you my test subject. I'm trying to decide what's better. Boyfriend doesn't fit because you are one hundred percent man."

He let out a gruff laugh. This was getting interesting.

"Lover"—her shoulders did a little dance—"sounds a little tawdry. Like we're reducing the relationship to sex when it's so much more. I wish there were a word that summarized an adult relationship with a person you love."

Love. She'd said love. His hands gently squeezed her outer thighs. The sensation spreading through his body was indescribable. He could dodge any speeding bullet, fight off an entire enemy contingent, climb every mountain.

"Last night was—everything." Her voice cracked, and her eyes went misty.

That was a lot to live up to. "Careful. You're going to give me a big head." Her cute chortle immediately told him how she took that with his erection poking her.

"I'm not just talking about your prowess in bed."

"Did you use the word prowess because you knew I'd like it?" Her using it in reference to him satisfying her made him even harder. He snuck his hands under her shirt—his shirt—but semantics weren't important when she wouldn't be wearing it in a minute.

"Maybe. It's your heart that made me fall for you. Well, I might have started falling the first time I saw you with Boss."

"Really?"

"You two were pretty adorable at your reunion. Though I wasn't ready for anything romantic then. But you wore me down and made me fake it until it was something I could handle. I feel like the me I used to be. Happy and more confident than I've ever been." She lowered her face to his.

"*Mmm*. I like all those things. I'll do my best to make sure you stay that way."

"Um, do you think you could get Boss to go to his bed while we . . . " She untied the drawstring of his sleep pants.

"Boss, you heard the lady. Go to your bed."

Boss gave a plaintive whimper, raising his snout toward the bacon.

"Go to your bed." John used his stern voice.

Boss hung his head and slunk away, casting a sad look at them before he disappeared from the kitchen.

"He's breaking my heart, but I don't think I can do this with him watching."

That John encountered nothing but bare skin when he ran his hands up her outer thighs to her hips backed up his decision to temporarily disappoint his dog.

"You can give him the bacon when we eat. All will be forgiven, and everyone will be happy."

Chapter Fifty-Eight

AMERICAN SOLDIER – Toby Keith

When John opened Elizabeth's front door, Boss raced inside. John didn't even knock—a sign of how quickly things had progressed the past two weeks. Was that all about to change? He headed to the kitchen on weighted legs. "Something sure smells great."

"Dinner's almost ready. You're later than I thought."

"Sorry about that. Colonel Holmstrom needed to see me."

"Is everything okay?" she asked, a guardedness in her voice. Her eyes narrowed, taking him in.

"Not exactly. The captain for Charlie Company, who replaced my team, was injured yesterday."

Her mouth formed a silent O. She didn't ask, so he didn't give her details that would only make her worry.

"They need someone to step in ASAP, as they've got a brand-new first lieutenant on his first deployment."

"They want you to go?"

"Holmstrom asked. I don't want to go right now, and I don't have to . . ."

"But you're being drafted for this mission?"

"The colonel wants somebody who knows the area and has a relationship with the locals to keep from losing the trust we've built. I replaced Elauria, so he knows the area too, but he's married and his wife's expecting their third kid in two weeks. He missed the birth of number two." No way John could ask Elauria to go in his place. "The company that deploys next is still training. They need their captain here. Since I'll be transferring out, I'm replaceable here, and the reason I was tapped for promotion early is that I'm good at what I do. If anything were to happen to one of the team that I could have prevented, I'd have to live with that."

Elizabeth sighed, not meeting his eyes.

He gave her several moments to take it all in. "I know this timing totally sucks. If I say no, it goes in my record. It's not like they'll force me out, but it could slow things down for my next promotion."

When she finally met his gaze, he couldn't read the look in her eyes. Was it hurt? Anger? Disappointment? Or worse —was she throwing in the towel and surrendering? Was she not willing to fight for what they could have after she helped him realize he hadn't fought for relationships in the past?

"We haven't talked about how we could make this work long-term. That's on me," she started.

"We both thought we'd have more time."

"A while back I asked about goals you haven't met. You brought up marriage and family, but we didn't talk about career goals. What are your plans and things you want to accomplish?"

He stood a little straighter. "With this promotion, I'm on track to make lieutenant colonel before I hit my twenty years, but I'm not saying I'll get out then. Full colonel is a nice pay bump and commands a lot of respect. I'm not sure I'm cut out to be a general. I can be diplomatic, but dealing with politicians? I'd rather face down a band of insurgents."

Elizabeth gave him a slight smile and head nod. "I can't see you enjoying the political side of things. For the record, you don't have to hit a rank to impress me. You already have my respect for your mad skills and service. I'd rather you do what you love and be happy."

"I love my team and what we do, but to move up, I have to do the staff slot as a major, whether here or at SOCOM. That they fast-tracked me for promotion and selected me for a position with the SFAB—"

"I know SOCOM is Special Ops Command, but what's the SF . . ."

"SFAB. Security Forces Assistance Brigade, where we partner with our allies to train their military. Sometimes called Special Forces Light."

"Does that mean it's not as dangerous?"

"Typically," he sought to give her some reassurance.

"Would they come here to train, or do you go there?"

"I'd still have to do some six-month deployments."

She gave a slight grimace. "How long does this new position last?"

"A minimum of two years. Then I could be extended or reassigned."

"Back here?"

"That's a definite possibility, unless I screw up or . . ."

"Say no now?" She drew in and slowly released a long breath. "How soon will you leave?"

"Depends. I hoped you'd be willing to take care of Boss."

"Of course."

"And I still get him when I come back?" he defaulted to humor.

"I might hold him for ransom." She cracked the hint of a real smile. "Make you work off his care."

"I'm happy to do that." That she was trying to keep her sense of humor too released some of the tension coiled in his gut. "Then I leave as soon as I can update some paperwork. One of the guys on my team has a son who'll mow the grass at my house. I'll leave you a key. Will you go by and check on it every couple of weeks for me?"

"You don't want to list or rent it now?"

"I don't have time to set that up, and I'll need a place to stay when I get back." Unless she was offering, but it would be pushing things to ask.

"How would you feel about having a short-term renter in there?"

"Which one?" He could see where she was going with this.

"Your pick. I think Ariana is ready, though being close to town would open up job opportunities for Mayala. It could also be good for Wren. Give her a few months on her own, knowing she has to transition from there. You don't have to decide right now. Think on it."

"I will." It's not like he had a lot of time, though. He placed a hand on Elizabeth's hip and pulled her to him. "Since you understand you can't talk about where I am, and I know you won't, I promise I'll be in touch as often as I can." He was doing things differently this time. Not going dark like he had with Britney. *It will be different. It will be different. Boss will be okay.* If he and Elizabeth could get

through this short separation so early in the relationship, they could figure out the next steps to make a long-distance relationship work once he moved—at least until she was ready for more. "I'll text Colonel Holmstrom to let him know."

"Can that wait until tomorrow?"

"They need to start pulling the paperwork in the morning and book my flight."

"You're not leaving tomorrow, are you?" The despair in her voice pierced him like a saber.

"No. Probably the next day, though." He should have brought her flowers, but she already associated them with bad things.

"You weren't kidding about soon." She sighed. "I guess you can't push it back a few days because your girlfriend is new to all this, huh?" She attempted a smile.

"If it were up to me . . . but not really." At least she was trying to stay strong.

"Has Boss eaten?" She took the casserole dish out of the oven.

"Not yet."

She pulled out the bag of dog food and filled Boss's bowl. "You stay, boy. And you . . ." She crooked a finger at John. ". . . come with me. We'll eat later. We have something else to do."

He followed her to her bedroom.

Chapter Fifty-Nine

HOW DO I LIVE – LeAnn Rimes

They'd PLAYED with Boss after dinner and made love again. Now, Elizabeth lay next to John, unable to sleep. Taking him to bed had enabled her to hold it together after he broke the news. It's not like he'd asked for this assignment. But in the darkness, her heartache grew as the minutes ticked by.

Moving slowly so as not to wake him, she eased from bed. She slipped his shirt over her head. *I'm holding onto this one. If only she could keep him here instead.* This was so unfair.

Boss lifted his head when she came down the steps. "*Shh,*" she whispered as he got to his feet. He stood there a moment, then traipsed to the front door and waited. "Might as well."

She quietly opened the door and followed Boss outside. While he sniffed her azalea bushes, she sank into one of the

rocking chairs. Tears flowed unchecked, and a soft sob escaped.

Boss came up the steps and rested his face on her leg. He didn't yet understand. At least they'd have each other from the start to make John's absence a little easier. She wiped away tears with the sleeve of John's soft T-shirt and rubbed Boss's head. He lay next to her chair as she rocked and listened to the frogs and crickets.

The sky was clear with only a sliver of moon to give light. Tiny dots of stars shimmered through her watery eyes. The screen door squeaked, and she dipped her head. John stopped a foot away. His bare feet were all she could see of him.

"Did Boss wake you to go out?" He caressed her shoulder.

"I think I woke him." Her voice came out broken and rough.

John squatted next to her. "Oh, darlin'. I never wanted to make you cry." He rested one hand on her knee. Pain dulled his eyes, and he gently brushed away her tears with a callused thumb before getting to his feet. "Come here."

She took the hand he extended. He sat on the swing, and she settled back against his chest. His arms wrapped around her.

He pressed several tender kisses to her temple. "Are you mad?"

"Yes."

"At me?"

"No." The word came out weakly. "At the Army."

He kissed her temple longer and harder this time. "I'll tell them I won't go."

As tempting as it was, she couldn't let him do that. "You

337

can't risk derailing your career." Not when that was clearly important—maybe as a wife and family.

"If you shoot me in the foot, they couldn't send me."

"I'm not shooting you." She looked to see if he was serious.

He grinned at her. "You're right. You might get in trouble. Nobody would believe I shot myself, though. Maybe I could break my arm."

"That idea has some merit." Except if anything happened to someone on the deployed team, they'd both have to live with it. She tightened her grip on his arms. "I wanted these next few months with you. I feel like we're being cheated."

"I wanted the time too. It won't be the same, but we'll message and talk when we can. It's only three months, then I'll be here for at least a month. I'll take leave and you can take vacation. And after that, I'll come up at least one weekend a month. You can come to Florida, or we can meet halfway."

"Is that really the kind of relationship you want?" She couldn't see him settling for a few days a month. She wanted more. With him, she wanted it all, or as much as his career in the Army allowed.

"No, and certainly not forever, but I'm not walking away from the best thing I've ever had."

She wasn't either. Not when he'd changed her life so completely these past few weeks. But she also wasn't rushing to make major life changes with her career or abandoning The Oasis when they'd had so little time together. Not after Adam. Though far from ideal, she'd see how the relationship fared separation, first by thousands of miles, then shorter time and distance. Then she could decide what

she was willing to sacrifice for a chance at the future she again envisioned.

"You never told me if there's a special meaning to this symbol on your necklace." He lifted it from her chest, turning it to see from different angles.

"My sister, Jennifer, gave it to me when I graduated with my master's. That's an infinity symbol in the center, and the other knots are to show that choices we make and each twist in life has a purpose in connecting us. The symbol represents growth and new beginnings."

"I like that. Thanks for telling me." He rubbed his thumb over it. "Are we staying out here to watch the sunrise or . . ."

"That's a few hours away." She turned her face up to his to nuzzle him with her nose.

"As long as you're in my arms, I'm good. But you probably need some rest so you don't fall asleep listening to your clients."

"True."

"Have you ever done phone or video sex?"

Oh, my. "No. But I'd be willing to try if you'll teach me. For now, let's go inside and see if you can help me get to sleep with the real thing." She squeezed his arms.

"Yes, ma'am." He spread his arms to free her. "I'm not going in until you leave for work either. So, if you need anything in the morning . . ."

She'd miss everything about him. Would she be able to let him go now and in the future without coming to resent him or his job? Was she strong enough to face the possibility of losing him when she already wondered if she could live without him?

Chapter Sixty

FAR AWAY – Nickelback

John parked Elizabeth's car in the passenger drop-off zone at the airport, unable to swallow the lump in his throat. He'd needed a ride since he was taking a commercial flight instead of the usual military transport. It was an easy decision to leave his truck at The Oasis where it'd be safe and serve as a reminder that he planned to come home to her. They'd gotten a little more time together on the drive over, but he failed at his mission to keep the mood light. They were out of time, and this would be a hard goodbye.

"I need to grab a baggage cart. Will you put the leash on Boss, please?" The small regional airport wasn't busy, but the last thing he needed now was Boss getting loose when he had to go.

He pushed the cart to where Elizabeth leaned against the car's open trunk, clutching the leash to keep Boss close

to her side. She'd put on her brave face, but her smile didn't reach her eyes.

He could relate.

It had been less than forty-eight hours since he told her the news. She was taking it well, but the test was still to come. They'd only been a couple less than a month. That wasn't half as long as he'd been with Britney. Look how that turned out.

Elizabeth wouldn't cheat on him and sure as hell wouldn't go back to her ex, but what if she decided this wasn't the life she wanted? Or that he wasn't good enough for her? Even though he'd hoped to impress her with his career goals, his insecurities reemerged with a vengeance. He would have asked Elizabeth's advice, but now that he was sleeping with her—and doing that as much as possible in the limited time they had left—he knew she'd say she was too biased to give him counseling advice.

Last night, they told the women at The Oasis about him leaving and later called his father. John had just told his dad and wife about Elizabeth the previous week. This deployment tanked his plans to take her to meet them. Instead, they'd met over video chat and promised to visit when he returned.

He loaded the last of his gear and bags, then drop to a knee and rubbed Boss behind both ears. "Elizabeth will take good care of you. You look after her too, okay?" Boss didn't understand what was going on, but he'd be in good hands. "I'll send you treats and toys." Boss licked his cheek.

John got to his feet. He pulled Elizabeth into his arms, breathed in her honeysuckle scent, and memorized how her body fit with his.

"You take care of yourself." Her voice cracked with emotion.

"I will. I promise. Thanks for the cookies. The guys will appreciate them. You'll make me the most popular guy in camp."

Britney hadn't baked him cookies or even asked about sending a care package like Elizabeth had. Everything was different with this deployment. The woman he was leaving behind. Flying out on a commercial airline, which would delay him getting into a mission mindset. He'd previously served with two of the men in Charlie Company and his explosives guy, Cruz, was replacing another injured member, but, for the most part, he didn't know these men or how they operated as a team.

He'd need to earn their confidence and get up to speed quickly—for the safety of them all. Injuries sustained by Charlie Company's captain and two of his team were stark reminders of the dangers of operating in that part of the world. There weren't Medevacs available for immediate extraction or combat hospitals staffed with skilled trauma surgeons and life-saving supplies. He'd never been afraid of dying, but this deployment he had serious motivation to come home safely.

He'd listed Elizabeth as a joint beneficiary with his dad in case anything happened to him. He didn't tell her. In the event of his death, he wanted her to have the money to take care of Boss and supplement her mission with The Oasis. Writing his death letter to her had been the hardest, yet easiest, he'd ever written. He prayed she wouldn't ever read it—even if it was a damn good letter.

"I love you, and I love what we have going on," he told her.

She hugged him tighter. "I love you too. More than I imagined possible."

His heart swelled under her smile. "When I get back,

FAKING IT WITH THE GREEN BERET

it's going to get even better. I want to take you somewhere. The time I came to the Friday night dinner, you mentioned wanting to see the Northern Lights. It should be the perfect time to see those. Or pick a place. I'll go anywhere with you."

"And I'd go anywhere with you—except where you're deployed."

"Trust me you don't want to go where I'm going. It's hot. There's no AC. There's no indoor plumbing. It stinks. And I'd be distracted and fighting off all the men who'd all be staring at you." He winked rather than go on to mention the poisonous spiders and snakes and armed gunmen. "I'll get in touch as soon as I can. There's a five-hour time difference, but we'll try and set up a regular date. We can do karaoke night."

"Oh, that'd be . . . fun."

"You're gonna turn the speakers down if I do, aren't you?"

"I hadn't *planned* to." She spoke slowly, and a smile spread across her beautiful face.

"I'll think of some duets we can do. Right now, I want to kiss a girl," he sang, lowering his mouth to hers.

They kissed, ignoring everything and everyone around them until Boss nuzzled his snout between their legs. John slipped his fingers under Boss's collar and eased him back.

"Get in the car, Boss."

Instead, the dog pulled toward the baggage cart.

"Afraid not. Stay with Elizabeth. She'll have treats for you." He led Boss to the car and wrangled him inside.

"Thanks for the ride and taking care of him. He may mope around for a few days, but he's got you. He'll be okay."

John kissed Elizabeth again, then pushed the cart toward the entrance. He stopped to look back at her

watching him instead of leaving. After he checked his bags, he went to his gate to wait for the first of his three flights and twenty-three hours of travel to Chad. He cued up the new song list he'd started and sent the first song to Elizabeth as his daily reminder he'd be thinking of her and missing her.

Chapter Sixty One

LOVE SHACK – B-52's

JOHN SETTLED into the makeshift communications room in their camp—sometimes referred to as the Love Shack. It was the only place the guys got five minutes of privacy other than the latrine, which was not where you wanted to video chat with your girl. He set up his laptop and checked the lighting before initiating the call to Elizabeth.

"Hey there, darlin'." He basked in her sultry smile. The first week or two apart had been the hardest, but they'd settled into a routine with daily messages to keep connected.

"How's your week been?"

"Good, other than the guys giving me a hard time about singing "Miss You Like Crazy" after you sent me that yesterday." It was worth any teasing, though. Today he'd sent her "Made to Love" by one of her favorite artists, Toby-Mac. They'd both broadened their musical repertoire over

the past month with their daily song exchanges. "Um, were you not quite ready for our date?"

"Because I'm fully clothed?" She stared at the camera, reading him like a book. "That's because we need to talk first."

Uh, oh. In the history of the world, nothing good ever followed those words. Dammit, he'd been doing his best to stay connected with Elizabeth these past two months. He hadn't seen this coming. His core tightened and he steeled himself.

"We're fine, but it's about Boss."

"What? Is he okay? What did the vet say?" It should have been a relief that it wasn't about them, but now panic of a different kind formed a knot in his throat. She hadn't mentioned any concerns after taking Boss in for his routine check, dental cleaning, and updated rabies shot.

"He's fine, but the vet had asked if we would be interested in breeding him."

"He is the best dog ever, but don't people usually want purebreds for breeding?"

"That's what I asked. After what the vet said, I had him run a DNA test. Boss isn't who you think he is. Turns out he's not part springer spaniel."

"Okay. That was kind of a guess." Because he wanted it to be, and Boss did have spots.

"He's not part Rottweiler either."

He picked up the thread of where she was going and didn't like it. "But his head is shaped like theirs."

"Close. Have you heard of Catahoula Leopard dogs?"

"A what?" It sounded like something she made up to prank him.

"I hadn't either. It's a breed out of Louisiana known for

herding and hunting large game. They're intelligent, loyal to their owners, and have lots of energy."

"Sounds about right."

"That's what the DNA results confirmed."

"Not even part Clydesdale, huh?"

She rolled her eyes and laughed. "Less than one percent. He is slightly over the top of the size range though. Come here, Boss. Say hi to your daddy."

Boss's big face filled the screen before giving John a view of the top of his head as the dog nuzzled his face to Elizabeth's screen.

"I still love you, boy. Guess I'll have to do some research on Chattahoochee Leopard dog?"

"Catahoula."

"Oh."

"I'll send you the info in an email."

"How's he taking it?

She laughed again. "Pretty well. We were more worried about you."

"Yeah. It does take some of the fun out of it, but I don't think we should change his name."

"I agree."

"Our next dog, we may have to adopt a cocker spaniel and name him Joe Cocker."

"We'll talk about that later. We're short on time. I had an idea to cheer you up."

"Oh, yeah? 'Cuz I'm taking this kind of hard."

"That's not what should be hard." Her voice dropped to that sultry tone that definitely made parts of him hard.

"What do you have in mind to make me feel better?" Their first video sex chat had naturally been a little awkward, but he'd talked her through it. Since then, she'd gotten more

comfortable. For now, this was what they could do, being separated by an entire ocean, but he definitely looked forward to getting home to her and doing things with her.

"We're going to play poker. Strip. Poker." She grinned at the camera and shuffled a deck of cards.

"I should warn ya. I'm pretty good at poker."

"That's okay. I have an advantage. I wear earrings and a necklace."

"I'll see your earrings and raise you a combat boot."

"I love you."

"I love you more. But we've only got ten minutes left before Garcia is knocking on the door for his turn to chat with his wife. So, I'll even take one boot off to get started. I'm trusting you not to cheat."

"I'd never cheat. I don't even mind losing a few hands."

She claimed to lose the first hand to a paltry pair of fives. He'd take it as a win, especially since she left it on her earrings and seductively removed her shirt to reveal the lacy black bra from the lingerie set he'd ordered for her. It looked even better on her than the model, though he was biased because he *loved* this woman.

A few more weeks and he'd be home. He prayed this time would be different with only good surprises and no "Another Somebody Done Somebody Wrong" songs to be played.

Chapter Sixty Two

COMING HOME – Keith Urban

THE MOOD in the plane's cabin grew more and more electrified now that they were flying over land. They were almost home.

John could sleep almost anywhere and long flights home after deployments usually provided the best sleep he'd had in months. This time, sleep eluded him. Memories of his last homecoming ate away at his confidence.

It didn't help that he'd missed last week's standing video date with Elizabeth due to being out on a mission. They sent each other their usual daily messages but hadn't talked in almost two weeks. The upside was that kept him from telling her their planned departure date, which was subject to last-minute changes or delays. His plan was for his first sergeant to drop him off out at Elizabeth's place where he'd get a nap and be waiting when she got home from work.

Though she didn't love surprises, he hoped she'd like this one.

He'd visualized their reunion, even a few worst-case scenarios, since things rarely went down the way he pictured. While it couldn't possibly be worse than his last homecoming, it could hurt more. This time, he knew genuine love.

He'd also had an epiphany. One that could change everything.

He believed they wanted the same things, and that she viewed him as good enough. That she would take the risk on a guy like him, even after this sudden deployment and separation. Nevertheless, anxiety churned in his gut as the plane touched down in the bright North Carolina sunshine.

As the jet taxied toward the hangar where a small crowd had gathered to welcome the men home, John peered past Cruz to look out the window. One day, maybe soon, there'd be somebody in that group waiting for him. Not just anyone. Elizabeth. More than anything, he wanted her to be the one.

"You forgetting something, Captain?" Cruz asked.

John stared at him blankly for a second.

"Your homecoming tradition is legendary in Third Group." First Sergeant Clark grinned across the aisle.

Duh. How could he forget? He fished his phone out of his pants pocket. He scrolled past all the songs that he and Elizabeth had sent to each other to find the right one. He stood, grabbed the plane's intercom handset, and motioned for the men to stay in their seats.

"Before we deboard, I want to say it's been an honor serving with Charlie Company. You all performed admirably under difficult circumstances. I have a parting gift for you." He started Chuck Berry's "Back in the USA."

on his phone. Cheers erupted while he played air guitar to the familiar opening lick. He sang the first stanza with Clark, Cruz, and a few others joining him.

"Company dismissed," he proclaimed when the flight crew opened the door. "If you need anything, my number is 867-5309," he sang.

"What area code?" A younger team member asked.

"Seriously? I'm overdue for R and R. Call First Sergeant Clark or your momma."

Laughter filled the plane as the men surged to their feet. Keeping with tradition, John waited at the front and acknowledged each man as they exited.

"You were the right man to step in during a rough time," Clark said. "You boosted morale and kept everyone mission-focused. We may not officially be your team, but we'll follow you into battle anytime."

"Thanks. That means a lot. Let's go." John followed Clark. The men congregated at the base of the boarding stairs, which meant he had to uphold another tradition and kiss some asphalt. Why had he started that?

Over the cheerful voices waiting to reunite with loved ones, John picked out a distinctive bark. Jerking his gaze up, he glimpsed Boss running full-bore across the tarmac. That could only mean one thing. He scanned the crowd fifty yards away, his heart racing. When he spotted Elizabeth waiting with the gathered families, tears stung his eyes. Worries weighing on him fell away.

Clark had to edge past Boss, who tried to squeeze his way up the stairs.

"Stay boy," John commanded. Boss sat, his tail thumping on the asphalt for two beats until John's boots hit the ground. He nearly knocked John down before he could drop his pack.

With his paws on John's chest, Boss licked John's face.

"It's good to see you, boy, but I need to see Elizabeth. Come on."

"Captain." Cruz pointed to the ground.

"I've got something better to kiss first." He had a new and far better tradition to start. He strode past his men with Boss at his heels. Elizabeth worked her way to the front of the crowd. When John broke into a jog, she surged forward. He lifted her into his arms and crushed her warm, soft body to his a mere second before his mouth claimed hers in needy, possessive kisses. "You're here. How did you know?" he stopped kissing her long enough to ask.

"I made a few phone calls. Once I finally got in touch with Debbie from the Family Readiness Group for Charlie Company, she agreed that Boss and I needed to be here and added me to the notification list. I know you like surprises."

"Best surprise ever." He kissed her again.

"Well, I have another surprise. Wren's still in your house."

"That's not a huge surprise." He set Elizabeth down.

"You're not saying . . ."

"You're going to have to stay with me. At least for a few days—probably longer."

"*That* I will gladly do. I'd rather not move back into a tiny home all alone."

"You'd have Boss. Maybe."

"Maybe?" He hitched an eyebrow at the woman he loved.

"I'd lure him to my place with treats to get you to come over."

He laughed and lowered his mouth near her ear. "Darlin', you don't need to resort to using our dog. I'll come anytime." He winked, and her cheeks grew pink. "There's a

tradition I need to perform so these guys will go home. Then, you can take me home."

He turned to face the men. They watched him drop to his knees and touch his lips to the asphalt. He popped to his feet to cheers and laughter.

Elizabeth smiled, shaking her head at him. He wiped his sleeve across his mouth before kissing her again. This homecoming beat any scenario he'd envisioned.

Chapter Sixty Three

STUCK LIKE GLUE – Sugarland

For once, Elizabeth was up before John. After the deployment and travel and last night's lovemaking, he deserved to sleep past sunrise. She lay beside him, studying him for another minute before slipping quietly from the room.

She thought he would suspect, even anticipate, that she'd be at the airfield yesterday, despite the fact he hadn't told her anything more specific than he'd be home 'soon.' She'd tried not to overanalyze that he had a mission and couldn't video chat last week—and hadn't rescheduled. But she'd been determined to get as close as possible to his ultimate Bucket List experience. Boss was like his child, after all.

She'd pulled off that surprise. John also loved the American flags she'd placed along the front of her property and the welcome home banner hanging from the fence.

She had one more surprise—an even bigger one for a little later.

First, she set about fixing a breakfast fit for a hero. Bacon, fruit, eggs, fried potatoes, and premium coffee. She might be going a bit overboard, but she hadn't cooked for him for months.

"You've been a very good boy," she said to Boss when she had nearly everything prepared. She'd fed him before getting out the bacon, but he'd taken up station next to her the moment she'd opened the package. She took the cooked bacon out of the air fryer and gave him a piece. It disappeared in a flash, and he pleaded for more with his big eyes. "You didn't even bother to taste it. One more. Then you have to wait for John." She held out a second piece.

Instead of devouring it, Boss took it gently in his mouth and headed toward the stairs.

"Wait. Don't wake him." She grabbed another piece as a bribe.

Before she could stop him, Boss had pushed open the bedroom door. He stood at the side of the bed after laying the bacon near John's face.

John sniffed and opened one sleepy eye.

"Here, Boss." She motioned to him and waved the bacon until he came. She closed the door this time and went back to finish cooking.

It wasn't long before John shuffled up behind her. She turned the heat up to cook the eggs. He wrapped his arms around her and held her against his aroused body.

"Good morning." She turned her head, accepting his kiss on her cheek. "Sorry about Boss waking you."

"It's okay. Bacon was a nice treat, though I would have preferred you in the bed." His low, sexy voice heated her as his hands slid up to cup her breasts.

"You'll have lots of mornings with me still in bed. Since we picked up pizza last night, I wanted to cook for you."

"You've gone all out."

"I like having you home."

"Home. I like that word." He pressed a long kiss near her temple. "Have you booked our trip though? Are we going to see the Northern Lights or someplace where we can snorkel and I can see you in a bikini?"

"There might be snorkeling where I plan to take you. I didn't check that."

"Okay." He let go and reached for the coffee mug with the Special Forces logo that she'd set out for him. "So, where are we going?" He spooned sugar in before filling the mug, then gave a satisfied sigh after taking a sip.

"Tampa."

"What? Why?"

"You need to find a place to live, so I've found a few options with some land for Boss." She pointed the spatula at the print-offs on the kitchen table. "I thought we'd drive down so we can take him with us and see if any of them are a place we could call home."

"What are you saying?" He eyed her and picked up the property listings and leafed through them.

"I want to be with you, and not just every other week-end. I'm not saying I'd move there immediately. We could give it a few months for you to get settled, and, if things go like we hope, then I'd start transitioning my practice. Scale back my days here while I'm building there. That would give my patients time to find a new counselor and the tenants here time to move on—and out."

"You'd do that for me? Give up everything you've got here? Your home? Your work? Your independence?" He gave a lop-sided smile adding the last.

"I'm not totally giving up my independence. I'm trading some in for something better."

"Well, before you do all that—or any of it—have you made reservations for down there?"

"Not yet. I wasn't sure how soon you'd want to go and this time of year there are plenty of beach rentals. I thought we'd see the properties and enjoy a few days on the beach. Why?"

Based on his tone and look, something was up. Tampa wouldn't be a bucket list trip since he—or they'd—be living there, but they could plan something more extravagant later.

"Let's wait on all that until I talk to Colonel Holmstrom. Do you remember what you told me after you asked about my career goals?"

"Not exactly. I was kind of reeling from the news that you were leaving."

"You said something along the lines of you already respected me, regardless of my rank, and that you wanted me to do what I enjoy."

"Sounds familiar."

"While I was deployed, I thought about that and why I wanted to get promoted. It wasn't for the work I'd be doing. It was for pride and accomplishment. Thinking I could prove my worth to my mother and earn her respect and love. Then I had an epiphany. She was just a scared kid when she got pregnant and did what her parents wanted her to do. I'm a reminder of the choices she made that she can't undo. I can't change that, but I can let it go and stop blaming her for not being the mother I wanted. She may never give me her love, but I don't need to prove myself to her. I'm happy with who I am, and what matters is keeping the respect of the person who already loves me unconditionally. You."

Elizabeth wiped away the tears that came, not only because of how much she mattered to him, but because she knew just how freeing letting go could be. And healing. Rather than tell him, she'd had to let him come to this acceptance on his own. To believe he truly was worthy of all the things he wanted. And free to do what he wanted in life, for himself.

"'I'm proud of you."

"'Thank you. Because being with you is what makes me happy. And with Boushey's injuries, he can't return to his position, which leaves our unit short two captains if I move. However, if Boushey were promoted and took the training slot at SOCOM in my place, I could stay on with Bravo Company, or move to his slot with Charlie, and not have to deploy quite as soon. If Colonel Holmstrom is on board and only needs to fill one captain slot right now, then I'd stay here and probably make major on the next promotion list or one after that. But if you've got your heart set on moving to Tampa, speak now or you're most likely stuck with me. Because you and me, darlin', we're stuck like glue."

She laughed and threw her arms over his shoulders. "'I think the line says 'baby.'"

"'If you prefer baby I can stick to the lyrics, but I like calling you darlin'." He winked, and his hands gripped her waist.

"'I love the way you call me darlin'. And the only thing my heart is set on is being with you. Rank isn't important to me. I'd rather you do what brings you joy."

"'Does that mean I get to take you back to bed for a romp and nap after breakfast?" He lowered his forehead to touch hers.

"'Definitely. That'll bring us both joy," She nipped his lower lip and gave it a playful tug.

"One other thing I want to ask is what introductory classes you took toward getting your counseling degree."

She pulled back to get a clear view of his face. His very serious face. "Why?"

"I'm not saying I'd necessarily get a counseling degree. But it could make me a better leader if I understood why my team members did certain things and could help them when they come to me for advice. If I'm good at it, when I can't be an operator anymore, I could go into practice with you, counseling vets."

"There's definitely a need for that."

"I know. And my experience on the teams could make guys more willing to open up than talking to someone who can't relate to what they've experienced. I'm not an office kind of guy though. It's just something I'm thinking about for down the road."

"A different approach might be exactly what some vets need. Talking with a counselor while sitting in a boat or walking a dog through the woods. You could even wear combat boots."

"Now you're talking. I'll look into taking a class or two. Might help me know if you're psychoanalyzing me, because I do think you planted a few subtle suggestions to help me see things in a healthier way."

"I'm good at my job too. And I didn't want to go breaking your heart." This time, *she* broke out singing one of the songs John had sent her while he was away.

John immediately joined in. Together they sang, messing up the lyrics and laughing while Boss wove between them in a perfect kind of harmony.

Epilogue

Boss SCRAMBLED to his feet and loped to the front door, signaling John's impending arrival.

Elizabeth went to the kitchen to check on dinner.

"Hey, Boss. You have a good day?"

Elizabeth loved hearing John's cheerful greeting and their playful reunions on the nights she was home before him.

"Something smells fabulous," he called to her.

"Baby back ribs with baked sweet potatoes and green beans." And a treat for dessert. She took the potatoes out of the oven.

"Hey, darlin', do you have something to tell me?" He held something behind his back. Boss sat next to him, cocking his head to watch her too.

"I—love you?"

"I like hearing that, but I was thinking of something

Those words brought the biggest smile in history to his

maybe I'm pregnant, or we already have our first child."

But she was ready for more. "Two years from now,

ment laced that one, short word.

"Okay." His expression didn't change, but disappoint-

Here. Together with Boss."

"In a year, I see us pretty much where we are now.

road?"

do you see us in a year, or two, or five years down the

placed his hands on her hips, and pulled her close. "Where

"Okay, I deserve that." He laid the onesies on the table,

"Serious? Sure." She tried not to laugh.

discussion?"

"I was trying to be supportive. But can we have a serious

man—if that was possible.

reaction made her fall even more in love with this incredible

"Really? Because you were smiling pretty big." His

didn't get a treat.

the same hound dog expression as Boss's when told he

"Oh. Whew," he tried to downplay it, but his face had

her," she explained.

"Our receptionist is going to have a baby. Those are for

a grin, with just a hint of guilt. "So . . ."

"It looked like the one from that lingerie store." He gave

"You peeked in the bag?"

onesies she'd bought today, his gaze locked on her face.

"I do like good ones." He held up the pack of infant

learning to enjoy them.

about surprises." He loved them, though, and she was

to see what was behind his back. "You know how I feel

Her curiosity rose. She took a step toward him and tried

seen on his handsome face.

else." John wore a satisfied smile, different from any she'd

face. She smiled right back and looped her hands behind his neck.

"I'm hoping that smile means you're on board with what I envision. We've both grown and dealt with our pasts. We love each other, and I have no doubt I've found the right person."

"I definitely have too. With Boss's help. Good dog," John said. "I have something for you. Stay right here."

He jogged off to the bedroom, leaving her curious and her heart pounding. He was back before her mind could move past her first premature and unlikely thought. In his hands, he held his gun case. Not what she expected. At all.

She tried to hide the pang of disappointment.

He held it out to her.

"You're giving me your gun?"

"No, I was just hiding something in my old gun case because I knew you wouldn't go in there. Open it."

The latch didn't budge. "What's the combination?"

"The first day we kissed." His grin ratcheted up a notch.

"At the wedding?"

"No. I kissed you then. I'm talking about when you kissed me."

She dialed in the month and day she'd showed up at his house. This time the lock popped open. Inside was a square black velvet jeweler's box.

Her heart skipped a beat, and her lungs stalled. Had he really bought a ring? After he'd passed on the promotion and reassignment to SOCOM, they'd settled into life here. Neither had pressed Wren to move out of his house. They were taking their time and hadn't discussed marriage, though it had certainly crossed her mind more than once.

"You don't have to say anything. If you're not ready, I understand. It's been pointed out by a friend, who happens

to be a counselor, that I tend to jump in too quickly. But I know I love going to bed with you, waking up with you, and I want to keep coming home to you, whether it's from a day at work or a deployment. So, I want you to know I have this and whenever you're ready, let me know and I'll ask the question. Until then, I'm sticking around until you give me the boot."

"Your counselor friend sounds like a wise person."

"Oh, she is. Beautiful too. And great in bed."

She cleared her throat. "As I was saying, she sounds wise, but I feel certain she would agree that sometimes you know with absolute certainty what's right. Like this. Us. Ask me." The longing consuming her nearly made her beg.

"Seriously? You don't want to see the ring first?"

"I don't need to see a ring." Honestly, she didn't even need one. She saw his heart, and she wanted this more than she'd wanted anything in her life.

John licked his lips and swallowed, then took the gun case from her hands. He set it on the kitchen table and picked up the velvet box. "I hadn't planned what to say because I didn't think this would happen so soon."

That his words came out breathlessly sent chill bumps up her arms. "Then keep it simple." He'd already told her what she needed to hear.

"I'm asking you to take my name—or wait. You don't have to change your name if you don't want to. I know you like your independence," he stammered. "But I want to do life with you. Life with you." He sang, dropping to one knee, and opened the ring box. "Elizabeth, will you marry me?"

"Yes! I want to be your wife. And share your life and your dog. Have your children."

"Even if it means enduring my off-key singing?" He got to his feet.

"I would be disappointed if you didn't sing at least once a day. Or talk to Boss like you expect him to answer. You make me smile and laugh. I'm happier than I've ever been." Happier than she ever thought she could be and now the future she once dreamed of was becoming a reality.

"Right back at you." His hands shook as he took the ring from the box. "With you, I feel it's safe to love. Safe to leave when I have to and know you'll be waiting for me to come home. You give me a reason to come home." He slid the ring on her finger. "What do you say we practice baby-making to celebrate?" He toyed with the button on her pants.

"Practice? I think we've got that figured out."

"Yeah, but we both have a lot of time to make up for before we have to get serious and keep it in the bedroom."

"Are you afraid our sex life is going to get boring?"

He gave an indecisive shrug.

"Not a chance, soldier. Because I love you like a love song, baby," she sang near his ear. And it was a song she wanted to repeat, over and over and over.

♫

Dear Reader,

Thank you for choosing *Faking it with the Green Beret*. I hope you enjoyed John and Elizabeth and Boss's story. I had so much fun coming up with the story and characters. Reviews and ratings are very much appreciated. Amazon, Goodreads, BookBub or your favorite book site. I hope you enjoyed seeing *Faking it with the Bachelor's* Nate and Cecilia again along with some of the ladies from Nate's season on *Say Yes to the Rose*.

Linc Porter, who makes an appearance in this book is a member of the Army Bad Karma team. If you have not yet read the tastefully steamy (aka – there are sex scenes) Bad Karma Special Ops romantic suspense series, you can start with <u>*Desperate Choices*</u>, the prequel novella to the series. Then read <u>*Deadly Aim*</u>, <u>*A Shot Worth Taking*</u>, and <u>*In the Wrong Sights*</u>. You can also get my novelette, *Undercover Angel*, which is Tony and Angela's backstory FREE by subscribing to my <u>newsletter</u>.

I hope you'll accept your invitation to attend John and Elizabeth's wedding at The Oasis which takes place in the next book in the *Faking It* series, <u>*Faking it with the Colonel*</u>. Read on for a sample and tune in to my <u>newsletter</u> or social media to get updates of what's coming and when.

Happy reading.

Faking it with the Colonel
Excerpt

CHAPTER ONE

In his twenty-six years in the Army, Graham Holmstrom had been given a lot of orders. As a colonel, he usually was on the giving end these days. With anyone else, he would have thought the order he'd just been given was a prank. However, General McKittrick was not known for having a sense of humor. At all.

"Can you repeat that?" Graham asked.

"I know it hasn't even been a year since Bethann passed—"

"Last week marked seven months since . . ." Not even close to a year.

"I understand you're still grieving, especially with her death being so unexpected, but we brought you in to replace Thomsen for a reason."

"But what does that have to with me and . . ."

"Thomsen replaced Boatman for the same reason. Actually, it was Boatman's second time getting caught with an NCO's wife, so he retired quietly rather than get bumped

down to major or dishonorably discharged for conduct unbecoming. With Mateo going after Thomsen publicly, the entire unit knows what happened. Not a good look for command."

"But, sir, I would never—"

"He was married and he still ..." Graham pointed out.

"That's what Thomsen said too."

"Exactly. Now, you're single, sympathetic, an officer, and could be considered quite the catch. I'm hearing that some of the men have concerns their wives could be targets when they deploy since they're seeing a pattern. If you have a pretty, new wife that should alleviate their concerns so they can focus on their missions. Or, if you're not ready, we can find a new post for you."

The words delivered a solid kick to Graham's gut.

"Where?" he probed as his pulse quickened to pound near his temples.

"Where would you like to go? Vincenza? South Korea? Back to Fort Lewis?"

No. No! And no. Bethann's death hit the entire family hard. With Jace and Reece based here probably long-term, Graham wanted to stay at Fort Bragg if at all possible. "SOCOM?" He'd hoped to get a shot at his dream position in the JFK Special Warfare Center and School here at Bragg eventually.

"Don't we all. I don't have the pull to make that happen. You don't have to tell me this minute. Take some time to think on it. Go on a date or two."

A date? "I wouldn't have a clue where to start." It'd been nearly three decades since he'd had a first date.

"Surely, one of Bethann's single friends has expressed interest or you can check out some of the online dating sites."

"All of Bethann's friends I know are married." Mostly other officers' wives or friends from church.

"What about Maribelle Jepson?"

"Kurt's widow?"

"Been over two years since he died in action. She's still in the area, and the rumors my wife has heard is Maribelle's dating, and, uh, in the market for marriage."

"She's got at least a decade before she hits fifty-five. If she remarries before then, she loses her survivor benefits."

"Jepson was only an O-5. You're a full-bird colonel, with a good shot at making O-7. Hell, you might climb higher than that," McKittrick laid it on thick. "She comes out ahead. College benefits for her boys won't disappear and they're practically out of the house. Perk for you, in addition to her looks, is she knows what being wife to a Spec Ops officer entails."

McKittrick had a point, but Graham had never thought of Maribelle that way. She'd been Kurt's wife. Bethann's friend. That had all changed though.

"Just don't date a dancer from a strip club if you ever want to get assigned to SOCOM."

"No worries." An exotic dancer wasn't the kind of woman he'd be comfortable introducing to his adult kids or their spouses. "The only times I've been to those bars was as part of bachelor parties, and that was years ago." Not that he didn't admire a beautiful, barely dressed women, but he wouldn't jeopardize his marriage when he had the near perfect woman supporting him. Raising their kids. Holding things together when he'd been deployed over and over. Only now Bethann was gone—forever. "I'll think on it."

He missed having a companion, but he hadn't thought about dating yet, nor could he imagine his kids being thrilled about his dating so soon after their mother's death.

It would suck to get transferred overseas or even across the country now though. However, he wasn't going to disrespect his wife's memory by replacing her with some random woman for the good of his career. He needed time to think. To feel his kids out this weekend.

Maybe he could find a compromise.

Faking it with the Colonel Excerpt

CHAPTER TWO

After the ding from the incoming message tone assigned to Piper, *Erin picked up the phone to see the reply to her earlier text.*

ETA 5 minutes.

She must not have stopped on the drive here. "You two be nice to Piper. She'll want to pet you," Erin said to the two cats as if they understood her. As a long-term pet-sitting gigs went, it was an easy one. Even if they didn't answer and ignored her except for the occasional rub against her leg or foot, she tried to befriend them, though they merely tolerated her since she fed them and changed their litter boxes.

A few minutes later, headlights slowly approached, and Piper parked her SUV next to Erin's sedan. She took a breath before stepping outside.

"Hey, sweetie." Erin embraced her youngest daughter and Piper hugged her back even tighter. "I've missed you."

"I've missed you too."

Faking it with the Colonel Excerpt

The tightness in Piper's smile pulled at Erin's heart.

"Can I help you carry anything in?"

"I've just got the one bag." Piper studied the parked cars and exterior of the older condos as the hatch lifted, and she grabbed her duffle bag.

Erin led her in, making sure neither cat snuck out.

"Oh," Piper crooned, setting down the duffle. She dropped to her knees and held out a hand to the cats.

"The yellow tabby is Tink." The larger cat studied Piper for a long moment before edging close enough for Piper to scratch behind her ears.

"Tink, not Tank. Like an Army tank?"

"Tink is short for Tinkerbell. She even has a green collar with bells on it. I switched it out for now because it gets annoying when she and Smokey there engage in a game of chase at seven in the morning."

"Maybe they're on Army time instead of our night owl clock." Piper sat cross-legged on the floor and coaxed Tink closer. "I expected more of a camouflage motif décor."

"Mareena and Sydnee wear camo fatigues for work, but they are both beautiful and definitely girlie-girls when off duty from the little I saw before they deployed."

"Were they able to get you any connections with Special Forces guys?"

Smokey ventured closer to Piper. It'd taken three days after Erin moved in before Smokey didn't run from the room every time she got near. Piper was clearly the cat whisperer in the family, despite never having pets in their house.

"No. They're in a medical unit. They don't interact with Special Forces units. They did say there's a bar called Jumpy's that's known for being a hangout for the Spec Ops guys. However, can you see me hanging out at a bar at my

372

age offering to buy guys in their twenties, or even thirties, a drink if they let me pick their brains or will invite me to come shadow them for a few days or training for research for the TV series I'm writing." That hadn't been picked up yet. Which meant she had zero credibility.

"It could happen. You have a way of connecting with people."

"I'm volunteering twice a week at the USO on base and hoping I'll make a connection there. I worked a home-coming for the 82nd Airborne two weeks ago. One of the wives I talked with seemed receptive to introducing me to her husband, but I want to give him a few weeks home before I reach out. I've got five more months here, though I hope it won't take that long. Ian says Marty Blane is on board. He played a soldier in a military series a few years ago and has done several USO tours. He has a good follow-ing, so getting him attached would increase the chances of HBO, Netflix, Showtime, or Amazon picking up the series. Ian said Marty thinks he can get Chris Remington attached as lead."

"Chris Remington? He's officially on the Hollywood Chris' A-list now. I'd watch if he were in it."

"That's good to know." Erin chuckled. A younger demo-graphic could increase the appeal and chances of success.

"That's all great." Piper stroked Tink's fur, not meeting Erin's gaze.

"Are you nervous about your year abroad?" It was a big step.

"No. Well, a little. Dad's been texting about him and Madison and Connor coming over for Christmas and trav-eling around Spain."

"Oh. Kind of early to be planning that. What did your sister say?"

"That she and Connor where already going to Cancun with his family right after Christmas this year. Have you talked to Madison this week?"

"No. Why?" The weight in Erin's chest grew heavier.

Piper grumbled a sigh so loud that Tink shot away. "Dad texted how he'd 'have to come alone since Mom left me.' Then, he started in with saying maybe he'd invite Lucille."

"Is he dating?" She actually hoped he was, maybe then he'd give up the martyr routine.

"I don't think so. He was texting a bunch of random crazy stuff."

Erin nodded. It went with Phil's pattern.

"Madison wanted me to ask you to try to get Dad to go to counseling again."

Erin patted the space next to her on the sofa and waited for Piper to join her. "Madison hasn't been home for longer than a two week stretch between school and moving to Austin after graduation. She hasn't seen how bad it'd gotten the past two years. He's your dad, and it's not your place to tell her. She still thinks the car accident was because a deer ran out in front of him."

"What? You never told her?"

"He asked me not to and said he would handle it." There may have been a deer, but that wasn't the sole factor, and the police officer knew it. Why would Madison suspect her father would already be over the legal limit at one thirty on a Sunday afternoon?

"Can't you try counseling again? Before the divorce is final and can't be undone?"

That was Madison talking. "Honey, you know I went. He came once." And got all defensive. "The next week, he had business calls scheduled and couldn't"—AKA wouldn't

—"go. And the same too busy scenario played out the next week." But she'd continued to go. "I thought I could suffer through it, and it'd get better. But I wasn't helping the situation with my attitude. After the accident, I couldn't pretend or be complicit by being silent anymore. Next time he might seriously hurt himself—or some innocent person."

Piper nodded, though a few tears still escaped. "If I—"

"No. It's not your or Madison's fault. It's not just the stress from Dad's job. We had other problems and suppressed a lot of things rather than communicate and work them out. I'm working on myself, and I've been happier in the past year than I have in a long time. I like *myself* better."

"But you're having to live in somebody else's little apartment—"

"That's my choice. It works well with being here at Bragg since it's temporary. Part of the divorce settlement is to sell the house. I can buy or rent something practical once I decide where I want to be."

"Are you going to move to California if the series gets picked up?"

"I'm not planning on it, and I shouldn't have to be out there. They may even shoot here in North Carolina or in Georgia. Not that I need to be where they film. I'm tutoring seven students for finals and SAT. I'll teach the summer session at Fayetteville Tech, then online this fall semester while I'm at the beach writing the scripts. I'll know more after that. Don't worry about me. I'll be fine. And if Dad comes to Spain for Christmas, I can come over Thanksgiving or spring break. His plans may change."

Piper rolled her eyes and nodded. "Yeah, he'll probably have some project at work come up."

"I only need a few weeks' notice to get a ticket if he

can't come." Though she'd suck it up and buy one last minute if he canceled.

"He keeps saying 'Mom is going to marry some widowed two star general or divorced Special Forces guy now that she left me.'"

Erin laughed despite the question in Piper's voice. "Right. Eventually, I may date, but right now, the idea of getting married again is not even a consideration. The only widowed generals I know are the fake friend requests on social media. Half the time they don't use the right first name of the real military officer they're pretending to be or spell it right. And the 'I'm an honest man looking for a kind-hearted woman' in their bio? Or saying they're an Army doctor who went to Harvard?"

"I can't believe anyone falls for those scammers."

"You'd think everyone would be suspicious of those random requests by now," Erin agreed. However, her friend Cyndi had spent weeks messaging with a man from a random friend request. After he'd sent Cyndi a gift, she'd reciprocate by sending an expensive gift. Once her kids found out about her online boyfriend, they ran a search using his profile picture and found it was from a stock photo site. Her poor friend had been so embarrassed at falling for it. Erin knew better. "People get lonely and want to believe it's real."

"What about you? Aren't you lonely?"

"I don't have a network of friends here like I did in Charlotte, but with teaching, tutoring, writing, and volunteering, I keep busy and interact with a lot of people. I'm liking the freedom and independence to eat what I want, when I want. Make decisions without having to get approval. I'm going to live at the beach for four months."

"In the winter."

"Still, it's the beach. I have a real shot at the screen-writing for this series and it's something I would love to do. More than teaching creative writing or how to write a fabulous essay for the SATs. Now's the time to pursue my dream —before I'm chasing grandbabies."

"Don't look at me. I haven't had a date in six months."

"Maybe you'll meet some hunky guy in Spain." She tried to sound excited, though her stomach ached at the idea of her daughter and potential future grandchildren living overseas where she'd rarely see them. Madison had only been home once the past year, in part due to the tension from the separation. Hopefully, she'd come to accept it. "I thought we'd watch a movie tonight and tomorrow we can go shopping for anything you need for your trip. And you're helping me volunteer at the USO's bowling night."

Piper had a way better shot at meeting a single soldier her own age than Erin did, not that either were looking for a boyfriend in the face of major life changes.

Order your copy of Not Faking it with the Colonel

Faking It Series

Sweet (with some heat) Romantic Comedies

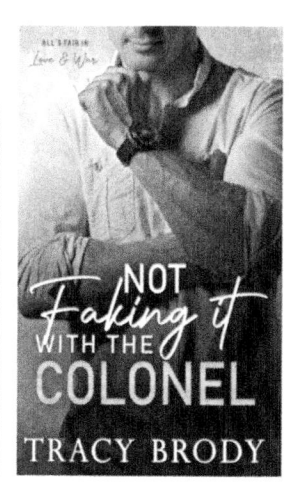

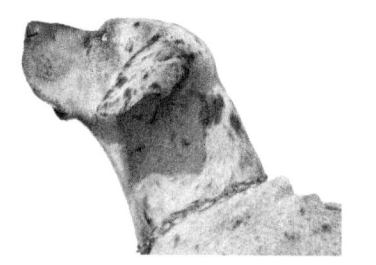

The Bad Karma Special Ops Series

Their love lives are as dangerous as their missions.

Bad Karma has never felt so good.

DESPERATE CHOICES

AWARD-WINNING AUTHOR
TRACY BRODY

Bad Karma has never been so worth it.

DEADLY AIM

AWARD-WINNING AUTHOR
TRACY BRODY

Bad Karma has never felt so right.

A SHOT WORTH TAKING

AWARD-WINNING AUTHOR
TRACY BRODY

Bad Karma has never been so real.

IN THE WRONG SIGHTS

AWARD-WINNING AUTHOR
TRACY BRODY

Acknowledgments

It was at my friend and neighbor Trudy M.'s celebration for getting her Masters that David Porter played "Friends in Low Places" and the idea of a soldier showing up in combat boots at his girlfriend's black tie affair came to me. Captain John Bryson worked perfectly as one of Nate's Army buddies in Faking it with the Bachelor. Thanks for the fun at the party Trudy and David, and all the fun I had writing this story.

Thank you Karen Long for the inspiration you provided for Elizabeth's mission, the Wren character and even a little of Ariana. The Lord put us together all those years ago on *The Unit* fan board for a reason. And a shout out to MSG Dale Simpson (US Army Ret.) for continuing to answer my calls, texts, and messages with military related questions. I appreciate you and your sense of humor. Whatcha wearing?

To my fabulous writer friends Jeanne Oates Estridge, Jilly Wood, C.S. Smith, Beth Long, and Janet Raye Stevens, thank you for your time and honesty and trusting that I'll put on my big girl panties and make the story better seeing things from your perspectives. Thank you, Ainsley, (Ph.D., LLC) Paula Huffman, and Lisa Von Colln, (MA, NCC, LPC, RPT-S) for being my sensitivity readers and helping me understand more about what real counselors do and say and what lines Elizabeth shouldn't cross.

To my copy editor, Laura, who was fast and knowledge-able. You rock as a writing coach and helped strengthen my

storytelling. Thanks also to Sarah Paige of The Book Cover Boutique for your skills on the excellent job and your patience in designing a cover that hit the right notes to portray Big John.

To JJ Kirkmon, you didn't get to edit this book, but you heard all about it while I was plotting and writing and helped me get inside a real tiny home. Looking forward to more adventures.

Thank you to our Armed Forces and their families for serving and sacrificing. You're my inspiration and heroes.

Lastly, much thanks and love to my family for their support and patience, allowing me to do what I love.

About the Author

Tracy Brody has a background in banking, retired to become a domestic engineer, and aims to supplement her husband's retirement using her overactive imagination. She began writing spec movie and TV scripts, however, when two friends gave her the same feedback on a script, saying that they'd love to see it as a book, she didn't need to be hit over the head with a literal 2" x 4" to get the message. She joined RWA® where A SHOT WORTH TAKING and IN THE WRONG SIGHTS won the Golden Heart® for

romantic suspense in 2015 and 2016. DEADLY AIM was a four-time finalist in the Golden Heart.

Tracy has written a series of single-title romances featuring the Bad Karma Special Ops team whose love lives are as dangerous as their missions. She is currently using her sense of humor to write romantic comedies in the Faking It series and has enough ideas to keep her busy writing for decades.

Tracy and her husband live in North Carolina. She's the proud mother of a daughter, son, and now a daughter-in-love. Tracy invokes her sense of humor while volunteering at the USO. You may spot her dancing in the grocery story aisles or talking to herself as she plots books and scenes while walking in her neighborhood, the park, or at the beach on retreats with friends.

You can connect with me on:
https://www.tracybrody.com/
https://www.facebook.com/tracybrodyauthor
https://www.tiktok.com/@tracybrodybooks4u
https://www.instagram.com/tracybrodybooks/
https://www.bookbub.com/authors/tracy-brody
https://twitter.com/TracyBrodyBooks

Sign up for my newsletter at https://www.tracybrody. com/newsletter-signup if you'd like to hear more about upcoming projects. You get access to free exclusive content including the tastefully steamy, behind closed doors scene of John and Elizabeth's first time being intimate.

There's also *Undercover Angel*, the back story of when Tony Vincenti of the Bad Karma Special Ops team and FBI Special Agent Angela Hoffman first worked together.